The Second Chinese Revolution

Ted Halstead

BOOKS BY TED HALSTEAD:

The Second Korean War (2018)
The Saudi-Iranian War (2019)
The End of America's War in Afghanistan (2020)
The End of Russia's War in Ukraine (2020)
The Russian Agents Box Set (2020) - A collection of the four books listed above
The Second Chinese Revolution (2021)

All books, including this one, are set in a fictional near future. Some events described have happened in the real world, and others have not.

To my wife Saadia, for her love and support over more than thirty years.

To my son Adam, for his love and the highest compliment an author can receive- "You wrote this?"

To my daughter Mariam, for her continued love and encouragement.

To my father Frank, for his love and for repeatedly prodding me to finally finish my first book.

To my mother Shirley, for her love and support.

To my granddaughter Fiona, for always making me smile.

All characters are listed in alphabetical order by nationality on the very last pages, because that's where I think the list is easiest to find for quick reference.

CHAPTER ONE

Shanghai, China

Chen Li Na glared at the man seated on the other side of her kitchen table. He had introduced himself as "Zhang Wei" which, as one of the most common names in China, was almost certainly a pseudonym.

Well, he was here to sell her a highly illegal product, so that made sense. But the price!

"Three thousand US dollars! And you can't even guarantee it will work!" Chen said, fuming and shaking her head.

Zhang gave her a thin smile. The truth was, he found the motion of Chen's long flowing black hair mesmerizing as she shook her head back and forth.

Normally Zhang's customers were delighted that he was willing and able to part with one of his devices. And, they usually cost twice as much.

But his boss wanted Zhang to sell this one cheaply. Well, Zhang's first lesson in this job had been – the boss is always right.

Aloud, Zhang said mildly, "It will be working before I leave your apartment, or I'll return your money. I want you to understand that the

Internet service this device provides can be interrupted at any time. Typically, every month or so. We normally restore it within a day, and there's no need for you to do anything."

Chen was still scowling. "Can't you do anything to make it more reliable?"

Zhang's smile disappeared. Too bad, he thought. When she wasn't angry, Chen was quite attractive.

This, despite the fact that Chen had done nothing to enhance her looks. No makeup Zhang could see. Her clothes were designed for comfort, not fashion.

Maybe it was the intelligence Zhang saw shining from her eyes. Or the remarkable expressiveness he saw in her features. Nobody who spoke with Chen would ever have trouble understanding her intent.

Well, Zhang thought ruefully, this wasn't a date. Time to focus.

"Remember, the American company that launched the satellites providing this Internet service isn't being paid. For that matter, they didn't intend to provide Internet service in China at all, paid or not. We're just lucky that at their scale of operations, we barely register," Zhang said.

"And nothing I do online can be traced back to me?" Chen asked intently.

Zhang shook his head emphatically. "When we started this business, it took us months of effort to access the Americans' system as an ordinary user. That was just to provide Internet access. They guard the level of administrative access that would be needed to track you like rabid wolverines."

Chen could hear the sincerity in Zhang's response and rewarded him with a smile.

Yes, she was gorgeous, Zhang thought with a sigh. Well, his boss had also been clear that he was to stick to business.

Lesson two had been – always follow the boss's instructions to the letter.

Zhang gestured to the case at his side. "If you have the cash to hand, I can proceed with setting up the equipment."

Chen had been told the amount before Zhang's arrival, and the pro-democracy organization she led had the necessary access to foreign currency through members in Hong Kong. Silently she reached into her purse and withdrew an envelope with the money. Chen hesitated and almost counted the bills before handing them over.

Then she realized there was no point. Chen had counted the money three times before Zhang's arrival.

Zhang opened the envelope and glanced inside. Then, he gently hefted the envelope up and down. The money next disappeared inside a pocket in Zhang's jacket.

Zhang smiled at Chen's raised right eyebrow. "American one-hundred-dollar bills. The weight was right."

Chen pointed at a small table next to the apartment's only window. "Will that work?" she asked.

Zhang nodded. "Perfect," he said and snapped his case open.

Minutes later, a small black rectangle sporting a parabolic antenna angled towards the window occupied the table. Zhang's organization called it a Gateway.

"Do you have a laptop?" Zhang asked. The question was mostly a formality. A Chinese woman in her twenties would certainly not be using a desktop PC. There was a chance, though, that she used a smartphone exclusively to access the Internet.

Chen nodded and pulled a laptop from the backpack at her side.

Zhang handed Chen his cell phone, which had three items on its display. A web address consisting of numbers and periods, a user ID, and a password.

"Use this web address to log on to the Gateway," Zhang said. "After you enter the user ID and password, you will be prompted to enter new ones. Neither we nor anyone else can access this Gateway without the user ID and password, so make sure they are ones you can remember. Never write them down."

Zhang paused and then asked, "May I use your restroom?"

Chen nodded, and Zhang left.

In fact, Zhang did need to use the restroom. But he could have waited. His real purpose in leaving was to give Chen privacy to change her user ID and password.

More instructions from his boss. Well, Zhang thought, it was only fair that three thousand dollars bought at least a little peace of mind.

The Chinese people were better off in almost every way than at any time in their history. Access to food, housing, health care – nearly all that was most important to the average person was vastly improved.

Except for privacy. For the freedom to express opinions critical of the authorities. For the ability to choose leaders who were not Party members.

No, in those areas, the government was unwilling to give anything at all.

Instead, the authorities publicly warned that all online activities were constantly monitored. Why? Because of the correct calculation that self-censorship through fear would be more effective than even the most active surveillance.

All thoughts that had passed through Zhang's mind many times before, he thought with a sigh as he finished washing his hands. Well, considering the business he was in, Zhang supposed that wasn't surprising.

"I expected satellite Internet service to be slow. But it's faster than the service I have now!" Chen said, smiling as she pointed to her laptop display.

Zhang nodded. "The Americans have launched thousands of satellites to support this service and are sending even more into orbit. So, if anything, the speed will only increase. But there are security precautions you must observe."

A frown replaced the smile that had been on Chen's face only a moment before. "I knew there had to be a catch. So, what are these precautions?"

Zhang shrugged. "Nothing too difficult. First, the Gateway's wireless signal is deliberately weak and should not be detectable through the walls of this apartment. Nevertheless, to be safe, you should unplug and secure it whenever you are not using the Internet."

Chen nodded without comment. Good, Zhang thought. That showed she had at least some common sense.

"Next, even though this Internet service is faster than the one you have now, you must not cancel your old service," Zhang said.

Chen looked startled. "Why not? That's a saving I'd expected to make up for this expense over time," she said, gesturing at the small black box.

"Practically no one your age living in a city like this does without Internet service. And nobody who has it then cancels it unless they move somewhere else. Many of our first-year customers who cut off their old Internet service then had their apartments searched, and their illegal device discovered. Finally, we realized what was happening and began providing this warning," Zhang said calmly.

Chen shivered. "I'm glad I wasn't an early adopter."

Zhang nodded. "You have a smartphone," he said, rather than asked.

Chen nodded back. "Of course," she said.

"And you pay for your cell phone Internet usage by the gigabyte, so you use your home network when you're in the apartment," Zhang said.

Chen nodded again but more slowly. "So, I need to continue to connect to my old Internet service when I use my cell phone at home."

"Correct," Zhang said. "First, because if your data use were to drop sharply, that would be a flag to the authorities, just as surely as if you stopped paying for Internet service."

"And I know many people who have been forced to hand over their phone to the police at checkpoints, and sometimes for no reason at all," Chen said bitterly.

"Yes. And any use of the Gateway by this phone would be immediately detected. Now, what would you do if the police took your phone once they returned it?" Zhang asked.

"I'd get rid of it as soon as I could buy a replacement and tell my friends the new number," Chen replied promptly.

Zhang shook his head. "An understandable reaction, but the wrong one."

"Why?" Chen asked, her head tilted in a way that Zhang correctly guessed meant genuine curiosity.

Good, Zhang thought. Chen might be young. But unlike many her age Zhang had dealt with, at least she didn't think she had all the answers.

"You know any phone collected by the police will have monitoring software installed on it before its return," Zhang said flatly.

Chen just nodded.

Zhang smiled. "The police are like anyone else. They don't like it when their efforts yield no results. When a phone they've put software on goes dark, that makes its user a priority target. At a minimum, for active surveillance. At worst, for a search of your apartment."

Zhang pointed at the Gateway. "That would be bad."

Chen frowned. "You've made your point. So, what should I do?"

"Continue to use the compromised phone for anything you're willing to share with the authorities. Making an appointment with a hairdresser. Looking up the hours a restaurant is open. Similarly, take it with you whenever you know you won't mind sharing your location with the police. From now on, sensitive communications should only be online through this Gateway, and this laptop should never leave your apartment," Zhang said.

Chen nodded but pursed her mouth with distaste. "I understand your advice and will follow it. But this is no way for people to have to live."

Zhang shrugged. "There, we agree. I and those I work for don't sell these devices just for the money. Before I go, do you have any questions?"

Chen shook her head. "Thank you. This will help," she said, gesturing towards the Gateway.

Zhang smiled and stood. As Zhang walked to the apartment door, he said, "You're welcome. And good luck."

Once Zhang reached the building's elevator, his smile gave way to a frown. The authorities were starting to focus more resources on finding users of this latest way to avoid official scrutiny.

Yes, Chen would need all the luck she could get.

SpaceLink Headquarters
San Francisco, California

Eli Wade stared at Mark Rooter, his SpaceLink project manager, in disbelief.

"Tell me that number again," Wade said quietly.

Rooter shifted uncomfortably in his chair. Not that any one-on-one encounter with the man in charge of one of the world's largest high-tech conglomerates was ever really "comfortable."

"A bit over one hundred thousand," Rooter said nervously.

Wade stood up and walked around his desk, finally coming to rest leaning against its front.

About a meter from Rooter.

"How did we come up with that number?" Wade asked.

"Well, we spotted data consumption that couldn't be accounted for by registered users. It took us some serious server time to do an analysis to reach that number because data is being drawn from multiple satellites. We have, though, identified it as a strictly regional issue," Rooter said.

Wade cocked his head. "And to sum up that region in one word, we could just say, 'China,' right?"

"Around China would be a better description. As you know, at the request of their governments, we haven't launched any satellites designed to provide coverage to either China or Vietnam. Since we were advised we wouldn't be allowed to sell terminals in either country, it also made business sense to agree to their request. But over the last two years, we have launched satellites to provide coverage to neighboring countries," Rooter replied.

Wade nodded. "Which countries?" he asked.

Rooter looked down at his notes. "Taiwan, Laos, Thailand, Mongolia, India, Nepal, Bangladesh, Kyrgyzstan..."

Wade shook his head, which Rooter knew was the signal to stop talking.

"How much of China could receive data from the satellites we currently have up to provide coverage to neighboring countries?" Wade asked.

Rooter coughed and looked down again at his notes, but the truth was he didn't need them.

"All of it," Rooter said soberly.

Wade stared at Rooter incredulously. "All of it?" he repeated with disbelief.

"Well, there are areas of China's interior where coverage would be too slow for video streaming but good enough for ordinary web browsing or low-quality video chat. But most people in China live near its eastern and southern coasts, so..."

Rooter's voice trailed off as Wade's glare finally penetrated.

"You do know I've got manufacturing investments in China, right? What do you think will happen to them once the Chinese figure out what's going on? In fact, I'm surprised I haven't heard from them already," Wade said, as his expression shifted from angry to thoughtful.

Rooter wondered if he looked as relieved as he felt. "I think the Chinese have probably had the same trouble we did understanding what was happening. We've spotted unauthorized user access now and then and cut it off but never made it a resource priority. Unpaid data use has never been more than a fraction of one percent, so it would have cost more than it was worth to stop."

Rooter paused. "Also, the scale we talking about matters too. One hundred thousand sounds like a lot of users to us. In a country like China with nearly one and a half billion people, it's again a fraction of one percent."

Wade grunted. "OK, so what are we going to do about this?"

Rooter frowned. "First, I'd like to do some more research and analysis on those unpaid users. Some things we've learned so far don't make sense."

"Such as?" Wade asked.

"Well, in the latest survey, average residential Internet speed in China was 7.6 megabits per second, ranking it number fifty-five in the world. Behind Sri Lanka," Rooter said.

"Really? I knew China lagged most other Asian countries in terms of Internet speed, but not that it was so far behind," Wade said, shaking his head.

Rooter shrugged. "One analysis I saw said it was a conscious resource choice by the Chinese government. They spend a lot to control and monitor Internet use. The people in charge probably see no need to spend even more to speed it up."

"OK, but what does that have to do with us?" Wade asked.

"Well, if we're reading the data correctly, it looks like nearly all unpaid users in China are just web browsing. Not much video streaming. Commonly accessed Chinese government websites are absent from data use records, making me think unpaid users are continuing to visit them from their old Internet service provider. It all adds up to way below average SpaceLink data consumption per unpaid user. It's one reason it took us this long to spot the problem. So, if they aren't using SpaceLink to stream video and everything else faster speeds would give them, why bother?" Rooter asked.

Wade nodded thoughtfully. "So, you want more time to collect and analyze data on these unpaid users, so we know what we're dealing with."

"That's it," Rooter said, relief obvious in his expression. "We're also working on options to pull the plug on these unpaid users. To do a comprehensive job, we'd have to require users in China's neighboring countries to adopt new user IDs and passwords, which I'd like to avoid. We could flush out most of them without inconveniencing our paid users, but we need a little more time to figure out the best way to do that."

"Fine," Wade said with a nod. "You've got the time. Let me know when you're ready to proceed."

"Absolutely," Rooter said and then stood and beat a hasty retreat from Wade's office.

Wade watched him go with a small smile, which then disappeared as he had a thought.

How long would it be before he heard about these "unpaid users" from the Chinese government?

Chapter Two

Zhongnanhai Compound
Beijing, China

President Lin Wang Yong grimaced as he walked into the room and looked around the crowded conference table. He'd told his chief of staff to keep the number of participants in this meeting manageable.

If he had to keep explaining "manageable" should result in empty seats at this table, Lin thought, it meant he needed a new chief of staff.

Lin waved all the standing officials to their seats as he took his at the head of the table. Looking at the assembled faces, he had to correct himself.

No, stopping Chinese subversives from accessing the Internet through American satellites was a complicated problem. Made no easier to address by the many agencies and offices with overlapping responsibilities for solving it.

Many of those sitting around the table had their offices nearby. The Zhongnanhai Compound included the central headquarters for the Communist Party and the State Council. It also housed his office as the General Secretary of the Communist Party and the Premier's office. The

Central Committee's headquarters and its highest level coordinating institutions, such as the Standing Committee, Politburo, and Secretariat, were also found here.

"Minister Song, please explain why I have called you all here today," Lin said.

This simple statement accomplished two things at once. First, Lin made it clear that the Ministry of State Security (MSS) now had the lead in solving this problem, even though the Ministry of Public Security (MPS) had been the primary agency so far.

Lin smiled to himself as he remembered an American journalist who had compared MSS to a combination of the Central Intelligence Agency and National Security Agency and MPS to the Federal Bureau of Investigation.

It was like comparing barracudas to goldfish.

Second, it demonstrated that Lin was unhappy with MPS' performance. Or he would have given advance notice to the meeting participants that MSS now had the lead.

Lin studied the reactions around the table. Everyone here was either a Minister or one of their Division Chiefs. All had long experience at controlling their expressions.

Lin saw with satisfaction he had put that experience to a severe test.

Minister Song had nodded and replied as though he'd been expecting Lin's instruction. Well, as the longest-serving member of the Politburo next to Lin himself, that was no surprise.

"We have no exact count of how many subversives are using the American satellite service. But we know the number is increasing. Many subversives we have tracked in the past have gone dark. A few may have gone overseas, but we are talking about dozens. Also, information ordinarily blocked by the diligent efforts of our MPS colleagues is reaching the public with unprecedented speed," Song said, shaking his head.

Lin smiled to himself. Well played. "Diligent" was a high compliment. But in the same sentence, Song had made it clear that MPS' best efforts had failed to produce adequate results.

The "Great Firewall" MPS administered had a technical and enforcement staff of over two million employees and cost billions annually for the hardware, software, and salaries needed to keep it functioning. Censorship administered through the Great Firewall made access to information the Communist Party didn't want Chinese citizens to have difficult to get, and kept tabs on subversives. That made the Great Firewall an essential tool for the Party to remain in power.

Knowledge is power. Lin knew understanding that cardinal principle was why the Party had stayed in charge in China while Communist regimes in Europe had crumbled to dust.

Lin returned his focus to Song as the Minister continued.

"To combat this threat, I first propose coordination between our Science and Technology Investigative Division and their colleagues at MPS. As you all know, the STI Division has long experience with monitoring telecommunications," Song said evenly.

Lin nodded to show his approval before MPS Minister Yu had a chance to react. MSS was usually focused on communications between Chinese citizens and foreigners. But now, the threat was Internet use routed through American satellites. Coordination made sense.

"STI Director Ma will now demonstrate the equipment that will begin this collaboration," Song said, nodding towards her.

Lin looked at Ma curiously. She was the only woman at the table. In fact, few women reached the top levels of the Chinese government. Currently, only two women were Politburo members out of over two dozen.

But it made sense that Ma had been able to rise to chief of her division. The STI chief would never advance to lead the entire MSS, so all the most capable and ambitious men had gone to MSS divisions like International Intelligence. Leaving the field clear at STI for a woman like Ma.

Ma removed a small black object from her suit jacket and placed it in the table's center. It looked like a hockey puck, Lin thought. Maybe a little smaller. Next, Ma took out a tablet not much larger than many smartphones and tapped an icon on its surface.

The object silently rose about a meter and then continued to hover for several seconds while every head around the table rose to track its progress.

Including his, Lin thought with a smile. Even though he'd been given this demonstration in advance and knew what to expect.

Ma tapped another icon on the tablet, and the object came to rest on the table as silently as it had risen.

Ma peered over her glasses and said, "This drone is designed to detect the wireless signal emitted by the device used to provide illegal satellite Internet service, called a Gateway. The signal is deliberately too weak to be intercepted through the walls of a building. But our experiments with captured Gateways show it can be detected a short distance through glass. Since Gateways must be stationed next to a window to connect to an American satellite, this gives us our opportunity."

The smile that now appeared on Ma's stern face made Lin immediately think of a hungry shark spotting a wounded fish.

"Thank you, Director Ma," Song smoothly interjected. "We propose that the role of MSS will be restricted to operating the drones and passing the location of intercepted signals to MPS. We will rely on MPS to provide priority targets for drone surveillance and to search the apartments where Gateways may be found."

MPS Minister Yu nodded thoughtfully. "So, MSS will provide technical assistance, but MPS will continue to carry out searches and arrests?"

Song smiled. "That is correct, Minister."

Yu shrugged. "MPS appreciates your cooperation with this important mission."

Lin beamed. Collaboration and consensus were always the government's goals in China, to the point that formal votes were nearly absent in the Politburo. Those goals were just as valid for meetings like this at the ministerial level.

"Minister Yu, I understand you also have a proposal," Lin said, nodding in Yu's direction.

"Yes, Mr. President," Yu said. "To our surprise, one of the first people we arrested when Gateways were initially discovered two years ago has just been released at a judge's order. The rationale was that the person was a teenager resident in the apartment where the Gateway was found, but there was no evidence he had used it to access the Internet. His parents, of course, remain in custody."

A disapproving murmur passed around the table. Some Chinese judges had the annoying habit of interpreting the law literally rather than carrying out its intent. Which, as far as Lin and the others around the table were concerned, meant doing whatever was necessary to keep the Party in power.

"Your proposed solution, Minister Yu?" Lin asked.

"Mr. President, I recommend that the burden of proof be explicitly shifted in law to anyone living in a residence where the Gateway is found who is sixteen or older. Also, that the minimum sentence be increased to ten years at hard labor, except for juveniles between sixteen and eighteen. For them, the sentence would be detention in a juvenile facility until the age of eighteen, and the balance of a five-year sentence to then be served as ordinary confinement," Yu said.

Some heads around the table nodded with agreement, while others remained still. However, there were no grimaces or frowns, let alone any sign that someone would speak out against Yu's proposal.

In spite of the fact that ten years at hard labor was effectively a death sentence. Lin thought idly that he'd have to get someone on his staff to check that point. Had anyone ever survived such a sentence, and if so, how long did they live after release?

Undoubtedly, the police would closely monitor any such survivor. No, check that assumption as well, Lin thought to himself.

Attention to detail was a key reason Lin had reached his present position.

Aloud, Lin said, "An excellent proposal, Minister. Please have your staff prepare a bill, and I will see that it is introduced at the National People's Congress."

This was, of course, a mere formality. Any bill with the President's support would become law, and quickly.

"I believe we have reached the end of the agenda unless someone has anything they would like to add?" Lin asked.

All the heads at the table shook, "No," as Lin had expected.

Lin rose and said, "Thanks to all of you for your service."

As everyone else quickly filed out of the conference room, Lin called out, "Minister Song, please stay with me for a moment."

The last person to leave was Song's deputy, who quietly closed the door behind him.

"I understand you have suggestions to share that must come only to me for reasons of security," Lin said.

"Yes, sir," Song said. "I have several ideas to address this problem more directly. However, all of them carry the possibility of adverse consequences. I will describe them in order, from least to most risky."

Lin nodded his understanding but said nothing.

"First, we could tell the American in charge of SpaceLink, Eli Wade, that he must cooperate with us or risk nationalization of his manufacturing operations in China," Song said.

Lin shook his head. "My first thought. But Commerce Minister Bao tells me we have more to lose than Wade from such a step. His electric cars, in particular, are a key part of our plan to reduce urban air pollution. Next?"

"Then I suggest we approach the American government on an informal basis. Tell them we would appreciate their help in convincing SpaceLink to stop its satellites from being accessed by Chinese citizens. Perhaps offer them something of value in return," Song said.

Lin pursed his lips. "I'd already thought about doing so, but until now hadn't considered it worth the effort. Now I agree it may be worth pursuing that option. The downside?"

Song shrugged. "Wade is well known as a man unlikely to bow to pressure. The American government needs Wade and his rockets more than anything we can offer. If Wade refuses and makes his decision public, it could be embarrassing to us. Worse, it could make more of our citizens aware that SpaceLink is an option through Gateways."

Lin shook his head. "I have already considered those points. I think most of our people will learn about SpaceLink and Gateways soon no matter what we do. We are past worrying about embarrassment. Send me a proposal with specifics. Next?"

Song hesitated and finally said, "We can destroy the SpaceLink satellites."

Lin smiled. "I recall our first successful antisatellite test in 2007 as well as you do. I presume you are speaking of an approach more subtle than a ballistic missile?"

Song nodded. "I'm sure you've seen the same reports I have. Laboratory tests suggest the space-based laser we now have in development may succeed in rendering a communications satellite inoperable. More importantly, we believe it could do so without being detectable from any ground-based observation."

"Well, that is important. I have no intention of starting a war with the Americans over this," Lin said.

"Of course, sir," Song said. "A reusable weapon like a laser is also a practical necessity. SpaceLink's service requires thousands of satellites to function. We're not sure exactly how many provide coverage to subversives in China, but probably at least two dozen."

Lin winced. "So many. And if we destroy or disable only satellites providing Internet service in or near China, suspicion will inevitably fall on us. Whether the damage is observed as it happens or not."

"That is undeniable, sir. That is why I am proposing we ask the Russians to assist us with the last two options," Song said.

"The Russians," Lin repeated. "Well, they certainly have been anxious to sell us their oil and gas."

"Yes, sir," Song said. "The Europeans have increasingly turned to renewable energy sources, and many other markets are closed to Russia for political reasons. We have been increasing our use of solar and nuclear power as well, so to accept all the oil and gas the Russians want to sell us would mean ending supply contracts with many smaller countries."

Lin nodded. "Doing so is not a real problem. We buy oil from countries like Venezuela to remind the Americans they can't stop us from doing so with their sanctions, not because we have any real interest in supporting Venezuela. But, how do you propose the Russians help us?"

Song hesitated. "Let me first emphasize, these two options are the riskiest for us, especially if the Russians are discovered..."

Chapter Three

FSB Headquarters
Moscow, Russia

Mikhail Vasilyev and Neda Rhahbar looked up from the files they were reading as Boris Kharlov entered the secure basement conference room. Vasilyev gestured towards the chair directly opposite him at the long wooden table, which had a file folder just like his waiting.

"Good morning," Vasilyev said. "We're expected to read through these before Director Smyslov gets here. We'll only have this one chance to ask questions before we leave for the airport."

"Well then, I'd better get reading," Kharlov replied. "Any chance of coffee?"

Kharlov had given up his Spetsnaz career years ago for a far more lucrative one as a warlord in separatist eastern Ukraine. While there, he had made himself useful to the FSB, which had called on Kharlov to assist Vasilyev and Neda's last Ukraine mission.

After an uneasy peace returned to Ukraine, Kharlov took the FSB up on their offer to work for them full time. It had been quite an adjustment.

Vasilyev shook his head. "No food or drink in this room. Apparently, any drop or crumb could compromise the electronics built into these walls keeping us safe from prying eyes and ears."

Kharlov opened the folder and sighed. "Reminds of my days with Spetsnaz, where we said 'Drive like madmen to the dock, wait three days for the ship.' I wonder whether the past year of training will have anything to do with this mission."

Neda looked up from her papers and smiled. "It's been fourteen months. And the answer is yes. Though not exactly in the way we expected. I suggest you start reading."

Kharlov grunted and began to do just that.

Half an hour later, the conference room door opened to admit a scowling Anatoly Grishkov.

As Grishkov aged, he looked more and more like his father, who had also been a policeman. Like him, he was shorter and more muscular than the average Russian, with thick black hair and black eyes. Grishkov's son Sasha was fourteen, and his other son Misha was twelve. Though both had black hair, otherwise, they thankfully looked more like his wife, Arisha.

Grishkov had worked together with FSB Colonel Alexei Vasilyev, Mikhail's father, on his first two missions. Before that, he had been the lead homicide detective for the entire Vladivostok region.

But after their first mission, FSB Director Smyslov had put Grishkov on "indefinite special assignment" as a Captain in the Moscow Police Department. This was a cover for his new job, which was high-priority overseas missions for the FSB.

After Alexei Vasilyev died during their second mission, Smyslov had assigned Alexei's son Mikhail as Grishkov's new partner. This assignment was no coincidence.

Smyslov knew that Grishkov was close to insisting on returning to police work after his second mission, simply because he thought his luck was unlikely to last for a third encounter with rogue nuclear weapons. He also knew Grishkov was not concerned for himself but felt a strong responsibility to Arisha and his two sons. Grishkov had a nearly superstitious belief that Alexei's son Mikhail would help Grishkov survive the mission.

Grishkov's third mission, which had taken him to Pakistan and Afghanistan, had nearly killed him. Though Grishkov had been cleared to return to duty after a lengthy hospital stay, Arisha had begged him not to do their fourth mission in Ukraine.

And she had cried, which had shocked Grishkov. Arisha was a woman Grishkov genuinely believed stronger than himself, and he had never seen her cry. He had finally ended the argument by promising to make Ukraine his last mission. Grishkov had, at that point, every intention of keeping that promise.

As his father had been, Mikhail Vasilyev was in excellent physical condition. Also, like him, Vasilyev was a firm believer in the value of hand-to-hand combat skills. Vasilyev was only a bit taller than Grishkov but was even thinner than his father. His full head of dark brown hair and his perpetual air of detached amusement had helped Grishkov recognize Mikhail Vasilyev immediately as Alexei's son.

That recognition had come only after Alexei's death. Alexei had been worried that knowledge of his son's existence would be used against him by the many enemies he routinely encountered in his assignments abroad, a worry which only intensified once Mikhail defied him and also began working for the FSB.

Grishkov had met Vasilyev's wife, Neda Rhahbar when she was fleeing Iran. The wife of Iran's leading nuclear scientist, Neda had defected to Russia when she learned her husband was making three nuclear test devices available for an attack against Saudi Arabia.

An accomplished nuclear scientist herself, Neda had been recruited to work in the FSB after her defection. Neda's first marriage ended when her Iranian husband died while setting off one of his nuclear creations.

Neda's expertise with nuclear weapons and language skills had served Grishkov and Vasilyev well on their mission in Pakistan and Afghanistan. That mission had also left Neda with a scar visible on one cheek and a smaller one on her forehead. Neither one appeared to trouble Vasilyev, who had married Neda soon after that mission concluded.

Grishkov wasn't surprised since even with the scars, Neda was still a strikingly beautiful woman with long dark hair and flashing dark eyes. He also knew that the sort of danger they'd shared could do a great deal to drive people close together in a remarkably short time.

That shared experience also gave them a certainty many couples never achieved. That no matter what, they could count on each other.

Vasilyev, Neda, and Kharlov all rose from the table and converged on Grishkov, whose scowl quickly gave way to a reluctant smile.

"It's so good to see you!" Neda exclaimed. "It's been months! How is your leg?"

Broken in two places, Grishkov's right leg had nearly been declared beyond salvage. The last time FSB Director Smyslov had seen them, he had pointedly told Grishkov that as a result, he would never again serve overseas with the FSB.

"I would not wish the months of physical therapy I went through on my worst enemy. But, thanks to a very competent team of therapists, I am fully recovered. In fact, I have been cleared for overseas deployment," Grishkov said.

Though Grishkov didn't know it, he had Director Smyslov to thank for his therapists' quality. He had called in a favor from the President to have therapists typically dedicated to Russia's Olympic team used for Grishkov's treatment, as well as their equipment.

"So, am I right to guess that the scowl on your face when the door opened was from Arisha's reaction to that news?" Vasilyev asked.

Grishkov's wife Arisha had been delighted by Smyslov's decision to retire Grishkov from FSB service after his mission in Ukraine and send him to relative safety as a Captain in the Moscow police force. Captains were well known to spend most of their time at a desk.

"Yes," Grishkov, and the scowl returned. "It took a visit to my home by the Director to return some semblance of peace."

All three of them stared at Grishkov in astonishment. "Smyslov came to your apartment?" Vasilyev finally managed.

Grishkov nodded glumly. "His security detail locked down the building's elevators and closed the stairs. Our neighbors probably won't talk to us for a month."

Vasilyev shook his head. "But here you are, so the Director must have been persuasive."

"Well, yes," Grishkov said with a shrug. "He promised that this mission would be far safer than our previous ones: no nuclear bombs, no terrorists, no criminals. And we won't be going to a country at war like Afghanistan. Though even that wasn't enough."

"Remarkable," Vasilyev said with a laugh. "And what convinced her?"

Grishkov gave a small smile in reply. "Arisha promised that I would come home to an empty apartment if the Director didn't tell her where I was going. At first, I thought that would get me a pass for this mission. Finally, though, he told her."

Vasilyev pointed at the folders on the table. "I just finished reading through our briefing, and our destination wasn't included. So, where are we going?"

"America," Grishkov said.

Simultaneously, the door opened behind Grishkov, and the burly, heavily bearded form of FSB Director Smyslov entered.

"So, you have spoiled my little surprise," Smyslov said, wrapping his arms around Grishkov in his trademark bear hug.

Finally releasing Grishkov, Smyslov waved them all to their seats.

"Grishkov had a chance to read these briefing papers when I visited him last night. Truly, Arisha reminded me that women have always had an equal role in making Russia a great country," Smyslov said.

"So, no nuclear weapon this time?" Vasilyev asked.

Smyslov shook his head. "No. But, your training over the past fourteen months wasn't wasted," he said, pointing at Kharlov and Neda.

Kharlov nodded. "So, we will be disabling a ballistic missile. Just not one with a nuclear warhead."

"Correct," Smyslov said. "You were training previously on methods to prevent the launch of an SS-18 ballistic missile. The rocket you will be disabling now will be even larger, but our experts believe one of those methods should still be effective."

Neda frowned. "But they don't happen to know which one?"

Smyslov shook his head. "The rocket is brand new, and so the information we have been able to obtain is limited. Frankly, even what we have is probably out of date. Eli Wade has been pushing his technicians very hard to improve the rocket's performance."

Neda tapped the file folder in front of her. "And this will be the first launch of his newest rocket, with a payload of over one hundred tons."

"Correct," said Smyslov.

Now it was Vasilyev's turn to tap his file folder.

"All that's here. But not a word about what I'll be doing. Am I right to guess that Anatoly will accompany me?" Vasilyev asked, gesturing towards Grishkov.

"Yes, but let me back up a moment. You are all being sent on a contingency basis. It is possible none of you will have to do anything and will simply be ordered home," Smyslov said.

Vasilyev nodded. "So, we don't need to know what would have to go right for us to enjoy an American vacation. But it won't take long before orders come one way or the other."

Smyslov nodded.

"And you're not optimistic," Vasilyev said flatly.

"No," Smyslov said.

"So..." Vasilyev prompted.

Smyslov sighed. "There are several reasons why I was forced to hold our meeting in this wretched secure conference room, rather than my office. Where I could have given you a sendoff meal worthy of the importance of your mission. Though my office is secure against all known eavesdropping methods, this room is supposed to be proof against even the unknown. And it was designed by my predecessor."

The rest of those at the table all looked at each other. They knew Smyslov's predecessor was now Russia's President.

"He is the one who established the rule that this room must be used to discuss assassinations," Smyslov added.

"Of who?" Vasilyev asked.

"I was ordered not to tell you, and when I walked in this room, I intended to obey that order. Now, though, I realize that would mean sending you all to a critical mission without understanding its objectives. Or having the opportunity to ask intelligent questions. Neither is acceptable," Smyslov said slowly and drew a deep breath.

"So, here are the details. The Chinese have asked for our help in acting against Eli Wade's satellite Internet program. They consider it a threat to national security. Our President has agreed. The Chinese are also trying to pressure Wade through the American government, but think success is unlikely," Smyslov said.

Vasilyev nodded. "Up to now, Wade has been launching satellites sixty or so at a time. This new model of his Spaceship would make that many hundreds at a time, so it must be prevented."

"Correct," Smyslov said. "The hope is that Wade would stop launches for some time while the cause of the Spaceship's failure was investigated."

Vasilyev shook his head. "But this Wade didn't get where he is now by being stupid. Surely, he would suspect a connection between Chinese objections to his satellite Internet service and the failure of his rocket that would launch many more. And couldn't he just continue using his old rockets?"

Smyslov shrugged. "Maybe. However, the Chinese turned to us because a check by the Americans of China's agents will show that none were active in Florida. And the American government is likely to insist on an investigation before any more of Wade's rockets are launched, old or new. Especially if the launch failure is...catastrophic."

Vasilyev nodded. "Very well, let's suppose the Florida operation goes perfectly. How long before Wade starts launching satellites from California? He already has an operational base there, doesn't he?"

Smyslov nodded. "You're right. It's only a question of time, and probably not much time at that. We would then have to move on to more direct measures. That's where you and Grishkov come in."

Vasilyev looked at Smyslov in disbelief. "Assassinate Wade? But surely the American reaction would be..." His voice trailed off.

"Yes, severe," Smyslov said irritably. "But only if you're caught. Obviously, we'll have to make sure the Americans have no idea who to blame."

Kharlov had been listening attentively but had said nothing. Now, though, he could no longer restrain himself.

"I am the new man here, so I apologize for asking a question that may seem obvious to the rest of you. Why are we doing this? Surely not just because the Chinese asked?"

Everyone else looked at Smyslov, who sighed. "No, you're right. There's more to it. The Chinese have promised to buy all our exports of oil and gas. More, they have agreed to make us their sole supplier, which would support our opening new production fields in Siberia."

Vasilyev nodded. "With the election coming up, I can see why our President would like to see such a deal go through."

Smyslov shook his head. "I would have resigned before approving this operation if I thought the President's political fortunes were all that was at stake. None of you know how serious our economic problems are, and that's very much by design. But if we don't make this deal with the Chinese work, we'll run through our foreign exchange reserves before the end of this year."

Neda slowly asked, "That sounds bad, but what does it mean?"

"An economic depression worse than the one that followed the collapse of the Soviet Union. Followed by revolution, civil war..." Smyslov's voice trailed off.

"We should never have let ourselves become so dependent on petrochemicals to support our economy," Vasilyev said.

"Agreed," Smyslov said. "But here we are. We can only deal with the world as it is, not as we wish it could be. For us, that means making the best of a bad set of options."

Then Smyslov looked at his watch.

"And for all of you, it means you must be on your way to the airport." Rising, Smyslov hugged them in turn, wishing each of them good luck as they left the conference room.

They were all able to fit in the elevator, but thanks to Kharlov's bulk, only just.

Kharlov looked at Grishkov and said in a low voice, "I understand you're the only one of us who has been to America before. What do you think of our chances?"

Grishkov grunted and replied, "I won't tempt fate by even trying to guess."

Chapter Four

Zhongnanhai Compound
Beijing, China

President Lin Wang Yong looked up from the folder on his desk as an aide ushered in General Yang Mingren, the Air Force Commander. As was proper, General Yang stood at attention before President Lin, whose titles included Chairman of the Central Military Commission. Or what the Americans would call the Commander in Chief.

Yang was taller than the Chinese male average, at one hundred seventy centimeters, or about five and a half feet. Lin was only a few centimeters shorter, which made his height still slightly above the Chinese average.

An objective observer would have said Lin's looks were just average, while Yang looked as handsome as everyone thought a fighter pilot should. Party officials were expected to marry and have the single child that up until recently had been government policy. Lin had done just that.

Not Yang.

A string of girlfriends left behind when Yang transferred from one base to another testified to his ability to convince one woman after another that he was finally ready to settle down.

He wasn't.

Yang's ambition was only part of the reason he had never married. Yes, a wife and, even worse, a child would have been distractions his career couldn't afford.

But even more fundamentally, Yang cared about no one but himself.

This was probably all that Yang and Lin truly had in common.

"Please, have a seat, General," Lin said, after judging that fifteen seconds was long enough to leave him standing.

It never hurt to remind the military that in China, the Communist Party was in charge.

"Thank you, Mr. President," Yang said impassively as he sat and adjusted his wire-frame glasses. As he approached late middle age, he now needed them.

Well, Lin thought, Yang's file did say the General's days of flying fighter jets were well behind him. But that's not what he needed him for today.

"I'm impressed with the progress you've made so far," Lin said, gesturing at the folder on his desk.

Yang just nodded. Good, Lin thought. He was smart enough to know there was a "but" coming.

"However, it appears that so far, you have done no testing of this new antisatellite laser weapon outside of the laboratory. Or have I missed something?" Lin asked.

"You have not, sir. I had just completed a draft of a request to the National Space Administration for an orbital test when Minister Song's office advised me of your interest. I have held the request in case you wish the test to...change its focus," Yang replied.

Lin nodded. "Perhaps soon. Would it be possible to reserve a spot on an upcoming launch on a contingency basis?"

"With your support, we could pick any available date. I recommend we select the next launch, due a week from now. Our original intent was to test our new laser weapon against a small satellite we put in orbit for that purpose last year. It has an electronic and communications package designed to send us telemetry on the laser's effectiveness up to the point that transmission will cease if the weapon is successful. If you decide to target the American satellites instead, that change will be easy to make," Yang said.

"Good. From your briefing papers, it appears this weapon's point is to allow the destruction of satellites while avoiding responsibility for doing so. How confident are you that it will be successful?" Lin asked.

Yang blinked, and for a moment, said nothing. Good, Lin thought. Only a fool would answer such a question without careful consideration.

"The weapon is coated in materials that should make its observation from the ground extremely difficult, even by the most powerful telescopes. The laser is designed to leave its target physically intact. For a communications satellite, the laser should be able to achieve the goal of rendering it inoperable by heating its interior components. We would stop firing soon after the target ceases transmitting," Yang replied.

"Yes, I read here you are hoping that even physical examination of the target satellite might not reveal the cause of failure," Lin said, tapping the file folder on his desk.

Yang nodded. "The Americans have retrieved satellites from orbit before. Naturally, there is a danger that once the target's interior cools, it will again be able to function. So, we must balance the goal of target destruction with our need to avoid responsibility for that act."

Then Yang hesitated, and Lin could see he was having trouble with what he would say next.

Long experience at this level of Chinese government told Lin that could mean only one thing.

Bad news.

"Yes?" Lin asked quietly.

"Mr. President, I must admit that a SpaceLink satellite would not have been our choice for an initial test of this laser weapon. Its 'sun visor' presents a unique challenge," Yang said.

Lin frowned and repeated, "Sun visor?"

"Yes, sir. When SpaceLink first deployed its satellites, there was an immediate outcry from astronomers. They complained that the reflected light from the satellites was too bright and interfered with their observations. Several years ago, SpaceLink included what they call a 'sun visor' on each satellite," Yang said.

"And you believe it will interfere with our weapon's performance," Lin said flatly.

"Yes, sir, but we still think a successful attack is possible. The visor is oriented to prevent sunlight from reflecting off the satellite and back to earth. At a minimum, we will probably have to use more power than we would have needed otherwise. We may also be forced to come a bit closer to the target. It may also be necessary to maneuver the weapon to strike a gap in the visor's coverage. And that raises another issue," Yang said.

Lin sighed. "What is that, General?"

"The SpaceLink satellites have a built-in capability to avoid other satellites that come too close. That capability activates automatically. We won't know if we can reach an effective firing range without triggering this SpaceLink auto-avoidance until we try it. However, I remain confident that despite these issues, we will ultimately be successful," Yang said.

Lin shook his head. "But even if you can destroy a single satellite, all you have said makes it seem unlikely you will reach your goal of destroying dozens with a single weapon."

Yang nodded. "Certainly not as quickly as projected in the briefing papers you have before you, which were for attacks on ordinary communications satellites. The number we need to target, though, should be manageable. I understand we will only be striking ones broadcasting a signal that can be used within China."

"Correct," Lin said.

Yang smiled. "Excellent. Though there are thousands of SpaceLink satellites in orbit, only a few dozen provide coverage that can be used within our country."

Then Yang's smile disappeared. "I regret, though, that I must advise you of a complication that has arisen just hours before our meeting."

Lin frowned. "And what is that, General?"

"The American military has announced that SpaceLink has been awarded a new contract to support their communications. There were few details, but we think we know the broad outline. In short, SpaceLink will provide backup to existing American military communications capabilities," Yang said.

Lin nodded slowly. "I read in the briefing papers that the American military signed a contract with SpaceLink several years ago providing them funds to evaluate their technology."

"Correct, Mr. President," Yang said. Though he did his best to conceal it, Lin could see that Yang was surprised both that he had read that detail and had been quick to make the connection.

Lin had noticed that other high-ranking officers besides Yang appeared to be surprised whenever their civilian counterparts proved competent.

That either meant too many high Party officials were incompetent or that the military was acquiring an exaggerated opinion of their abilities.

Or maybe both.

Neither would be good. Both together could spell real trouble.

These thoughts passed through Lin's mind in a flash.

Aloud, Lin added, "It appears the American military's evaluation is now complete."

"Yes, sir," Yang said. "For this operation, what we don't yet know is the importance the American military will attach to the destruction of a handful of SpaceLink satellites out of thousands."

Lin shrugged. "Maybe a risk we'll have to take." Then his eyes narrowed.

"How many GPS satellites do the Americans have?" Lin asked.

Yang replied without looking at his notes. "Thirty-one are operational. Nine are held in reserve, and three are currently being tested."

Lin nodded. "And the GLONASS satellites which serve the same purpose for the Russians?"

"Twenty-four are operational. As far as we know, they have none in reserve," Yang replied promptly.

Now it was Lin's turn to be impressed. Well, global positioning must be critically important for the Air Force.

"And the Beidou satellites which give us our global positioning capability?" Lin asked.

"The third phase of Beidou to provide global coverage was completed in 2020 with the thirtieth satellite launch. Since then, we have launched three more that are kept in reserve," Yang replied.

"Will any of these SpaceLink satellites be a backup to the American GPS satellites?" Lin asked.

And looked at Yang closely while he responded. The other questions had been part curiosity and part an effort to break Yang's focus.

For this question, he needed an honest answer.

"We don't know. But it is possible," Yang replied instantly.

Yes, a truthful answer, Lin thought. And the one he feared.

"I should clarify that my guess is based on our efforts in this direction. All of the dozens of commercial communications satellites we've built that are now in orbit are designed to allow switching to military use in case of emergency," Yang said.

"Including satellites we've sold to other countries?" Lin asked.

"Naturally," Yang replied. "Of course, we would clear that decision through your office."

Lin nodded, but he was actually alarmed. He wasn't surprised that such a "back door" was present. Lin already knew they had been built into many Chinese-manufactured computer and communications systems.

But it was one thing to gather data on foreigners remotely and untraceably. Taking over another country's communications satellite...

Yes. That might be a step too far unless they were engaged in war with the Americans.

Was Lin about to start one?

"Tell me more about how a SpaceLink satellite might back up the American's GPS capability," Lin said.

"First, it's important to recognize that there are major differences between them. GPS satellites orbit at an altitude of about twenty thousand kilometers. SpaceLink satellites orbit far lower, at about five hundred fifty kilometers. GPS satellites weigh over sixteen hundred kilograms, much of it accounted for by sophisticated electronics and transmission capabilities. SpaceLink satellites weigh a bit over two hundred kilos," Yang said.

"Understood. So, despite these differences, SpaceLink satellites could help replace damaged or destroyed GPS satellites?" Lin asked thoughtfully.

"Possibly," Yang said. "It would require combining the capabilities of multiple SpaceLink satellites. It might require changing their orbital positions. The calculations needed would require a supercomputer. Maybe more than one."

Yang paused. "Of course, they have had several years to make at least some of those calculations in advance. Once made, updating them would be much easier and quicker since the position of the GPS and SpaceLink satellites is relatively static within a month or so after launch."

Lin nodded. "And if you were in command of the American Air Force?"

Yang didn't hesitate. "I would do everything I have just described. If the Americans have invested that sort of time and effort over the past few years, I would expect them to react strongly to the destruction of multiple SpaceLink satellites."

"Yes. Well, it may not come to that," Lin said with a shrug. "But we must prepare in case the Americans are unwilling to listen to reason. Send me orders to sign to get your weapon on the next launch. We'll either test it on the satellite you put in orbit last year or on SpaceLink satellites providing uncontrolled Internet access to subversives. One way or the other that is going to stop."

Chapter Five

Beijing, China

Mark Bishop was the station chief at the US Embassy in Beijing, the highest representative of the CIA in country. He looked nothing like spies did in movies. Middle-aged, slim, medium height with brown hair, Bishop wore glasses and clothes that would have made him at home in any office cubicle in America.

There was absolutely nothing remarkable about Bishop.

Of course, Bishop was not on the Embassy's official directory as "CIA," nor was anyone else. However, as the station chief, he was a "declared" agent. That meant the Embassy had notified the Chinese government unofficially that Bishop was the CIA station chief. Just as years earlier, before his promotion, the Embassy had told the Chinese that Bishop was the deputy chief.

Some CIA agents assigned to the Embassy had also been "declared" to the Chinese, though others had not. The Chinese worked hard to find the rest, though Bishop was fairly confident there were always a few they missed.

Naturally, the Chinese Embassy in DC and their many consulates scattered around the US played the same game.

Now Bishop only had a few months left until he was due to be transferred to his new job at CIA headquarters in Langley, Virginia. It was another promotion, but Bishop was dreading the move. He'd joined the CIA to work in the field, not to push papers at a headquarters desk.

Yes, he'd be paid more. Yes, the papers would be important. Yes, he'd tell a lot of people in both Langley and overseas what to do.

It wasn't bad enough to make Bishop think about retiring.

Not seriously, anyway.

As Bishop looked around the empty restaurant, he had to smile. As the lamest of ducks, it had come as a real surprise to receive this lunch invitation from Minister Song, head of the Ministry of State Security (MSS). Keeping an eye on spies was only one of the many jobs on Song's list.

No, if he'd wanted to, Song could easily be seeing the Ambassador instead. So, why Bishop?

Well, Bishop was smiling because one reason might be to make a point. This was the very restaurant where Bishop had met several years ago with a Deputy Director of the Chinese Ministry of Foreign Affairs. By far the highest-ranking official to defect from China. Selecting this restaurant out of literally thousands for their lunch was Song's way of saying he knew Bishop had been involved in that defection.

But that had to be incidental.

There were few others at the Embassy who approached Bishop's level of fluency in Chinese. Certainly not the Ambassador, a political appointee who knew only a few polite phrases.

Bishop shook his head. Song had obtained a university degree in the United States, like many high-ranking Chinese officials. If he were worried about the potential for misunderstanding, Song would just speak in English.

No, only one reason made sense. Deniability. Whatever Bishop said after this meeting would be the word of a spy.

Bishop's smile widened despite himself. The Chinese were adversaries, but you had to admire them. They knew how to play the game.

No sooner had Bishop had that thought than the door opened to admit Song and his security detail. Several other men emerged from corners of the restaurant where they had been hidden from Bishop's view, apparently as an advance guard. At their signal, the men around Song took up positions around the restaurant.

Song walked directly to Bishop's table. Bishop stood and made the short bow required by custom, along with the usual pleasantries in Chinese.

Both men took their seats, and Song looked at Bishop with frank curiosity. Finally, he said in flawless American accented English, "I'd been told your Chinese is good but am still surprised. It's the best I've heard from an American without Chinese parents. In fact, if I'd heard you on the phone, I could have mistaken you for a Chinese citizen."

Bishop smiled. "Thank you, Minister. I consider that high praise."

Song nodded. "I've taken the liberty of putting us both in the hands of the chef. That will give us more time to talk."

"Of course," Bishop said. "I have to admit to great curiosity about the topic that prompted your invitation. I'm sure you know that, with great regret, I will soon have to leave China."

"Yes," Song said. "But I have an important message to convey before you go."

Then Song paused.

"Though we serve different masters, I believe we both understand that not all information should be shared with the public," Song said.

Bishop nodded but said nothing. Now wasn't the time to debate where to put that information-sharing line.

"We consider the ability to decide which information should be shared with all our citizens a matter of national sovereignty," Song continued.

Bishop again nodded but stayed silent. By using the term, "national sovereignty," Song was making it clear his government considered this a matter of vital national interest.

In other words, the Chinese were very, very serious.

It was also interesting that Song was saying nothing about the accuracy of information shared with the public, a point commonly stressed when China was challenged on censorship.

No, Song was saying that the issue was access to information, true or not.

"I'm sure you're aware that some of our citizens are obtaining access to the Internet through American satellites," Song said flatly.

Bishop did his best to keep his expression impassive, as he thought to himself incredulously, "That's what this is about?"

"Yes, but I understand this is an unintended by-product of making Internet service available to countries bordering China. I've also read that the company providing the service, SpaceLink, regularly discovers and terminates access to unpaid users no matter where they are located," Bishop said.

Song nodded. "I believe all you have said is true. However, the ingenuity of the people providing pirated Internet access appears more than a match for SpaceLink's security measures. The situation has now become intolerable. We believe there is only one solution."

Now we come to the deniable part, Bishop thought. The Chinese knew nobody would like their solution.

"SpaceLink must terminate its Internet service to all countries bordering China. We have been launching satellites designed to provide high-speed Internet service since 2020 and plan to launch more soon. China will take over the task of providing Internet service to all countries on its borders. Naturally, we will provide SpaceLink with fair compensation for the value of its contracts," Song said.

"Is this a matter you have discussed directly with SpaceLink?" Bishop asked.

Song shook his head. "No. We believe they would reject our offer. However, given the importance of American government contracts to SpaceLink and its parent company, we think they would listen to you."

Bishop shrugged. "Of course, I can do no more than convey your proposal. However, I must ask, why do you believe we would be willing to consider it?"

Song nodded. "Your government recently requested that China cease construction on an island in the South China Sea. Are you familiar with the request?"

Bishop was, and nodded. China's latest and most extensive effort to annex a vast swath of ocean territory, including much that was closer to other countries than to China. This was done by dumping thousands of tons of rock and sand on low-lying atolls to manufacture "islands" over which China then claimed sovereignty.

And on which China built military bases, in case any of its neighbors objected.

"If your government can convince SpaceLink to agree to our proposal, we will suspend construction on this island as requested. Further, we will not start construction on any other island in the South China Sea, pending a negotiated settlement agreeable to all countries in the region," Song said.

"Do you speak for President Lin in this matter?" Bishop asked.

The question was a formality, but Bishop had to ask for his report. He could see that Song understood this from his immediate smile.

"Of course," Song said.

A glance from Song to a member of his security detail was all that was necessary to start a procession of waiters bringing one course after another for their lunch.

The food was excellent, but Bishop hardly tasted it.

He couldn't imagine President Hernandez agreeing to the deal Song had just proposed. From what he'd heard of Eli Wade, Bishop doubted he would either.

So, if the answer was no, what would the Chinese do next?

CHAPTER SIX

Near the Chinese-Indian Border

Sergeant Xu was prone as he looked through the scope of his Zijiang M99 sniper rifle at the distant mountain where they thought the Indians had put their observation post.

No movement.

Then Xu swept his scope over the rest of the unofficial no man's land between Chinese and Indian forces.

Nothing.

Xu began backing away from their position, taking care to use movements drilled into him as the least likely to be observed from a distance. This was when the vegetation that had concealed them could if they were careless, betray them instead.

A glance to his side told Xu that his spotter, Corporal Guan, was both keeping up and using the same care with his movements.

Guan was grumbling about moving yet again, but he was careful to keep the volume below the level where Xu would have to take notice.

In some ways, Xu thought Guan had the more challenging job. Guan's 25/40×100 long-range observation binoculars had served the

People's Liberation Army (PLA) well for decades. They gave him a better field of view than Xu's scope, which was, after all, the point.

Otherwise, Guan couldn't warn Xu of danger, like soldiers coming to flank them while Xu was focused on a target.

But the binoculars and their tripod made Guan a more visible target and one that couldn't shoot back.

For decades their Indian sniper opponents had been armed with the Russian Dragunov rifle, which had an effective range of about eight hundred meters. That could be a bit more or less, depending on the sniper's skill and the scope fitted to the rifle.

Recently, though, the Indians had been armed with several more advanced sniper rifles. One, produced by the Italian company Beretta, was chambered to fire the .338 Lapua Magnum cartridge and would undoubtedly exceed the Dragunov's range.

But that wasn't the rifle Xu feared.

No. The one that concerned Xu was the American M95 Barrett .50 caliber rifle.

In theory, the Beretta company's rifle could match the Barrett's effective range of nearly two kilometers. His own gun was supposed to be able to do almost as well.

Before his last leave, Xu might have believed what he'd been told in training.

Nobody in his family knew more about Xu's military service than his specialty as a sniper. He certainly hadn't told any of them where he was now stationed.

But when he'd come home for a brief visit, there was his cousin Deshi. He was more like the brother Xu had never had. Thanks to China's old one-child policy, a real brother had never been a possibility for Xu's generation.

At his first opportunity, Deshi had pulled Xu aside and slipped him a USB drive.

With a grin, Deshi had refused to tell Xu what was on it, except that he should watch it alone with the sound off.

And that no, it wasn't pornography.

Soldiers weren't allowed to bring personal electronics with them on a front-line deployment, so Xu's old laptop had been in his bedroom right where he'd left it.

Xu's first thought when he'd walked into the room after everyone else had gone to sleep was how small it now seemed. Next, how long it took his laptop to boot.

Well, Xu thought with a sigh, soldiers loved to complain about military housing and equipment. It was easy to forget what civilians had to put up with unless they were rich.

Very few Chinese soldiers came from wealthy families.

As Xu slid the USB drive in place, he remembered just in time to turn down the laptop's volume. Knowing Deshi's sense of humor, the drive's content could easily turn out to be pornography after all.

But no. It had been far more shocking.

They were videos from a Western website blocked in China of the M95 Barrett's performance. And recent news reports from other blocked sites about fighting along the Chinese-Indian border.

Several of those reports said the Indians had purchased thousands of Barretts. And millions of rounds of ammunition.

And the Indians had been sold the technology to manufacture the bullets themselves.

Xu had to watch several of the Barrett videos twice to understand what was happening. These were American civilians! Who were firing the Barrett for...fun?

And they were making shots he knew his Zijiang M99 couldn't equal. Well, Xu thought bitterly, not with him at the trigger anyway.

Xu had plugged in headphones to hear the commentary and calmed a bit as he'd realized many of the men he saw shooting the Barrett were retired soldiers. OK, that made more sense.

Then he'd reached the last video, a news report describing a shot killing an ISIS fighter in Syria fired by a rifle he had never heard of, the McMillian TAC-50. The report said the TAC-50 was used by several military forces, including the American Navy Seals.

But this ISIS fighter had been killed by a Canadian sniper. From a range of over three and a half thousand meters.

Xu had never dreamed such a shot could be possible.

His hands shaking, Xu had deleted every file on the USB drive. Then he'd formatted the drive.

Xu was no computer expert. He had no idea whether any of the files could still be retrieved, but he wasn't going to take any chances.

Using a penknife, Xu pried the USB drive open and then snapped it into small pieces. Each piece went separately into the toilet on two different restroom visits.

The next morning after gulping down breakfast, Xu had pasted a fake smile on his face and told his parents he was going with Deshi to check out a new shop nearby.

As soon as they were out of sight of his parent's apartment building, Xu had grabbed Deshi's arm and pulled him into an alley after checking to make sure they were unobserved.

Slamming Deshi against the alley wall, Xu had snarled, "Who told you I was stationed at the Indian border?"

Deshi had laughed and shrugged. "Easy, cousin. Nobody told me. But where else are our snipers fighting? I figured if not now, then soon."

Xu's glare had softened as he could see Deshi was telling the truth. But he hadn't released his grip.

"How did you get the videos on that drive?" Xu had hissed.

"A friend with a Gateway. How else?" Deshi had asked as though the answer should have been obvious.

Xu's suddenly nerveless hands had dropped from Deshi's shoulders. Yes, how else, indeed?

Xu was sure a civilian caught with a Gateway would be punished, but not how severely. But a soldier, subject to military justice?

Then Xu had realized he was not the only one at risk.

Another wave of anger had swept Xu, and once again, he'd found himself holding Deshi up against the alley wall.

"You do know you've put all of us in danger, even your aunt and uncle?" Xu had asked furiously.

Deshi had shaken his head sullenly. "Too much drama, cousin. The police can't watch over a billion people every minute. You're out there risking your life, and this was stuff you needed to know."

That had made Xu stop and think and finally release Deshi.

It was true. The Barrett was a mortal threat, and he did need to know more about it.

After making Deshi swear he'd never repeat his use of a Gateway, they'd returned home.

Now, every time Xu was out with his rifle and spotter, he thought about those videos with the Barrett.

Those videos were the reason Xu was changing position about twice as often as he'd been told to in training. And why he was moving about double the recommended distance.

A gout of earth rose from their previous position, with bits falling on both Xu and Guan, followed by a distant *craaak*.

With a sheepish smile, Guan whispered, "Good call, sir."

Xu nodded absently, but in truth, felt no satisfaction.

Had the Indian sniper really been too slow to take the shot?

Or had they been dialed in the whole time, and the round fired as a deliberate warning?

Chapter Seven

The White House
Washington DC

President Hernandez smiled with genuine warmth as Eli Wade and General Robinson were ushered into the Oval Office, though for different reasons with each man.

Wade had always shared his belief that rebuilding America's crumbling infrastructure and restoring its educational system to its former world leadership should be top government priorities. For that matter, Hernandez saw SpaceLink as the best chance to get Internet access to the millions of Americans without broadband access. That would address a key infrastructure need as well as improve access to educational resources.

The fact that Wade had backed their shared beliefs with generous campaign contributions didn't hurt either.

As the Air Force Chief of Staff, General Robinson was at this meeting in part because Wade's company had just received a major Air Force contract. It was also due to Robinson's role as unofficial National Security Advisor, one he had refused several times to allow Hernandez to make official.

Robinson had told Hernandez he preferred to avoid the bureaucracy and media scrutiny that came with the title, and Hernandez had reluctantly agreed.

Hernandez and Wade were both busy men, and so pleasantries were brief. Robinson sat quietly as Hernandez explained China's request to Wade that SpaceLink stop providing satellite Internet access to countries surrounding its territory.

Wade frowned. "So, are you asking me to go along with China's request?"

Hernandez shook his head. "I think you know me better than that. First, I thought it was important you knew exactly what the Chinese were asking for, whether or not you decided to agree to it. Second, I won't lie. It would be nice to have the Chinese stop military construction in the South China Sea. But if you agreed to stop SpaceLink services around China, I doubt it would be long before they started up construction again."

Now Wade smiled. "Glad to see I backed the candidate with some common sense. So, what next?"

Hernandez spread his hands. "Up to you. It might be worth asking the Chinese how much compensation they'd be willing to offer for your backing out of a dozen or so contracts if only to buy time. Just out of curiosity, how much are you getting paid to provide SpaceLink services to those countries?"

Wade shrugged. "The only real money has come from Taiwan, which is funny in one respect. They already have the world's highest average Internet speed, and most of the population already has broadband access. But getting service to people in mountainous areas and on a few outlying islands was a government priority, and they were willing to pay a premium to be first in line."

Hernandez nodded. "Sounds like they'd be pretty unhappy if you cut them off."

"That's for sure. India wouldn't like it either, though they have many other companies working on improving Internet access. Anyway, I've already decided that short of a government order or a threat to withdraw your satellite launch contract, I'm not going to go along with what the Chinese want," Wade said.

Then Wade nodded towards General Robinson. "When I saw the General, I thought that's why he was here."

Now Robinson spoke for the first time, his voice a bit more gravelly than usual. "That's not how this administration does business, sir."

Wade leaned back in his chair and laughed. "Glad to hear it. Now, I may take you up on the suggestion that I pretend to be interested in negotiating an end to our SpaceLink contracts. I have manufacturing interests in China, and if they're going to be shut down in retaliation, a little time to prepare would be nice. I imagine some more time to think about what the Chinese will do next would help you too."

"Yes, it would. Speaking of your factories, I'm surprised the Chinese didn't start by threatening to close them," Hernandez said.

Wade shook his head. "They know it would be a dumb move for them, though they may end up doing it anyway. I have local partners with a lot more to lose than I do and friends in the Communist Party leadership. The technology in my main factory was great when we started, but we've made improvements in many fields since then that I've been very slow to incorporate in China. Especially in batteries. If they nationalize my assets, they know they'll never see that tech."

Hernandez frowned. "But you think out of frustration, they may do it anyway."

"You're right," Wade said, standing and offering first Hernandez and then Robinson his hand as he said, "Thanks for your understanding and support. I'll let you know whatever I hear from the Chinese."

Hernandez walked him to the door and said quietly, "We'll do the same, Eli."

SpaceLink DC Area Offices
Bethesda, Maryland

Eli Wade had expected Mark Rooter, his SpaceLink project manager, to be waiting for him when he arrived.

He hadn't been expecting Rooter to be holding a single piece of paper as though it were radioactive. As soon as Wade walked into the building entrance, Rooter handed it to him without comment.

Wade had finished reading it by the time they stepped off the elevator and into the top-floor conference room. Rooter knew Wade wouldn't want an audience for their discussion, so they were the only ones at the table.

"So, this message came to you directly by name from the Chinese Embassy here in DC?" Wade asked.

Rooter nodded. "They sure didn't waste any time. I figure their compensation offer is worth about twice the value of the contracts we'd be canceling. We have no financial reason not to go along with China's request to stop providing Internet service to the countries on their border."

"So, do you think we should do what the Chinese want?" Wade asked.

Rooter shook his head vigorously. "Absolutely not. Once we pull the plug on China's neighbors, who's next? Russia's neighbors? Saudi Arabia's? No, let's make it clear we won't let any country tell us not to provide Internet service to countries nearby, just because some of their citizens access our service without paying for it."

Wade smiled. "Exactly what I was thinking. So, what should we do instead?"

"Well, we've done some more research, and I think we've figured out what most of the Chinese users are doing with our service. They're accessing websites blocked by the Chinese government and sending each other communications they don't want the government to see," Rooter said.

"OK, that explains why their data use was low. Do you think we could pull the plug on them without inconveniencing our paying users?" Wade asked.

Rooter nodded but with a distinct lack of enthusiasm. "Yes. Our Chinese friends did a great job of counterfeiting our equipment. But we were able to zero in on the lower signal strength they built-in, so I'm sure we could disable all of them remotely."

Wade smiled. "Great job! But why do I feel that you're not so happy about this?"

Rooter shrugged. "This is your call, boss. But now that I know why these users want access to the Internet through our satellites, it doesn't feel like a victory to cut them off."

"I'm with you on that. The truth is, I haven't decided what to do. I might cut them off, or I might leave them alone, depending on what the Chinese government does after I refuse their compensation offer," Wade said.

Rooter just nodded, but Wade could tell he was relieved.

Wade frowned and said, "If the Chinese go ahead and nationalize my manufacturing operations, they'll hurt themselves more than me. I think that's why so far, they haven't even threatened to do so. If they do nationalize, though, I want options. Especially if they give me inadequate compensation."

"Options. You mean, besides cutting off non-paying users or letting them stay connected," Rooter said slowly.

"That's right," Wade replied. "You've analyzed what they're calling the 'Gateway.' Am I right to think we could produce those same devices easily and cheaply?"

"Well, sure. They're just a copy of our standard satellite Internet equipment, with a deliberately weaker Wi-Fi signal. I suppose to make them harder for the authorities to detect. If we wanted to, we could crank them out fast and cheap. But if we sold them in China, wouldn't that give the authorities there a valid reason to complain?" Rooter asked.

"It would. But I never said I'd sell our version of Gateways," Wade said with a smile.

Rooter stared at Wade. "You mean...just give them away?"

Wade nodded. "Do we have any way of getting in touch with the organization selling these Gateways? I don't want to involve anyone working for us who is now actually in China."

Rooter shrugged. "The head of our Singapore regional SpaceLink office is originally from China and still has good contacts there. Whether any of them could help with this, I don't know. But it's our best shot."

Then Rooter hesitated. "Not my business, boss, but who have we got running things on the manufacturing end in China? If we go down this road, it could work out badly for them."

"You're right," Wade said. "And never hesitate to tell me what you're thinking. I can miss important details just like anyone else. Not this one, though. Our last American citizen employee there got on a flight to LA this morning. I've been pulling our top people out of China one at a time since this business started."

"Good," Rooter said. "You think the people we have left in China are safe from retaliation?"

"With that government, you can never be sure, but I think so. All we have left in place besides factory workers are Chinese middle managers and technicians. The authorities know none of them would have had any policy-making role in the company. Besides, they're exactly the people the government would need to squeeze value out of my plants," Wade said bitterly.

Rooter nodded. "That makes sense. OK, I'll get my people working on our Gateway version. Now that I think about it, the best approach would be a version letting us dial the wireless strength up or down. That way, if this business somehow blows over, we can use the equipment anywhere."

Then Rooter paused and snapped his fingers. "We were just about to make a lot more units anyway to go with the SpaceLink satellites that will be launched by the new Spaceship next week in Florida. I'm going to go right now and get that production run held and replaced with a new variable wireless signal design."

Wade grinned. "Perfect! Now we'll be covered no matter what the Chinese do. Go to it!"

As Rooter nearly ran from the conference room, Wade mentally kicked himself. Never, never invite the wrath of the gods through the cardinal sin of pride. It was as though all those Greek legends Wade had read in his youth had taught him nothing.

Nationalize his manufacturing assets in China. Arrest his American staff in China. Get the American government to lean on him.

Wade shook his head. No, he couldn't think of anything else the Chinese could do to him.

Then Wade grimaced.

That left what he couldn't imagine.

Chapter Eight

Russian Embassy
Washington, DC

Boris Kharlov peered over the cup of coffee he was holding at Neda Rhahbar. They had come to the Embassy cafeteria for a break, since now at mid-afternoon, it was deserted.

Unlike everyone else at the Embassy, they had no desk where they were supposed to be working during fixed hours. Instead, Kharlov and Neda had spent days studying technical documents of the rocket they were supposed to destroy.

If, indeed, those orders arrived. So far, they had only been told to prepare and wait.

"Did you notice the sign marking the space just across from the Embassy as 'Boris Nemtsov Plaza'?" Kharlov asked.

Neda shook her head. "No. A Russian, I'm guessing. Who was he?"

"Ah yes," Kharlov grinned. "This other Boris was before your time in Russia. He was a political opponent of the previous President."

"When you say 'was,' I suppose you mean he's now dead," Neda said.

"Yes," Kharlov replied. "He was shot multiple times within sight of the Kremlin while accompanied by his girlfriend. She was untouched. Nemtsov died instantly."

Neda frowned. "Well, if this happened so close to the Kremlin, surely the crime was recorded on video. I've walked in that area many times, and it's full of cameras."

"You're right. There was a recording of the murder," Kharlov replied. "Unfortunately, the camera with the best view of the area was obstructed by a parked municipal vehicle, so the recording's image quality was poor."

Neda's eyebrows rose. "But surely a murder so brazen didn't go unpunished!"

"Naturally not," Kharlov said solemnly. "The then-President took personal charge of the investigation. The prime suspect died when police surrounded his apartment building in Chechnya, and he blew himself up rather than surrender."

Neda looked at Kharlov incredulously. "Isn't Chechnya almost two thousand kilometers from Moscow? How did he get that far despite a nationwide manhunt for Nemtsov's killer directed by the President himself?"

Kharlov shrugged. "A reasonable question. However, the incident's outcome did save the government the expense of a trial."

"OK, I get it. You think Russian government agents killed this Nemtsov, and then someone else was killed to cover it up. I guess the Americans do too, and that's why they named the space across the street from our Embassy after him," Neda said.

Kharlov shook his head. "I haven't said I think anything. But I do agree with your assessment of the conclusion drawn by the Americans."

Neda grimaced. "Well, the Americans' opinion of us doesn't seem to have improved much since they named that plaza. Every single time we've left the Embassy, they've had men following us."

"Good," Kharlov said with an approving nod. "I'd wondered whether you'd noticed them. The authorities here are quite capable and seem to have devoted significant resources to following us as unobtrusively as possible."

"Yes, I saw that too. Multiple teams, switching off to make detection more difficult. Well, I bet they're getting bored," Neda said.

Kharlov laughed. "I'm sure you're right. Yesterday, I thought I saw the last team call it a night before we got back to the Embassy."

Each evening since their arrival at the Embassy, they had walked together to a restaurant for dinner. At first, they had stuck to the three closest, one Mexican, one Chinese, and one Italian. Then they had walked further down Wisconsin Avenue into Georgetown. Last night they had turned onto M Street and went to within sight of the Potomac River and the Key Bridge leading to Virginia.

Each time Neda and Kharlov had done nothing but window shop and eat dinner. No dead drops. No clandestine meetings. As they'd been trained, their conversations were limited to comments about details observed during their walk.

Yes. By now, their watchers surely realized there was indeed nothing to see.

Neda looked up sharply. "That's the whole idea, isn't it? Get the Americans bored, so they stop paying attention to us."

Kharlov nodded. "That's my guess. It helps explain why there was such a rush to get us here, even though the launch we may or may not target is still days away. After all, we could have reviewed the SpaceLink rocket's details in Moscow."

"So, let me go back to that other Boris," Neda said.

Kharlov frowned and twirled his finger in the air, the signal that the cafeteria was probably monitored by Embassy security.

"Obviously," Neda said with a shrug. "Do you really think anyone cares what we think of the previous President?"

Kharlov grinned and said, "No, you're probably right. I guess old habits die hard. When I served in Spetsnaz, he was still very much alive."

"So, any misgivings about what happened to Nemtsov on that bridge?" Neda asked.

Kharlov sat back in his chair and thought for a moment before answering. "We saw what Russia would be like with a weak leader in the 1990s under Yeltsin. Nobody wants to go back there. That leaves the question of whether killing your opponents makes you strong or just feared."

Kharlov paused and then shook his head. "Shooting Nemtsov sent four messages. The first, doing it within sight of the Kremlin, said opponents aren't safe anywhere. The second, doing it while Nemtsov was with his girlfriend but leaving her untouched, said we don't care who sees us do it. The third, blaming the killing on perhaps the least credible suspect in Russia, said we're only going through the motions of a cover-up. Because we want you to know we did it. The fourth, making sure the suspect died, too, said there would be no official reason to continue the investigation. Such as it was."

Neda frowned. "Maybe the fifth was that they didn't care what anyone outside Russia thought."

"True. And besides naming the plaza across the street after Nemtsov, another truth is the Americans and Europeans didn't do much. But while we're on the subject of assassinations, you're really thinking about Vasilyev, yes?" Kharlov asked quietly.

Neda looked up quickly and jerked her head in a way that Kharlov knew was meant to remind him they were probably under observation.

Kharlov shook his head. "Naturally, I won't discuss either our mission or his here. But you are worried about him, aren't you?"

Neda said nothing and just glared across the table at Kharlov.

"And I understand you have something of a soft spot for Grishkov too since he helped you make it out of Iran," Kharlov said flatly.

Neda's glare, if anything, intensified.

Kharlov nodded. "Well, then think about this. The best chance that their mission is called off is that we are successful with ours."

Neda frowned and then slowly nodded.

Then she stood and put down what was left of her coffee.

Kharlov rose as well and grinned. "Yes, let's get back to it."

Chapter Nine

Qinshan Nuclear Power Plant
One Hundred Kilometers South of Shanghai, China

Plant Complex Director Wu walked up to Qinshan Senior Manager Tan, who tried to keep the groan he felt from reaching his face. What now?

Tan turned away from the technician he had been speaking with, who had the sense to scurry off. The Director coming down to reactor operations was never good news.

Putting a smile on his face he knew had to look insincere, Tan said brightly, "Good morning, sir! How are things looking today?"

"Well, better than I thought. You know I had questions about the safety of the extra fifty megawatts we started squeezing out of this old lady a few years ago. But so far, I haven't found anything wrong," Wu said.

Tan breathed a sigh of relief. Qinshan was the oldest nuclear plant still operating in China, and had been built over thirty years ago. Much of its non-nuclear equipment like turbines, pumps and motors had recently been replaced in a major refit. But the reactors themselves had been left untouched.

Tan was beginning to feel his age as well. Sadly, he mused, a refit wasn't an option for him.

Tan hadn't been looking forward to retirement after reaching sixty. But he was starting to change his mind.

Wu was Tan's boss, even though Wu was ten years younger. That didn't bother Tan. He had plenty to deal with, and didn't have any interest in adding more work.

"I'm glad to hear it, sir. We've been doing our best," Tan said with all the confidence he could muster. But he knew from Wu's expression that something else was coming.

There was nothing Tan could do except grit his teeth and hope for the best. It had been three months since Wu had been appointed to oversee both the Qinshan and Fangjiashan nuclear plants. Since only about ten kilometers separated the two plants, Tan had to agree that made sense.

And since Fangjiashan was twenty years newer than Qinshan, it was also logical that Wu was more concerned about his plant's safety.

None of that made Tan's life any easier.

"I know my concerns may seem excessive. But you know why I was appointed," Wu said, his eyes glittering.

Tan swallowed hard. Yes. He knew.

Just before Wu's appointment, there had been an accident at Qinshan resulting in the release of a small amount of radioactivity. Tan's old boss had done everything right in response. There had been no casualties and only a brief interruption in power production. Nobody outside the plant had any idea that there had been a problem.

But Tan hadn't seen or heard from his old boss since. And Tan knew better than to ask what had happened to him.

"This past weekend, I drove to Shanghai, for the first time since I moved here. Do you know what I noticed?" Wu asked.

Tan knew. Just as he knew, he had to play along with Wu while he made his point.

"No, sir, what?" Tan replied.

"Thanks to traffic, it took me over three hours to get into Shanghai proper, even though the city limits are only a hundred kilometers away. But you know what has happened to the farms I remember were in this area when I visited Shanghai as a child?" Wu asked.

"They're gone, right?" Tan said, his heart sinking.

"Exactly so," Wu said. "Instead, there are industrial plants, apartment buildings, shops of all sorts. I'm not going to say every square meter between here and Shanghai has been paved over. But it's not for lack of trying."

Tan had to nod agreement. The growth of Shanghai's suburbs had indeed been spectacular, even by Chinese standards.

And much of that growth had been in the direction of this nuclear power plant.

"So, if something serious went wrong here, how many people do you think could be affected?" Wu asked.

Well, there it was, Tan thought bitterly. As though he could do anything about where Qinshan had been built.

"I'm not sure, sir. Quite a few, I'd guess," Tan said stoically.

Wu nodded. "I'm not sure either. My guess, though, would be in the millions."

Tan didn't know what to say to that. Especially since Wu was probably right.

But apparently, Wu hadn't been expecting an answer because now he was thrusting a plant-issued windbreaker towards Tan.

"Let's take a walk," Wu said and led the way to a door outside the plant.

It had been quite a while since Tan had been on one of the maintenance walkways that circled the reactor buildings. He had no trouble, though, remembering the cold, spray-filled breeze that blew in from Hangzhou Bay.

Qinshan was surrounded by water on three sides.

Waving his arm at the bay, Wu asked, "Does our location remind you of anywhere in Japan?"

Tan wasn't a fool and answered immediately. "I'm sure you're thinking of Fukushima, sir."

Wu nodded. "You know, the last estimate I saw said that cleanup there will take about forty years."

Tan winced but said gamely, "Yes, sir, but we don't see tsunamis here like the one that hit Fukushima."

"That's true," Wu said. "But what about typhoons?"

Tan shrugged. "China has been hit by typhoons before, but I checked when I started working here. The weather has never been a problem at this plant."

"You're right again. But do you know when and where the last big typhoon struck China?" Wu asked.

Tan shook his head.

"Typhoon Mamie in 1985. It made landfall along a stretch of coast from south of here up to Shanghai. A thousand factories had to shut down. Over six million trees were blown over. Nineteen rivers overflowed. More than a hundred thousand homes were damaged. A million people were directly affected," Wu said and then paused.

"Of course, this plant hadn't yet been built. That happened five years later," Wu said.

Tan nodded slowly. "I didn't know that," he said with grudging respect. "You are suggesting we should take precautions against the sort of seawater infiltration that damaged the Fukushima plant. In the event of storm-driven waves that make it past our current physical barriers."

"Correct," Wu said. "I know you will need additional resources. Draw up an action plan for my review, and I'll get it to Beijing."

Tan nodded. "Typhoon season is just beginning, which I suppose is what started you thinking about this. But you know there's no chance we'll get what we need approved in time for any big storm that comes our way this year, right?"

Now Tan got to see one of Wu's rare smiles. "Even I have to admit that 1985 was a long time ago. I think this time the odds are with us."

Part of Tan thought if he saw it, Wu would be afraid of his own shadow.

Another part, though, wished Wu hadn't just said that.

Chapter Ten

Shanghai, China

Chen Li Na had been making good use of her Gateway. She had used it to accelerate her efforts to recruit and organize a rapidly growing network of pro-democracy activists who all had one thing in common.

None of them believed the Communist Party should have a monopoly on power.

Chen's problem was that's about all they agreed on.

The single largest group was unhappy with China's economic problems and believed Party mismanagement and corruption were to blame.

Chen's parents had been among the many victims of one corrupt official, a man who demanded bribes to turn on water service to residences. He had the bad luck to be among the one percent of such officials to be arrested and turned into a national example.

When police searched his lavish home, they found over twenty million American dollars' worth of various currencies.

The next largest group were victims of the Hukou residence permit system. Anyone who had not been fortunate enough to be born in a large city like Shanghai could not simply move there. At least, not legally.

Chen had been lucky to have world-class software programming skills that had made several Shanghai companies actively recruit her. All had included a residence permit among their inducements.

But that made Chen one of the fortunate few.

At a minimum, all migrants from the countryside to the city were required to obtain a temporary residence permit. But that required a job offer, and those were increasingly scarce these days. And if the factory or construction company closed, the permit couldn't be renewed.

Naturally, some migrants came without a permit at all.

This meant any work those migrants found would be at the lowest pay.

And that, lacking a residence permit, no child the migrant had could be enrolled in a school in the city where the parent worked. About a fifth of all children in China had to live apart from their parents as a result.

Over sixty million children were separated from one or both of their parents most of the year while they attended school in rural areas and lived with grandparents or other relatives.

No residence permit? No access to subsidized housing. Or government health care. Or welfare, pension, or social security payments of any kind.

And if you had a problem with any of that, the authorities had a simple solution. You could be sent back to wherever in rural China your official records said you belonged. Even though, in some cases, you might have never actually lived there.

Never mind. Government records were never wrong.

That principle also applied to the social credit system, which had become a growing source of resentment to government authority. Large enough to give the residence permit system real competition for the title, "most hated Communist Party policy."

The social credit system took the concept of a financial credit score found in other countries and added a long list of other factors. These resulted in the possibility of reward or punishment, depending on a person's behavior.

So, you could get a high score from paying bills on time, donating blood, giving to charity, and avoiding any action that annoyed officials or businesses. That could mean less waiting time at a hospital or a discount for a hotel stay.

The government placed a much higher priority on using the system to punish bad behavior.

Such as? Well, it was a long and continually growing list. Failing to sort recyclables correctly. Jaywalking. Making a restaurant reservation and failing to show. Eating on public transport.

And doing anything – anything – that made an official believe they should lower your score.

For example, complaining about governmental incompetence or inaction. Or failing to pay a bribe.

Want to know why your score is low? Or who was responsible for lowering it?

Too bad.

Though, to be fair, there was one way you might find out what the authorities said you had done wrong. Score-lowering infractions, along with full identifying information on the miscreants who had committed them, were sometimes posted online.

And sometimes shown on electronic displays at major city intersections.

The consequences of a low score went beyond the denial of loans or employment that people with a low credit score experienced in other countries.

By 2019, the last year the government released official numbers, twenty-seven million people had been denied permission to buy airline tickets. Six million had been refused high-speed rail tickets.

The consequences didn't stop with the person who had the low score. Want to get your child into the right private school? Or a public university?

Well, their school grades might be good enough. But if one or both parent's score was too low, then the child's grades wouldn't matter.

Chen smiled as she looked at her sleeping girlfriend, Tang Yanfei. Chen might be doing well for her young age, but on her income, she was still lucky to afford this apartment within Shanghai city limits, only a short distance from her office.

Tang's job didn't pay nearly as well. Chen accepted no rent from Tang and instead had her buy groceries and contribute to the water and power bills.

Chen loved Tang, but she was always practical. The apartment, so close to her office, was in her name alone.

A long commute would have left Chen with no time for what she thought of as her "other job." Organizing resistance to the Communist Party.

As she looked around the dark apartment, though, Chen had to sigh. There was no bedroom. Chen was sitting up on the bed that folded out from her sofa, in what during the day was her living room.

Chen leaned over and carefully brushed Tang's hair away from her nose and mouth. She had always been a restless sleeper.

Chen frowned. Her mental inventory of groups with grievances against the Party always ended with her own. Same-sex couples.

True, overt employment discrimination had mostly stopped. Chen's company knew about Tang but didn't care.

A new "legal guardian" system helped cover issues married couples took for granted. Visitation rights at hospitals. Inheritance.

But there were many other rights denied to same-sex couples. Starting with the right to have children, either through in vitro fertilization or adoption.

And in Chinese society, the government pretended same-sex couples didn't exist. Cultural references in any form were banned, particularly in television programs and movies.

Chen had grown up feeling there was something wrong with her. It was a feeling she hated and still struggled with even after three happy years with Tang.

Chen smiled as she looked at Tang, who was still sleeping peacefully. She owed her a great deal. First, her sanity.

Just as important, Tang was her right hand in organizing resistance to the Party. Tang was the only person who had her absolute trust.

Yes, Tang was still sleeping. But what had woken Chen? Normally, she was an even heavier sleeper.

Chen checked her phone. At night, it had been set to activate only for emergency alerts. No activity.

Well, nothing in her tiny apartment was moving. Something outside?

Still holding the phone, Chen pulled her drapes back a fraction and looked outside.

What was that?

Chen had to squint to see it. A small black disk hovering next to a window two floors down.

Her heart thudding in her chest, Chen lifted her phone and focused its camera on the hovering disk. She made sure the drone filled the screen center before pressing the button that would send the recording directly to the phone's removable SD card.

It wouldn't do for the recording to show enough background to allow her building to be identified.

Chen stopped recording once the drone began to rise silently towards the floor just below hers. Then she backed away from the window after carefully closing the drapes behind her.

At this hour, there was minimal sound or video for a drone to collect. That just left one other possibility.

Wireless signals.

They were looking for Gateways.

Chen shook her head. The government would never rest until it had hunted down all its opponents.

Organizing was important, but now that phase was over.

It was time to act.

CHAPTER ELEVEN

Near the Chinese-Indian Border

Sergeant Xu looked down at the food in his bowl with a distinct lack of enthusiasm. The cooking he'd enjoyed during his recent leave with his family had reminded him of how breakfast, and for that matter every meal, was supposed to taste.

The food doled out by military chefs was never wonderful. Here at a front-line deployment, though, what was turned out by temporary field kitchens could best be described as...edible.

If you were really hungry.

Corporal Guan grinned as he saw Xu's expression and correctly guessed its cause.

"Your mother's cooking spoiled your appetite for what our chefs can manage?" Guan asked innocently.

Xu scowled but said nothing. Noncommissioned officers like Xu didn't normally eat with enlisted men like Guan, but everyone knew the relationship between a sniper and his spotter was different. Each depended on the other to stay alive in a way that encouraged close cooperation.

In this case, for Xu, that meant keeping his temper when provoked.

Besides, Guan was right, not that Xu would ever admit it.

Instead, Xu just growled in a low voice, "I don't see why any of us are here in this infernal frozen wilderness. Just about all the rest of China is warm and pleasant. As far as I'm concerned, the Indians are welcome to it."

Xu felt a sudden breeze behind him, and then Guan pale and jump upright, followed by all the other soldiers in the dining tent.

Years of drilling propelled Xu upright as well. Please, he thought, please don't let it be...

The unmistakable voice of Colonel Chang directly behind him telling the soldiers to resume their meals told Xu that his prayers were going unanswered.

Maybe Chang didn't hear what I was saying, Xu hoped desperately, as he fixed his gaze a few meters away on one of the thick wooden posts supporting the dining tent.

"Sergeant, Corporal, I think I'll join you. Lieutenant, please get us all a fresh cup of tea, and then take a break. I'm going to spend a little time talking to these men," Chang said.

Xu dared to feel a bit of relief. At least, it didn't look like Chang was going to have him punished on the spot for defeatism, so maybe he didn't hear Xu after all.

A lot of officers would have done that automatically, as Xu knew well. Chang had the reputation of being a good officer who treated his men well, even if he was a bit odd.

"I read the report of your last patrol with interest," Chang said, and all the soldiers within earshot relaxed, including Xu and Guan. Interest in a report was a perfectly normal reason for an officer to speak with an NCO like Xu.

Chang took a sip of his tea and frowned. Putting the cup back down, he said, "From your description, I could see that you took unusual precautions during your patrol. I do not doubt that those steps are what kept you alive, so we could speak today."

Xu did his best to keep relief from his expression. Chang had failed to hear his comments, or he wouldn't be praising him now.

"I had intended to stop by briefly to tell you this but was glad to hear you ask an important question as I arrived. Why are we all here on the border with India?" Chang asked rhetorically.

Now Xu tried hard not to wince, though he doubted he'd been successful.

"I will begin with a question of my own. Have you ever heard of Alaska?" Chang asked.

Xu nodded doubtfully, while as a mere corporal, Guan did his best to look simultaneously attentive and invisible.

"Good. Now, from what you've heard, would you imagine Alaska is as cold and snowy as where we are now?" Chang asked.

Xu nodded again, wondering where this was going.

He was also starting to see why Chang had the reputation of being a bit odd.

"America bought Alaska from Russia in the 1860s, just after the American Civil War. The Russians sold it because they believed the Americans might seize it otherwise. They also feared the British, who ruled Canada, might take it instead. Since Russia had recently lost a war to the British in Crimea, they much preferred to have the Americans on the other side of the Bering Strait, rather than the British and their navy," Chang said.

"That all makes sense, sir," Xu said. And it did. But what did it have to do with anything?

From the smile Chang gave him, for a horrified instant Xu thought he had asked the question aloud.

But no. Chang said, "It makes sense to you. And it did to many Americans. But others considered the purchase of Alaska unwise. The man in the American government who negotiated the purchase was named Seward. So Americans who opposed the purchase called Alaska 'Seward's Icebox' and 'Seward's Folly.' In the end, though, the Americans were repaid handsomely for their investment of seven million dollars. Do you know how?"

There was just one thing Xu thought he knew about Alaska, and he used that knowledge now.

"Sir, don't they produce oil in Alaska?" Xu asked.

"Excellent, Sergeant. Indeed they do, in substantial quantities. Long after Alaska's purchase, of course. In fact, before oil was even considered a resource. Now, let us imagine for a moment that the Americans had declined to purchase or seize Alaska, and the Russians had kept it. How could that have mattered?" Chang asked.

Xu frowned with thought, and then his eyes slowly widened.

"Sir, the Americans and Russians were mortal enemies for decades, and each built a vast nuclear arsenal targeted at the other. A large Russian territory in North America might have been a decisive advantage!" Xu exclaimed.

"Perhaps," Chang said with a smile. "Or, it could have led to a nuclear conflict between the two countries drawing in many others. Maybe including China. And then, you and I might not be talking here now."

That brought Xu up short. Yes, in hindsight, it did seem remarkable that with the thousands of nuclear weapons on both sides, none had ever been used against the other.

"So, Sergeant, what lesson would you draw from our discussion about Alaska that might apply to the territory where we now sit?" Chang asked.

Xu looked at Chang with new respect. "Sir, it seems land that appears worthless today might become much more valuable in the future. Maybe in ways that now we can't even imagine."

Chang stood and, smiling, patted Xu on the shoulder. "Just so, Sergeant. I'm pleased to see that you're as good at using your head as you are at keeping it out of sight of Indian snipers. Continue to do both."

Moments later, Chang and his aide had left the dining tent, and Xu and Guan were looking at each other.

"I feel just like I did when we dodged that round yesterday," Guan said.

Xu's laugh was short and sharp as he said, "You and me both."

CHAPTER TWELVE

Russian Consulate General
San Francisco, California

Mikhail Vasilyev looked out from one of the Consulate General's windows at the pedestrians and traffic below, without really seeing either. Anatoly Grishkov swirled the coffee dregs in his mug and fought the impulse to get another cup. He knew, as usual in any office, it would be no better than the last.

Detailed maps of San Francisco covered most of the large conference room table.

The remaining space was occupied by several large-scale blueprints of San Francisco's tallest buildings. Other blueprints were neatly stacked on a small side table.

It was a sizeable stack. It turned out there were plenty of tall structures in San Francisco, despite Vasilyev's vague hope that fear of earthquakes might have kept their number in check.

They had a schedule of events that would bring Eli Wade out from his home and office's safety, compiled from both public and covert sources. It gave them a starting point, but no more than that.

Wade was notorious for canceling some appearances at the last moment and dropping in at other events with no notice. Publicly this was often chalked up to the billionaire's eccentricity.

Vasilyev had noted, though, that one reporter had suggested one fact did more than any other to explain Wade's behavior.

The people at the events Wade attended or skipped nearly always needed him more than the reverse. So blacklisting him, for example, wasn't practical.

Several of the most experienced diplomats at the Consulate General had worked hard to annotate the schedule, focusing on the events where it was believed Wade was most likely to attend.

Heading that list was a charity event Wade was hosting himself that he had never missed since founding the charity over a decade ago. That fundraiser would be an ideal opportunity.

Except they weren't sure they would receive orders to act before the event.

"I think we should go downtown to get an in-person look at some of these buildings. Enough days have passed since our arrival that I think official curiosity in our movements has dropped sufficiently. Besides, we will look like we're taking in the sights," Grishkov said.

Vasilyev just nodded and continued looking out the window.

"Honestly, I don't know why our consulate was put way out here. There are no American government buildings nearby or other foreign consulates. Was it a punishment of some sort by the Americans?" Grishkov asked.

Grishkov didn't care one way or the other. But he knew he needed to get Vasilyev talking about something inconsequential before moving on to what was really bothering him.

It worked. Vasilyev glanced up and replied, "We asked for this location."

OK, now Grishkov was curious. "Do you know why?"

Vasilyev shrugged. "Not for sure. But you remember the park we walked through yesterday, called Presidio?"

Grishkov nodded. "Yes, very nice and impressive views, but surely not the reason we're at this location."

"Well, it was impressive enough that the Americans offered it as a possible UN location, though the mostly European selection committee picked the much closer New York City. However, when this mission opened in the 1970s, the Presidio was an Army base," Vasilyev said.

Grishkov nodded thoughtfully. "Yes, that was mentioned on several of the signs in the park. Are you suggesting we were conducting electronic surveillance of American military activities?"

Vasilyev smiled. "Well, whether we were or not, as you saw yesterday, it has been many years since the Army left. The base was closed along with many others after the end of the Cold War."

"Yes, and this consulate was closed for years due to American sanctions. It's fortunate we were finally allowed to reopen it, or this mission would have been far more difficult," Grishkov said.

Vasilyev sighed. "Yes. Fortunate."

"OK, let's have it," Grishkov said. "You haven't been yourself since Smyslov told us about our mission."

At first, Vasilyev started to object, and then he paused.

Grishkov sat back, his arms folded. He was glad Vasilyev had remembered on his own that, by necessity, the FSB officers here had been informed of their mission. Both to provide documents to assist with its planning, and with Vasilyev and Grishkov's subsequent exit from America.

Which was likely to be hasty.

So while it was possible their conversation was being monitored, it was unlikely. Standard FSB procedure was to disable listening devices in any rooms where planning for a declared mission was in progress. Vasilyev had reminded Neda before they left that she had no such protection since the FSB had given the Embassy in Washington no details about their mission.

Instead, the Embassy had only been told Neda and Kharlov would carry out their mission, if ordered, well away from Washington and without their involvement.

"Sorry," Vasilyev said shortly. "I was thinking about Neda again."

Grishkov nodded. "Of course you were. But being separated from her isn't the only reason you've been distracted."

"No, you're right. I don't like anything about this mission. That we're doing this at the bidding of the Chinese. That it's our weakness that lets the Chinese make such demands," Vasilyev said bitterly.

"Or that we're being forced to kill a man whose only crime is making it easier for the Chinese to learn facts their government would rather keep hidden," Grishkov added.

"Yes. Understand me. I will carry out my orders and know you'll do the same. If Smyslov says we risk returning to the Yeltsin period or worse if the Chinese don't buy our oil and gas, I believe him. To avoid that outcome, sacrificing one agent's conscience is a small price to pay," Vasilyev said.

"Well, you can make that two agents," Grishkov said. "I don't like doing this either. But I disagree with you on one point. There's just one thing about our orders I do like."

Vasilyev raised one eyebrow inquiringly but said nothing.

Grishkov laughed. "Remember that the Chinese are going to try to pay Wade off and might succeed. If that doesn't work, maybe when Neda and Kharlov blow up Wade's Spaceship, he'll reconsider the wisdom of going up against over a billion Chinese. If either of those things happens, then we can just fly home to Moscow."

Vasilyev shook his head. "You've read everything we have on Wade, including the assessment of the FSB's psychologists. Do you think either outcome is likely?"

"No," Grishkov replied promptly. "But I've lived longer than you. That means I've had more chances to be proved wrong. I'm hoping this is one of those times."

Chapter Thirteen

Three Gorges Dam
Hubei Province, Central China

Hydropower Director Peng looked down from the top of the dam to the vista below. It was truly spectacular. Water flowing through the spillway created a constant thunder that reminded Peng of the raw power under his control.

It was power on a scale difficult to fully grasp. The dam had the world's largest installed power capacity, at over twenty-two thousand megawatts. In 2020, they had set the world record in annual power production at over one hundred four terawatt-hours.

They had also set several less fortunate records.

Flooding upstream in the Yangtze River in 2020 had sent an unprecedented seventy-five million liters of water a second to the dam. The only way to cope with that volume had been to discharge well over half as soon as it was received, at a rate of nearly fifty million liters of water a second.

Despite the record water release, the dam's reservoir approached its rated limit of one hundred seventy-five meters for the first time. It ended up topping one hundred seventy meters.

Three hundred thousand residents bordering the river were evacuated. Multistory buildings were submerged.

Peng had subsequently been put in charge of the Three Gorges Dam and all of the many other dams on the Yangtze River's numerous tributaries. The critical problem identified after the near-disaster in 2020 had been refusal among other dam managers to coordinate water release, with each most concerned about possible damage to their facility. Plus, maintaining their power production quotas.

Peng had to admit that those dams were important. Though none were as large as the Three Gorges Dam, together, the top four subsidiary dams produced twice as much power. The largest, Xiluodu, was the world's third-largest power producer.

Unfortunately, Peng still needed Beijing's clearance to take any action that might affect power production. Still, Peng was confident that in a crisis, the government would back him.

Peng would risk damage to Xiluodu or any other dams if he had to because the Three Gorges Dam had to remain intact.

If the Three Gorges Dam collapsed, the flooding it would unleash would kill millions. It would be a disaster unprecedented in scale and scope, not just in China but worldwide.

Peng was determined to prevent that. At any cost.

Dam Manager Shen wasted no time scurrying through the biting wind to Peng's side. As though to encourage Shen, a sudden shift in wind direction sent spray from the spillway over the dam's side.

Drenched from head to toe and teeth chattering, Shen pulled his supposedly waterproof jacket tighter together. Peng, who had narrowly missed being soaked himself, tried to sound sympathetic.

"Sorry to drag you up here, Shen. But it's not just for the view," Peng growled.

Shen peered over the side, his miserable expression quickly replaced with one of pride. "It's always worth it," he said.

Peng nodded. Shen had many faults. But he made up for them with what Peng considered the most important virtue.

Total dedication to his job.

"Look down towards the base," Peng said quietly.

Shen did as Peng had ordered, and his look of pride disappeared. Peng had thought Shen looked miserable before, but now a better word might be despairing.

"So, do we have a tiger after all?" Peng asked even more quietly.

Shen didn't answer at first, his attention still focused on the view below. Then shaking himself like a man waking from a nightmare, he turned to Peng.

"I remember my senior engineer's words," Shen said evenly. "Don't describe a kitten as a tiger, he said. I thought his statement an invitation to bad luck at the time and told him so."

Shen looked down to the dam's base again and sighed.

"It looks like bad luck has accepted our invitation. The deformation at the base is visibly worse, just as our latest engineering survey suggested. You know as well as I do that with the men and equipment here, we can only manage the problem, not solve it," Shen said angrily.

Peng nodded. Shen was only speaking the truth.

"Very well. Tell me about your management efforts," Peng said.

"The leading cause of deaths from the dam has been landslides in areas it has affected. We've spent over a billion American dollars on engineering projects to identify and mitigate that risk, with considerable success. I believe we have that problem under control," Shen said.

Peng softly clapped his hands, making Shen start with surprise, and then his eyes narrow. Was Peng mocking him?

No. Peng said, "I've read your comprehensive reports. I agree with your assessment. At a minimum, you've bought us some time."

Shen inclined his head slightly, acknowledging the praise. "Water release management is the main tool we have to keep further deformation in check. Power production must continue, of course. However, maintaining the dam's structural integrity is now the absolute top priority."

Peng nodded but said nothing. He had discovered that Shen's predecessor had engaged in an unofficial competition with the Itaipu Dam, on the border between Brazil and Paraguay, for the title of world's greatest power producer. Ironically, there was no evidence that Itaipu's managers were even aware of this competition.

It had, though, played an essential role in the trial of Shen's predecessor for gross abuse of government resources and the endangerment of thousands of Chinese citizens.

Shen would never see his predecessor again.

China officially acknowledged executing about a thousand people a year for a variety of offenses. Amnesty International and many other human rights organizations said they had evidence the number was far higher.

Peng and Shen knew nothing about that discussion. But they were both aware that execution of your predecessor was one way a vacancy might open up. One that might help your career.

It also had its intended effect. Anyone whose career advanced as a result would do whatever they could to avoid the same fate.

"How can I help?" Peng asked.

Shen looked at Peng sharply, and Peng had to fight back a smile. He knew exactly what was passing through Shen's mind. China's bureaucrats were no better known for a burning desire to help their subordinates than those of other countries.

Visibly making up his mind, Shen said, "Please continue to press the dam managers upstream to give our water management requests top priority. None of them face our challenges. All they risk is, at worst, failing to meet their power production targets."

Peng nodded and said, "I certainly will."

And he meant it. Before the National Assembly approved construction of the Three Gorges Dam in 1992, many had argued that the power China needed from hydro sources could be obtained at far less risk by only building dams on the Yangtze River's upstream tributaries.

Usually a rubber stamp for the President and the Politburo, a full third of the Assembly refused to vote for the Three Gorges Dam's construction.

Maybe more in the Party should have listened to the dam's critics, Peng thought.

Then Peng shook himself. No. There was no point in reliving the past. They had to live in the present and face its problems head-on.

Maybe it was time to give Shen some reassurance. "Though typhoon season is about to start, I think there's no need to panic. After all, in the years since 2020, we've had no repeat of that year's scare," Peng said.

From the look Shen gave him, he knew exactly what Peng was trying to do. Still, he did manage to reply, "I'm sure you're right."

"I think we've seen enough for today," Peng said. "Let's get back inside." Shen nodded, and they walked together back to the elevator going to the power production management level.

Taking in the view one last time as they walked, Peng reflected that he was now one of the few privileged to see it. The Three Gorges Dam had been a prime tourist destination until recently. There had been boats full of camera-toting visitors and buses bringing others to the dam's viewing platform located some distance below Peng's current vantage point at its crest.

No longer. Deformation had been spotted as far back as 2020 through satellite images made available online and had finally become too obvious to deny.

Peng scowled as they reached the elevator. Covering up the problems with the dam's structural integrity was all well and good.

But could those problems really be managed?

Chapter Fourteen

Near the Chinese-Indian Border

Sergeant Xu had talked over their last patrol with his Lieutenant, an officer on his first border deployment. For that matter, Xu suspected the young man was straight out of the Academy.

Of course, that was the sort of question Xu could never ask.

His Lieutenant had offered no objections when Xu suggested changing the time of their patrol. Xu had given quite a bit of thought to the change and was almost disappointed when he didn't have to explain.

Almost. One of the first lessons you learned in the Chinese Army was taking yes for an answer and keeping your mouth shut afterward.

Xu had no way to know it, but that lesson worked equally well in any country's armed forces.

Not that Corporal Guan was a big fan of the change. For that matter, like most enlisted men, he was not in favor of change in general.

In a way, Xu didn't blame him. Like most enlisted men, Guan had learned the hard way that change was rarely to the good.

Today's change, though, was designed to keep them alive.

Neither Xu nor Guan had detected the Indian sniper and, almost certainly, his spotter. But the shot that had nearly hit Guan had given Xu a pretty good idea of where they had been.

Of course, they wouldn't have stayed in the same precise spot. But Xu doubted they'd moved far.

Armed with this knowledge, Xu had spoken with the company weather officer. At first, he had been puzzled by Xu's request. Once the weather officer had understood its purpose, though, he'd cooperated enthusiastically.

Armed with a topographical map, Xu's guess of where the sniper had been, and the weather officer's charts, he had learned several details that should be useful.

First, that today would be cloudless.

Second, the period when the sun would be shining directly into the eyes of the Indian sniper and his spotter.

Of course, the simplest way for the Indians to deal with the problem would be to avoid deploying a sniper at that time. The Chinese side didn't keep snipers out constantly, and Xu doubted the Indians did either.

But something told Xu he was out there. Waiting.

Several methods helped to reduce glare so a sniper could still zero in on his target.

But they all affected accuracy.

If Xu was going to go up against a Barrett again with any hope of success, he needed an edge. And an Indian opponent arrogant enough to think he could hit him first, sun or no.

Xu and Guan were making their way to the position Xu had picked out for their patrol using another change Guan didn't like.

There was only one trail from their base camp to the patrol area. Today, they wouldn't use it.

The grass and low brush on both sides of the trail were no particular obstacle for a man with a rifle. Guan's long-range observation binoculars and tripod only weighed a bit over twenty kilos, even with their case. But, Xu had to admit, the case was a bit bulky.

So, Xu compromised. They would stay off the trail. But they wouldn't venture very far from it, so the terrain was still reasonably easy to navigate.

Then Xu had it again.

The same feeling he had when a round had nearly hit Guan.

But they were still out of sight of that sniper. Xu was sure of it.

It didn't matter.

Xu held up the clenched fist that meant "hold" in a surprisingly large number of the world's armies.

Guan froze.

Xu looked in every direction. Nothing.

An instant of frustration swept Xu, and he nearly decided to march on. After all that effort...

No.

Xu made the hand signal telling Guan they were returning to base.

Guan turned to obey, but when he did, he tripped and fell. The case holding his spotting binoculars and its tripod left his hand and flew towards the trail.

A loud roaring filled Xu's ears, and the earth seemed to rise to meet him.

Then everything went black.

When Xu opened his eyes again, he was confused to be looking at Colonel Chang. Then he looked around and realized he was in the base medical unit.

Xu's uniform had been cut off and bandages were wrapped around him at many points. But, he was relieved to see that nothing appeared to be missing.

"Sergeant, I must not have been clear enough when I told you to keep your head down. I meant to keep all your parts intact," Chang said with a smile, gesturing towards Xu's numerous bandages.

"Yes, sir," Xu said tiredly. "How is Corporal Guan?"

Chang nodded approvingly. "The right question, Sergeant. The Corporal is in about the same shape you are," he said, pointing towards the bandaged figure lying at the other end of the medical unit.

"Which is to say, lucky to be alive. Or, maybe not so much luck as skill. After we heard the explosions, the men sent to retrieve you said they found you some distance from the trail. Too far to have been thrown there by the explosions, they thought," Chang said, in a tone that made it clear he expected an explanation.

"Yes, sir," Xu replied. "I didn't think the trail was safe."

Chang looked at Xu thoughtfully. "Well, you were right about that. If you'd been even a meter or so closer to it, we wouldn't be having this conversation. The trail had been mined, and the mines set to detonate simultaneously as soon as one was triggered. We're not sure how yet, but I had the mine fragments collected and sent back to headquarters for analysis."

Xu shook his head and immediately regretted the action. "Sir, I don't understand. We have remote cameras, drones, and even aircraft covering that area, right? How could the Indians have mined the trail without being detected?"

Chang nodded shortly. "That's a good question, Sergeant. Since you and your spotter appear to have been its first victims, I'm going to clear you to receive a highly classified answer. The Indians may have developed a mine-laying drone small enough to avoid detection. Probably operated at night, using GPS and infrared sensors to place the mines."

Xu thought about that for a moment. Then Xu asked, "Sir, do you know how long it will be before we're cleared to return to duty?"

Chang smiled. "Good attitude, Sergeant. But you and your Corporal will be here a little longer. The good news, though, is that the doctors have decided neither of you need to be evacuated to a regional hospital. So you'll both be back on patrol soon."

Chang paused, and now his smile made Xu think of a hunting tiger spotting unaware prey. "I believe Headquarters will approve my proposed response to this latest provocation. It's time to remind the Indians they aren't the only ones who can produce surprises."

Chapter Fifteen

Wenchang Satellite Launch Center
Hainan Island, China

General Yang Mingren sat restlessly in front of a console at the Mission Command and Control Center.

Power had been cut to the console. Yang had been both amused and annoyed to see that, in addition, a combination of black fabric and electrical tape had been used to conceal and immobilize the console's buttons and switches.

Mission Director Gao had smiled apologetically when he'd seen Yang's reaction, explaining that experience had proved the steps were necessary.

Yang had immediately thought about a few ill-advised flights with non-pilots in the back seat of combat aircraft and told Gao he understood completely.

Yes. Far too much was at stake to risk failure because of a mistakenly tripped switch.

A large digital display occupied most of the wall directly in front of Yang, showing the Long March 5B rocket on the pad. Not China's latest rocket, but that was fine.

The maiden flight of the Long March 7A from this same spaceport in 2020 had failed. Yang was happy with tried and tested.

Even better, less than half of the Long March 5B's twenty-five thousand kilo payload capacity was needed for the Air Force's new laser weapon. Two commercial satellites were also included in this launch, which would be critical to maintaining security for this mission.

Yang had previously overseen the launch of an Air Force communications satellite from the Jiuquan Satellite Launch Center in the Gobi Desert near the Mongolian border. That had the advantage of being far from prying eyes and the sensors of American reconnaissance aircraft, which continued their provocative flights off China's coast.

This launch, though, had to go from Wenchang. Hainan Island was China's most southern territory, aside from the "islands" it was building in the South China Sea. At only nineteen degrees north of the equator, its low latitude was necessary to launch the Long March 5B's heavy payload.

At Jiuquan, Yang had discovered there was both a Launch Control Center and a Mission Command and Control Center. He had spent all his time in the Launch Control Center because all he cared about was a successful launch. Not because Yang took it for granted that if the launch were successful, the satellite would function.

But because Yang knew that if the satellite didn't work, there would be nothing he could do about it from Jiquan.

At Wenchang, though, he was at the Mission Control and Command Center. This time, there would be a mission for him to command.

Yang watched as the launch countdown clock crawled towards zero. He was calmed by the quiet, purposeful hum of activity all around him as dozens of technicians worked. It was a familiar sound for a high-ranking military officer like Yang.

As the clock reached zero and the Long March 5B's engines lit, Yang tensed involuntarily. Over ninety percent of China's launches over the years had been successful. But two failures in less than a month in 2020, not so long ago, had made many dependent on China's launch capability skittish.

This time, though, luck was on his side. Yang watched with relief as the rocket climbed smoothly into space. Cheers erupted around Yang, which he found himself joining.

And why not? Few other countries could match China's space capability, so their pride was deserved.

Even better, today, China would deploy a new capability no other country could equal.

The words were foreign, so during his first launch at Jiquan, Yang hadn't understood that "payload fairing" and "nose cone" meant the same thing. Now, though, Yang understood that they had reached the next critical step in the launch as the display in front of him reported the rocket had reached deployment altitude.

The sudden hush around him told Yang everyone else knew it too.

Then on the display came the words, "payload fairing separation successful," followed quickly by "payload separation successful." That meant the two commercial satellites and the weapon were free of the rocket and ready for movement to their operational positions.

More cheering, but this time very brief. Because now control passed to them, and they ceased being spectators.

About half of the technicians in the Mission Control and Command Center with Yang were responsible for ensuring that the two commercial satellites would reach their assigned positions and begin broadcasting.

The rest were under Yang's command and dedicated to the laser weapon. They already knew which SpaceLink satellites to target in an attack plan that Yang had designed to remove those broadcasting to China as quickly as possible. Yang was only there in case something went wrong.

Yang scowled as he thought again about the plan's only weakness. The distance between the satellites meant eliminating all of them would take hours, in fact nearly a full day.

Then Yang's expression cleared as he saw the technicians send the weapon towards its first target.

Yes, it might take a while to rid the space above China of the cursed American satellites threatening the Party's control of the information available to its citizens.

But it would also take time for the Americans to realize what was happening. And anyway, what could they do to stop the attack?

Chapter Sixteen

SpaceLink Pacific Mission Command Center
Vandenberg Air Force Base, California

SpaceLink project manager Mark Rooter frowned as he looked at the display. There were thousands of SpaceLink satellites circling the globe, and every so often, one would fail.

But two within an hour? And both, while not really "close" to each other, still closer than any other satellite.

Huh. Both satellites were providing Internet coverage to countries bordering China. A coincidence?

Rooter charted the two satellites that had gone dark and then located the one closest to the second to fail.

Hmm. That third satellite also gave Internet service to a country bordering China.

Well, that wasn't so surprising. After all, those satellites would be close to each other, right?

Rooter pulled up the optical feed from the satellite he'd just identified. He'd pointed out to his boss Eli Wade that it would be useful to see what was around the satellites in case of problems. He was sure, though, that the fact optical sensors were both light and dirt cheap was really what had convinced Wade to agree.

It was lucky that these satellites had the optical sensors since they were only present on satellites launched within the past two years. Rooter had suggested they avoid publicly announcing the presence of the sensors, and Wade had agreed.

Rooter suspected, correctly, that Wade had agreed to both proposals so easily not because he saw their value. Instead, it was to make it easier to refuse Rooter's other more expensive requests.

Of course, as his boss, Wade could say no to anything Rooter suggested. But as long as he considered Rooter a valued employee, Wade would do whatever he could to keep him happy.

Within reason.

Rooter was about to justify Wade's belief that he was worth keeping.

Well, Rooter thought, nothing to see here, it seems. He panned the view from the third SpaceLink satellite in every direction. In some of those directions there was nothing but the blackness of space, punctuated by the pinpoints of distant stars. The satellite's broadcast antenna was naturally pointed at Earth, and there the view was spectacular.

Every time Rooter saw a view of Earth from space, it reminded him of why he'd worked so hard to get to his present position as SpaceLink's project manager.

OK, it was crazy. And paranoid.

But Rooter calculated the position of the second satellite to go offline relative to this one. And then, he focused the optical sensor in that direction.

Nothing. Rooter increased the sensor's gain to its maximum resolution.

Still nothing.

Rooter was simultaneously relieved and annoyed. OK, time to move on to other possibilities.

But he left the sensor running and the monitor on, just in case.

Rooter sat down at the adjacent console and pulled up production records for the two malfunctioning satellites. Yes, they were both manufactured at the same time, at the same facility. So, maybe the explanation was...

Whoa! What was that?

For an instant, a flood of white light poured from the monitor relaying the optical feed of the third satellite.

Then the monitor's screen turned jet black.

A quick check confirmed that power was still going to the monitor, and switching it to a different input source confirmed that the monitor was working fine.

There was no longer a signal coming in from the third satellite.

So, did that mean... Yes. The third satellite wasn't working either. Dead, just like the other two.

A production problem could account for two failures, or maybe even three. But all within less than two hours?

Fingers flying over his keyboard, Rooter pulled up the digital recording made by the third satellite's optical sensor while he'd been researching production files.

Then he played back the last few minutes at half-speed.

There! Rooter couldn't say he saw anything directly.

But he could see that something was blocking the light from several stars. And whatever that something was, it was moving closer to their satellite.

Rooter almost forgot to freeze the playback at a moment before the monitor flooded with light but hit the right key just in time.

Then he reached for his phone.

"Boss, where are you?" Rooter asked Wade without preamble.

"Santa Barbara," Wade answered.

Rooter winced. Now he remembered Wade had told him he was taking his long-time girlfriend on a shopping and dining trip to Santa Barbara, a pretty seaside town well known for having plenty of places to do both.

It was rare for Wade to take a day off. And heavens knew Wade worked hard enough to deserve one, boss or no. Ordinarily, Rooter would have apologized and hung up as soon as Wade reminded him he wasn't in the office.

But Rooter didn't hesitate.

"Boss, I need you at Vandenberg as soon as you can get here," Rooter said.

There was a long pause. "You can't tell me why I suppose," came Wade's resigned voice.

"No, boss," Rooter replied. "Not over an open line."

"OK," Wade said. "An hour or so," he said, and the line went dead.

By the time Wade walked into the command center, Rooter had the fourth satellite's optical sensor directed towards the attack he expected any minute.

Sure enough, Wade only had time to ask, "So, what's the problem..." when a bloom of bright white light from the nearby monitor announced the destruction of the fourth satellite.

Rooter pointed at the monitor and said, "Someone's destroying our satellites. That's the fourth. I think they're using a laser. And I think it's the Chinese."

Wade looked around the command center, which would typically have had many other staff at work on various tasks.

Wade and Rooter were the only ones present.

"I gave everyone else the day off," Rooter said evenly.

Wade nodded. "Good thinking. It makes it easier for us to talk about this. So, tell me why you think it's the Chinese."

After Rooter had finished his explanation, Wade sat silently for a few moments, clearly thinking over what he'd just heard.

Then, Wade nodded sharply. "You're right. It's the only way to account for the satellites' destruction that fits the facts. So, what can we do about it?"

Rooter smiled and answered with a question of his own. "Remember I told you we needed to enhance the thrusters on the satellites and switch from ones consuming krypton gas to xenon?"

Wade frowned. "I do. I remember approving the request because you said they might need more power to avoid other satellites successfully."

"Right, and I meant that," Rooter said. "But I had another agenda, too. I didn't talk about it then because I was thinking about a scenario like this. I was worried you might refuse my request as paranoid."

Wade pointed at the digital display, showing four dull red dots representing satellites no longer communicating with the Command Center. Or anyone else.

"Well, now the threat couldn't be clearer," Wade said.

"And I propose we take direct action to combat it," Rooter said as he typed rapidly.

The image on the digital display shifted to show the stars blocked out across much of the screen. Part of the SpaceLink satellite was also visible.

Rooter kept typing. Now the image occupied just half of the display.

After more typing, Rooter had a very similar image on the other half of the screen. Yet, it was immediately clear they were not the same image.

"These are images from just before the laser struck two of our satellites. You can see the images are similar. It's not a coincidence. I think the Chinese weapon had to approach the satellites exactly this way because of the sun visor, which would reduce its laser's effectiveness. They'd either have to circle to the rear of each target satellite, which would take a lot of time and fuel, or do this. The visor has a gap where we have the main antenna sending the Internet signal," Rooter said.

"I think I see what you mean. So, we know exactly which way they're coming," Wade said.

"Right. And as soon as we spot the weapon, we go to meet them. At our satellite's top speed," Rooter said with a tight smile.

Wade sat back. "I sure see why you wanted me here for this one. If I take this over to the Combined Space Operations Center, they'll buck it up to the Pentagon, and they'll ask the White House. By the time we get an answer, we won't have a satellite left anywhere near China."

The Combined Space Operations Center (CSpOC) was practically walking distance from SpaceLink's Command Center at Vandenberg. With responsibility for command and control of all American military activities in space, an attack like this was exactly the sort of threat CSpOC had been created to address.

Rooter nodded. "I couldn't agree more, sir. This is self-defense, plain and simple. But if we're going to try to limit our losses to just one more satellite, I need your decision now. That weapon's moving fast."

Wade sat still, thinking hard. But for less than a minute.

Then he looked up at Rooter.

"Do it," he said simply.

Rooter walked over to the next console, where only a few keystrokes revealed an image like the ones on the other monitor. But this one covered the entire screen, and all the stars were clear.

So far.

"I wouldn't mind another pair of eyes, sir. Anything passes in front of those stars, sing out," Rooter said tensely.

Wade nodded and said, "Got it."

"Some time in the next ten minutes. I haven't had time to calculate the weapon's speed more precisely than that," Rooter said.

"Understood. Are we sure there's just one weapon?" Wade asked, his eyes still on the screen.

Rooter's gaze involuntarily shifted from the screen. "I sure hope not," he said.

"Well, the track of satellites the weapon attacked can certainly be accounted for by a single attacker. If you hadn't been here, it's probably all they would have needed," Wade said.

Rooter shrugged. "Well, a lot's going to depend on who's operating this weapon. If they're quick enough to react, they may be able to avoid a collision. And ramming is the only weapon we've got."

The next minutes crawled by.

Finally, Wade was the first one to spot something. "There," he said, pointing at the right edge of the screen. "It looks like it's sliding over towards the middle of the display."

Rooter nodded. "And if it moves as fast as it did the other times, it won't take long to reach firing position."

But Rooter just stood there.

Wade looked at Rooter, confused. "Shouldn't you get our satellite moving?"

Rooter shook his head, his gaze still fixed on the display. "I've got to let him get closer. So he won't have time to change course. We're only going to get one chance at this."

It felt like forever, but a glance at the bottom of the screen told Wade it had been less than a minute when Rooter pressed a switch on the console.

Then Rooter sat down in the chair in front of the display and leaned forward.

Wade was about to say something, but Rooter's smile stopped him.

"That thing's exactly where I thought it would be. I'd already programmed the course and maximum speed. The hard part I did before you got here, disabling the automatic collision system," Rooter said.

"Right, the system we had to install to avoid colliding with other satellites in orbit. How long before we know..." Wade started to ask.

This time the bright light from the monitor flared on and off so quickly both men had the same thought.

If we'd blinked, we might have missed it.

"Well, that was sure different than last time," Wade said. "What do you think it means?"

Rooter shrugged. "If I had to guess, I think they fired the laser just before our satellite struck their weapon. Either way, we've lost all contact with the fifth satellite."

"So, how can we find out whether we destroyed or disabled the Chinese weapon?" Wade asked.

Rooter pointed at the monitor displaying the orbital positions of all SpaceLink satellites. Now there were five glowing a dull red.

"It's simple. Sometime in the next hour, another one of these lights will change from green to red. Or it won't," Rooter said.

He was typing while he spoke. The monitor that had been displaying the optical feed from the fifth satellite now showed an image from another one.

"This is from the sixth target satellite, assuming the weapon survived and continues on its current course. Since there have to be limits to the weapon's fuel, I think staying on course is a given. So, we both go back to looking for darkness covering the stars," Rooter said.

Wade nodded. "But this time, they'll know what to expect."

"Right. So, they might shoot from further away if they have the power. Or circle our rear if they have the fuel. Either way, we've lost the advantage of surprise."

"But, it'll take them at least half an hour to get to the next target, right?" Wade asked.

"Yes. Probably a bit longer, even if they increase their speed," Rooter replied.

"Good," Wade said, looking away from the screen and pulling out his phone.

And then he stopped.

Who was he going to call, and what was he going to tell them?

Chapter Seventeen

Wenchang Satellite Launch Center
Hainan Island, China

General Yang Mingren looked up at the main display screen dominating the Mission Command and Control Center's front. It was scattered with green circles, representing the SpaceLink satellites targeted in today's operation.

There were also four red symbols, each with a line drawn through them. All had been confirmed to have ceased transmitting after the new laser weapon had attacked them.

So far, everything had gone perfectly. They were right on schedule. Yes, it would still take many more hours to destroy the remaining targeted satellites.

But they were going to succeed with this mission.

Yang smiled to himself. Who was he trying to convince, anyway?

Long experience, though, had taught him that disaster usually struck when skies were clear. Not when you had seen the thunderclouds gather and were well prepared.

Now Yang had to suppress a grin at his own expense. Could any thought have marked him more clearly as a pilot?

Yang returned his focus to the small monitor directly in front of him, which would shortly show the weapon's approach to the fifth targeted satellite.

Yes, Yang and the officers he was working with had important plans, and accomplishing this mission played an essential part in their success.

Success gave its architect credibility. And Yang needed President Lin to believe every word he said.

"Approaching the fifth target," the lead technician announced.

Yang settled back to watch the show. It had gone just as planned the first four times, and no matter what his nerves said, there was no reason to believe this time would be any different.

At first, it wasn't.

But after a few minutes, Yang could see the lead technician talking with another one and pointing at his monitor.

"Report!" Yang said.

"Sir, I don't understand this," the lead technician said. "The target is moving."

Yang scowled. "We discussed this. Did you keep out of range of the target's automatic collision system?"

"Yes, sir," the technician said hurriedly. "But it's not trying to avoid us."

"What do you mean? What is it doing?" Yang asked, genuinely puzzled.

"Sir, it's coming straight at the weapon at a speed it shouldn't be able to reach, and I can't change course in time to avoid a collision," the technician said.

For a horrified instant, Yang couldn't believe what he was hearing.

Then he had several thoughts in quick succession.

One of the Americans has figured out what we're doing.

What we thought we knew about the American satellites is either wrong or out of date.

A weapon in space with only one engine can't make sharp turns.

Aloud, he said just two words.

"Fire now!" Yang bellowed.

The technician did so immediately, and one of the green symbols on the main display was quickly replaced by a red one, as the satellite ceased transmitting.

Yang started to breathe again. "Status of the weapon?" he asked.

"We have lost contact with the weapon, sir," the technician said.

"I don't understand," Yang said. "How could you miss from that range?"

"I didn't, sir," the technician said sullenly. "But shorting out the satellite's electronic systems or even disabling its thrusters couldn't prevent the collision. They deliberately waited until we were too close to miss. By the time we detected the target's movement, it was already too late."

He paused and then added, "That's why I didn't fire earlier. It wouldn't have mattered."

Yang ground his teeth in frustration.

The laser weapon had been coated in materials designed to absorb every wavelength of light. Every attempt to discover it through radar or lidar should have failed as well. Not that a communications satellite should have carried either.

So how had the Americans not only detected the weapon but been able to target it for collision?

Yang shook his head. Right now, it didn't matter.

The cost of a SpaceLink satellite was publicly quoted as about two hundred fifty thousand American dollars. Yang had destroyed five of them, so well under two million dollars in total.

Yang didn't know exactly how much the laser weapon had cost to develop and deploy.

But he knew it was more. A lot more.

There would be no way to report this as anything but the failure it was.

But Yang wasn't finished yet.

No, he had one more card to play. And this time, a single worthy target.

Qinshan Nuclear Power Plant
One Hundred Kilometers South of Shanghai, China

Qinshan Senior Manager Tan jerked his head up with surprise as Plant Complex Director Wu appeared behind him.

Tan had left strict instructions to his staff to warn him whenever Wu came to the plant. Tan sighed as he realized Wu must have told everyone at the plant not to let him know of his arrival.

Since Wu outranked Tan, of course, they would follow his orders.

Against all expectations, though, Wu was...smiling.

"Good morning," Wu said cheerfully. "Please, let's take another walk outside. I have a few questions for you."

Tan nodded as he quickly pulled on his plant-issued windbreaker. Since Wu's last visit, he always kept it handy.

Wu wasted no time walking up to the pallets of burlap bags that had been delivered the previous day, that were now stacked up against the concrete containment vessel protecting the reactor.

While he walked beside Wu, Tan looked at the water lapping around them on three sides and shivered. Only partly from the cold. How could he have looked at the sea all around him for so many years, and failed to spot the danger?

Wu patted the closest pallet and then pointed at the nearby piles of sand. Each pile was covered with blue plastic sheets, which were secured to the ground with multiple metal stakes.

"It looks like you have here two of the key ingredients for sandbags. Bags and sand. But what about labor? If a storm threatens the plant, our staff will be busy securing the reactor and will have no time to fill these bags," Wu said.

Tan nodded. "I thought about that. I've spoken with the warden at a prison not far from here. He will supply workers to fill our sandbags whenever I ask."

Wu looked skeptical. "Really? We have no authority over the warden. Why should he help and risk the escape of his prisoners?"

"At first, he refused," Tan replied. "Then I pointed out that if disaster befalls this plant, the radioactive contamination that would be released might reach his prison very quickly. Probably too quickly to allow the evacuation of his prisoners and staff."

"Not to mention his evacuation," Wu said, nodding. "Well, you did nothing but tell the truth. So, how were you able to get all this so quickly?"

Wu's arm swept around the dozens of pallets of bags and vast piles of sand.

Tan smiled. It was an impressive sight, after all. And it was nice to see someone else appreciate it.

"Burlap bags and sand are surprisingly cheap, especially when ordered in quantity. It took my entire discretionary budget for items like official travel and a small amount of my personal funds, but I was able to make it happen. I checked a long-range weather forecast a few days ago, and there is a typhoon brewing that might head this way. So, I decided better safe than sorry," Tan said.

Wu's next action surprised Tan.

He bowed. And to a depth showing genuine respect.

"Well done, Tan. I'm sure you know as well as I do that if we get a real monster storm like the one in 1985, sandbags won't be enough to save the plant. But they should give us enough time to do a safe shutdown and avoid a total disaster like Fukushima," Wu said.

Tan recovered from his surprise rapidly enough to politely return Wu's bow. "Thank you, sir. I also appreciate your quick approval of my increased request for next year's budget. If Beijing provides the funds we're requesting, then we could do a proper job of making this plant typhoon-proof."

Wu nodded. "I am already researching other vulnerable plants and have contacted several other plant managers for information. You remember the damage storms did to the Three Gorges hydropower plant in 2020?"

Tan nodded. "Yes, sir. It does seem that so-called once a century storms are becoming more common."

Wu smiled thinly. "Yes. Ironic that hydropower and nuclear power plants, which have done nothing to contribute to climate change, seem destined to become its first victims."

Then Wu's smile changed and became genuine as he patted Tan on the shoulder. "Well, at least with good men like you on our side, we still have a fighting chance. Let's get inside out of this cold."

Tan hurried after Wu towards the plant's entrance door, while the wind picked up as if to hurry him along. Shivering, Tan looked back at the storm supplies he'd managed to assemble.

He couldn't help asking himself the same question that always seemed to be his last thought before he tried to sleep.

Would it be enough?

Chapter Eighteen

Russian Embassy
Washington, DC

Boris Kharlov looked up as Neda Rhahbar walked into the conference room they'd been using to prepare for their mission. He was about to ask Neda why she looked so tense when the answer walked in behind her.

Alina.

She had been Neda's debriefing officer when she went to the Russian Embassy in Tehran to defect. Neda's husband had been plotting to provide three Iranian nuclear test weapons as part of a broader attack on Saudi Arabia. Since there was no American Embassy in Tehran, she had thought the Russians were the only others powerful enough to stop him.

Given the stakes, Alina had not been gentle. She had tried to force details about the plot from Neda, even threatening her with expulsion from the Embassy and into the arms of Iranian security forces.

Neda had refused, insisting she would not provide details on the weapons' location until she was safely out of Iran. Alina had finally agreed, and Neda had eventually reached Moscow and been recruited to the FSB.

Alina had even been their control officer on their last mission in Ukraine. So, Neda had learned to work with Alina.

But they were not friends.

Kharlov had met Alina on that same mission in Ukraine and had been impressed with her competence. But he understood Neda's misgivings.

Kharlov thought of himself as a reasonably handsome man in excellent physical condition. The many girlfriends he'd had over the years would have agreed with that assessment. They might have been even more flattering if he'd chosen any of them as a spouse. However, neither his activities in Russian Spetsnaz special forces nor as a warlord in Ukraine's breakaway eastern provinces had been conducive to marriage.

Ordinarily, Kharlov would have wasted little time trying to date a woman as attractive as Alina. Long blond hair, a trim figure that hinted at excellent stamina, and a face pretty enough to adorn a magazine cover were all excellent incentives.

Until you looked at Alina's icy blue eyes. One glance was enough to know they had seen much their owner would prefer to forget.

And help anyone who saw them realize Alina's fit physique was not there to attract suitors. Instead, it was a byproduct of the continuous training needed to ensure she could deal with any threat, whether or not she had a weapon.

Yes, Kharlov mused, a date with Alina would undoubtedly be memorable. However, he preferred encounters where he didn't have to calculate the odds of survival.

Alina gave Kharlov a smile that made him wonder how many of his thoughts had been visible on his face. Then she closed the door behind her.

"I've cleared the floor. We may speak freely," Alina said, sitting down at the head of the conference table.

Neda sat next to Kharlov. On the side away from Alina.

Alina next gave Neda a smile that told both her and Kharlov she'd noticed.

"I have received new orders from Moscow. Your mission is to proceed," Alina said.

Kharlov nodded. "So, the other Chinese efforts have failed."

Alina shrugged. "I was told nothing of those. But to take the risk represented by your mission, certainly yes. I have been directed to emphasize certain aspects of the orders you have already received and to add one new element."

Kharlov and Neda both sat quietly, knowing Alina would proceed without prompting.

"You must not injure or, worse, kill anyone you encounter while on this mission. That is true even to avoid capture. Understood?" Alina asked.

Both Kharlov and Neda replied, "Yes." They knew from their training that a nod was not sufficient.

"The rocket you will sabotage must explode at a high altitude, and its course must be unaffected before its destruction. If you cannot accomplish this, you must allow the launch to proceed. Understood?"

Both Kharlov and Neda replied, "Yes" again. The Spaceship weighed over five million kilos and was over one hundred twenty meters tall. Allowing it to fall intact on a populated area would be considered an act of war by the Americans.

Or by anyone else, for that matter.

"Now, the new element. Neither of you may allow yourselves to be captured. If it appears capture is imminent, you must take one of these capsules," Alina said, sliding two small plastic containers across the table.

Kharlov grunted. "And I'd thought the life of a warlord was risky."

Neda looked at the containers as though they were venomous snakes. "So, now we know why we weren't told this part in Moscow. And why I'm on this mission with Kharlov rather than my husband. He might have had something to say about this."

Alina shrugged. "Maybe. I think Kharlov's training with rockets and explosives played a role too. But knowing Vasilyev, I'm sure you're right that he would have objected. Remember, though, that if you're successful, it's possible I won't have to give capsules to him and Grishkov."

A look of fury and loathing appeared on Neda's face that briefly made Kharlov think he would have to restrain her.

But no. It disappeared as quickly as it had appeared, as Neda regained her self-control.

Alina still noticed.

"Please remember that I didn't write these orders. Nor, I suspect, did Director Smyslov. I think it is very likely this part came from the President himself. Remember, he was the FSB Director before Smyslov," Alina said.

Then Alina paused. "For many years, we have relied on exchanges to free captured agents. As recently as 2010, we swapped four persons in our custody for ten Russian agents arrested by the Americans. The President must have decided the Americans would react to the discovery of our role in sabotaging one of their rockets with something besides an exchange offer."

Kharlov nodded. "Yes. Perhaps by destroying one of our rockets in retaliation, maybe killing many Russian citizens in the process."

"Correct," Alina said. "Knowing our President, he would feel obliged to respond, likely setting a cycle in motion that would end with a nuclear exchange."

Kharlov had been watching Neda out of the corner of his eye while he kept Alina talking. He admired Neda's outward composure when he could practically feel the hatred radiating from her in the seat next to him.

At least Neda wasn't lunging across the table toward Alina, which Kharlov had thought a real possibility for a moment.

"When do we leave?" Neda asked.

"As soon as you can gather your materials," Alina said, waving her hand over the table.

Neda said nothing and began folding and stacking the papers covering the table.

As Kharlov stood to help her, he asked Alina, "How will we get to Florida?"

Alina smiled. "The same method we used in Ukraine. We will be using the regularly scheduled diplomatic mail run between the Embassy and our consulate in Houston."

Kharlov frowned. "My knowledge of American geography may be lacking. But is Florida really on the way to Houston?"

"It is not. However, we will turn off the normal route once we reach a city called Chattanooga, in Tennessee. It is close to Georgia, a state bordering Florida. We have detected FBI surveillance several times during this run, but it has never continued past Tennessee and usually stopped well before then," Alina replied.

"I'm sure this detour will cost us some time, yes?" Kharlov asked.

"Not too bad. It will take us about nine hours to get to Chattanooga and the same time to get from there to our destination in Florida. Driving direct would have taken about fourteen hours, so a short delay, but one worth making to maintain security. Most of the time, the FBI doesn't bother following this mail van, but..." Alina shrugged.

"Agreed. As you say, security must take priority," Kharlov said as he folded the last of the papers they had used to prepare for the mission.

Kharlov had been curious about their upcoming trip. But in truth, he'd been more concerned about avoiding an eruption between Neda and Alina.

So, he was not looking forward to the answer to his next question.

"Who will be our driver?" Kharlov asked.

Alina smiled. "To begin with, I will. I still have much detail to cover regarding your mission. And even more regarding our subsequent departure from Florida. I see you've collected all your papers, so let's head to the basement parking lot to begin our trip. Your clothes have already been packed and loaded."

Kharlov nodded and followed Alina out the door, careful to stay between her and Neda.

A glance back at Neda told Kharlov that was a good idea.

Kharlov sighed. It was going to be a long drive to Florida.

Chapter Nineteen

Zhongnanhai Compound
Beijing, China

President Lin Wang Yong once again let General Yang Mingren stand for a while after an aide escorted him to his desk.

In fact, Lin ignored Yang totally for several minutes while he once again reviewed the report on his desk of the laser weapon's failure.

Then, Lin pointedly did not invite Yang to take a seat. Instead, he asked him, "General, do you have anything to add to your report?"

Yang reached into his jacket pocket and withdrew a single folded sheet of paper. Placing it on Lin's desk, Yang replied, "Just my letter of resignation, which I wished to present to you in person, along with my profound apologies for this failure. My deputy stands ready to try again with a different weapon we have been developing."

"A different weapon," Lin repeated slowly. He looked at Yang for a moment, who was still at attention, staring straight ahead.

Finally, Lin made his decision.

"Have a seat, General. Describe this weapon," Lin said in a tone making it clear he expected the description to be succinct.

Yang didn't disappoint him. "It is a missile fired from a modified Russian Sukhoi SU-34. We plan to destroy the entire payload of the next American rocket launch. It will carry four hundred satellites and is due to launch soon from Florida. Most of those satellites are planned for deployment to countries near China."

Lin nodded. "I am aware of this planned launch. Has your new weapon been tested? Can a missile launched by an airplane destroy a target in space?"

"We have not tested this weapon against a target in space. But the Americans have already proved an air-launched missile can destroy a satellite," Yang replied.

"Really? When?" Lin asked.

"In 1985. An American F-15 fired an ASM-135 missile from an altitude of about eleven kilometers and destroyed a satellite weighing about one thousand kilos orbiting at an altitude of over five hundred kilometers," Yang replied.

"1985," Lin said, shaking his head. "Can your plane fly that high?"

"We have flown the SU-34 at altitudes over fifteen kilometers high without problems. We are confident the missile will perform as well as the American model, if not better," Yang replied.

Lin grunted skeptically. "You thought so as well for the laser weapon, didn't you?"

"Yes, sir," Yang replied stoically. "But the laser weapon did work and destroyed five American satellites. Our failure was not anticipating the American's quick detection of our attack and then using one of their satellites to ram our weapon in response. But the Spaceship's payload will have no such capability. We will strike the payload as soon as it separates from the rocket before the satellites move into their assigned positions."

Lin was unconvinced but still curious. "Tell me about the missile that will destroy the payload."

"We are using the outer casing of the Russian Kh-47M2 Kinzhal missile. It was built to withstand the rigors of supersonic flight over a range of more than two thousand kilometers, so using it saved our designers much time. It was also easy to mate to the Russian-built SU-34 jet. The engine is our design since it had to work both within the atmosphere and in space. The warhead is made of tungsten, with no explosive content," Yang replied.

"Why not?" Lin asked with a frown. "Wouldn't an explosive warhead be more effective?"

"Yes, sir," Yang replied with a nod. "However, we must consider deniability. The destruction caused by explosives would be detected as such by the Americans. But an inert object striking a satellite or payload might be explainable as an accidental collision with a small asteroid or piece of space debris. It has happened before, and once it was even our fault."

"Really? When?" Lin asked.

"In 2013. By a piece of debris caused by our 2007 antisatellite test, the only one we have publicly acknowledged. We used a ground-fired SC-19 ballistic missile for that test, a modified version of the Dong-Feng 21 missile still deployed today. The debris damaged a Russian scientific research satellite. Of course, we denied responsibility. The Russians never pursued a claim against us, so I see that incident as validating our approach," Yang replied.

Finally, Lin had no more questions. He frowned as he considered Yang's proposal.

Then he shook his head.

"No. I have other plans for that rocket in Florida, which you do not need to know. You're dismissed," Lin said.

Yang saluted and turned on his heel. He had nearly reached the office door when he heard Lin's voice behind him.

"Wait," he said.

Yang turned around, trying hard to keep the hope he was feeling from showing in his expression.

He doubted he'd been successful.

"Yes, sir?" Yang asked.

"Do the Americans have any more of these Spaceships ready to launch?" Lin asked.

"Yes, sir. They have one in California already tested and scheduled for launch later this month, assuming Florida's deployment is successful. A third has just been manufactured and is undergoing final readiness checks in Florida, a short distance from the launch facility. The one in California is due to launch four hundred SpaceLink satellites, like the one the Americans are about to send into orbit. The newly manufactured Spaceship is intended for a test of military cargo transport," Yang replied.

"Very well. For now, I will keep your resignation letter. But I will wait to accept it depending on your new weapon's success against the rocket in California. If indeed this American billionaire is foolish enough to launch it," Lin said.

"Yes, sir. We will be ready for your order," Yang said.

Yang hurried to the building's entrance, his mind full of all that had to be readied in a very short time.

Yang reached the entrance just as the Army Commander, General Shi, was arriving. Probably to discuss the Army's role in the "border crisis" with India that President Lin had engineered to distract China's citizens from the Party's inept management of the economy.

And much else.

General Shi looked exactly like the tanker he had been for his entire career before moving into command positions. Short and squat, Yang mused that Shi would have had no trouble fitting into the small tanks available when he began service as a mere private.

Shi had barely met the military service's old height standard at one hundred sixty-two centimeters, or about five and a quarter feet.

Yang frowned as he remembered reading that the height standard had been lowered by two centimeters just a few years ago. Even though Chinese adults' average height had been increasing for years, thanks to improved nutrition made possible by a growing economy.

It turned out the change had been necessary to widen the recruitment pool to include brighter and more educated recruits. Needed because more advanced equipment was finally being made available for the Chinese military. To use such equipment effectively, intelligence and education were what mattered.

Not height.

Yang had been impressed to learn that Shi was one of the rare service commanders to have risen from the enlisted ranks. It said quite a bit about his energy and drive and made Shi an especially valuable ally in his plans.

As Yang approached, Shi said nothing. Instead, he merely raised his right eyebrow.

Translation: Do you still have a job?

Yang nodded curtly as he passed Shi on the way to his vehicle.

Shi gave Yang a slight smile and nodded back.

Translation: Glad to hear it. I look forward to continuing our collaboration.

Yang had nearly lost it all today.

That could never be allowed to happen again. There was only one way to make sure Yang could never be fired.

The military needed to take control from the corrupt and incompetent politicians.

Yang had been working on a plan to do just that with General Shi for months. Until today, though, he'd believed the moment had not yet arrived to execute it.

Yes, Yang nodded to himself as his driver and escort vehicles drove through Beijing's busy streets back to his office.

It was now or never.

CHAPTER TWENTY

Cocoa Beach, Florida

It had been well after midnight when they had arrived at the small house Alina had rented as a base for their mission. Boris Kharlov had pled exhaustion, so Alina and Neda Rhahbar had shifted back and forth as drivers during the nearly eighteen-hour drive from Washington DC via Tennessee.

Kharlov's real purpose had been to keep either Alina or Neda busy talking at all times. He was sure leaving them together for any length of time would have had unfortunate consequences.

Kharlov's initial hope that Neda's anger at the prospect of a suicide pill being presented to her husband by Alina would cool on its own had faded with each passing kilometer.

As Alina and Neda took turns at the wheel, Kharlov had engaged each in conversation, trying to ease the tension that hung in the van like a fog.

It had only worked to a point. All Kharlov had achieved was to prevent Neda from starting a physical confrontation between the two women.

Kharlov wasn't sure how such a contest would have ended. Alina certainly had far more experience in hand-to-hand combat. But Kharlov had seen sheer determination triumph over superior capabilities before.

And Kharlov had been sure he didn't want to be in the same small space while Neda and Alina settled their differences.

As was his habit, Kharlov had woken with the dawn. He didn't need much sleep, and that was fortunate. The few hours he'd managed had left him energized, and Kharlov began brewing a large pot of coffee in the surprisingly well-stocked kitchen.

Once coffee had begun to trickle into the pot, Kharlov looked around him with approval.

Windows on all sides of both the kitchen and the living area. Though the house was not new, the furnishings appeared to have been recently replaced.

A blinking red light near the entrance to the house announced the presence of a security system.

So, not flashy, but upscale.

A few minutes later, Neda padded into the kitchen in stocking feet, looking in all directions around her.

"Have you seen her?" Neda hissed.

"Not yet. Here, have a cup of coffee. It's fresh," Kharlov said as he poured one from the pot.

Neda grimaced but accepted the cup and sat down at the small kitchen table.

As Kharlov had hoped, Neda relaxed slightly as she sipped her coffee.

Kharlov poured a cup for himself and remained standing.

"You know, I believe Alina when she said she didn't write our orders," Kharlov began.

At the mention of Alina's name, Kharlov could see Neda's immediate reaction.

It was not positive.

Kharlov held up his hands. "Yes, she could have been more delicate in explaining the consequences for mission failure, both for Vasilyev and Grishkov and for us. But we know she is no diplomat. In her way, I think she was just trying to be honest. And you have to admit we needed to know our options here."

Neda frowned and sat silently for a moment, clearly weighing Kharlov's words.

Finally, she nodded reluctantly.

"OK, maybe I have been focusing my anger at our situation on her when she didn't deserve it. But it's hard for me to stomach the idea that my failure could lead directly to my husband's death. Even worse, it's making me fear obsession with that worry will hurt my performance on this mission," Neda said glumly.

"Good morning," Alina said as she walked into the kitchen, carrying a small bag.

Both Kharlov and Neda stared at her.

Alina's long blond hair was gone. In its place was short hair, dyed a mousy brown.

She pulled a mug from the cabinet and held it towards Kharlov, who was still standing in front of the coffee pot.

"Coffee, please," Alina said.

Once she had taken several deep swallows, Alina sighed and gestured towards Kharlov. "Let's sit. We have much to discuss."

Kharlov was careful to take the seat closest to Neda.

"First, I see you both noticed my new haircut," Alina said.

Kharlov nodded. "I must say I'm impressed. By necessity, I've had to cut my own hair several times. The results were never flattering."

"Don't be too impressed. The hair you saw before was a wig," Alina said with a shrug.

Neda looked at Alina suspiciously. "It certainly looked like yours. We were together for days on our last mission in Ukraine, and I'd have known if you were wearing a wig then."

"Good eye," Alina said, nodding with approval. "The wig was made of my own hair by our technical staff in Moscow. Changing our appearance is vital to this mission, and this was an easy part of meeting that requirement. Harder, for me anyway, is changing my eye color to brown. I hate wearing contacts, so I won't put those in until we leave for the mission."

Kharlov's eyebrows rose. "So, I assume that means changes in appearance are in store for us as well?"

"Yes," Alina said with a short nod. "But a few other details before I go into that."

"Right," Kharlov said. "Like how we're going to get onto the island where the Spaceship will be launched."

"I was about to tell you that," Alina replied. "You won't."

Kharlov and Neda both stared at Alina in disbelief.

"We won't?" Neda repeated, finally. "We must upload instructions to the rocket that will result in its destruction. It is certain such instructions can only be sent directly to the rocket via a dedicated line from the control center on the island where the launch will take place. Without access to that line, this mission will fail."

Alina shook her head. "I understand why you would think so, but we have discovered a weakness in the American command and control system. First, remember that this rocket is launched by a business, not the American government. So, it is not using a network secured to government standards."

Neda and Kharlov both nodded and visibly relaxed. Yes, it made sense that a business would be more vulnerable than a government.

"Now, that does not mean no attempt was made to avoid exactly what we plan to do. The designers of the network connected all of its launch centers via high-speed fiber optical cable. For the most part, the network is designed to transfer data allowing rocket activities to be monitored simultaneously from all launch centers. However, there is also a capability to allow rocket operating software to be transferred to all launch centers," Alina said.

Neda shook her head. "But surely there is a way for them to ensure that the type of code we plan to upload is only coming from the center in command of that particular launch, correct?"

Alina smiled. "There is. But the network designers miscalculated. Or maybe, it's better to say they outsmarted themselves. Since they built the network and operate it, naturally, they know the time it takes a signal to travel from origin to destination. So, a time limit was set for transmission of a critical command to the rocket."

Kharlov nodded. "So, a critical command from the launch center in California to this one in Florida would be automatically blocked as invalid."

"But how does that help us?" Neda asked with a frown. "Surely this network cannot be accessed through the Internet?"

"No," Alina acknowledged. "But we can access it on this island, posing as public utility workers."

Neda shook her head stubbornly. "I think you underestimate their network engineers. We may not be far from the launch center, but I still think their software will detect we are not on the same island."

Alina arched one eyebrow. "Even if that additional distance is under one hundred meters?"

For once, Neda was at a loss for words. Finally, she repeated, "Less than one hundred meters? How is that possible?"

"We have located an access point from which we can reach the fiber optic cable just after it leaves the island with the launch center to the island where we are now sitting. We are certain a command sent from there will be treated as valid," Alina replied.

A bit smugly, Kharlov thought.

"I am sure access points to this cable are monitored. And I saw many cameras mounted along roads on our drive to this house," Kharlov said flatly.

"True," Alina replied. "This cable's direct access path is indeed monitored. But you will approach it underground after entering a separate underground conduit that has been unused for years."

"Have you confirmed that the connection exists in reality, not just on paper?" Kharlov asked.

"No," Alina said, shaking her head. "There was no time. Besides, it makes no sense to go to the location until we are ready to use it. If the paper doesn't match reality, there is no time to make an alternate plan before the rocket launches anyway."

Kharlov grimaced, and it was clear he was anything but satisfied. "At least tell me where you obtained this information and how sure you are of its accuracy," he said.

Alina hesitated but finally nodded. "Normally, I would not divulge sources to agents in the field, but since your lives are so directly on the line, agree you have the right to know. We obtained most of this information from a SpaceLink employee. He was identified as likely to respond positively to our approach after we ran a credit check on all employees we thought would have access to the necessary information."

Kharlov frowned. "Well, now we know how you obtained the software code we have been using as the basis for our attack on this rocket. But isn't it likely that company security detected such a wide-ranging inquiry?"

"No," Alina said, shaking her head emphatically. "A vast quantity of data on all Americans is available to anyone willing to pay a credit reporting bureau. We go the extra step of making the inquiries through several small banks we own, of course via multiple cutouts. Americans' lack of privacy, particularly from these credit reporting bureaus, has been a real boon to our operations here."

"So, if you identified the target through a credit bureau, he had significant debt problems. But access to the variety of information you obtained from him suggests a high-ranking employee. Wasn't he well paid?" Kharlov asked.

Alina smiled. "Very," she said shortly. "But he spent his money even faster than it came in. Gambling is a highly efficient means to do so."

Kharlov cocked his head, puzzled. "Gambling? I know gambling is legal in Nevada and Atlantic City. But I thought it was illegal elsewhere. I suppose it shows I have much to learn about this country."

"That realization is always the beginning of wisdom," Alina said with a grave nod.

Neda smiled despite herself at Kharlov's discomfort.

"Native Americans living in reservations are allowed to operate casinos in many states, including Florida since they are considered sovereign nations in some respects. Casinos also function as a form of reparations not requiring money from taxpayers. This SpaceLink employee had never been near a casino before and quickly became addicted to gambling. There is such a casino about a two-hour drive from here," Alina said.

"Very well," Kharlov said. "But what if this employee has a sudden attack of conscience? Or is arrested for some other reason and decides to trade his knowledge of someone willing to pay for information about SpaceLink's network for his freedom?"

"That can't happen," Alina said, shaking her head even more emphatically.

"And why not?" Kharlov asked.

"Because he had a motor vehicle accident and did not survive," Alina said coldly.

Once the silence that followed her statement had stretched on for several seconds, Alina said, "You may as well know that I managed this aspect of the mission. I picked this man among several candidates first because he was unmarried and had no children. I also confirmed through surveillance he was not in a relationship with either a woman or a man."

Neda's face showed no expression as she said neutrally, "So, you kept the damage to a minimum."

Alina shrugged. "You could say that. For the mission, though, it's more relevant to say the man won't be missed. His death has been ruled an accident by the police, and the case closed. We know of no one asking questions about that conclusion."

Neither Kharlov nor Neda asked whether the accident had been real or staged. Or whether Alina had handled that too.

Looking at Alina, they already knew the answer to both questions.

Kharlov frowned. "So, the prohibition on injuring or killing Americans during this mission only applies to us?"

Alina shook her head. "That's not the right way to put it. I had several days to plan, prepare and assess before execution. The risk was minimal since the target providing information was a civilian, and the attack on the rocket was not yet underway. By contrast, the danger you will encounter will most likely come from armed police while you are carrying out the attack and making your escape. That is why the prohibition applies to you."

"Very well," Kharlov said grudgingly. "You said that you obtained most of this information from this SpaceLink employee. What about the rest?"

"Nearly all came from public records. Incredibly, some of what we needed was placed by local authorities on the Internet. Most American states have laws requiring information relating to utilities they regulate to be easily accessible. Other information required an in-person visit because the records were not available in digital form. The closest I came to security was a clerk who asked for my utility company ID. She barely looked at it, let alone made any attempt to confirm my identity," Alina said, her upper lip curling in contempt.

Kharlov nodded. "Which brings me to my next question. I assume we will all have utility company IDs. But what happens if someone does call the company?"

Alina looked at Kharlov, puzzled. Then her expression cleared, and she said, "Of course, you only played a brief part in one FSB mission, the one in Ukraine. We don't leave such details to chance, particularly for a high-priority operation like this one. An agent is in place at the utility company that supposedly issued our IDs. Their computer system will confirm both the IDs and the work order we will use to carry out the mission are genuine."

Kharlov's eyes narrowed suspiciously. "How did you have the time to place an agent at an American utility company? Let alone one with access to multiple systems?"

Alina sighed. "Very well. He is not our agent. He is from G2."

"The Cubans!" Neda exclaimed. "Are we sure we can trust him?"

"You are right to worry. I wouldn't trust just any operative from another intelligence service, even one where our ties go back as far as they do with the Cubans. As it happens, I trained this particular agent myself in Moscow when I took a break from field operations. It is not a coincidence. It is one of the reasons, along with our previous experience working together, that I was put in charge of this mission," Alina replied.

"Good," Kharlov said. "Now, let's imagine we are successful in accomplishing our mission. How will we get back home?" he asked.

"I will drive the van that will take us to the location with the access point. It will have a removable decal bearing a utility company logo. While you carry out the mission, I will provide overwatch. Once you complete the mission, I will switch the decal and license plates and drive us to Key West. A fast boat will be docked there for our use in reaching Havana," Alina said.

"How long will all that take?" Neda asked.

Alina shrugged. "Impossible to be sure. Fortunately, we are driving to Key West on a weekday, and it is not currently prime tourism season. Still, seven hours is optimistic. Once there, we can leave immediately for Havana, which is less than two hundred kilometers away."

"If you need a break, I was trained in the operation of any powered vessel. I presume this fast boat does not use sails," Kharlov said.

"You presume correctly," Alina said with a smile. "And fortune seems to be with us so far. The forecast is for clear skies and no delay for the rocket's launch, and that's good news for our trip to Cuba as well. Swells should be moderate and allow us to reach Havana in a few hours. Once there, you will depart on the first available flight to Europe. There are many flying from Havana, so you should both be back in Moscow by the following day."

"I suppose that leaves transformation of our appearance. What will that involve?" Kharlov asked.

Alina said nothing and instead reached into her small bag. Her hand emerged with a gleaming straight razor.

Alina put it on the kitchen table with a wicked smile.

"This was my father's, and I brought it with me just for this mission. This model is the ZTV Dvuhzakovnaya," Alina said.

Neda cocked her head curiously. "Just when I think I've mastered Russian, I'll hear another unfamiliar word. What does 'Dvuhzakovnaya' mean?"

Kharlov stared at it, shaking his head. "Double forged, which explains how even now it's in such great shape. ZTV stands for Zavod Trud, labor factory, and Vacha, the town in Nizhny Novgorod where the factory was located. ZTV used to make combat knives for the Red Army in Soviet days, and plenty of them are still around. I saw some in Chechnya."

Alina nodded. "ZTV also made surgical instruments. They began making razors in the early 1800s and stopped around 1970 as straight razors went out of fashion. You can see from the stamp on this one that it was made in 1924."

"A real antique. So, what do you propose to do with this one?" Kharlov asked, still staring at the razor.

"Oh, I think you know," Alina said, her smile broadening as she fixed her gaze on Kharlov's beard.

Neda's answering laugh was quickly joined by Alina's.

Wonderful, Kharlov thought glumly as Alina stood to begin her task. For now, at least, the conflict between these two appeared to be over.

But at what a cost!

Chapter Twenty-One

Zhongnanhai Compound
Beijing, China

President Lin Wang Yong impatiently gestured for Army Commander Shi to take a seat.

"I hope you have good news for me," Lin growled.

So, though every effort had been made to restrict the information, the news Shi had learned about the Air Force attack on the American satellites must be true.

It had not gone well.

General Yang was indeed fortunate to have his job still.

I wonder how?

These thoughts passed through Shi's head in the time it took him to nod acknowledgment of Lin's question.

"I do have good news, sir. You asked us to keep the Indian military occupied on our mutual border without allowing the conflict to escalate to one with major casualties. We have done exactly that. Further, we have made the Indians show their hand," Shi said with satisfaction.

"How so?" Lin asked, his curiosity overcoming the annoyance he was still feeling at Yang's failure.

"Reports from our front-line snipers confirm our suspicions that the Indians have deployed two key capabilities to our border. First, the American-made Barrett sniper rifle, firing a round even capable of penetrating light armor. Second, a mine laying drone. Best of all is that we obtained this knowledge without losing any of our soldiers, despite the Indians' best efforts," Shi said.

"Yes, I saw the report that two of our soldiers were injured. But they are expected to return to duty?" Lin said.

Shi nodded. "In a few more days. In the meantime, I would like your authorization to send a message to the Indians. It should not lead to a major escalation."

Shi then explained his proposal. Lin considered it for a few moments and then shrugged.

"Approved," Lin said. Shi was right. It shouldn't cause any real problems.

"Now, on to new business," Lin said.

Shi was careful to keep his expression neutral in response, though internally, he groaned. What new adventure was this?

"I told you previously to freeze construction work on the new bases we're building in the South China Sea. I had hoped that would induce the Americans to stop the deployment of new Internet satellites reaching inside our borders. But, they refuse to see reason. So, I want you to resume work. More, I want you to accelerate it," Lin said.

"Yes, sir," Shi said with relief. This was just more of what they'd been doing for years and should pose no problems.

But Lin wasn't done.

"When I say speed up, I mean I want the latest base you're building to be ready by next week. And by ready, I mean able to launch aircraft to defend our airspace. Can you do it?" Lin asked.

Shi's mind raced furiously. The last report he'd read said the new "island" had already been built with enough rock and dirt to keep it reliably above sea level.

Fortunately, Shi had anticipated the freeze being lifted at some point. So, ships were still on station nearby with the materials needed to build the hangers, bunkers, control buildings, and runway required for a functioning base.

But that left planes.

"Sir, as Army Commander, I am in charge of all military construction. But I have no authority over the deployment of aircraft to the base once it is ready," Shi said carefully.

Lin shook his head impatiently. "Don't concern yourself. General Yang will do as I order. And be sure you understand this. The base must be ready for full combat operations. I will order the defense of our airspace as soon as our planes can fly. The Americans and their allies must learn there are consequences for refusing our just requests."

Shi automatically said, "Yes, sir. We will be ready," but his mind was racing. Slapping together a few temporary structures together and declaring a base "ready" was one thing. But Shi would not be the judge of whether this new base in the South China Sea was able to conduct "full combat operations."

No, that would be Air Force Commander Yang.

And all for what? To proclaim sovereignty over thousands of square kilometers of empty ocean?

"Very well, General, see that you are. I will expect regular reports on your progress. You're dismissed," Lin said.

Shi rose, saluted, and left.

Like most high Party officials, Lin had never served in China's military. Shi had checked, and Lin had registered for selective service as required. But, of course, had never been drafted.

Too bad. Maybe if Lin had spent any time in the military, he'd have known better than to dismiss his Army Commander with less respect than Shi would have given a Private.

As Shi reached the building entrance and his waiting car, he realized Yang might have been right all along.

Maybe it was time for President Lin to go.

As Shi settled into the staff car's back seat and it sped back to his headquarters, he smiled.

Shi realized Lin had given him a precious gift. Unscheduled meetings between military commanders were always viewed with suspicion by the Ministry of State Security (MSS). But now they had the perfect cover.

An operation absolutely requiring close coordination between the Army and Air Force, ordered by Lin himself.

Yes. Now Shi could speak with Yang far from the many eyes always watching in Beijing.

And decide whether it was time for the military to take charge from bumbling incompetents like Lin.

Chapter Twenty-Two

Cocoa Beach, Florida

Boris Kharlov did his best to keep a smile from his lips at the transformation Alina had worked on Neda Rhahbar's appearance.

The glare Neda sent his way suggested his attempt had not been successful.

Well, then why not say what he was thinking?

"We will be passing through Miami on our way to Key West. Perhaps we should try your new look at one of its many nightclubs?" Kharlov asked, doing his best to look as innocent as possible.

Kharlov could see immediately that his attempt at humor had not been successful.

Alina put a restraining hand on Neda as she moved to stand. Kharlov had the strong impression Neda had been about to demonstrate her unarmed combat skills.

Though Kharlov was confident in his abilities, and knew he was certainly stronger, he had heard stories about Neda's prowess both in training and in the field.

Alina was right, though. This wasn't the time to put Neda's reputation to the test.

"Workers in this country have far greater latitude in their appearance on the job than in Russia. The shade of red I have dyed her hair would not be encountered on a utility work site in Moscow. Here, though, it is nothing surprising," Alina said.

"And her green eyes?" Kharlov asked. "Surely not a combination found in nature!"

Alina shook her head. "Perhaps you have never seen it. But though it is one of the least common combinations, it does exist. It is not even the most rare. That honor falls to red hair and blue eyes."

"And the tattoos?" Kharlov asked.

"Removable, of course. In the event we are recorded somehow, another false trail for investigators to follow. And another difference between Neda, FSB agent, and the person caught on camera," Alina replied.

Kharlov knew Neda would not appreciate comments on Alina's skill in using makeup to conceal all traces of the scars on Neda's face. But Alina's comment had made it clear doing so had nothing to do with vanity. Instead, it was to avoid revealing Neda's true identity.

So instead Kharlov just grunted, and said, "I'm sure her hair color will be considerably harder to return to normal."

"Usually you would be right. Fortunately, the FSB's technical staff has long experience with all aspects of disguise, and this challenge is relatively simple. There is a plastic container in the back of the van large enough for Neda to immerse her hair. Into the container will go a chemical solution formulated to remove the dye I used without trace," Alina said, and then smiled and nodded towards Neda.

"You are lucky to be following in my footsteps," Alina said. "I used exactly this process during my first field mission. The solution in use then worked perfectly to return my hair to its original color, but stripped it in the process. It also left behind a horrible smell like nail polish remover. I visited the FSB lab after I returned to Moscow. You will find your experience much improved."

Kharlov sighed. "I don't suppose any magic tricks are waiting in that van to restore my normal appearance," he said, unconsciously rubbing his newly bare chin.

Alina shook her head, and said gravely, "Perhaps part of a bear pelt we could glue to your face and neck? No, I'm afraid not."

Seeing Kharlov's expression and his futile efforts to frame a suitable response, both Alina and Neda collapsed in laughter.

Looking at them, part of Kharlov was still furious. Both in Spetsnaz and as a warlord in separatist Ukraine, it had been a rare day when anyone dared to laugh at his expense.

But the larger part was glad to see Neda had truly overcome her earlier anger with Alina. Kharlov knew they would have to function as a team to have any chance of success with this mission.

"In any case, I see your skin reacted well to the salve I gave you after your shave. This morning I see little evidence of irritation. How does it feel?" Alina asked.

Kharlov grudgingly nodded. "It's fine. If I didn't know better, I'd say I never had a beard at all. Your father taught you well."

Alina smiled. "You are the first man I have shaved since he passed. It brought back good memories for me. More important, a straight razor is the best way to avoid the telltale nicks and redness that usually show recent beard removal."

Alina paused and looked both Kharlov and Neda over, finally nodding with approval.

"As long as an image is not collected at a short distance by a high resolution camera, I think it will be difficult to match either of you with your true identity. Now, do you have everything you need before we depart?" Alina asked.

Kharlov and Neda both nodded silently.

"Very well. It should only take us a few minutes to reach the target location," Alina said.

Moments later they were all in the van, now sporting a utility company logo. The sky was just beginning to lighten with dawn's approach.

As Alina eased the van into traffic, Kharlov said with a frown, "I thought you said the logo could be replaced after we finished the mission and were on our way to Key West. But I saw no seam or other evidence that the utility company logo there now is removable."

"Good," Alina replied, as she kept her gaze fixed on the road ahead. "That means the FSB technical staff is doing their job. Commercially available removable signs are based on magnets. That means a certain thickness is necessary to ensure a proper seal. But this sign's grip is chemical, not magnetic."

"Chemical," Kharlov repeated with an even deeper frown. "How does that work?"

"We apply a specially formulated clear chemical solution to the entire van, both to ensure a uniform appearance and to give flexibility on where to place a logo. The sign is made of a very thin sheet of plastic, made to bond with the chemical once it has dried. Though this bond is highly stable, logo removal is still easily accomplished by sliding a fingernail under its edge at any point and pulling. However, this method has many limitations, and so is only used for the highest priority missions."

Kharlov nodded. "I wondered why I had never heard of this technique before. What are these limitations?"

Alina halted at an intersection with a stop sign, looked both ways and then drove on before replying.

"The clear chemical solution takes nearly two days to dry completely. It also has a short shelf life. Production of the plastic signs requires a lead time of about a week. Both the solution and the signs are only made in Moscow, and must then be flown to wherever they are needed. So, this is only the second time I have ever used these materials in a mission."

"I appreciate your taking the time to explain this," Kharlov said slowly. "It helps keep my mind off speculating about what could go wrong with the mission."

"Understood," Alina said. "We are nearing the target location. I will advise through your earpiece if I see police approach, which is a real possibility. They are always on heightened alert during launch days. Remember, none of us may be taken."

"You mean, taken alive," Kharlov said quietly.

Alina shrugged. "Just so," she said as she made another turn and began to slow.

Kharlov could see Neda's hand already reaching for the rear door as the van came to a stop.

Moments later, they were at the manhole cover that showed where the disused access tunnel was located. Crumbling asphalt around it revealed the manhole had been in a road at one point, but now it was surrounded by weeds.

The sky was a bit lighter, but true dawn was still some way off.

In the gloom they couldn't see the short stretch of water separating their island from the one housing Cape Canaveral. But the unmistakable smell of the sea told them they were close.

The secondary road they had turned onto to reach the manhole had no traffic, at least so far. But that was sure to change before long.

It only took Kharlov moments to unfold and place barriers around the manhole cover indicating it was now an active work site.

Alina nodded, satisfied. "Good. I will move the van nearby where I can observe any approaching traffic and provide warning. I know you will work as quickly as possible."

Without waiting for an answer, Alina drove off.

She left Kharlov and Neda standing in front of the manhole cover. Each was carrying a bag.

Kharlov's was much larger.

He opened it, and extracted a tool which he used to pry the manhole cover loose. As it fell to the side, Kharlov sighed with relief, and Neda looked at him curiously.

Kharlov smiled. "I was worried something out of use this long might be rusted shut. So far, so good."

Neda smiled back. "I wondered what you had in that big bag. Glad to see it's tools, not weapons."

Kharlov just raised an eyebrow in response, and pointed his flashlight into the newly revealed hole. Metal handrails glinted back in the gloom.

"Our luck is holding," Kharlov said quietly. "I'll go first."

Holding his bag in one hand, Kharlov swung his bulk onto the ladder. Neda was always surprised by Kharlov's speed and agility in spite of his mass.

Of course, Neda never saw the many hours of daily exercise Kharlov devoted to making such performance possible.

Almost immediately, Neda heard "clear" over her earpiece, and followed Kharlov down. It turned out few handrails had been necessary to allow access to the tunnel, which was barely tall enough to let Kharlov stand.

The light from Kharlov's flashlight showed the way ahead was unobstructed.

"Proceeding to objective," Kharlov said for Alina's benefit. A single "click" told Kharlov and Neda his message had been received.

Now the flashlight showed a sharp bend in the tunnel ahead.

Kharlov glanced back to see that Neda was keeping pace right behind him. He said quietly, "We should see the junction with the tunnel we need to access as soon as we make this turn."

But they didn't.

Neda drew her breath in with a sharp, disappointed hiss. "All our work was for nothing," she said, disgusted.

To her surprise, Kharlov smiled. "Fortunately, you have a soldier with you. Who had the foresight to bring the right tools."

A few moments later, they were standing in front of the concrete wall revealed earlier by the flashlight. Its smooth texture contrasted sharply with the rough, pitted surface of the tunnel they had been walking through so far.

Kharlov bent down and pulled a small, round object from his bag. Frowning with concentration, he tapped several small buttons on its front, and was rewarded with a "beep" and a digital display reading "1:30."

Kharlov peeled away a strip of paper, revealing an adhesive patch on the other side of the device.

"What is that thing?" Neda asked. Her tone, though, suggested she had already guessed the answer.

"With luck, our ticket in," Kharlov said, as he pressed the small round object against the smooth concrete wall.

It stayed attached, even when Kharlov gently pulled on it.

Seeing Neda's puzzled look, Kharlov grinned. "It would be bad if it fell off and rolled after us. We need to get back to the other side of that bend in the tunnel behind us."

Neda wasted no time following Kharlov's instruction.

Kharlov pressed the largest of the small buttons on the device.

The digital display began counting down to zero.

Kharlov rounded the turn in the tunnel, and saw that Neda had moved on some distance towards the manhole. He nodded with approval.

Caution was always warranted when dealing with explosives. Especially ones planted by someone else.

A muffled roar was followed by a plume of dust that rounded the turn in the tunnel, but had largely dissipated by the time it reached Kharlov and Neda.

Alina's alarmed voice immediately sounded in their earpieces. "What's happening down there?" she asked.

Kharlov replied tersely, "Stand by," and led the way as they both returned to the concrete wall that had blocked their way forward.

The wall was still there, but a large hole showed where the device had been planted, along with cracks radiating outward from the new opening.

Kharlov removed a sledgehammer with a folding handle from his bag, gesturing for Neda to stand back. Snapping the handle into place, he checked to make sure Neda was safely out of range of his swing. Satisfied, Kharlov began with the area of the wall closest to the hole.

It took only a few minutes before it became obvious this was a contest Kharlov was destined to win. Less than ten minutes after he'd started the hole was large enough to admit Kharlov, and Neda followed quickly behind him.

Only now did Kharlov update Alina. "We had to remove an obstacle blocking our way to the objective. Now approaching."

Alina's voice was low and furious. "Your removal method sent up a dust plume that can be seen from some distance. Police are likely to be here soon."

"Understood," Kharlov replied calmly. "Will report when mission complete."

Neda said nothing, but Kharlov could see she was worried.

Well, he knew Neda placed a higher priority on mission success than her own safety. Since if they failed, her husband Vasilyev and their friend Grishkov were up next.

Kharlov had willingly risked his life for friends and comrades many times. But he didn't remember feeling that he would actually prefer his own death to theirs.

And knowing they would feel the same way about him.

Yes, Vasilyev was a lucky man.

Neda spotted the fiber optic cable first. She stepped forward confidently, reaching down into her bag for the optical splitters she would need to access the cable.

Once Neda had them in place, she glanced backwards at Kharlov. As expected, he had already removed the optical transmitter and attached it to a bulky portable power supply.

Neda connected the optical splitters to the transmitter, and then pressed its power button.

A solid green light announced a stable connection. Good.

But the hardest part was still ahead.

Holding her breath, Neda gently slid the thumb drive with the virus designed to destroy the rocket into the transmitter's USB port. Their transmitter was set up to send any data inserted into it immediately, so the "data being sent" light began blinking amber at once.

Only a few seconds later, the blinking amber light was replaced with a single solid green light.

Data sent.

Her hands blurring, Neda disassembled everything and shoved the small items into her bag, while Kharlov stored the optical transmitter and its power supply.

"Mission accomplished. En route," Kharlov said over his earpiece to Alina.

"Understood," came Alina's crisp acknowledgement.

It only took a few minutes for them to reach the tunnel exit.

But it was a few minutes too long.

Kharlov's head was just emerging from the manhole when he heard over his earpiece, "Hold position! Police on scene!"

At the same instant a blinding light transfixed Kharlov, just as he was about to go back into the tunnel.

A voice over a loudspeaker said, "Police. Come out slowly, with your hands over your head."

There was no choice. Kharlov did exactly as he was told.

His eyes were still dazzled by the light being trained on him, but Kharlov could see at least one thing.

There were no certainly no spinning red and blue lights, and he didn't think the police vehicle had its headlights on either.

So, that explained why Alina had failed to spot the police vehicle's approach until it was too late.

It also suggested this policeman was no fool.

"Who are you, and what are you doing here?" the policeman demanded.

"Officer, we're with Brightlink Cable Services," Kharlov said. "We were sent here to repair an outage."

"You said we. Is someone else down there?" the policeman asked.

"Yes, sir. We always work in pairs. Can I show you our work order?" Kharlov asked. They had discussed this scenario in advance, and agreed that their documents had to include both of them. So, they would escape or not together.

"Reach for it slowly," the policeman replied. Kharlov's eyes had now adjusted well enough that he could see the policeman had a pistol trained on him.

Kharlov's hand went very slowly to the upper right pocket of his utility coverall. He was careful to make sure that a folded piece of paper was the only thing visible as his hand reemerged.

As planned, the other item now in Kharlov's hand was the capsule Alina had given both of them in case they were about to be captured.

"Walk four steps forward, and keep your hands up," the policeman ordered.

Kharlov did as he was told.

"Slowly place the paper on the ground. Then walk backwards three steps," the policeman ordered.

Kharlov obeyed the order, and then stood stock still.

The policeman kept his pistol steady as he walked towards the paper. It never wavered as he retrieved it and then walked backwards to within a few steps of his vehicle.

The policeman glanced at the paper and then shook his head.

"When I saw your van I called and asked if there were any cable or Internet outages in the area. I was told no. How do you explain that?" the policeman asked.

"The line we're repairing is a dedicated high-speed Internet fiber optic cable. It's only used by businesses, and none of them are open yet. Whoever you talked to doesn't know about the outage because so far customers haven't complained yet. My boss sent us out, though, because pretty soon they will. Just call the company and ask for him. His name's right on the form," Kharlov said.

The policeman glanced again at the form, and then at Kharlov.

Then he shook his head.

"We'll sort this out at the station," he said, tossing a pair of handcuffs to Kharlov's feet with his left hand, while keeping the pistol steady in his right.

"Put those on, and then tell whoever's down there to come up," the policeman ordered.

Part of Kharlov admired the policeman's instincts, which were spot on in doubting Kharlov was who and what he claimed.

A much larger part regretted that he would now have to choose between putting on the handcuffs and taking the capsule.

"Take no action," came Alina's terse voice over his earpiece.

"Officer, please reconsider calling my boss," Kharlov said. "I'm not asking you to call some bogus number. Call the company direct and ask for him by name. He really is a supervisor there."

The policeman shook his head, annoyed. "Put the cuffs on. If I have to tell you again, I'm going to add resisting arrest to..."

He never finished the sentence.

A slim arm wrapped around his neck, and after a brief struggle the policeman was lying on the ground unconscious.

Kharlov was already at the manhole, looking down towards Neda. "Let's go," he said.

As soon as Neda emerged, Kharlov replaced the manhole cover.

Both of them then hurried towards Alina, who was dragging the policeman towards his vehicle. Kharlov helped her get the man's limp form into a prone, face up position in the back seat.

Alina pulled a syringe from one of her pockets, and removed its cap. Next, she swiftly injected its contents into the policeman's neck.

Alina took out a piece of paper from another pocket, and used the syringe's needle to attach it to the policeman's uniform where it was plainly visible.

The policeman had a body camera, which Alina removed. She gestured for Kharlov to do the same with the camera attached to the front windshield. That took more effort, but in moments Kharlov had it secured in his bag.

Closing the patrol car's rear door behind her, Alina began walking towards their van without a backward glance.

Kharlov had closed the front door and was about to follow, when heard the radio in the vehicle's front making noise. He couldn't hear what was being said, but could guess.

The policeman was being asked for a status update.

Kharlov opened the door, keyed the radio receiver's handset, and in his best attempt at an imitation of the policeman's voice said, "10-24. Nothing here to report. Resuming patrol."

The radio was silent for a moment and Kharlov held his breath. Did whoever was on the other end actually know this policeman? He doubted his attempt at impersonation had been very good.

"10-4," was the reply Kharlov had been hoping for, and he felt a wave of relief when it was the one he got.

Kharlov replaced the handset and closed the door behind him.

A few seconds later, Kharlov was moving towards the van. He was impressed to see that Alina had used his time on the radio to remove the utility company logo on its side and replace both the front and rear license plates.

Kharlov might have been less impressed if he had known the plates had been held in place by magnets designed for rapid replacement.

Alina started the van's engine as Kharlov climbed into the passenger seat. He looked back and saw that Neda was already in the rear seat.

From Alina's expression, Kharlov thought it was fortunate Alina had been occupied with the van's logo and plates while he'd been dealing with the radio call. It would be a long walk – and swim – back to Moscow on his own.

It took less than fifteen minutes for them to cross to the mainland.

The tension radiating from Alina made it seem much longer.

Kharlov understood. They had to cross two separate bridges to reach the town of Cocoa, where the rocket they were hoping to destroy had been built.

Businessmen might have their limitations, Kharlov thought. But at least in such matters, money could be counted on to make them do the obvious. It made sense to build a huge rocket as close to where it would be launched as possible.

The bridges made Kharlov tense too. They would be the perfect place to apprehend three foreign saboteurs.

There would be no hope of escape.

But unlike Alina, Kharlov doubted the police were aware of their actions. He had thought of telling Alina about his brief radio conversation with the police dispatcher, but a look at her had convinced Kharlov it would be better to wait until she asked.

After they crossed the second bridge without incident, though, Alina appeared to decide that for the moment at least they were safe.

Keeping her eyes on the road ahead, Alina said just one word in a low, furious voice.

"Report."

Kharlov nodded. "I will begin at the end, because it is most relevant to our escape."

Then he recounted his conversation with the police dispatcher.

Alina glanced at him thoughtfully. "You said the '10-24' code you used meant 'assignment completed' and that you used it because you believed the policeman had been sent specifically to investigate the dust plume you caused."

Kharlov nodded silently.

"And how did you happen to know that code?" Alina asked.

Kharlov shrugged. "You kept repeating there was a good chance we would encounter police during this mission. As a smuggler in separatist

Ukraine, I often found it useful to understand police communications, and they all use codes of some type. Here they are not even secret. I was able to look them up online."

"Well, that may have bought us some time," Alina said.

Kharlov relaxed fractionally. Was he off the hook?

"Now, let's talk about the explosives you used in that tunnel. As team leader, I know exactly what we were authorized to bring on this mission. Explosives weren't on that list for a reason. Where did you get them?" Alina asked.

No. Not off the hook.

"First, it was a single charge, designed to breach a reinforced steel door for hostage rescue. I brought it with me to Moscow after our last mission in Ukraine, " Kharlov said.

Alina looked at him in disbelief. "So, it was in your checked baggage all the way from Moscow to Washington, and then you brought it into our Embassy?"

"I was a smuggler for many years. Do you really think concealing a single small charge was such a challenge? Besides, nobody at the Embassy even asked us to open our suitcases. Apparently we were expected," Kharlov said.

Alina shook her head. "Didn't it occur to you that examination of the explosive's residue could lead straight back to us?"

"How?" Kharlov asked stubbornly. "You don't think I'm dumb enough to use a Russian device, do you? It was German. And no, not East German. It was made just a few years ago. If someone in the FBI is very capable, they will trace it back to a shipment stolen from a German company supplying GSG-9."

"GSG-9," Alina repeated. "The tactical unit within the German Federal Police. And do you happen to know what became of the rest of that shipment?"

"Not all of it," Kharlov replied. "But several charges had already been used in thefts from jewelry shops and bank branches in Germany and Belgium when I obtained the one I just used. Zero connection to Russia."

Alina nodded, but said nothing.

"Look, I'll admit I didn't tell you about the charge because I knew you wouldn't let me use it. But without it, we couldn't have succeeded in this mission," Kharlov said.

Alina sighed. "You have a lot to learn. First, we don't know yet whether the virus will work. More important, though, the top priority for this mission was not success. It was avoiding detection of Russian involvement. We have a backup plan in place in California."

Neda's eyes flashed as she looked up at the mention of Vasilyev and Grishkov in California, but she stayed silent.

"Fine. So why did you bother saving us, then?" Kharlov asked.

"Idiot," Alina said, shaking her head. "The capsules were always a last-ditch option, for use only if we were all about to be captured. It's likely your dead bodies would have eventually have been identified as those of FSB agents. Our efforts at disguise were designed to make an image match difficult, not to fool a full forensic examination."

Kharlov frowned. "We were being followed by the authorities in Washington. Won't they notice our sudden disappearance, and perhaps connect us to this incident?"

Alina shook her head again. "As far as the Americans are concerned, you didn't just disappear. You don't need the details. So without you two in their possession, either dead or even worse alive and able to answer questions, there is nothing to connect the rocket's destruction to Russia."

Alina paused. "It should have occurred to you that successfully uploading the virus to the rocket made your rescue imperative. Two dead

Russian agents near a buried fiber optic cable would be bad enough. But if that cable was found to be the means for the rocket's destruction?"

Alina shook her head. "As we already discussed, that outcome was and is unacceptable."

"Fine," Kharlov said. "But what about the policeman? What did you inject into him? And what was on that piece of paper you attached to his uniform?"

Alina sighed with exasperation. "Neda, I have to express my admiration. Your husband's life is at stake in all this, and I have yet to hear a single question from you."

Neda smiled softly. "Don't give me too much credit. Kharlov is asking the same questions I would have, so there's no need for me to speak."

Alina grunted, and turned right.

"Very well. I injected the policeman with a powerful sedative. The note was a warning I had already prepared to avoid attempting to wake him with a stimulant, because it would interact with our drug and risk his life."

Kharlov raised an eyebrow and asked, "Isn't risking the American policeman's life also against orders?"

Alina shook her head. "The threat is empty, and designed to buy us more time. As soon as the policeman starts talking, the hunt for us will intensify. In particular, they will know to look for two women and a man in a van."

"You're right. We need to switch vehicles as soon as possible!" Kharlov exclaimed.

Alina gave Kharlov a look that he thought, with a flush, could best be described as pitying.

"That is our first destination. A vehicle is ready for us, and we will be there shortly."

"So that's why we're travelling west? I thought Key West was south," Kharlov said sullenly.

"We are no longer going to Key West. The scale and speed of the search about to be launched for us makes that impossible," Alina said.

Kharlov shrugged. "Just as well. I was never enthusiastic about an escape route that included an eleven thousand meter long bridge, which I understand is the only way to drive to Key West. So, will we take a boat from somewhere else on the Florida coast?"

Alina shook her head. "I considered that, but no. It is the next obvious option, and once the policeman begins talking, the search for us will be in the hands of the FBI. They will cover the obvious first."

"Very well," Kharlov said. "So, where are we going?"

Alina smiled. "Laredo."

Chapter Twenty-Three

Shanghai, China

Chen Li Na had accomplished two things by uploading the video she had captured of the Gateway-hunting drone. Of course, it had been critical to warn Gateway users that the government was using a new means to find them.

But in a way, the footage of the drone's silent search had been even more important as a motivator. Small, black, and relentless, its progress in the dark of night was the stuff of nightmares.

What sort of government felt comfortable adding this creature to its arsenal?

Chen had been gratified to see the flood of requests from other Gateway users for something concrete to do in response. Today they were going to take their first real step.

Most people in Western countries had the vague idea that hacker toolkits were only available on the "Dark Web." Far from it. For months anyone with a Gateway had been able to access the most basic of what hackers called toolkits. Software written to allow penetrating and attacking networks, toolkits would typically have been no great threat.

After all, toolkits had been available in Western countries for years. Many were even free.

In fact, much hacking software was widely distributed and bounties paid by major companies for its successful use.

As long as "success" fit the definition of those companies. That meant "white-hat" hackers identifying vulnerabilities companies could fix before "black-hat" hackers exploited them.

It didn't work that way in China, though. Hacker toolkits had long been available only to military and civilian intelligence agencies.

Fat and happy behind the Great Firewall, Chinese companies and government agencies believed they were safe from online attacks.

Now they were going to discover how wrong they were.

The classic problem of coordinating nationwide action was the need to maintain security. The only way to achieve real security was to use the time-honored revolutionary strategy- the cell. The members of each cell were only able to initiate contact with those within it and did not know about activities outside their own cell.

When Chen uploaded the footage of the Gateway-hunting drone, she discovered there was an organization coordinating the activities of those cells.

When it congratulated her, gave her an advanced hacker toolkit and an assignment.

And told her the organization's name.

Forward.

Evidently, Chen thought, Forward's leadership had decided that only a genuine revolutionary would reveal the existence of such drones.

And Forward already knew all about her prowess in writing software.

One other detail Forward knew impressed Chen, and for the first time gave her real hope that the Chinese government might be vulnerable after all.

Forward had specific, detailed information on how a particular government system could be accessed remotely. Ordinarily, learning this would have required probes that would have been detected, and the vulnerability then quickly addressed.

Chen could see only one explanation. Someone with both access and expertise at the relevant government office had provided that information to Forward.

The hack that was about to be executed had been Chen's work. The content she was about to see displayed, though, had been provided by someone at Forward.

If it worked.

Chen was in a taxi stuck in midday traffic, just as she had expected. Traffic was always bad in downtown Shanghai.

Also, as always, digital signs at the intersections both before and behind her displayed the names and "crimes" of particular citizens. Ones the authorities had decided needed to be shamed into changing their ways.

Until, at exactly noon, the messages on the signs all changed.

Now the display was replaced by a single line of text displayed for three seconds, immediately followed by another:

Forward Says

Stop Slandering Citizens

Allow Free Elections

Permit Free Speech

Stop Censorship

End Party Tyranny

Then the display flickered and went dark as power was cut to the entire system.

Chen fought hard to keep a smile from her face, but it wasn't easy. Part of her code had prevented a power shutdown commanded by system software.

Someone had been forced to find a physical switch.

Chen had focused the camera in her phone on the sign the entire time and concentrated on capturing the best possible image. Part of her, though, had been waiting for the taxi driver to object.

The objection had never come. As the sign darkened and Chen lowered her phone, her heart leaped when she saw what the taxi driver was doing.

His phone was also up and recording.

Chen passed the driver money that covered both the fare and a generous tip, saying, "I'll get out here."

The driver nodded his understanding.

Chen walked as quickly as she could without seeming to run. Fortunately, she had planned well.

Shanghai's subway system was the world's second-largest, with four hundred fourteen stations. One of those stations was only steps away.

It took less than two minutes for Chen to board the first train she found leaving the station.

By then, police had already begun confiscating the phones of everyone they could find anywhere near the hacked signs. But it was already too late.

Shanghai just had too many people. And they almost all had phones.

Members of Forward had used Chen's code to hack the hated "shame display" signs in every major Chinese city. The same message had been displayed on all of them.

Gateway owners uploaded recordings of the message to dozens of sites. Quickly removed by Chinese censors, they were still seen by millions.

Forward had announced themselves to China's citizens and the Party.

What would they do next?

Chapter Twenty-Four

Cape Canaveral Air Force Base
SpaceLink Launch Command Center

SpaceLink project manager Mark Rooter stood next to his boss Eli Wade as they both looked out the vast expanse of glass in front of them at the rocket about to launch into the clear morning sky.

It was an awe-inspiring sight. Wade had dreams of using this very rocket model to send crews to the Moon and then Mars.

Today, though, no crew would be on the rocket. Instead, there would be four hundred SpaceLink satellites, enough to replace the satellites destroyed by the Chinese and add more for even better Internet coverage.

Wade smiled to himself at the thought. Yes, it was time to send a message to the Chinese.

Attacks on SpaceLink satellites would have consequences. Ones the Chinese wouldn't like.

"How's the launch looking?" Wade asked, glancing at the three displays in front of Rooter. They were full of graphs and data that, from Wade's vantage point, meant nothing.

Not that he couldn't have figured out the data on the displays if he sat down and took the time. But that's why he hired people like Rooter. So he wouldn't need to do that.

"Everything's green. Even the weather is cooperating," Rooter said.

"Great! But you still look worried," Wade said.

At first, Rooter looked startled, and then he laughed. It had the sound of coming from a man who hadn't laughed in some time.

"Sir, if the first launch of a new rocket model this size didn't worry me, you'd need a new project manager," Rooter said with a smile.

"Got you," Wade said with a nod. "So, ten minutes to go?"

"That's right," Rooter replied, glancing up at the large rectangular clock with a red digital readout suspended from the ceiling. And impossible for anyone in the launch center to miss.

Rooter knew Wade could see it and understood what the display meant. Pointing that out would have not only been rude, though. It would have missed the point.

Wade was just as nervous as he was.

Rooter had been present for every one of the dozens of rocket launches that had been necessary to establish the constellation of SpaceLink Internet satellites. For each one, he'd wondered if this would finally be the time it became routine.

It never did.

One part of each launch was always the same, though. Somehow, time seemed to both slow to a crawl each time Rooter looked up at the countdown clock and pass by in a blur as he monitored the hundreds of things that could go wrong with a launch.

Before he knew it, Wade was chanting the same refrain that had been familiar since the Apollo program that took crews to the Moon.

"T minus nine, T minus eight..."

Fire gushed from the bottom of the massive rocket, propelling it upwards. Slowly at first, then faster and faster.

Until it was out of sight.

A large display hung from the ceiling at the launch center's front now showed the rapidly receding launch center from the perspective of the rocket's bottom, where a camera was sending back a steady stream of images.

A sudden flurry of activity at several consoles caught the attention of both Rooter and Wade at the same moment that a red alarm bar appeared on all of Rooter's displays.

"What's causing these pressure fluct...?" was all Rooter had time to say.

Before a blinding flash from the ceiling display was replaced with static.

And all his displays showed zero incoming data from the rocket.

Now one of the technicians near Wade stood up and gestured at his headset, where he had just received a message.

"Sir, NASA tracking reports the rocket has broken up. Multiple fragments are now appearing on their radar," the technician said.

Into an echoing silence that had been a buzzing hive of activity moments before.

Rooter sat down heavily. It wasn't the first rocket they'd lost.

But it was the first in a long time.

And the very first of their newest type. After so many successful tests of every component...

"What happened?" Wade asked quietly.

Rooter shook his head. "It doesn't make any sense. Something went catastrophically wrong with stage separation. But the pressure readings didn't make any sense."

Wade nodded and gestured for Rooter to follow him. Rooter's first instinct was to object, to say he couldn't walk away after a disaster like this.

Two things immediately stopped him. First, Wade was his boss and could ask him to do whatever he wanted.

Next, there was nothing here for Rooter to manage. Finding the explanation for the rocket's explosion would take hours, if not days.

Rooter wasn't looking forward to the "it's not your fault" pep talk he knew was coming. At least he knew Wade well enough to know he wasn't about to be fired.

Wade swiped the access card to the conference room door and motioned for Rooter to precede him. Rooter sat down, and Wade closed the door.

Then Wade sat down right next to him with an expression Rooter didn't understand.

Wade was angry. But not at him.

His next words cleared up the mystery.

"Could this have been the Chinese?" Wade asked.

Rooter sat back, astonished by the question.

That possibility had not occurred to him. At all.

But the more he thought about it, the more sense it made. The Chinese had certainly pulled out all the stops to destroy the satellites they had broadcasting an Internet signal that could be picked up within China.

OK, they had the motive. But how?

"Let's assume the Chinese did this. They'd either need access to the rocket or to the launch center. I guess we should start by reviewing the logs showing exactly who that was and if there's anything we missed in their background checks. And if any of them had a big recent bank deposit," Rooter said sourly.

"What about an attack through the network? I know this rocket is monitored through our other launch centers, so access has to be possible. Maybe someone breached our security," Wade said.

Rooter shook his head. "Not possible. Monitoring data that's outgoing is allowed anywhere in the network. But uploading software code or sending a command to the rocket can only be done from this launch center."

Wade cocked his head. "You seem sure about that. Couldn't a command have a launch center authenticator included if they were able to reproduce it?"

"No way," Rooter said emphatically. "The network is set up to check that the command or software update was sent with essentially no lag. In other words, from this launch center. If it was sent from anywhere else the system would know, and alert us immediately to an attempted breach. We've tested it multiple times, and it's always worked."

Wade grunted, and Rooter could see he wasn't convinced.

"OK, but you're going to check network activity logs, right?" Wade asked.

Actually, it's probably the last thing Rooter would have done on his own, but why not? It wouldn't take long, and then they could move on to the real culprit.

Rooter was sure it was someone with physical access to the rocket who'd probably been paid a handsome sum to carry out the sabotage.

Maybe someone at the launch center right now.

The thought sent a wave of anger through Rooter that surprised him with its intensity.

No. Whoever was smart enough to do this without being caught in time wouldn't be dumb enough to hang around.

So, check to see if anyone had picked now to go on vacation. Or call in sick.

Wade interrupted the jumble of thoughts passing through Rooter's mind.

"Look, I know we've both got a lot to think about here. Why don't you check on those network activity logs, and I'll get us some help with this investigation. People who can, for example, check to see if anyone here recently opened an offshore bank account," Wade said.

Rooter realized he hadn't even answered Wade's last question and had been sitting frozen with his thoughts. Shaking himself, he nodded.

"Right, boss. I'm also going to check if anyone has picked now to go on leave, either on vacation or calling in sick. I can't think of anyone off-hand, but we've got a lot of people here, and some of them are contractors," Rooter replied.

"Good. I'll let you know who I can get to help us later this morning. Once you find anything, tell me and only me. We still don't know who we can trust here. Until we settle that, we can't decide what we should do next," Wade said.

Rooter nodded, sickened by the realization that Wade was right.

Until they got to the bottom of this, SpaceLink was going to be frozen in place.

And that, Rooter thought bitterly, had to be exactly what the Chinese government wanted.

Chapter Twenty-Five

The White House
Washington DC

President Hernandez looked up from his stack of papers as General Robinson walked into the Oval Office.

"Good morning, General. I understand you have an update on the explosion of that rocket in Florida," Hernandez said.

Robinson nodded. "Yes, sir. I just finished speaking with Eli Wade. They don't know how it happened, but they suspect China was behind it."

"Well, I had the same thought. After that Chinese laser attack on SpaceLink satellites, they're the obvious suspects. But sometimes rockets do blow up, and it was the first operational flight of this new Spaceship model. I'm going to need real proof before I can go public with an accusation," Hernandez said.

"Agreed, sir," Robinson said. "Wade called me because I knew about the laser attack, and this latest disaster happened at an Air Force base. However, I think this investigation will require resources well beyond what's available to military law enforcement. I've referred the matter to

FBI Director Finegold and made sure our military investigators know the FBI has the lead."

"Good," Hernandez said. "I'll call Finegold after we're done and tell him this is a top priority. Did he say who he's putting in charge?"

Robinson nodded. "Yes, sir. Bob Hansen."

"Excellent. I remember Hansen from when he stopped the Chinese effort to snatch one of their defectors from Dulles Airport a few years back. And wasn't he also involved in the arrest of those five Chinese agents trying to force dissidents who had made it here to return to China to face trial?" Hernandez asked.

"Yes, sir, in 2020. He's now been promoted to heading up all investigations for the Assistant Attorney General for National Security. Hansen is on his way to Florida right now," Robinson said.

"OK, so we'll wait to hear from the FBI. While we're on the subject of China, I wasn't happy to hear they've restarted construction on another one of their so-called islands. Is the Air Force monitoring that situation?" Hernandez asked.

"Not directly, sir. The Japanese have that job, since this newest Chinese provocation is in waters they also claim near the Senkaku Islands," Robinson replied.

"I'm sorry to hear that, General. Don't we have any assets in the area?" Hernandez asked.

Robinson hesitated. "Well, sir, it's not my place to discuss this, but I did see a report that the USS *Oregon* is nearby."

Hernandez grunted. "Right, it's General Robinson, not Admiral. As I'm sure, our friends in the Navy would be quick to remind you. *Oregon* is a *Virginia* class attack sub, right?"

"Yes, sir," Robinson said with a resigned smile.

"Funny how the *Oregon* keeps turning up at one crisis point after another, isn't it, General?" Hernandez asked.

"You're referring to its involvement in recent incidents in the waters off Korea and Saudi Arabia. I'd say that shows the Navy's good judgment in sending their best assets where they're most needed," Robinson said.

Hernandez laughed. "I keep trying to name you as National Security Advisor, and you keep turning me down. More comments like that, and I'll make you Secretary of State instead!"

Robinson winced. "Please, no, sir. I meant what I said before. I'll be a lot more effective staying under the radar."

Hernandez nodded, still smiling. "Fine. But tell me how you just happened to get a report on a sub deployment between China and Japan."

Robinson pursed his lips ruefully. There was a reason Hernandez had made it to the Presidency.

Very little got past him.

"For its past several deployments, the *Oregon* has been the testbed for advanced munitions, including ones that also interest the Air Force. The weapon they are testing in the Pacific now is one of those, sir," Robinson said.

"Interesting," Hernandez said, nodding thoughtfully. "You know, if it turns out the Chinese were involved in destroying our rocket, I'd like to make them regret it without going all the way to a nuclear exchange. Can you get me a report on this new weapon's capabilities without alerting anyone in the Navy or, for that matter, the Air Force that I'm the one asking?"

"Yes, sir," Robinson said. "I think a lot of our allies in the region would be happy to see something unfortunate happen to one of China's so-called islands. I'll get back to you later today."

Moments later, Hernandez was again alone in the Oval Office.

Yes, Hernandez thought to himself.

It was time for the Chinese to learn that you couldn't keep pushing others in the region without, at some point, having someone push back.

Hard.

Chapter Twenty-Six

Shanghai, China

Chen Li Na didn't like anything about this meeting in her apartment. She might trust Forward as an organization. The message she had helped them display on signs at traffic intersections all over China proved they were allies in fighting against the tyranny of Party rule.

But just how good was Forward's security? Particularly since they were willing to arrange something as risky as an in-person meeting?

Say this woman was a State Security agent. She could well be waiting until she had discovered as much of Forward's organization and its allies as possible before calling in the arrest teams.

So the fact that nobody had yet broken down Chen's door was no comfort at all.

Chen had no problem risking her own life in the struggle for freedom. As far as she was concerned, ending the Party dictatorship was worth the risk.

But the danger to her girlfriend Tang Yanfei did bother her. Yes, Tang was also part of the struggle.

But Chen knew that Tang's less important role was unlikely to expose her to arrest. No, if Tang ended up in prison, it would almost certainly happen because she had been swept up with Chen.

A soft knock at her door provided a welcome interruption to Chen's thoughts and even made her smile.

That wasn't a State Security knock.

Chen opened the door and stood rooted there for several moments.

The woman in front of her looked nothing like the person Chen had expected. Someone dull, gray, and anonymous.

No, this woman was the opposite of that.

Chen was average height, or maybe a little above. This woman exceeded her height by almost half a meter, making her one of the tallest women Chen had ever seen.

Her dark hair was cut short, unlike Chen's long flowing tresses. But many of the woman's individual strands were colored in a pattern that seemed at once random and, as her hair moved, picked with deliberate care by an artist.

Her makeup was delicate and had been applied sparingly. Yet it succeeded in accenting the woman's high cheekbones, full lips, and seemingly bottomless eyes.

Her perfume was just as subtle as her makeup. But it seemed to have been made just for her.

Chen was suddenly very glad that Tang wasn't present to see her staring at this visitor.

"May I come in?" the woman asked with a smile that said this wasn't the first time her appearance had provoked such a reaction.

"Please," Chen replied with embarrassment and an awkward wave towards her sofa.

The woman gracefully sat and said, "First, let me introduce myself. I am Wang Yan."

Which meant "glamorous" in Chinese. When Chen had been told to expect this name by Forward, she'd already thought the popular name was probably an alias. Now Chen thought that was nearly certain. A name probably chosen to match Wang's job as a model or actor.

"I know you must be wondering why I insisted on meeting you face to face. First, it is because I decided the information I have for you could not be trusted to any network and had to be delivered in person," Wang said.

Wang held up a USB drive she had just pulled from her purse but made no move to give it to Chen.

"Second, I need to be sure you understand the risk you are taking by agreeing to help launch this attack on the government. I trust the man who provided the information on this drive with my life, and I know you will do your utmost to keep the attack from being traced back to us. But make no mistake. The government will do everything in its power to find you," Wang said, locking eyes with Chen as she delivered her warning.

Chen, with difficulty, broke contact with Wang's gaze and asked, "What is the target?"

"The Shanghai Stock Exchange," Wang replied, observing Chen for her reaction.

Chen did not attempt to hide it. It was astonishment.

The Shanghai Stock Exchange was the world's fourth-largest, with a market capitalization of over four trillion US dollars. It was one of the best protected cyber targets on the planet.

Wang's smile told Chen her reaction had been seen and understood.

"You don't see how such an attack could be possible. First, as with the attack you helped mount on the shaming signs, we have help from someone inside the Exchange's network. Next, most of the network's security measures are focused on preventing data removal or alteration. We're not going to do either," Wang said.

"You're going to shut down the Exchange completely," Chen said with a sharp intake of breath.

"Yes," Wang said, pleased that Chen had come to the realization on her own.

"But there have to be multiple backups to, well, everything," Chen said. "There's no way we'll be able to keep the Exchange down long, even if we're initially successful."

Wang nodded. "Not long, perhaps. But panic will grow with every passing minute the Exchange is offline. And it will take much longer before everyone is reassured that nothing was stolen."

Chen frowned.

"So, are we doing all this for at best a few hours of chaos? Just to prove something as important as the Exchange is vulnerable? If we can't remove or alter any data, there's no way Forward could make any money from the attack..."

Chen's voice trailed off as she saw Wang's smile grow wider.

Finally, Chen shook her head.

"I'm an idiot. Of course, advance knowledge of the shutdown could be used to make profits once the Exchange reopens."

Wang nodded. "Yes. We will need to avoid doing too well, though. There is certain to be an investigation afterward to uncover those people who made the greatest profits. They will become the prime suspects."

"And I suppose Forward needs money to carry out the struggle," Chen said, trying to keep cynicism out of her tone.

Wang heard it anyway and smiled. "Believe me, there are less risky ways to make money in today's China. And if I weren't sure what we make from this attack will go towards ending Party rule, I wouldn't be sitting here."

Just a glance was all Chen needed to be sure Wang was being honest. Like any pretty woman, Chen had been told many lies and knew how to tell them from the truth.

Besides, no woman with Wang's looks would ever want for money.

Chen made her decision.

"I'm in," she said decisively. "When will we attack?"

Wang laughed, a silvery sound that made Chen's heart lurch.

You love Tang, she told herself fiercely.

And it was true. Chen really did love Tang and believed she would never betray her.

Chen was discovering, though, that anyone could be tempted.

"We will attack when you are ready," Wang said, handing Chen the USB drive she had held up before.

Her hand barely touched Chen's as she did so.

It didn't matter. Chen's heart had lurched before. Now it nearly stopped.

Wang added, "Based on the work you did before, we're sure you won't need long. When you've finished, please upload it to Forward using your Gateway just as before."

Not trusting herself to speak, Chen simply nodded.

"Good. On behalf of Forward, I want to thank you. We have more attacks planned if this one goes as well as we hope. Never forget that you're an important part of our struggle against tyranny," Wang said.

Moments later, Wang was gone.

Chen sat still on her sofa for several minutes, her head spinning, trying to regain control.

What had just happened?

Shaking herself, Chen made two decisions.

The first was to say nothing to Tang about the visitor other than two true statements. A woman had dropped off a USB drive containing information. And Forward needed Chen's help to use that information to launch another attack against the government.

The second was even more straightforward.

No more in-person meetings.

Chapter Twenty-Seven

Health First's Cape Canaveral Hospital
Cocoa Beach, Florida

Bob Hansen had flown into Cape Canaveral Air Force Station Skid Strip with a team of six other FBI agents the same day the rocket exploded. The small FBI jet's landing on the asphalt runway had been bumpy, just as he'd been warned.

The "Skid Strip" had been built in the 1950s to provide a landing spot for the SM-62 Snark, a long-range nuclear cruise missile later rendered obsolete by the development of ballistic missiles. The Snark had no wheels and so literally had to skid to a stop for data to be retrieved when it was being tested.

Wheels would not have been necessary if the Snark had ever been launched against the Soviet Union.

Now used only by Air Force cargo aircraft to deliver satellite payloads, Hansen's flight hadn't been cleared to land on the "Strip" until General Robinson had intervened personally. Which hadn't happened until Hansen's flight was already on its way.

So, Hansen had not arrived in the best of all possible moods.

Now, this county sheriff was trying his patience even further.

As anyone who knew Bob Hansen could have testified, patience was not a quality he possessed in great supply.

One of Hansen's first steps in any investigation was to review incident reports from local law enforcement.

The report of a possible explosion just over the bridge from Cape Canaveral had leaped from the page like a flare. Doubly so when the information included the fact that the deputy sent to investigate had been sedated with the injection of an unknown drug.

"Sheriff, I understand your concern for the health of your deputy. I'd be worried about one of my agents if he were lying in that hospital bed, too," Hansen said, gesturing towards the unconscious deputy.

So close, Hansen thought, trying to avoid visibly gritting his teeth. He'd talked a doctor into administering a mild stimulant to wake the deputy so he could give Hansen a description of whoever had drugged him. But the sheriff had turned up just before the doctor could give him the shot.

"But whoever did this is almost certainly a foreign agent, and right now is probably on their way out of the country," Hansen said.

"You already said that," the sheriff said stubbornly. "Next, you're going to tell me they blew up that rocket this morning."

Hansen was under direct orders not to tell anyone other than his superiors in the FBI anything he learned during the investigation.

Instead, he just glared at the sheriff and let his silence do the talking.

For the first time, the sheriff seemed to hesitate but then shook his head.

"If that's true, then why not just kill him? If foreigners did this, why run the risk of leaving him alive?" the sheriff asked.

It was a good question, and one Hansen had already asked himself. There was only one explanation that made sense.

Orders.

Whoever carried out the attack had been told not to leave any bodies behind. Which suggested a government that cared about American retaliation, not terrorists who would proudly boast about blowing up a rocket in Florida.

Plus, nobody so far had tried to claim credit for the attack.

But Hansen wasn't going into any of that with this sheriff.

So, try another tack.

"Your deputy was investigating a report of a possible explosion, right?" Hansen asked.

"That's right," the sheriff said with a frown. "But he radioed back that there was nothing to report."

"Uh-huh," Hansen said. "Are you sure that was your deputy on the radio? Did whoever he was talking to know him?"

That made the sheriff stop and think.

"Well, no," the sheriff said slowly. "I remember approving the dispatcher's shift schedule. We just hired someone new, and she would have started on the graveyard shift. She would have been on her last hour or so when he called in."

Then the sheriff shook his head and reached for his radio. "If that was him. I've got to get some men back there to check that area again thoroughly. We looked again when we found him unconscious but didn't find anything."

Now it was Hansen's turn to shake his head.

"Don't do that. I've got men there already. There was an explosion underground. That's why you got reports of a dust plume just before dawn." Hansen said.

The sheriff swore and then pointed at his unconscious deputy. "Look, I want the people who did this just as much as you do. But you saw the note they left. How can you guarantee the warning they left is an empty threat?"

"I can't," Hansen said. "All I can do is tell you what I did before. I talked to our medical experts, and none of them know of a drug interaction that could do what the note claims. But I won't lie to you. Especially if these are foreign agents, they could be using a drug we've never seen."

Hansen paused. "I think it's a lot more likely this is a bluff to buy time. One that's working. And every minute we stand here talking is more time they have to get away."

The sheriff scowled and shook his head. "Look, he's got a wife and two kids. You don't know him, but I do. He's a good man, and I'm not going to risk his life based on a guess. Now, you can get a court order and make a doctor give him a shot, but I'll bet by then he'll be awake anyway."

Hansen had already considered getting a judge to do just that but wasn't so sure that one would cooperate. And the sheriff was right. It would take too long.

"Fine," Hansen said evenly. "One last thing for you to think about, then. Like you said, you know him, and I don't. If we could ask him, would he want us to give him that shot?"

That made the sheriff stop and think.

Finally, the sheriff swore and said, "He never called for backup. I know he's going to be kicking himself over that. And he should because he knows better. If he finds out I stopped you from waking him up long enough to let whoever did this get away, he's going to be even madder than I am now."

Hansen had asked the doctor who had come with him to the deputy's bedside to wait while he spoke with the sheriff, and he was still standing nearby. Trying, unsuccessfully, to look like he wasn't listening to every word.

Now the sheriff gestured to the doctor and said brusquely, "Give him the shot."

The doctor nodded and removed a syringe he had already prepared from one of his pockets.

"Sheriff, for what it's worth, I told Mr. Hansen earlier I was willing to do this because I think it's safe. Your deputy is sleeping, not in a coma or anything close to it. The stimulant dose I'm going to give him might not wake him up. But there's no way it's going to hurt him," the doctor said.

With that, the doctor administered the injection.

At first, Hansen thought the doctor had been too cautious with his dose because there was no reaction from the deputy.

There was no change in the digital readouts on the many pieces of equipment hooked up to the deputy either. Hansen didn't blame the sheriff for his obvious relief as the deputy's breathing continued normally.

After several minutes, though, the deputy's eyelids fluttered open. He looked around weakly, obviously disoriented.

"Where am I?" the deputy mumbled.

The doctor replied, "Cape Canaveral Hospital. How are you feeling?"

The deputy shook his head. "Throat hurts, but not too bad. My head aches, but I've had worse. What happened?"

"We were hoping you could tell us," the sheriff said.

"Sheriff," the deputy said, grimacing as he tried to sit up straighter in the bed.

The sheriff shook his head. "Just lie still. I've got a man from the FBI with me. He's got some questions for you about whoever did this."

"FBI," the deputy repeated and then shook his head.

"This won't take long," Hansen said. "First, how many were there?"

The deputy was still for a moment, clearly thinking about his answer.

"I only saw one. But I'm pretty sure there were three," he said finally.

Hansen nodded. "Describe the one you saw."

The deputy described Kharlov, adding, "He had an accent, but it wasn't really strong. I think he's been here for a while. My guess would be he's from somewhere in Europe, probably eastern Europe."

Hansen nodded again but was thinking to himself it probably meant the man had capable language instruction. Not that he had been living in America for a while.

And he certainly wasn't Chinese.

"Why do you think there were two others?" Hansen asked.

"There were two names on the work order that supposed Internet service company tech showed me. One was supposed to be him. The other name was a woman's, who he said was still in the tunnel," the deputy said.

"Ok, and the third person?" Hansen asked.

"Well, I'm sure that was a woman. The last thing I saw before I blacked out was an arm across my throat. I'm sure it was a woman's," the deputy said bitterly, shaking his head again.

"So, you don't think the woman's name on the work order was the person who attacked you," Hansen said.

"No," the deputy said. "I heard someone in the tunnel moving after the man exited. And I had the manhole in view the whole time."

The deputy paused. "Unless there was another way out of the tunnel that would have let her get behind me."

Hansen shook his head. "There wasn't. It was dug by a company that went bust after the dot com boom bottomed out in 2000, and there was only one way in or out."

The deputy looked relieved, and Hansen sympathized. Letting someone get the drop on you was bad enough. At least three to one odds made it a little easier to swallow.

"One last thing. Why didn't you call for backup?" Hansen asked.

The deputy sighed. "I should have. When I saw the van, I called the company on its logo, and they said they had no reports of Internet outages. So, I already knew something was fishy when I saw that guy coming out of the manhole. But I had him cold, so I thought I could handle it."

"Back up a second. Describe the van you saw," Hansen said.

The deputy did, right down to the company on the logo and its license plate number.

Hansen nodded. Maybe this would finally give them something concrete to go on.

Then Hansen gestured to the FBI specialist he'd brought with him.

"This is a sketch artist. Please work with him to help us produce an image of the man you saw we can distribute to border crossing points. If we hurry, I still think we have a chance to stop them," Hansen said.

"Happy to do it," the deputy said, and Hansen could hear the sincerity in his voice.

"I got a real good look at him," the deputy added.

"Good!" Hansen replied. Just as sincerely.

The saboteurs might have succeeded with their mission, Hansen thought. But getting out of the country might not be as easy as they thought.

Chapter Twenty-Eight

Approaching Ziyou Island
South China Sea

General Yang Mingren glanced over at the Army Commander, General Shi. He appeared to be enjoying the helicopter trip to this artificial island even less than Yang, and that was saying something.

It was the second helicopter flight today for both of them. Even with extra fuel tanks, no helicopter in China's inventory had the range to travel straight to this newly built island. Instead, they had to take one flight to a helicopter carrier and then another to the island.

It had been the first time Yang had seen a Type 075 helicopter carrier, and he had to admit it was impressive. Well over two hundred meters in length, he'd been told it carried thirty helicopters along with a detachment of Marines.

The first Type 075 had started sea trials in 2020, just a few months after a minor fire on board had been extinguished and the damage repaired. A second was now operational, and a third was under construction.

Yang hadn't bothered asking why they'd needed to move to a different helicopter rather than wait for the same one to be refueled. He already knew the rule was for every hour a helicopter spent in the air, it needed two for maintenance.

It wasn't quite that bad for his own service's jet aircraft. But close.

Besides, it had been good to stretch his legs for a few minutes. And even better to use a real bathroom.

Yang had smiled when he heard how quickly Shi turned down the lunch offer before the second flight. But the truth was, his stomach had lurched too at the thought.

Flying in a helicopter over the Pacific was a challenging experience even for a pilot like Yang, who had plenty of time at the controls of planes facing rough weather.

That was the problem, though, Yang realized. This time, he wasn't at the controls. Without the distraction provided by a frantic struggle to keep his craft in the air, Yang had nothing to think about but his stomach.

Yang looked down at the rapidly expanding dot that the pilot had announced was "Ziyou Island" and shook his head.

Who named these, anyway? "Freedom" from what? All the amenities of civilization, even the few ordinarily available at a forward Chinese military base?

The last report Yang had read said the base wouldn't be ready on time. Shi had insisted it would and offered Yang this opportunity to see for himself.

It would also offer them the rare chance to talk with no one else nearby to overhear.

The closer they got, the more "Ziyou Island" made Yang think of an anthill he'd kicked over as a child. Everyone was moving quickly.

A few soldiers were even running from one spot to another.

The only stationary objects were the ships. Several surrounded the island, laden with supplies of various types.

Several temporary buildings were indeed in place. There were also plenty of tents.

Yang was glad they wouldn't be on the island long enough to experience sleeping in one.

The helicopter finally settled on a crudely marked landing pad, gently enough to avoid the "clack" of his jaws coming together that had marked their arrival on the helicopter carrier.

Islands did have one advantage over ships. They weren't always moving.

Once the helicopter's blades stopped turning, Yang and Shi exited and saw an Army colonel was hurrying forward to meet them.

The colonel gave Shi a crisp salute and barked, "Welcome to Ziyou Island, General Shi! I am Colonel Xia, and it will be my honor to brief you on our progress."

Shi nodded, and returned the salute. "Colonel, this is General Yang, the Air Force Commander. Treat any question from him as coming from me. Let's go straight to your briefing."

"Yes, sir. Please follow me," Xia said, leading the way to the closest temporary building.

Well, Yang thought to himself wryly, this island's size did have one advantage.

Wherever you were going, you wouldn't have to walk far.

As they walked inside, Yang saw with approval that Xia had kept it simple. One whiteboard and two chairs.

It went without saying that Xia would be standing.

It didn't take long for Xia to finish his briefing. If he were to be believed, Shi's troops would indeed finish constructing the airbase on time.

Yang was still skeptical.

"Colonel, you still have bulldozers grading the surface area designated for the runway. How will you pave it in time for my planes' arrival?" Yang asked.

"Sir, we will meet the deadline by using landing mats," Xia said.

"Landing mats?" Yang repeated with a frown. "I've seen them used for cargo helicopter landing pads. Are they safe for jet fighters?"

"Yes, sir. At our direction, a state-owned company purchased mats and associated equipment several years ago from a firm in the United Kingdom. Our company reverse-engineered the mats and equipment and then put them into production for our sole use," Xia said.

Yang grunted and thought for a moment. Now, this rang a bell. The UK company had sued in a Chinese court and was still waiting for a hearing date.

Yang remembered being amused by the UK company's belief that it was doing anything but enriching several Chinese lawyers.

"Describe these landing mats," Yang ordered.

"Yes, sir. They are aluminum panels designed to be inter-locked by troops with only basic instruction. After grading is complete, we will lay down a geotextile membrane to suppress dust before installing the panels. The panels will be secured to the ground with multiple anchor stakes. Of course, I will personally inspect the work before declaring the airstrip ready for use," Xia said.

"See that you do, Colonel," Yang growled.

Then Yang was surprised by a question from Shi. "How much do each of these panels weigh, Colonel?" Shi asked.

"About fifty-one kilos, sir. We are using panels rated to support heavy cargo aircraft. More than required by your orders, sir, but I did it for two reasons. First, they don't take much longer to assemble than the lighter version. Next, we'll be ready in case you need to resupply this base quickly by air or send more troops," Xia replied.

Shi nodded. "I wondered when I saw the heavy weights listed on the cargo manifests of the ships offshore, and now I have my answer. Well, I left those details to you, and agree with your decision. General Yang, your thoughts?"

Yang also nodded. "Agreed, General. I'd much rather have a paved runway. If there's no time for that, though, a temporary runway designed to carry the weight of even cargo aircraft is the next best thing for my fighters. I do have one more question, though."

Yang paused and pointed at the whiteboard. "Your presentation was quite thorough in every respect but one. How do you plan to fuel my aircraft?"

Xia tried hard to keep his expression impassive but failed. "Sir, ordinarily, we would have fixed fuel storage structures and buried, reinforced supply lines leading from those structures to your aircraft. However, we don't have the time for that. So, we are using temporary plastic fuel lines, which we will have replaced with properly buried metal pipes within a few days."

Yang glanced at Shi, who shrugged.

Yang wasn't happy. But with this timetable, it wasn't a surprise.

"Colonel, there are two primary risks to my aircraft. The first is a soldier who tosses his cigarette anywhere near a temporary fuel line. The second is enemy attack. Given current military realities, I'm much more worried about the first," Yang said.

"Sir, if I catch any soldier with a cigarette or a lighter on this island, I'll shoot him myself," Xia said.

Yang nodded, satisfied. He could hear the sincerity he was looking for in Xia's voice.

Turning to Shi, Yang said, "General, please make addressing the fuel situation the top priority here. Even ahead of a paved runway, which I hope will follow shortly."

"Understood, General," Shi said. Fixing a cool stare on Xia, Shi said, "I'm sure the colonel is aware that temporary fuel lines and the explosive ordnance carried by your combat aircraft are a dangerous combination."

Xia nodded rapidly. "Yes, sir. General, I will report to you directly as soon as the work is complete."

"Very well, Colonel. Obviously, you have a lot of work to get to, so I'm canceling the tour you had planned. I'll walk around the base with General Yang a little later. Please make sure we're not disturbed in the meantime," Shi said.

Yang wasn't surprised to see that Xia didn't like that at all, though he did his best to keep that from his face. He sympathized since no officer would be happy to have his superior wandering unchecked around his command.

Luckily for Xia, in this case, Yang and Shi weren't doing it this way to catch him out.

"Yes, sir," Xia said, saluted, and left. Within moments, Yang and Shi had the building to themselves.

Shi stood and walked over to a small table nearby with a kettle and the fixings for tea. He poured a cup for each of them and then sipped from his.

Shi grimaced but shrugged.

Yang reached for his cup nevertheless. He could see from the steam rising above it that at least it was hot. Only a fool would expect a gourmet brew under these circumstances.

"Sorry about the fuel situation. I didn't know it was this bad until just now," Shi said.

"Not your fault. Not the Colonel's either. We both know who's really responsible," Yang said bitterly.

From a lifetime of habit, Shi looked around the empty building before responding. Even then, all he did was nod.

"We also know there's no real military reason for the chances we're taking here," Yang said. "The Americans didn't stop the launch of the Spaceship carrying more Internet satellites, so this base was the supposed price for their defiance. How much sleep do you think they've lost as a result?"

"Not much," Shi said. "But what about that Spaceship blowing up? What sort of a message did that send?"

Yang looked at Shi sharply. "Are you suggesting we did that? How? Did you hear something?"

Shi held up his free hand. Yang was sure he would have held up both if one wasn't still holding a teacup.

"I've heard nothing," Shi said. "But you have to admit, it's quite a coincidence."

Yang grunted. "Maybe. But it's not the first time the Americans have lost a rocket."

"True," Shi said, nodding. "Still, if it turns out we were behind it, everyone here should keep their head on a swivel. This base is a long way from help if the Americans decide to get revenge."

Yang shrugged. "We have thrown one provocation after another at the Americans, and they have yet to do anything. You remember the Hainan Island incident in 2001?"

Shi nodded but said nothing. An American reconnaissance aircraft had been rammed by a Chinese fighter jet and forced to land on Hainan Island. All twenty-four crewmembers had been interrogated for the next ten days, and their EP-3E was held even after their release. It was finally returned to the US three months later disassembled after they had squeezed every useful bit of information from it.

They had even forced the Americans to apologize for the death of the Chinese airman who had rammed his jet into their plane. And pay for the food they had fed the American prisoners.

"Anyway, the real point is that neither of us should be out here. We both know the real prize is hundreds of kilometers north," Yang said.

Shi nodded again and sighed.

At first, Yang thought Shi would continue his silence, but finally, he said, "You're right. I've been waiting for us to move on Taiwan since I joined the Army. We're no closer today than we were then. Instead, we're wasting time in places like this and the Indian border."

"That's right," Yang said, nodding vigorously. "If either of us wants that to change, we have to act."

Shi still looked uncertain. "Are you sure you have reliable men ready to carry out your part of the plan?"

Yang did his best to project total confidence as he replied. "Yes, I am sure. Even better, Lin's successor is looking forward to his promotion."

Shi looked both startled and unhappy. "You have spoken with Vice President Gu directly? Was that wise?"

Yang shrugged. "I'm still here. If Gu was content to remain where he is, I'm sure we'd both be in custody right now."

Yang knew there was no point in telling Shi he wouldn't betray him if he were arrested. The interrogation methods used on those the Party considered traitors would force the truth from anyone, and quickly. Pretending otherwise was wishful thinking.

Shi clearly understood the logic in Yang's statement.

But Yang could see Shi was still worried.

So Yang added, "I also pointed out to our friend that if he were to change his mind about our arrangement, he would still be at risk. Above all, the Party would wonder why we thought it safe to approach Gu with details of our plans."

Shi grunted agreement. "A good point. Gu has made no secret of his ambitions. And with every day that has passed since you met Gu and he failed to report you, his guilt has grown."

Shi paused and still looked uncertain. Then he straightened and looked Yang in the eye.

"I will need more time to convince all those necessary in my command that action must be taken. If I misjudge anyone, I will need more time on top of that to silence them. Still, I will soon be ready to begin concrete preparations. Do you have a target date for our strike?" Shi asked.

Yang smiled and began telling Shi all the details of his plan.

Soon the military, not the Party, would be in charge in China.

Chapter Twenty-Nine

En Route to Laredo, Texas

Boris Kharlov had kept himself busy on the first part of their drive out of Florida searching their sedan's radio for news programs. They had abandoned their van outside Orlando after first burning the logo Alina had removed from it before they left Cocoa Beach.

Kharlov's eyebrows had climbed as he saw how quickly the plastic logo was consumed once lit.

Alina had nodded and said, "The solution applied to the van's surface to provide the chemical bond keeping the logo in place was just as flammable. Remember I mentioned drawbacks were preventing commercial use?"

They were driving just a few miles per hour over the speed limit, which kept them firmly in the right lane with almost all traffic passing them on the left. Kharlov agreed with Alina's speed, though. It was the wrong time to risk an encounter with traffic police.

Anyway, their speed was high enough that not long after Kharlov found a station focused on news, its signal began to weaken, and he had to start searching again.

In the back seat, Neda Rhahbar smiled at his frustration and held up her phone so Kharlov could see it.

"I'm going from one news site online to another back here. If we were successful, we'll know," Neda said.

Kharlov nodded but said, "I'll stick with old technology, if you don't mind. We'll see who gets there first."

Alina paid no attention to either of them and stayed focused on the traffic ahead. In particular, she was looking for any sign of slowing traffic that might announce an upcoming roadblock.

All their heads turned to the radio when the news came, though, that the rocket had exploded.

When the broadcast continued to include the details that the explosion had happened at high altitude and caused no casualties, all three of them cheered.

Alina slowly exhaled, only then realizing just how tense she had been. "Well done, you two," she said quietly.

"How long until we get out of Florida?" Kharlov asked.

Alina frowned. "It will be some time yet. It is about an eight-hour drive from Cocoa Beach to the Alabama border on this road."

Kharlov nodded. "Right. I forgot that we are passing through what they call the 'Panhandle.' And about another fifteen hours of driving after that to reach Laredo?"

"Yes," Alina replied, nodding. "You should also add several hours to account for gas and meal breaks. Plus congestion around the major cities we will pass. We need to talk about what we'll do after we reach Laredo."

Kharlov shook his head. "No, I think we should discuss my departing before we reach the Mexican border."

Alina frowned and shook her head. "My orders specify that I am responsible for returning you both safely to Russia. I can't do that if you wander off on your own."

"Your orders didn't anticipate what happened in Cocoa Beach. I am the only one that policeman saw. We collected his body and dashboard cameras, but he will certainly provide a likeness through a sketch artist once he regains consciousness. He got a good look at me and appeared both intelligent and observant," Kharlov said.

Alina shook her head. "Even if they distribute such as a sketch to agents at every border crossing, the chances of matching it to you are low."

"Maybe," Kharlov said with a shrug. "But he also saw my work order, with a woman's name on it. He must have heard Neda moving in the tunnel. And though he didn't see your face, he must have seen your arm. A woman's arm. So, he knows there were two women and one man there."

Alina chewed on her lower lip and shook her head even more stubbornly. "No. Neda could have come out through another exit, and so there could be just one woman and one man."

Kharlov's eyebrows rose. "Really? They will search that tunnel and confirm it had only one way in or out. That was under observation by the policeman from the moment I exited, including when he would have heard Neda's movement in the tunnel. No. They will be looking for two women and one man."

Alina sighed, defeated. "Very well. What do you propose?"

"Once we near Laredo, exit the highway and let me make my way across the border on foot. I will make my way south and then back to Russia. I'm sure the FSB staff at our Embassy in Mexico City will be able to help make arrangements." Kharlov said.

Alina looked at Kharlov incredulously. "There are so many problems with what you've just said, I hardly know where to start."

Kharlov shrugged. "Well, we have plenty of time. Start at the beginning."

Shaking her head, Alina said, "I will do just that. Crossing the border near Laredo will require either a boat or swimming across the Rio Grande River. People drown attempting that every year."

Alina held up her hand as Kharlov started to object. "Fine. You were Spetsnaz, and you know how to swim. Let's suppose you survive the river crossing. The Mexican side is lined with criminals called coyotes, who routinely rob and kidnap anyone crossing the border who has not paid them in advance. Of course, they usually encounter victims going in the other direction, but they will see you as prey the moment they spot you regardless."

Kharlov grinned wolfishly. "They will not find me so easy to capture."

"Perhaps not," Alina replied. "But you will be alone and in unfamiliar territory. They will know every rock and tree and travel in heavily armed groups. I think you underestimate the danger."

"Very well. Propose a better solution. Or tell me there is no risk in having all three of us cross the border together," Kharlov replied.

Alina said nothing for several minutes as she continued to drive and scan the highway ahead for roadblocks.

"You are right that traveling as a group is a risk. And the policeman will produce a sketch. I have trouble believing it will be enough to identify you. But if you are detained, the risk of your identification as an FSB agent is indeed unacceptable," Alina said and paused.

"Fine. Your plan is approved in all but one respect. You must not contact our Embassy in Mexico City under any circumstances," Alina said.

"Why not?" Kharlov asked. He was sure he looked every bit as surprised as he felt.

"Because your departure on a flight from Toronto to Moscow via Paris, along with Neda, was recorded by Canadian authorities yesterday. That's after both of you had your Canadian entry registered after leaving

Buffalo via the Peace Bridge. As a matter of routine, your travel was reported to all our other posts in the region except Havana," Alina said.

Kharlov nodded slowly. "Two other agents who looked like us, with diplomatic passports in our identity. So if the Americans check on what we did after we shook their tail, there is an explanation."

"Yes," Alina said. "One that leads them in the exact opposite direction of Florida. We often have diplomatic staff on temporary duty in Washington also serve in Canada, so nothing is surprising there. It's only about a ten-hour drive."

"And above all, we must maintain the security of the mission. Very well. I will figure out some way back home without the Embassy's assistance," Kharlov said stoically.

"Don't be ridiculous. Of course, you must have help. I will give you a card with contact information for a retired FSB agent who is now an independent contractor in Mexico. The name on the card is a pseudonym. His real name is Evgeny," Alina said.

Neda had been sitting silently in the back seat but now stirred. "Surely not *the* Evgeny?" she asked.

Alina glanced at the rearview mirror curiously. "Well, yes," she said. "But you haven't been in the FSB long enough to know him. How did you hear of Evgeny?"

Now Neda looked uncomfortable. "I feel foolish for speaking. Vasilyev told me stories about Evgeny that he said were passed down by his father. He said I should never repeat them, not even to others in the FSB."

Alina nodded. "Your husband was right about that. Evgeny never wanted fame, and I always thought one of the reasons he retired was because he had become too visible."

Kharlov pursed his lips thoughtfully. "If the man is such a legend, it's surprising he was allowed to retire. Perhaps his contractor status is just a cover?"

"Well, anything is possible," Alina said uneasily.

Neda and Kharlov both had the same thought. Kharlov's guess sounded uncomfortably close to the truth.

"Once we get to Mobile, we will stop to buy food and gas. Kharlov, then you will take over the driving until Houston when it will be Neda's turn. I will take the final leg once we are near Laredo, and then after crossing the border, we should reach Monterrey in about three hours," Alina said.

"So, I should meet you in Monterrey, then?" Kharlov asked.

Alina nodded. "Eventually. First, if you successfully cross the border, find a safe location as soon as possible and contact Evgeny. He will get you to Monterrey and arrange transport for all of us out of Mexico."

"Understood," Kharlov replied.

Alina gave him a sharp look but said nothing. She knew it wouldn't help.

Overconfidence had killed many agents, including ones even more capable than Kharlov.

Time would tell if it was about to claim another victim.

Chapter Thirty

Highway US-59 South
10 Kilometers Northeast of Laredo, Texas

Neda slowed their sedan, and at Alina's signal, prepared to exit US-59 South, the highway they had been on since leaving Houston. As Alina had calculated, they needed gas. Filling up at the next highway rest stop should be enough to get them to Monterrey, as long as they didn't spend too much time idling at the border.

"So, a few points before we part company," Alina said. "I recommend you wait until nightfall to cross. There are security lights at several points along the river, but they are easily avoided. Vegetation, including salt cedar and carrizo cane, is plentiful and should be used to shield you from view until you begin your swim, which will be about fifty meters from one side to the other. Avoid snakes since several species are poisonous. However, attacks in this area are uncommon."

"Great," Kharlov said with a smile. "Well, this was my idea, so I suppose I can't complain."

Alina arched one eyebrow but let the comment pass.

"As usual, the only real danger is the two-legged variety. Avoid anyone you see. Persons headed north across the Laredo area border are far more likely than average to be single travelers trying to avoid apprehension. Most persons crossing in other regions are part of family groups who actively seek to surrender themselves to the Border Patrol and claim asylum. In this area instead, dozens of border agents are assaulted each year, and over ninety percent of apprehensions are of single adults."

Kharlov frowned. "Why the difference here?"

"Perhaps because of heavier than average drug smuggling activity. This area on the Mexican side is controlled by the Cartel del Noreste (CDN), the rebranded and reorganized version of the Zetas. Their second greatest income generator is kidnapping, which will be your primary danger once you cross the border," Alina said.

"Let me guess. You've been to Mexico before," Kharlov said.

Alina shrugged. "Several times. Now, if the CDN captures you, make sure they see your card with Evgeny's alias. It should prevent you from being killed rather than ransomed, which is what would happen if they decided nobody would pay for your release. Just say you are Evgeny's employee and refuse to give any other details. If you make something up, they will be suspicious."

Kharlov shook his head. "You seem convinced I'm going to walk straight into their arms. Many in both Chechnya and Ukraine have discovered I'm not so easily killed or captured."

Alina looked at Kharlov expressionlessly. "If I thought you had no chance, I wouldn't have approved your plan. All that is left now is to wish you good luck and take you to a point within walking distance of the river."

"No, we've already discussed this. A lookout notice is certainly circulating with my likeness and the notation I am traveling with two women. Drop me off in town, where I'm sure I'll find plenty of taxi drivers willing to take me close enough to the river that I won't need to walk far. I've already got an address picked out," Kharlov said.

Alina gnawed at her lower lip and finally nodded. "Fine. Grab something quick to eat before you get in the cab. It may be a while before your next meal, and there's still plenty of time before nightfall. Good luck."

Kharlov nodded. "Thanks for all the good advice. I'll look forward to seeing you both in Monterrey."

Neda smiled and said, "Good luck from me too. Enjoy your swim!"

The Rio Grande River
Near Laredo, Texas

Kharlov's stomach was actively questioning his earlier choice of food. It had been quick, filling, and cheap. And it had tasted fine, especially compared to what Kharlov had often been forced to eat in the field.

But it brought to mind an old saying. Cheap doesn't always mean a bargain.

However, it wasn't Kharlov's principle misgiving. No, that was his insistence on taking a taxi to a spot near the river, a garage on the city outskirts, rather than letting Alina drop him off.

The taxi driver had accepted his fare readily. When he'd asked whether Kharlov needed him to wait, the driver had appeared to believe Kharlov's explanation that he was picking up his repaired car. The driver had even smiled gratefully when Kharlov gave him a generous tip.

But as soon as he drove off, Kharlov saw the driver had a phone pressed to his ear.

Maybe he was being paranoid.

But as the taxi disappeared, Kharlov noticed that the garage was very quiet, with only a single mechanic at work. And only a few cars were present, none of them anywhere close to being fully repaired.

This garage was probably not the first choice for most heavy-tipping, English-speaking customers.

So what else would Kharlov be doing here, the taxi driver was probably wondering.

Or maybe, Kharlov thought bitterly, he'd already guessed.

So, call another cab, and try his luck at another spot?

Kharlov quickly discarded the idea. If the driver had alerted criminals on the other side, they wouldn't be looking for him only at this stretch of riverbank. No, his best chance would be to cross before word had an opportunity to make it to this area.

It was almost dark enough to cross right now. It surely would be by the time Kharlov walked from here to the river.

Kharlov was right. And so far, luck appeared to be with him. He had seen no one, and no lights were visible on either side of this stretch of riverbank.

Best of all, heavy clouds prevented the light of a quarter moon from providing more than a faint glow. Kharlov was confident he could cross without being observed.

Compared with the swims Kharlov had endured in Spetsnaz training, crossing the Rio Grande was no challenge. Not particularly cold, and only a fraction of the length he'd faced back then. Best of all, no full combat pack was doing its best to drag him to the river's bottom.

Kharlov grinned to himself as he grasped some vegetation to pull himself up the riverbank's southern side. Alina had been right. It was a cane plant of some type.

Welcome to Mexico!

Kharlov froze as he heard several voices and crouched dripping as they came closer. He couldn't make out what they were saying and only knew a few words of Spanish anyway.

A light snapped on about ten meters away and played back and forth along the riverbank. Fortunately, it came nowhere near Kharlov.

So, they'd been alerted but hadn't spotted him yet.

The light vanished, and the voices went silent. All nearby movement ceased.

Kharlov knew that didn't mean the coast was clear. Instead, he was sure the men whose voices he'd heard earlier were watching and waiting.

There was nothing for him to do but watch and wait as well.

The minutes crawled by as Kharlov wondered whether he was dealing with professionals or amateurs. Would they stay quietly in place until dawn, or maybe beyond?

No.

After only about half an hour, the light snapped back on—this time, only about five meters away.

The light played back and forth on the riverbank but never came close enough to reveal Kharlov. Mainly since he had used the...what had Alina called it... carrizo cane to hide his position from anyone viewing from a distance.

Then the light went off once more.

Kharlov heard the voices again. But this time, they were receding.

Another half-hour passed.

Slowly, the total stillness present during the first half-hour wait was replaced with ordinary insect and small animal sounds.

So, a single lookout might have been left behind. But the larger group, at least, was gone.

Probably.

Kharlov had to account for the fact that years of experience in the varied wilderness territories of Russia and Ukraine might not apply directly to this setting.

Well, Kharlov had to move out at some point. And be well away from this river by dawn.

Or even better, to the hotel he'd identified in Nuevo Laredo by then.

His decision made, Kharlov began to move out. And immediately cursed under his breath, as he discovered the carrizo cane that had made such excellent concealment was not so easy to leave.

At least, leave quietly. Kharlov still suspected a lookout was lurking nearby. It's what he would have ordered. And he'd have left one of his best men.

So, Kharlov moved as though he knew for a fact a man was watching and waiting nearby. Someone just as good as him.

There! The distinctive sound of metal on metal. Just the faintest "clink" but impossible to mistake for anything else. Probably something like a canteen or thermos brushing up against the lookout's weapon.

Well, Kharlov was a bit thirsty too. But he'd paid attention to one of the first lessons of his Spetsnaz training about eating and drinking in an unsecured area.

Be sure you enjoy your last meal.

Kharlov crept towards the position revealed by the noise. Made even more cautious by the realization the sound might have been made deliberately to lure him forward.

Not this time.

Guessing the lookout would be facing the river, Kharlov had taken the extra time to circle around him. His hunch had paid off, and Kharlov found himself looking at the back of the lookout's head.

Alina had given Kharlov one of the new Udav pistols, firing the equally new 9x22mm cartridge. Though more powerful than the

Makarov it replaced, this was not the reason for Alina's choice. She had explained the Udav's reliability was superior and had tested as more likely to survive exposure to water, sand, and even mud.

In short, just the weapon to take for a swim in the Rio Grande. Kharlov was no fool, though, and had used the plastic pouch Alina had given him to store the Udav in his jacket.

Kharlov never even considered taking out the Udav. Firing it here would be like sending up a signal flare.

Instead, Kharlov calculated the distance between him and the lookout. The vegetation between them. The lookout's crouching posture and the time he would need to turn around to face Kharlov's attack.

Much of the difference between Spetsnaz training, or special forces training in any nation's military, and regular military training was the degree of repetition. You didn't just learn to do something. You did it so many times it became as natural as breathing.

Or, Kharlov thought as his arm tightened around the lookout's neck, making sure the enemy stopped breathing.

His attack had been entirely successful. Unfortunately for Kharlov, his luck that night was abysmal.

Kharlov's focus had, by necessity, been total during the few minutes required to plan and execute his attack.

Those few minutes, though, had been the same ones used by the lookout's companions to return to check on him.

Kharlov allowed the lookout's lifeless body to slip from his grasp and stood up. At the same moment, blinding lights switched on him, and a voice yelled a Spanish command.

Kharlov guessed correctly that it meant, "Hands up!"

His first thought was – Lights, twice in two days?

Several options went through Kharlov's mind in an instant.

Run. Fight. Surrender.

His least preferred choice was the only one that seemed to offer any hope of survival.

Slowly, Kharlov raised his hands.

"I work for..." were the only words Kharlov had time to say before a sharp pain in the back of his head was replaced by a long fall into blackness.

Chapter Thirty-One

Qinshan Nuclear Power Plant
One Hundred Kilometers South of Shanghai, China

Qinshan Senior Manager Tan shivered in the whipping wind and rain as he watched while some men from the nearby prison filled sandbags. Other prisoners moved the just-filled sandbags where Tan thought they would do the most good.

The forecasters had been right. The danger from the typhoon had turned out to be just as real as they'd warned. Another "once in a century storm," like the one that had damaged the Three Gorges Dam in 2020.

The prisoners had nearly failed to appear. The warden had tried to back out of his promise, saying that the weather was too dangerous for him to risk his guards.

It went without saying that the prisoners were expendable.

The warden still wouldn't budge when Tan reminded him of the danger that a reactor breach would pose to everyone at the prison, including him personally.

But he changed his mind when Tan gave him a graphic description of what would happen once radioactive materials reached the prison. Yes, radiation sickness was truly not a pretty way to die.

Tan had not enjoyed the conversation. But he told himself that he wasn't making threats.

He was simply telling the truth.

Plant Complex Director Wu appeared beside him, just as he'd promised.

The last time Tan had been surprised to see Wu because he'd asked his staff to warn him of Wu's arrival. Today Tan knew they were too busy preparing to shut down the plant.

But he was still surprised to see Wu. This time because Tan had been told after he'd last spoken to Wu that the only road to the plant had been closed because of the typhoon.

"I'm pleased to see you, sir. Has the road to the plant reopened?" Tan asked.

Wu grunted with amusement. "No. But anyone they might have had manning the roadblock has gone, probably to a drier location. I just drove around it."

Tan nodded. "Good that you have a four-wheel drive vehicle, sir. Were you able to get authorization to close the plant from Beijing?"

Wu shook his head. "No. Everyone I could reach insisted the plant must remain open. Said that the power we produce was vital to typhoon relief and rescue operations. I was promised help to keep the plant safe from the typhoon."

Tan looked at Wu with dismay. "Help? What sort of help could they possibly get us in time? As it is I'm not sure these sandbags will give us enough time to shut down the plant safely."

Wu shrugged. "I'm just telling you what they told me. I'm not saying I believed them."

Now Tan moved from dismay to shock. "Sir, you know as well as I do what will happen if we allow this plant to be inundated. We are much closer to a major population center than Fukushima was, and..."

Wu lifted his hand. "I know all that, Tan. Sorry, I should have told you at the start that I have no intention of obeying Beijing's orders. We will shut down this plant immediately."

Tan felt two conflicting emotions. A wave of relief.

And a surge of nausea.

"Sir, if we defy Beijing's orders..." Tan began.

"We will be executed," Wu finished for him with a nod.

Then he added, "I will try to argue that you were simply following my orders, and had no idea Beijing had ordered the plant must remain open. But even if I am believed, you will be executed as the plant's senior manager, who must be held responsible in all cases. They'll probably also argue you should have confirmed my orders with Beijing."

Tan stood silently in the rain, watching as the last sandbags were filled.

Then he turned to Wu and said, "If that's what it takes, so be it. Do you have the codes needed for the shutdown?"

Wu nodded. "The men who designed the shutdown procedure had enough sense to realize communications could be cut in an emergency. As you know, your authorization codes will be required as well."

Tan pointed out where he wanted the last sandbags to be placed. Eager to escape the wind and rain, the prisoners hurried to finish their task.

Then Tan turned to Wu, and gestured to the water rising on all sides around them.

"We've done all we can here. I think we've bought ourselves enough time to do a proper shutdown, but we have to hurry."

Wu nodded, and followed Tan towards the plant as the typhoon did its best to slow them.

Wu looked at the rising water as they reached the plant's door. He doubted they had time to finish shutting down the plant before the water came bursting through.

But there was no point telling Tan that. All they could do was their best, and hope.

Even if, no matter what, there was no hope for Wu and Tan.

Chapter Thirty-Two

Near Nuevo Laredo, Mexico

Boris Kharlov's eyes opened just enough to let him see his surroundings. He hoped whoever was guarding him wouldn't realize he had regained consciousness.

Time to take stock. Head throbbing, but not too bad. Maybe a concussion. Probably not a skull fracture, or the pain would be sharper.

Sitting in a wooden chair, with his hands cuffed behind him. Metal cuffs, not zip ties.

And he was still wearing his clothes. With his pistol and both knives removed, of course.

But leaving him with his clothes on was an amateur move on their part. One they would soon regret.

Without moving his head, Kharlov could see only a single guard. He was standing next to a grimy window, which showed it was still dark outside.

So, Kharlov thought, he hadn't been unconscious long.

The floors were no cleaner than the windows. Kharlov doubted that anyone had lived here in some time.

The guard's attention was focused on the view outside the window, though he did glance at Kharlov now and then. So far, he seemed to think Kharlov was still unconscious.

Unfortunately, as long as the guard stayed where he was, he was well out of Kharlov's reach.

So, perhaps not total amateurs.

Kharlov sat quietly, keeping his eyes nearly closed, and listened.

He was nearly certain no one was in the room with him besides the single guard.

But there were definitely more men just outside. At least four or five, from the sounds he was hearing.

Kharlov waited until the guard had once again glanced at him, and then returned his view to the window. Then, he carefully moved the fingers of his right hand towards his shirt's left cuff.

Next, Kharlov probed the cuff with a fingernail, until he teased a thin piece of metal from inside the fabric.

The guard looked at Kharlov. Had he spotted his movement?

No. The guard's view returned to the window.

Kharlov had practiced using this tool to pick handcuffs open until he could do it with very little effort. There was really just one challenge.

Doing it without the telltale audible "snick" that would alert the guard to his success.

The problem was that he had no way to know what model of handcuffs these were, or their condition.

Well, slow and gentle might work. If it didn't, he had to be ready to lunge at the guard as soon as his hands were free.

That probably wouldn't work out too well, though.

Kharlov was certain he could overcome the guard before the man could bring the pistol at his waist to bear.

But without making enough noise to alert the four or five men outside?

Doubtful.

So, best to wait for an opportunity. If he could just get these cuffs unlocked without alerting the guard.

Kharlov tried to focus equally on the delicate task of picking the handcuffs open, while simultaneously watching the guard for his reaction to any sound he made.

Yes! Kharlov relaxed a fraction as he could feel the cuffs loosen, without any sound he could hear. And if he couldn't hear anything, the guard shouldn't have either.

Sure enough, the guard's focus on the window remained unchanged.

Now, he just had to wait for the right moment.

Which appeared in no hurry to arrive.

Kharlov tried willing the guard to move closer, so he could be sure of disabling the man without making enough noise to alert his compatriots outside.

Apparently, that only worked in the movies.

After what felt like forever, but Kharlov knew could have only been about an hour, the door opened.

In the doorway stood a squat, heavily muscled man sporting numerous tattoos. Kharlov saw he was holding his Udav pistol, and repressed a visible reaction with some difficulty.

To Kharlov's surprise, the man spoke to the guard in English.

"Did he give you any trouble?" he asked.

The guard shrugged. "He's been awake for about an hour, but he hasn't moved or said anything."

OK, Kharlov thought with a sigh. I've got to stop underestimating these men. I just hope he didn't hear me unlock the handcuffs.

Apparently not, because that's all the guard had to say.

Kharlov opened his eyes fully and looked around him. As he'd thought, they were the only ones in the room.

"Ah, you are awake. Well, you're lucky we found your boss's card in your clothes before my men decided to let you sleep permanently. Or have some fun with you before you died. Pedro was a good man, and you killed him like it was nothing," the gang leader said, keeping the Udav aimed squarely at Kharlov's head.

The leader had left the door open behind him. Kharlov could hear more men moving, and revised his estimate of their number upwards. Probably their number now included this man's bodyguards.

Kharlov was careful to keep his expression neutral. "I'm sorry I had to do it. But Carlos was expecting me, and your man was in the way."

"Carlos" was the alias on the card Alina had given him to contact Evgeny.

The leader reached in his pocket, and shook out a folded piece of paper. It contained a sketch bearing a remarkable resemblance to a certain Boris Kharlov.

Kharlov couldn't read the Spanish surrounding the sketch. But he had no trouble understanding the many zeros in the Mexican peso amount printed in large type at the paper's bottom.

"We wondered why a white guy like you didn't just wait in line to walk into Mexico like any other gringo. Turns out you're wanted on both sides of the border. You're lucky your boss was willing to pay even more than they're offering," the leader said with a toothy grin.

A grin that told Kharlov the leader saw the chance to earn multiple payments for Kharlov.

Kharlov wasn't going to leave here unharmed just because Evgeny handed over a big bag of cash.

That left one important question. Did Evgeny know what he was about to walk into?

The leader's head jerked backwards as several of the men outside called out.

"Your boss is right on time," he said, and then gestured to the guard, who was still standing by the window.

"Keep an eye on him. If he makes a run for it, shoot him," the leader said.

The guard nodded and removed the pistol from his waist. He held it in an easy, familiar grip that told Kharlov he had used it before many times.

And was the one standing here today.

Yes, it was an important point to remember. These men clearly had no military training. But they had the benefit of a Darwinian selection process that weeded out obvious incompetents.

A man commanding a criminal band this large could afford to hire the best from whoever remained.

Minutes later, the leader was back, still holding his Udav. This time, he was accompanied by a slight, nondescript man with thinning brown hair holding a briefcase.

Kharlov had trouble suppressing a groan. This was the famous Evgeny? His already low estimate of their survival chances plummeted still further.

The gang leader appeared no more impressed than Kharlov. But something was apparently making him hesitate.

Evgeny noticed as well.

"I'm glad to see that you recognize the make of the briefcase. It will save me the trouble of explaining how this will work," Evgeny said calmly.

The leader nodded slowly. "Yes, I've seen Antonio's work once before. You leave the briefcase with me, and once you and your man have reached a safe distance you call me with the disarming code."

Evgeny nodded. "Correct. And if I either fail to call you with the code, or haven't left the agreed payment inside the case, you contact Antonio and he will fix the problem."

The leader nodded again. "Yes. I've only heard of one time when that was necessary."

"Well, Antonio doesn't sell his cases to just anyone," Evgeny said with a thin smile.

"Fine," the leader bit off, with poorly disguised frustration.

Evgeny turned to Kharlov and asked, "Are you injured?"

At the same time two of the fingers on Evgeny's right hand moved in a manner that, if others had noticed it at all, would have been dismissed as a nervous tic.

For someone from the FSB, the signal meant, "I am about to launch an attack. Are you ready to assist?"

Kharlov had found this the easiest part of his months spent in FSB training, since most of the body signals were familiar to him from his Spetsnaz days.

During training he had thought several times to ask whether the FSB had borrowed them from Spetsnaz or vice versa, but in the end Kharlov had decided it didn't matter.

A slight shrug with only his left shoulder gave Evgeny the response, "Yes."

Aloud, Kharlov said, "I've got a headache, but I think I can walk."

Evgeny pointed at Kharlov's hands, which still appeared to be handcuffed behind his back, and said to the leader, "Please remove the handcuffs, and I will give you the case and we will be on our way."

Frowning, the gang leader jerked his head towards the guard, and leveled the Udav pistol at Kharlov's head.

"Take off his cuffs while I cover you," he said to the guard.

Turning to Evgeny, he said, "If either you or your friend feel like trying anything, remember how many men I have waiting outside."

The guard appeared distinctly unenthusiastic about his orders, but moved quickly to obey them.

"And don't even think of trying to take him hostage," the leader said. "I'll have no trouble shooting you both."

Evgeny shook his head, and looked towards Kharlov.

"He knows better than that," Evgeny said, patting his briefcase. "No need for heroics, when the payment is right here."

The guard was walking towards Kharlov, at the same time reaching inside his shirt pocket for the handcuff key.

What happened next took place so quickly Kharlov thought it was closer to a magic trick than combat.

Evgeny somehow covered the distance separating him from the Udav pistol before Kharlov knew he'd done it.

More important, before its holder became aware he was no longer holding the pistol.

Evgeny pushed the gang leader off balance with his left hand, at the same moment that the Udav spoke twice.

The guard fell dead at Kharlov's feet.

The leader had regained his balance and was reaching for another pistol when Evgeny shot him twice as well.

Kharlov had barely managed to get his hands free when the Udav came sailing towards him.

He caught it perfectly, so that it was not just in his hand, but ready to fire.

Evgeny smiled and said, "Yours, I believe." Then he removed the second pistol the gang leader had been too slow to retrieve.

Evgeny and Kharlov were covering the only door from two different angles. If the men outside had any sense, they'd realize trying to rush inside would be suicide.

Three gunmen in quick succession proved they did lack such sense, and were soon stacked in or near the doorway.

But what happened when someone with more intelligence or experience decided to set a fire on the side of the house?

Or what if they had a grenade?

Kharlov was about to ask Evgeny how he thought they could escape when he could hear the answer. The distinctive sound told him first. Confirmation came from a shouted word in Spanish repeated by several of the men outside that he had no trouble understanding.

"Helicoptero."

"Better get down," Evgeny shouted over the rapidly swelling noise outside.

One of Kharlov's first military lessons had been to obey orders immediately, and worry about understanding them later.

Heavy caliber rounds punching through the walls above them made Kharlov glad he had wasted no time in joining Evgeny flat on the floor.

The professional soldier in Kharlov was surprised at the volume and intensity of the fire pouring out of the helicopter. Police with automatic rifles firing from its interior certainly couldn't account for it.

But Kharlov had trouble believing the obvious alternative.

A military helicopter.

Less than a minute later, the roar of automatic weapons fire was replaced with the rapidly diminishing sound of helicopter rotors.

"You OK?" Evgeny asked, as he rose from the floor.

Kharlov rose as well, shaking off some of the dust he had acquired from the none too clean floor.

"I'm fine," Kharlov said. "Your friends out there, I hope?"

Evgeny nodded. "I asked them to be careful with their aim, but I'm not really surprised. If these were elite troops, I wouldn't have been able to bribe them."

With that, Evgeny walked confidently towards the helicopter. Kharlov recognized it immediately as an American-made Black Hawk, and the weapon he'd heard as an M134 Minigun, a 7.62×51mm six-barrel rotary machine gun with a two thousand round per minute rate of fire.

Kharlov followed Evgeny. These had better be friends, he thought, or this is going to be a really short walk.

A half dozen Mexican soldiers were walking around the scene, checking that all the gunmen present were dead. From what Kharlov could see that appeared likely, but as a professional he approved of their priorities.

Kharlov's concerns receded as Evgeny was warmly greeted by an officer whose bearing told him this was the unit's commander.

Rapid fire Spanish followed on both sides, and Kharlov quickly saw the officer's smile replaced with a deep frown.

Then Evgeny held up his cell phone's screen, followed by more Spanish in a much lower voice, spoken even more quickly.

A chime sounded on the officer's cell phone, which he pulled out from his uniform pocket.

Now the frown was still there, but it wasn't nearly as deep.

Finally, the officer shrugged and gestured for both of them to get on board.

The officer quickly followed, to the pilot's evident surprise.

The officer snapped something brief in Spanish to the pilot, who reddened and immediately started the helicopter's engine.

A minute later, they were soaring over the Mexican countryside, at what felt like the helicopter's top speed.

Evgeny sent Kharlov a warning look he had no trouble understanding.

No questions.

They sat quietly for nearly an hour. For almost half that time, Kharlov heard the officer speaking rapidly and often impatiently in Spanish into the helicopter's radio.

Then the officer put the handset down for what turned out to be the last time. Kharlov could see a small smile on Evgeny's face, which disappeared so quickly at first he thought he'd imagined it.

No, he hadn't. Evgeny at last sat back and relaxed, and Kharlov realized only then how tense Evgeny had been to that point.

Kharlov could tell from his training and the sun's position that they were flying almost directly south. To where?

It turned out the answer was, another Black Hawk helicopter. This one had exterior fuel tanks attached, and was sitting in a large open field surrounded by several jeeps and a fuel truck.

Their Black Hawk settled down next to it. The officer and Evgeny immediately exited their helicopter without a word.

Kharlov wasted no time following them.

He noticed this Black Hawk had no minigun. Instead, he saw with relief it had been configured for VIP transport, with plush leather seats that looked far more comfortable than the jump seats they'd been on for the past hours.

The helicopter's engine started at once, and they were quickly airborne.

Kharlov noticed that the officer was still with them. But the pilot was the only other Mexican soldier on board.

Evgeny sent Kharlov another look.

He needn't have bothered. Kharlov knew he'd get an explanation once it was safe for Evgeny to give one.

Kharlov's watch and cell phone had been taken from him while he was unconscious, so he wasn't sure how many hours were passing. But he did understand why the external fuel tanks had been necessary.

The pilot had been on the radio several times during the flight, but Kharlov had understood none of the Spanish conversations. However, he had taken comfort from the calm, professional tone of the exchanges.

Including the one the pilot was having right now with whoever was in what Kharlov assumed was the control tower for the airport dead ahead. Clearly, a civilian airport, since Kharlov could see the logos of several commercial airlines on the planes below.

Or, Kharlov corrected himself, perhaps a dual-use facility. There were many in Russia, and he knew they were common in many other countries as well.

But no. As they came closer to the airport, Kharlov could see only civilian aircraft. Their helicopter settled to a landing next to an Airbus A350 bearing the logo of Spain's national carrier.

A military jeep was driving at high speed towards the helicopter before its rotors had stopped turning. A fuel truck was right behind it.

The Mexican officer and the pilot jumped out of the helicopter. As soon as the jeep pulled up, the Mexican officer began speaking in Spanish to the officer in the back seat.

There was another man next to the officer in the jeep's back seat, wearing a shirt and tie.

He was carrying a briefcase, and looked nervous.

Kharlov noticed that both the jeep's camouflage pattern and the uniform of the officer it contained were different than the ones he had seen in Mexico.

Where were they?

"We have a few minutes alone, so I will update you now," Evgeny said. "We are in Guatemala City, and if all goes well are about to board a flight to Madrid."

Evgeny handed Kharlov a passport. When Kharlov opened it, he recognized his photo as one of several Alina had taken just after shaving off his beard in Cocoa Beach. The name and date of birth were not his, and he quickly committed them to memory.

Evgeny's approving nod told Kharlov he had done as expected.

"I appreciate your help," Kharlov said. "I hope everything you've done for me won't be too disruptive to your operations in Mexico."

Evgeny stared for a moment in what, Kharlov slowly realized to his embarrassment, was disbelief.

"I will be on the plane with you," Evgeny finally said.

"I'm sorry," Kharlov said sincerely. "You don't know me, but I do understand what it's like to lose everything and have to start over. I regret being the cause for having it happen to you. I owe you a debt you can call on me anytime to repay."

Evgeny looked at him coolly for a moment, and finally shrugged. "It's really Alina you should thank. When she told me to expect your contact, at first I thought your military experience would allow you to cross the border unobserved. Once I had time to check, though, I found out your likeness had been given to the Mexican authorities. And from the many informants there to the cartels. I then told her your capture by one or the other was nearly certain."

"Do you know if Alina and Neda are safe?" Kharlov asked.

Evgeny nodded. "I'm pleased to see you care. Neda is on her way to Paris, and from there will fly to debriefing in Moscow. Alina will soon be en route to her next assignment. You have no need to know the details, but all is so far going according to plan."

"Of course I care," Kharlov said with a frown. "I worked with them before, and would risk my life for both."

"Risking your life is normal and expected in these missions. Alina risked much more than that for you. She risked her career," Evgeny said, shaking his head.

"How so?" Kharlov asked.

"When I was contacted by the cartels with their ransom demand, I told Alina we should let them kill you. I told her after your failure to follow orders in Cocoa Beach you deserved it. Alina objected strongly, and pointed out your dead body could still be tied to the mission. I replied that though greedy and often incompetent, this particular gang could be counted on to dispose of your body without trace," Evgeny said, and then paused and shook his head again.

"Alina told me if I refused to rescue you, she would resign, and we would no longer be friends," Evgeny said quietly.

Kharlov could hear from the way Evgeny said the words that he still had trouble believing Alina had spoken them.

"And how is it that you, a retired contractor in Mexico, know about my failure to follow orders in Cocoa Beach?" Kharlov asked.

Evgeny smiled. "As I hope you've guessed by now, I'm a bit more than that. I was actually in charge of all active field operations in North America until today. If we do make it back to Moscow I may end up in charge of no more than a desk, or start collecting a pension."

"Is it really so bad?" Kharlov asked. "After all, we did succeed with the objective in Florida."

Evgeny's laugh was short and sharp. "That's the only reason I didn't include 'unmarked grave' in the list of possible outcomes. But your unauthorized use of explosives ensured the Americans know their rocket's detonation was no accident. They may not yet know it was us. But they're not stupid, and might still figure it out."

Kharlov shook his head stubbornly. "I don't see how."

Evgeny ignored his comment, and continued. "Then there is the small matter of the funds I expended on our escape, and the cost of re-building our operations in Mexico. I don't envy my successor."

"I had no idea I was causing such trouble," Kharlov said sincerely. "I can only repeat that I will do whatever I can to repay you for your help."

"Assuming we both make it back to Moscow, and we're both still working for the FSB after our debriefings, I may well hold you to that. But as I said, I'm not the one you most need to thank," Evgeny said.

"Yes, I understand. By the time I get back to Moscow I hope I'll have thought of an appropriate way to express my appreciation," Kharlov said.

Evgeny's attention was focused on the distant conversation between the Mexican and Guatemalan officers, and so it took a moment for Kharlov's statement to register.

When it did, Evgeny's reaction was completely unexpected.

Deep disappointment.

"Surely she would not have picked someone with such limited intelligence," Evgeny said, evidently to himself, since he was still watching the distant conversation. Which had become quite animated.

To the point where Kharlov had to ask, "What are they saying? Can you hear anything?"

Evgeny shrugged. "Not really, but I know what they're saying anyway. I gave that Mexican officer enough money to let him live comfortably anywhere he wants. But that could change if he has to give too much to that Guatemalan officer. And he's rightly worried that if he doesn't get us on that plane, I might find a way to take back some or all of the money I sent him today."

"How will we know which way this goes?" Kharlov asked.

Evgeny nodded towards a truck in camouflage colors idling next to the terminal building.

"I'm betting that truck is full of soldiers loyal to this Guatemalan officer. Who are loyal because of the money they're expecting from this trip to the airport," Evgeny replied, and then gestured towards a set of metal stairs attached to a small vehicle with a driver at the wheel.

"So the question is whether the stairs or the truck start moving towards us. Oh, and that silent fellow with the tie sitting in the jeep will be the immigration officer who needs to stamp our passports for departure. He has to be paid too, out of the Guatemalan officer's cut," Evgeny said.

"A delicate negotiation. I see why it's taking a while," Kharlov said, and then paused.

"Was that comment about 'limited intelligence' directed at me? What have I done that seemed so stupid to you?" Kharlov asked.

Evgeny's attention remained focused on the distant conversation, but he shook his head. "It was the wrong thing to say. Now that I think about it more, it's not intelligence you lack, but experience. You joined Spetsnaz at a young age, were then a warlord in separatist Ukraine, and next immediately began your FSB training. So, you have never been in a serious relationship."

"No," Kharlov said with a shrug. "As you say, time and circumstances never made that a real possibility. So?"

Evgeny smiled, and at first Kharlov thought it was because the Guatemalan officer had lifted his radio to his mouth, and the vehicle with the stairs had begun moving towards them.

But no. "Alina would have never risked her career as she did for someone she simply liked. If she survives her next assignment and finds you in Moscow, I expect her to make that clear to you. In her own way."

Evgeny said, "Get out your passport," as the jeep also began moving towards them.

Then he added, "Your file says you have fought Chechen terrorists and Ukrainian human traffickers, survived a buried nuclear detonation, and helped retrieve a stolen Russian thermonuclear weapon before also helping to destroy an American rocket. Correct?"

Kharlov nodded silently.

Evgeny's smile broadened. "Now at last you face a real challenge. A relationship with a strong Russian woman."

His right eyebrow arched as he handed his passport to the man with the tie who had just reached the helicopter.

"Good luck," Evgeny said.

Chapter Thirty-Three

Qinshan Nuclear Power Plant
One Hundred Kilometers South of Shanghai, China

Senior Manager Tan looked up from his control board at Plant Complex Director Wu, and smiled.

"Please check these readings, Director. I think we've done it," Tan said.

Wu looked over Tan's shoulder intently at the many dials and gauges that displayed data critical to the reactor's operation.

Or, in this case, to its safe shutdown.

For several tense minutes, Wu said nothing as he reviewed the data displayed by the control panel.

A half-dozen plant workers within earshot did their best to appear busy with their tasks while waiting for Wu to speak.

Then Wu exhaled in relief and patted Tan on the shoulder.

"Congratulations. I didn't think we had time, but I've never been happier to be proved wrong," Wu said with a broad smile.

All the plant workers nearby cheered and clapped, and soon everyone else at the plant was too.

They all knew how close they had come to disaster.

In the control room, seawater was around their ankles. In many other levels of the plant, it was still higher.

But it wasn't rising anymore, and the rain outside had finally stopped.

The outside door to the plant swung open, admitting a platoon of soldiers with a scowling officer at their head.

The officer marched up to Wu and asked, "I am Captain Jin. Where are Manager Tan and Director Wu?"

Wu looked at Jin and replied, "I am Director Wu, and sitting next to me is Senior Manager Tan. What do you want?"

Jin nodded with satisfaction. "You are both under arrest. Before I escort you both to prison, you are to restart this reactor, which you have shut down in violation of direct orders to keep it in operation."

Wu shook his head in disgust. "Look down, Captain. What do you see?"

"Water," Jin said defiantly. "So what?" He waved at all the control equipment around them. "This is all still working. So that proves you can restart the reactor."

The reaction from everyone in the room was the last one the Captain had expected.

They all laughed. Loudly. Some of the men actually doubled over.

Jin's face contorted with anger, and he pulled out his pistol. The soldiers behind him raised their rifles.

"If I have to shoot every man here, I'm going to follow my orders and get this reactor restarted. Now, are you going to do as I say, or am I going to save the government the cost of trying you two?" Jin snarled.

Wu shrugged. "Death by your bullets is far preferable to death by radiation poisoning, and every man here knows it. Did your superiors give you the codes needed to restart this reactor? Did you bring anyone with you who knows how to enter the control codes for this plant?"

Jin hesitated. "No to both. They said you two know how to restart the reactor, and I should force you to do so before taking you to prison."

Wu nodded. "Well, then we have a problem. The water here is nothing compared to what has seeped into the reactor area itself. If we try to restart it now, the explosion and fallout that result will be many times worse than at Fukushima. You have heard of Fukushima, right, Captain?"

"Yes," Jin said sullenly. "But that doesn't change my orders."

Wu noticed, though, that some of the soldiers behind the Captain were looking at each other with alarm.

"Captain, did your superiors tell you that water from the storm had entered the reactor?" Wu asked.

"No," Jin replied.

"I'm not a soldier," Wu said. "But it seems to me that if something important has happened that your superiors should know about, you should tell them. Our communications have been cut off because of the typhoon."

Then Wu gestured towards the radio strapped to Jin's belt.

"But are military communications working?" Wu asked.

Jin stood seething for several moments. Obviously, he wanted nothing more than to ignore what Wu had said and continue trying to force him to restart the reactor.

But Jin had noticed his men's reaction as well. Even if he didn't believe Wu, it was obvious some of them did.

Finally, Jin decided a status update would be prudent.

"Guard them," Jin ordered, pointing at Wu and Tan. "Make sure they don't do anything while I'm on the radio."

All the soldiers lowered their rifles, and several surrounded Wu and Tan, who looked at each other and shook their heads.

Jin moved back towards the exit door and had an increasingly agitated conversation that none of them could overhear.

When he walked back, Jin was still seething. But now, for a different reason.

"I have new orders," Jin announced. "Pumps and other equipment are on the way and should arrive later today. All plant workers are to remain at work until the reactor is safe to restart. A new plant manager is on the way."

Then Jin pointed at Wu and Tan. "These two men are still under arrest and are to be sent for trial immediately. Restrain them."

Two soldiers began to place plastic handcuffs on Wu and Tan.

Several plant workers moved towards the soldiers, and one Wu couldn't see shouted from the back of the room, "This isn't right! These men saved us!"

An angry murmur swept through the room, and more plant workers started to move towards the soldiers.

The soldiers looked at each other uneasily, and several raised their rifles again.

In a loud, clear voice, Wu said, "Captain Jin is in charge here until the new plant manager arrives. You must obey his orders. I know you will all do your best to remove this water and get the plant operational again. It has been an honor to work with you."

Then Tan spoke. "Director Wu is right. You must follow Captain Jin's orders. I also have been honored to work with you."

The plant workers looked at each other, and from their expressions Tan could see they still weren't happy.

But they stopped moving towards the soldiers.

Both Wu and Tan were marched out of the plant and into the back of an unmarked green van. Benches were bolted to both sides of the interior. Each was chained to a bench across from the other.

Wu and Tan both noticed that a TV news crew had video equipment pointed in their direction as they entered the van, but nobody in the crew made any effort to speak to them.

Moments later, the van lurched into motion.

Tan looked at Wu with admiration. "That was quick thinking, sir. Just a few seconds later, and I'm sure those soldiers would have started shooting."

Wu nodded absently. "And nothing the workers did could have saved us. Good men would have died for no purpose."

Tan asked quietly, "Do you think we have any chance, sir?

Wu shook his head. "No. But we go to meet our ancestors knowing that we did our duty. Death comes for us all, sooner or later. At least we die with a clear conscience, and our heads held high."

Chapter Thirty-Four

Three Gorges Dam
Hubei Province, Central China

Hydropower Director Peng was looking at the gauges that measured the dam's reservoir level when Dam Manager Shen walked to his side.

"You will want to know whether I have checked personally to make sure these readings are accurate, sir," Shen said.

"Good," Peng said with a smile. "We are beginning to understand one another."

But there was no smile on Shen's face when he replied.

"Sir, the readings are accurate. The stress being inflicted on this dam is just as bad as the gauges say. The typhoon has now passed. But another storm system is on the way from the south. We don't have the equipment or materials to shore up the dam well enough to survive," Shen said somberly.

"Help is on the way," Peng said confidently. "I'm still an officer in the Army reserves. I was able to use military radio communications to call on some old colleagues of mine from the Army and explain the situation.

I've been told that General Shi himself has ordered troops and equipment to be sent immediately."

Shen brightened for a moment and began to speak but then paused and shook his head.

"Sir, that's good news, but nothing the Army does will matter if we can't get Xiluodu to cut back on the water they're sending downstream. The storm has cut all phone and Internet service from here, so I can't even ask them to reduce their water flow. Anyway, I know their manager. It would take more than a plea from either of us to have him risk his precious power quota," Shen said bitterly.

The Xiluodu Dam, the world's third-largest, was still considerably smaller than the Three Gorges Dam because it was further upstream. But it had the most significant impact on the water sent downstream to the Three Gorges Dam. And since the typhoon had weakened considerably between the two dams, Peng knew it couldn't have faced the same challenge as the Three Gorges Dam with its reservoir level.

Peng smiled. "I have even better news for you, then. A helicopter should arrive here any minute to take me to Xiluodu. You are right about their manager. But with me standing in front of him, you can be sure the water flowing down to you from Xiluodu will slow considerably."

Shen looked more than dubious. "A helicopter, sir? Who is crazy enough to fly one in this weather? The typhoon has just passed, and another powerful storm is on the way. For that matter, even if you can persuade someone to fly, do you think you'll survive the flight?"

Peng's smile widened. "The pilot is another friend of mine from my Army days. He's just as crazy as I am."

Then Peng sobered. "And consider the alternative. If I stayed here with you and did nothing, would I be safe?"

Shen looked at the gauges again for a moment and then sighed. "No, sir, I suppose not."

A plant worker emerged from the elevator to the upper level and waved at Peng, who nodded and said to Shen, "Well, that's my ride. I've also asked for military assistance at Xiluodu, just in case I've underestimated the danger there. At a minimum, they should be able to set up radio communications between Xiluodu and Three Gorges."

Shen bowed to Peng and said, "Sir, I admire your courage. Good luck on your journey."

Peng bowed back and said, "Good luck to us all, Shen."

Then he hurried to the elevator, where the door was being held open for him by the same plant worker who had waved to him earlier. Peng nodded his thanks and then looked out at the scene as the doors closed shut.

Would this be the last time he saw the Three Gorges Dam?

Peng shook his head, trying to will away such thoughts. Not if he had anything to say about it, he thought savagely.

The wind buffeted Peng as soon as the elevator doors opened.

Much worse, water whipped up by the wind sprayed over him from the reservoir.

Not just once or twice. Continuously.

That shouldn't be happening, Peng thought immediately.

And it couldn't unless the reservoir's level was critically high.

His teeth chattering, Peng hurried to the helicopter pad. To reach it, he had to travel most of the dam's length to the pad, set just beyond it.

Well, there was the helicopter. But where was the pilot?

There. Peng saw the pilot, Captain Zhong, just a short distance away.

Zhong was doubled over and vomiting.

Peng frowned. From the appearance of the ground at Zhong's feet, he'd been emptying his stomach for a while.

Peng waited until Zhong had straightened and unsteadily wiped his mouth on his sleeve before approaching him.

Peng handed him a handkerchief and a bottle of water he'd been saving for the flight.

It looked like Zhong needed it more.

Zhong emptied part of the bottle on his face and then wiped it more thoroughly with the handkerchief. Next, he swallowed the rest of the bottle.

"That's better," Zhong said with a sigh.

Then Zhong focused on Peng for the first time.

"Peng," he spat, shaking his head and cursing, before finally pausing for breath.

"You have no idea how close you came to making my wife a widow," Zhong said.

"I'm sorry," Peng said sincerely. "But it really is urgent."

Zhong nodded. "I know. It's the only reason I'm still talking to you. I saw how high the water is in the reservoir before I touched down. But help is almost here. You can't see them yet, but troops and heavy equipment should reach this dam within the hour."

"That's good, Zhong. But it's not enough. Unless I can get to Xiluodu, the water they're sending us will make any attempt to shore up this dam pointless. The typhoon has cut all communication. Their manager is also unlikely to cut back the flow of water enough unless I'm standing in front of him," Peng said.

Zhong shook his head. "Just like the old days, Peng. You're the only one who can save the day. Well, you're not my commanding officer anymore. It's Captain Zhong now. And you're just a reserve officer who hasn't been called up. So, you have no authority to give me any orders. I came here as a favor. And I meant what I said before. I'm not going to make my wife a widow."

Peng nodded. "I understand. Let me ask one last favor. To get out of this wind, you can walk with me to the elevator, which will take us to the dam's control room. Along the way, you can experience what the reservoir's level means. Then you can talk to the dam's manager and decide whether staying is safer than going."

Zhong shrugged. "Honestly, I stopped listening once you said, 'get out of this wind.' Let's go."

They had only gone a few meters towards the elevator when both of them were drenched from head to toe.

Teeth chattering, Zhong yelled, "Can't you release some of this water from the reservoir?"

Peng shook his head. "We're already at maximum release volume. Flooding downstream is already a certainty, but nothing communities in this area haven't dealt with before. But if this dam collapses..."

Zhong turned around. "Fine. I'm convinced. Let's get to the helicopter."

Both of them ran as fast as they could, with the wind buffeting them from side to side.

Zhong and Peng both clambered aboard the helicopter. Peng's nose wrinkled at the smell.

Zhong had begun vomiting well before reaching the Three Gorges Dam.

"Strap in," Zhong said as he started the engine.

Once the rotors had begun to turn, Zhong turned towards Peng. Shaking his head, he tightened Peng's flight harness so much that he had to make a real effort to breathe.

"Trouble breathing?" Zhong asked.

Peng nodded.

"Good," Zhong said. "That means no matter how badly we get shaken, there's some chance you won't be vomiting next to me. Not that it would matter much to how the cockpit smells at this point. But I can't afford the distraction."

"Understood," Peng forced out through clenched teeth.

Zhong fastened his flight harness and asked, "What have you had to eat today? I'd just like to know what to expect."

Peng shook his head. "Nothing. Not my first time in a helicopter."

Zhong laughed. "You were always smarter than me. After all these years flying, I thought I could take anything. I was wrong."

Then they both sat still as the wind rocked the stationary helicopter from side to side.

Zhong looked at Peng, who looked back at him silently.

"Good," Zhong said. "You do remember something about helicopters. If I don't wait for a break in this wind, it's going to be a real short trip."

Another minute passed, and finally, there was a pause in the rocking. Zhong immediately pulled up on the helicopter's collective, and it lurched into the air.

Then Peng corrected himself. The control in Zhong's hand was a mixing unit, a device that combined the inputs from both the cyclic and collective and then sent along the "mixed" input to the helicopter's control surfaces.

In truth, Peng was trying to occupy his thoughts with anything but what a corner of his brain insisted was his imminent death.

It took several minutes for them to reach what Peng thought of as a safe altitude.

Several very long minutes.

But Peng was almost immediately proved wrong.

What felt like a giant hand appeared determined to press them down into the ground, and the altimeter wound down with alarming speed before Zhong was able to regain control.

And they were less than five minutes into their flight.

Zhong hadn't been exaggerating. Nothing about this was safe.

The entire flight was much like the first five minutes. Several times Peng had been sure they were finished. In particular, he would never forget the sound of tree branches scraping against the helicopter's bottom one time before Zhong was able to wrestle it back upwards.

Zhong was shaking and sweating by the time Xiluodu's helicopter landing pad was finally in view.

As though resenting their success, the wind sent a gust that left their helicopter careening at an angle so sharp Peng was certain they were finished.

Gripping the edges of his seat, Peng closed his eyes and was sure his last thought would be, "We tried."

And then Peng opened his eyes to find they were on Xiluodu's landing pad.

Peng looked across at Zhong, who was trembling as he wiped his hands on his pants.

A sudden wave of nausea struck Peng, and he fumbled with his flight harness, finally managing to free himself and fling open the helicopter door.

Just in time. Peng had told the truth about having had nothing to eat that day.

But it appeared his stomach hadn't fully processed the previous day's meals. And his stomach continued its determined effort to empty itself long after nothing was left.

Peng's eyes finally refocused to see a bottle of water and a scrap of cloth in front of his face.

Held there by a still shaky Zhong, who was, however, able to manage a smile.

"No handkerchiefs in the Army, but at least the cloth is clean," Zhong said.

Peng repeated the routine he had seen Zhong perform what seemed like a lifetime ago with the bottle and the cloth.

"Thank you, Zhong," Peng said once his face was clean. "I owe you."

Zhong gestured dismissively. "As usual, you're trying to do the right thing. Feels good to help. Now, let's get out of this wind."

Peng wasn't sure who supported who as they made their way to the dam's upper entrance.

What if they'd changed the entrance code?

Peng had the thought just as he entered the code he knew into the elevator's keypad.

The elevator door slid open, and Peng breathed a sigh of relief.

As the elevator descended, Peng asked, "Did you see any troops or equipment approaching this dam on the way here?"

Zhong shook his head. "No. But that doesn't mean much. At the end there, I could have missed an entire division marching anywhere but right in front of us."

As the elevator door opened, Peng heard a distinctly unfriendly voice to his right.

"Director! What brings you here in such terrible weather?"

Peng thought to himself that the unpleasant, whining voice of Xiluodu Dam Manager Jiang had one virtue.

It was instantly recognizable.

"Jiang, it is precisely this terrible weather that brings me here. The Three Gorges Dam is at immediate risk of collapse. You must sharply lower your water release rate at once!" Peng said.

Jiang nodded but said nothing for several moments.

Finally, Jiang said, "My manners! You both look exhausted. Let's sit down in the conference room, and I'll get us some tea."

Jiang gestured towards a glass-walled room to the right with a large table. And chairs.

Peng realized he was indeed exhausted. And Zhong looked close to collapse.

Peng nodded curtly, and a few moments later, they were seated at the conference room table. A plant worker appeared with a tea service, and shortly they were all warming their hands on steaming cups.

Well, at least this part of the dam's operation is well organized, Peng thought.

"So, what about it, Jiang? This helicopter pilot brought me here through what you rightly just called 'terrible weather' so I could save the Three Gorges Dam and prevent a terrible disaster that will kill thousands, or maybe even millions. Will you follow my order?" Peng asked.

"Well, I must first consider my standing orders from headquarters in Beijing regarding power production from this dam. We have indeed met our quota for this month. But we have not yet met it for this quarter. If we reduce our water release rate as much as you wish, I am concerned that meeting the quarterly quota may be impossible. So, I will have to ask Beijing for authorization," Jiang said.

Peng pointed to the phone in the center of the table. "Fine. Let's do that now. We can speak to headquarters together."

Jiang shook his head with what appeared to be regret. But Peng could tell from the gleam in his eye that it was actually poorly concealed satisfaction.

Jiang had been a dam manager nearly five years longer than Peng when he had been named Director overseeing all of the Yangtze River dams. Peng's appointment was one Jiang had always bitterly resented.

And now his petty vindictiveness was going to get a lot of people killed, Peng thought.

He knew what Jiang's next words would be before he spoke them.

"I'm sorry, but the weather cut both our landline and cell phone service. Our Internet service, too. And we've heard on the radio that another storm is on its way, so I think it will be some time before we can reach Beijing," Jiang said.

Jiang's tone was even and reasonable. But Peng knew Jiang was anything but willing to listen to reason.

Still, he had to try.

"Look, you have the authority to override any rules or quotas when it's necessary to safeguard the lives of our citizens. If you're worried, I'll put the order in writing. You can blame me if anyone in Beijing later objects," Peng said.

Jiang shook his head again, but this time he made no effort to conceal his satisfaction.

"Sorry, no. I'm not going to take that chance. And nothing you can say will change my mind," Jiang said.

Both Peng and Jiang jerked upright as Zhong slapped both his hands on the table with enough force to shake it.

"He's not lying," Zhong said to Jiang, pointing at Peng. "I've just seen the Three Gorges Dam from the air. The reservoir is full, and the dam near collapse. You have to listen."

Then Zhong turned to Peng, "Captain, why are we wasting time with this weasel? You're the Director, right? Just tell the workers here what to do so we can save the Three Gorges Dam!"

Before Peng could say anything, Jiang stood up, his face contorted with rage, and pointed at Zhong. "Who are you to speak to me that way?"

Without waiting for an answer, Jiang swung to Peng. "So, 'Captain' is it? I knew you served in the Army before, but not that some there still follow your orders. Well, tell this fool that this is not the Army and that you can't force me to do anything against Beijing's orders."

Peng took a deep breath and shook his head. "It's true. Unless I can reach Beijing, I can't make him reduce water flow from this dam that could cause them to miss their power quota."

Zhong stared at Peng in disbelief. "Go to the plant workers directly. Surely they will understand the need to act."

Jiang sneered. "And tell them to raise the reservoir level of this dam to a dangerous level to prevent a supposed, unconfirmed risk to the Three Gorges Dam? Against my orders? Orders from the man with authority to fire them on the spot? I don't think so."

Peng looked Jiang in the eye. "I'm not lying about the danger, Jiang. If you don't do as I say, the Three Gorges Dam will collapse, and you'll be responsible. You won't be fired after the investigation. You'll be executed for gross negligence."

Jiang looked back at Peng defiantly. "I don't believe you, and I don't care about your threats. The Three Gorges Dam is all you've ever cared about. Well, Xiluodu and the other dams count too. It's about time you were reminded of that."

The silence that followed was absolute.

Peng's mind raced as he tried to come up with some alternative that would work.

It was clear nothing he could say would change Jiang's mind.

From Zhong's glare at Jiang, Peng could see he was thinking about a more direct approach.

Peng was about to tell him that it wouldn't help when the elevator doors opened.

Five soldiers in full battle gear emerged, led by an officer holding a small envelope. Peng squinted through the glass and could see that he was a full Colonel.

Peng waved to him, and the Colonel gestured to his men to follow him.

The Colonel entered the conference room and said. "I am Colonel Dai. Is one of you Director Peng?"

Peng nodded tiredly. "Yes, I am, Colonel."

Dai nodded and lifted his envelope. "Good. These orders signed by General Shi say that we are to assist you as needed in securing all Yangtze River dams from collapse. I also have troops and equipment at the Three Gorges Dam who are already at work doing what they can to support your staff. I have more troops and equipment awaiting your orders nearby. How can we help?"

Peng turned to Jiang. "Now you see that Beijing does take this crisis seriously. Order your staff to reduce the flow of water through your turbines by three-quarters immediately."

"I will not," Jiang snapped. "I don't answer to these soldiers. I won't do anything you say until I have authorization directly from Beijing."

Peng turned towards Dai, intending to ask him whether military communications were available to call their headquarters.

But Dai had already removed his pistol from his holster and was pointing it directly at Jiang.

"Arrest this man," Dai told his soldiers. Two soldiers immediately stepped forward and, grabbing Jiang by each arm, yanked him to his feet.

"Get him out of here," Dai said. "We have work to do."

Then Dai turned to Peng. "Come with me, please."

Ignoring Jiang's protests as soldiers dragged him to the elevator, Dai stood in the middle of the control room with his hands on his hips.

"May I have your attention!" he began.

It was an unnecessary request. Every eye in the room was already on him.

Dai pointed at Peng. "You all know Director Peng," he said rather than asked.

Nevertheless, everyone present nodded.

The room suddenly became much quieter as the closing elevator doors cut off Jiang's frantic protests.

Dai lifted the envelope he was carrying. "I have orders here signed by General Shi, Army Commander. They say I am to support Director Peng in doing whatever is necessary to prevent any dam's collapse on the Yangtze River. My troops will arrest and remove anyone who fails to obey Director Peng's orders. Do any of you have questions?"

The silence that followed was absolute.

"Good," Dai said.

Then he nodded towards Peng, who quickly gave the orders that he hoped would save the Three Gorges Dam and all the millions who lived downstream from it.

As the plant workers rushed to carry out Peng's instructions, he told himself that there was still time to avoid disaster at the Three Gorges Dam.

There had to be.

CHAPTER THIRTY-FIVE

The South China Sea

Captain Jim Cartwright sat up and ran his hand through his closely cut, prematurely graying hair as Lieutenant Commander Fischer approached him with the type of printout that always meant one thing.

New orders for the USS *Oregon*.

Short and thin with sandy hair, Cartwright thought for maybe the hundredth time that Fischer looked like a much better fit for submarines than an officer like him who stood over two meters tall without shoes.

This would be their last deployment together. After Fischer's recent well-earned promotion, he was about to get his own command.

Cartwright frowned and shook his head.

"Are they serious? We haven't tested a single one of these new weapons, and they want us to use one on a Chinese base?"

Fischer nodded. "My first reaction was the same, Captain. But it did work perfectly when it went through surface ship trials. And the underlying Tomahawk missile design has been around for decades."

Cartwright grunted. "Maybe so. But you know as well as I do none of that is the issue. Once that Tomahawk breaches the surface, it's going to be visible to anyone who happens to be in range to look. At least, until it's able to lower itself to cruising altitude."

"Well, Captain, we'll have two things going for us there. This Tomahawk's surface is coated with a radar absorbing material that should reduce its return to the point it can't be identified as a missile. And its launch profile should minimize the time its altitude is high enough to allow detection at all," Fischer said.

"Yes, and you know the tradeoff there, too," Cartwright said. "Depressing the missile's flight trajectory so quickly comes at a fuel cost that will mean a significant range reduction. So we have to move closer to the target."

"Yes, sir," Fischer acknowledged. "But so far, we've seen no hint of Chinese submarine activity out here."

"And how long do you think that's going to last? You've seen the reports on how quickly the Chinese are building new submarines. If you were a Chinese admiral, don't you think you'd park one or more on the approach to their newest and most advanced base?" Cartwright asked.

"Yes, sir, I would," Fischer said thoughtfully.

Then he grinned. "Glad to have one last opportunity to learn from the best. So, along with getting that new course laid in, I'll stop by sonar to remind them about that report the Chinese have deployed their first Type 095 sub."

Cartwright winced. "The new *Sui* class. Yes, please do. I just wish we knew more about that new type."

"Yes, sir," Fischer said with a shrug. "I still wouldn't trade places."

As the first Block IV *Virginia* class attack submarine to be completed, the *Oregon* incorporated numerous upgrades to both passive sonar and propulsion that made its detection extremely difficult.

Unless it was, say, launching a Tomahawk missile.

That thought went through Cartwright's head in an instant. But it didn't stop his immediate response to Fischer.

A smile and the words, "Me neither."

Chapter Thirty-Six

SpaceLink DC Area Offices
Bethesda, Maryland

Eli Wade and Mark Rooter both stood as Bob Hansen entered the secure conference room. Hansen made sure the door had closed behind him and then grasped first Wade's and then Rooter's outstretched hand.

"Welcome to SpaceLink," Wade said. "I'm Eli Wade, and this is SpaceLink project manager Mark Rooter."

"Good to meet you both," Hansen said. "Before we get started, I've got some forms for you both to sign. I know you've both been through this routine before."

Wade and Rooter both nodded and barely glanced at the paperwork before signing in multiple places. They knew they were acknowledging receipt of classified information and their understanding of the penalties for divulging it.

"OK, first I've been told to make it clear I'm telling you everything we know so far," Hansen said.

Seeing their reaction, Hansen shook his head and added, "I wish it were more. But the White House has told me to give you everything we've got, which we normally wouldn't do during an active investigation. But I agree that nothing about this incident is normal."

Hansen put a sketch of a man's face on the table facing Wade and Rooter. "Have either of you seen this man before?"

Wade shook his head and turned to Rooter. "Mark?"

Rooter shook his head as well and asked, "Who is he?"

"The same day as the rocket's explosion, we told you to cut the launch center's connection to the fiberoptic cable linking it to your wider network. That's because we believe this man tapped into it," Hansen said.

"How could he do that?" Rooter asked incredulously.

"There was an old access tunnel that connected to the one with your cable just after it left the island with your launch center. He used explosives to get from one to the other," Hansen replied.

"Explosives? Didn't anyone notice that?" Wade asked.

"They did," Hansen replied with a nod. "A deputy was sent to investigate and caught the man in this sketch as he exited the tunnel. Before he could put him in custody, though, an accomplice choked him from behind and injected him with a powerful sedative."

"Did he survive?" Wade asked and then paused. "A stupid question. Of course, he did. Otherwise, you wouldn't have this sketch."

"No questions are stupid. I still have plenty myself," Hansen said.

Then he added, "You're right, of course. As soon as the deputy helped us make the sketch, I had it distributed to all ports in Florida and land border crossing points in Texas. Airports too, but I doubt the three of them will try to leave the country that way."

"Three? How do you know that?" Rooter asked.

"Sorry," Hansen replied. "The deputy heard someone else in the tunnel besides the man, and we've confirmed that there was only one exit, which the deputy said he had under observation until he was attacked. So, at least three people."

Rooter shook his head with disgust. "You said they accessed our cable right after it left the island?"

Hansen nodded.

Rooter turned to Wade. "Boss, that's how they were able to defeat our main safeguard. Our system was programmed to accept commands only if they were issued with close to zero lag. But the island with the launch center is so small that an upload from just across the bridge would have registered as valid."

Hansen nodded and asked, "Have you been able to isolate and examine the code used to cause the explosion?"

Rooter shrugged. "Yes, but I've never seen anything like it. Most of it is spare and even elegant. But I'm almost certain it was originally intended for another target. I can see where some of the software was removed and replaced with much more hastily written code. Not that it mattered for its effectiveness."

"Understood," Hansen replied quietly. "Do you have a copy of the code for me?"

Rooter nodded and passed Hansen a USB drive. "You'll want to make sure whatever you use to examine this isn't connected to a network of any kind."

Hansen smiled. "I'm not a tech guy. But even I am sure our people will be careful with software that could blow up a rocket. Do you know yet how it was done?"

"I think so," Rooter replied. "Pressure fluctuations during stage separation caused one of the fuel tanks to rupture and explode. Those fluctuations were programmed by someone who knew exactly how much pressure it would take to produce that result."

"And how would they know that?" Hansen asked.

Rooter shook his head with frustration. "The obvious answer is one of our employees, but we've checked, and I know you have too. We've looked into everyone working at SpaceLink, including contractors, and haven't found anything remotely suspicious."

Hansen nodded. "What about former employees?"

Rooter cocked his head, clearly thinking over the question. Then, he said slowly, "We haven't been in business that long, and there's a lot of competition to get a job with us because of the salaries and benefits we offer. The same is true for the contractors we have. I was going to say we haven't lost anyone, but that's not true."

Wade nodded. "Steve Naylor."

"Who was he?" Hansen asked.

"One of our senior engineers. He died in an auto accident less than two weeks ago," Wade replied. "The only employee to die since I founded the company," he added sadly.

Hansen nodded and said, "Please pass his details to me as soon as you can. Would you say he knew enough to help someone design this code?"

Rooter paled. "Steve? Oh, yes. And if he did, then maybe his death was no accident."

"I'd already planned to check on that," Hansen said. "I'll let you know whatever we find."

"Now, about those explosives. Have you had enough time to learn anything from them? Like, were they Chinese?" Wade asked.

Hansen shook his head. "I understand you have reason to think the Chinese government targeted your rocket. However, notice that the man in this sketch was certainly not Chinese. Neither were the explosives."

Wade let out an exasperated hiss. "So, where were the explosives from then?"

"They were stolen from a German company supplying their Federal Police. Some of those charges were used to open vaults during robberies in Germany and Belgium," Hansen replied.

"So, do you think this man might be German?" Wade asked.

Hansen shrugged. "He might be. From his appearance, he could be from any European country. The deputy spoke with him and thought his accent was East European. But he could have been faking the accent. The truth is, we don't know where he's from."

"Except, he's not Chinese," Wade said, shaking his head.

"That doesn't mean they're not behind it," Hansen replied. "The Chinese could have hired these people. In fact, that's what I'd expect if any operation might cause serious trouble with their trading relations."

"So, these were just mercenaries?" Wade asked.

Hansen shook his head. "I doubt it. Pulling off an operation like this would take a lot of resources. I'm guessing a national intelligence service, but that doesn't narrow it down. I can think of more than a dozen that could have done it and don't like us much."

"But why would any of those countries help the Chinese?" Wade asked.

Hansen looked at Wade thoughtfully. "That's a good question," he said. "There are other agencies with people able to give a better answer than I could. Offhand, I have no idea why any other country would take a risk like this for the Chinese."

Hansen was writing notes rapidly as he added, "I may not have the answer to that question, but at least I know the right people to ask."

Wade nodded. "We've already put safeguards in place at this launch center and the one at Vandenberg so that the last attack can't be repeated. Is there anything else we should do to improve security?"

"Let me ask you first, do you plan to go ahead with the launch of SpaceLink satellites using your Spaceship from Vandenberg?" Hansen asked.

Wade and Rooter both nodded. Wade said, "Now that we know it wasn't a technical fault on our side but instead an outside attack, why wouldn't we proceed?"

Hansen pursed his lips and shook his head. "And are these satellites also going to provide Internet service to countries bordering China?"

Wade nodded emphatically. At the same time, Hansen noticed Rooter was looking at Wade with some concern.

"We are absolutely pressing forward. In fact, I'm moving up the launch schedule. There may not be any proof China was behind the attack on our rocket in Florida, but I can't think of anyone else with a motive. I'm going to make them sorry they did it," Wade said darkly.

"Has it occurred to you the Chinese may have realized that might be your reaction? And decided if it was, to deal with their problem more directly?" Hansen asked.

Wade looked surprised. Hansen was pleased to see that Rooter instead looked relieved.

"Boss, I'm glad Mr. Hansen here raised this because I was sure worried about it. We need to up your security in a major way," Rooter said.

Hansen nodded. "I've been cleared to offer you an FBI security detail as long as the threat from China persists. Once your new satellites are in place, I'd assume that there would no longer be a reason to target you, so it shouldn't be long."

Wade shook his head. "Out of the question. We've said nothing publicly about the threat from China. How would I explain being followed around by a squad of G-men?"

Hansen started to speak, but Wade lifted his hand to stop him. "Yes, I know. Your men are capable of protecting me without being too obvious. You don't know how many people I have following me around with cameras. Somehow I've become something of a celebrity. My house is practically a fortress because of all those so-called paparazzi. I'll stay there until this is over."

Hansen shrugged. "Of course, that's your call." Then he slid his card across the table and stood.

"If you change your mind, or if anything else comes to mind, call me anytime. I'll be in touch as soon as we learn anything further. Good luck with your launch," Hansen said.

Once Hansen had left, Rooter turned to Wade.

"Boss, we both know there's at least one time you're leaving the house soon, and so does everyone else in California," Rooter said.

Wade nodded. "The annual charity fundraiser. You're right. It's my charity, and I'm certainly not going to miss it. But now that I've moved up the schedule, it's going to be right after the launch."

"Yes, but if God forbid something goes wrong with that one, we both know you'll keep at it until our satellites are all around China," Rooter said.

Wade just shrugged. It was true.

"OK, so here's my idea. There's someone I know from my time in the Navy who just retired from the Seals. I've heard he's started a security consulting business right here in the DC area. I know he'll be discreet. Let me get him on this," Rooter said.

Wade was uncertain but then looked at Rooter and saw his anxiety level. Even if he didn't believe the Chinese would send an assassin after him, he didn't need his project manager worried about more than the launch. That was more than enough to keep Rooter busy.

"Fine," Wade said. "Meet with him before we head back to California. Make sure he understands I've already got a close protection detail, all faces the paparazzi and press are used to seeing around me. Whatever he'll do will be extra security, not a replacement for the men I already have. Also, that this job lasts only as long as the Chinese threat does. As Hansen said, that should be over as soon as we do the Vandenberg launch."

"Got it, boss," Rooter said.

"Now, the Spaceship that we just built in Florida. It passed its readiness tests yesterday, right?" Wade asked.

"Yes, sir. That one's slated to do a test of rapid munitions deployment, with a dummy load and monitoring instruments the guys at Defense are providing us," Rooter replied.

Wade nodded. "Good. How is the manufacture of our modified run of Gateways going? The ones that can be switched from low to high powered wireless signal production?"

"Almost done, boss. As you directed, the default setting is low power," Rooter replied.

"Excellent. Now, last question. How long before we can get another rocket ready to deploy more satellites once we get this Vandenberg launch behind us?" Wade asked.

"Well, sir, it shouldn't take more than a couple of extra days. As you ordered, we're running satellite production nonstop, so assembling and fitting the payload is all we still have to do," Rooter replied.

"Great. I'm just thinking through some contingencies. But I think that once this Vandenberg launch is a success, the Chinese will see there's nothing they can do, and we'll be finished with this," Wade said.

"Yes, sir," Rooter replied.

Like the boss says, Rooter thought, this should all be over soon.

And maybe if I tell myself that enough times, I'll actually believe it.

Bresca
Washington DC

SpaceLink project manager Mark Rooter stood as retired Seal Team Six Commander Dave Martins approached his table.

"Good to see you, Commander! I'm glad you could make it on such short notice!" Rooter said warmly.

Martins grasped Rooter's outstretched hand firmly and grinned as he shook his head.

"Wrong on all counts, Mark. First, I'm retired, so call me Dave. Second, anytime a billionaire's company is ready to pay for my meal at a Michelin-starred restaurant, I'm there. I just hope I'll be able to help you with your problem," Martins said.

Then Martins paused and looked around the private dining room. "You're off to a good start. This room tells me both that you're serious about security and that you're not worried about spending money to achieve it."

Rooter smiled. "Money's not my problem. A billionaire who won't listen to my advice is."

With occasional pauses as the food was served, Rooter explained the threat posed by the Chinese. Martins listened intently and waited to ask questions until Rooter had finished.

"So, even if your highly paid outside expert tells Wade he should have his bulletproof limo drive right into the building's underground garage on the night of his charity event, he won't do it?" Martins asked.

Rooter shook his head. "No. Wade says he's not going to do anything different. Says if he did it would 'let the terrorists win.' I had trouble even getting him to approve hiring outside help. You and anyone coming with you are going to have to stay out of sight. Especially on the day of the event."

Martins grunted. "That won't be a problem. I know the head of your current security detail. Delta Force before he retired. He'll have hired capable men to assist him in close quarters protection. But I'm sure he's never had to consider long-range assassination with a scoped rifle as a serious threat before."

Rooter looked startled. "Do you think that's possible?"

"Not only possible but nearly certain. I've been to downtown San Francisco many times, and I know where the charity event will be held. Several nearby buildings could serve as the base for a scoped rifle attack," Martins replied.

"How will you prevent it?" Rooter asked.

Martins shrugged. "If Wade is determined to make the same public entrance as in years past, I'll need two things. First, all the information you can get me on the tenants of the target buildings. In particular, whether any of the offices are unoccupied or recently rented. Second, I'll need you to rent office space for me and two others in the building hosting the event. Tell me which spaces are available, and I'll let you know the offices to rent."

"OK, I see where you're going with offices unoccupied or recently rented. Once you've got those identified, though, why not just post guards on each one?" Rooter asked.

Martins shook his head. "Those buildings will have hundreds of offices between them. I'm guessing at least a couple dozen unoccupied or recently rented, maybe more. Again, you won't need us at all if Wade will just use the event building's underground garage."

Rooter sighed. "Believe me, I've tried hard to convince him, but he won't budge. So, what will you and your men do to stop the attack?"

"Counter-sniper. We'll each take a building and try to spot the assassin before he fires," Martins replied.

Rooter sat quietly for a moment. "That doesn't sound easy. I'm also going to put you in touch with Bob Hansen from FBI HQ. He's offered to help with security, but Wade refused to have his men involved. I think, though, that Hansen could help you coordinate with both the San Francisco FBI office and local law enforcement."

"Excellent," Martins said. "I was going to do the coordination piece anyway, but having someone from the DC level in the FBI who already knows what's going on will be a big help. I don't want anyone mistaking us for possible assassins."

Rooter wiped his mouth with his napkin and stood. "Great," he said. "I'll start getting together the information you need, and see you tomorrow in San Francisco."

Chapter Thirty-Seven

Near the Chinese-Indian Border

Sergeant Xu sat up in his hospital bed as Colonel Chang walked in, accompanied by an officer wearing a uniform Xu had never seen. His eyes widened as he saw what the officer was carrying.

To Xu's surprise, they went to Corporal Guan's bed first.

Chang nodded, and the officer propped the long case he was carrying against the small table next to the head of Guan's bed. Then he undid its latches and revealed its contents.

The rifle in the case gleamed in the bright overhead lights of the field hospital and was clearly brand new.

"I'd like to formally present you with this Barrett sniper rifle, captured by this Lieutenant and his men last night. For security reasons, there will be no introductions," Chang said.

"Thank you, sir," was all Guan could manage through his astonishment.

Then the two officers brought the other case to Xu's bed. Once it was open, Xu could see his looked quite different.

"Its owner was firing at us while we approached. Because of him, I lost one of my men," the Lieutenant growled.

Xu swallowed as he looked at a dark patch on the well-worn rifle's stock.

"It could use some cleaning," the Lieutenant said with grim satisfaction.

Xu realized the Lieutenant had to be from the "Night Tigers" special forces unit based at Sichuan. Its origins dated all the way back to World War II, before the Revolution.

Xu's opinion of Colonel Chang went up several more notches. He'd never heard of a Night Tigers deployment on the Indian border before. Xu was sure it had taken Chang real effort to get that approved.

A private Xu had never seen before now walked into the room carrying a clipboard, and Chang nodded towards him.

"Of course, a hospital is no place for such weapons. This private will have you sign acknowledging receipt of these rifles and then store them in the armory. There you will find the ammunition for them, also captured by the Lieutenant and his men," Chang said.

"Thank you, sir," was all Xu could think of to say as well.

Chang smiled. "I'm also pleased to inform you both that the doctor tells me you will be discharged later today. Sergeant, you are free to begin familiarizing yourself with this rifle immediately. I understand it will be a significant adjustment from your present weapon. Of course, it will be your call whether or not to use it on patrol."

"Yes, sir," Xu said. "I appreciate the opportunity."

Chang nodded, pleased with the sincerity he could hear in Xu's voice.

"Sergeant, be aware that thanks to the work of the Lieutenant and his men, the enemy will probably change location once they return. I'm told that they left gifts behind in case the enemy is foolish enough to reoccupy their old position. Some, easy to find. Others buried more deeply and designed to remain inert for several days after they're planted," Chang said.

Then Chang turned to Guan. "Don't worry, Corporal. I'm not expecting you to trade in your spotter's gear and become a sniper yourself. But I understand every spotter must become familiar with his sniper's weapon and its capabilities. And since you run the same risks and are also in a hospital bed, I would say you've earned it."

"I appreciate that, sir," Guan said.

Xu and everyone else present could hear that he meant it.

Now Xu realized giving them the rifles had been done only partly to level the playing field with the Indian snipers who had so far been out of his reach. Word of these "gifts" would travel around camp within minutes. Xu was sure morale was about to skyrocket.

He certainly felt better.

Chapter Thirty-Eight

Russian Consulate General
San Francisco, California

Mikhail Vasilyev looked at the McMillan TAC-50 that had been placed on the cloth covering the conference room table and let out a long, low whistle.

Anatoly Grishkov nodded and said, "It appears no expense is being spared to support our mission. Unless I'm mistaken, this is the famous rifle that made the shot for the world's longest confirmed kill. An ISIS terrorist in Syria several years ago, I think."

Vasilyev frowned. "Yes. A Canadian sniper made the shot. I just wish I had a target as worthy of his fate."

Grishkov nodded again. "True. ISIS with their black flags and videotaped beheadings are just as over the top evil as the SS were with their skull and crossbones insignia and mass killings."

Vasilyev ran his hands over the stock and shook his head. "But on one point, I must disagree. I've been informed this rifle was purchased for not much more than the price recommended by the manufacturer.

Twelve thousand American dollars. And another two thousand dollars for the Leupold Mark 4 LR/T 16x40mm scope."

Grishkov stared at Vasilyev in disbelief. "That wouldn't even buy you a decent used car in Russia, let alone a beauty like this! Next, you're going to tell me it was easy to get!"

Vasilyev shrugged. "It was difficult only in the sense that it is a gun in high demand. Oh, and California happens to be the only state where possession of this particular gun is illegal. So our agent had to drive out of state, in this case to Wyoming, to make his purchase."

"I'm impressed that we were able to produce the documents required for such a purchase in time for this mission. But then, I suppose America is the primary target for FSB operations," Grishkov said.

"I was impressed too, at first," Vasilyev replied. "But after speaking to the agent who made the purchase, I see it wasn't so difficult after all."

"Really?" Grishkov asked. "What about those documents? Or was he dealing with a criminal?"

Vasilyev shook his head. "No, purchase from a criminal would have been too risky, especially for a valuable weapon such as this. It was easy because no documents were required for the sale."

"I'm confused," Grishkov said. "This is a .50 caliber sniper rifle, capable of punching through light armor. Surely documents and permits are required for its purchase."

"No," Vasilyev replied simply.

Seeing Grishkov's exasperated reaction, he quickly added, "First, I should point out that laws on firearms purchase vary from one American state to another. I mentioned that possession of this rifle is not legal in California. But in Wyoming, there is no state license or permit required to buy a rifle of any type."

Grishkov frowned. "But what about the Federal government? Don't its requirements apply in every state?"

Vasilyev nodded. "Yes. And every licensed gun dealer is required to conduct a background check of a Federal database. However, no check is required if a purchase is made from a private individual."

Grishkov's frown deepened. "That makes no sense. Why wouldn't any criminal simply purchase from an individual?"

Vasilyev shrugged. "A reasonable question. However, first, note the word 'required.' Some private sellers carry out Federal background checks, though the law doesn't force them to do so."

"I presume, though, that a private seller could be asked in advance what he requires to make a sale. A criminal could just avoid a seller who required anything more than payment," Grishkov observed.

"True, except for cases like ours where choice is limited because we are looking for a weapon in high demand. The seller we used had a fairly common requirement of his own. Our agent was required to bring a valid government-issued ID," Vasilyev said.

"So he could carry out a background check," Grishkov said, nodding.

"No. The seller said specifically that our agent would not be required to wait for a background check," Vasilyev said with a smile.

"So, this entire conversation is intended to ...wait, there is an American expression I was taught...'push my buttons,' isn't it? Because you know I was a police officer before joining the FSB?" Grishkov said, scowling.

"An excellent use of an American idiom," Vasilyev said solemnly. "Though I would have preferred 'yank your chain' instead."

Seeing from Grishkov's expression that his patience was now truly at an end, Vasilyev hurriedly added, "The ID request had a serious purpose. Many criminals would prefer not to provide an ID, even a false one, because it would include a photo that would have to match the buyer's real face. Police can sometimes trace copies of fake IDs back to their producers, who know their clients' real identities. And if the weapon they've sold is used in a crime and is subsequently traced back to them, then they have evidence to provide the police."

Grishkov shook his head. "If they're so eager to help the police, why not do a background check as well?"

"One practical reason is that it would affect sales. Also, many private sellers object in principle to interfering with what they believe is the right of all Americans to own guns," Vasilyev said.

"Well, at least our agent was able to get this beauty quickly," Grishkov said, patting the rifle's stock.

"You'd think so. But it took over an hour to complete the transaction, much to the agent's annoyance. After a fifteen-hour drive to reach the seller," Vasilyev said.

"So, the seller ran a background check after all?" Grishkov said hopefully.

Vasilyev shook his head. "No. He examined each of the hundred dollar bills provided in payment thoroughly with two different pieces of equipment. While two unsmiling, well-armed men stood by the seller in case of problems. It seems the seller had been paid in counterfeit currency in a past transaction and was determined not to repeat the experience."

Grishkov nodded and then frowned. "When you say our agent had to provide a government-issued ID, I presume it was not a national ID card issued by the Federal government. America does remain one of the few countries without one, yes?"

"Correct. The closest substitute is a driver's license issued by each American state, but of course, not everyone drives. States also issue IDs that aren't tied to driving. Requirements vary from state to state, and in many are easy to meet. Wyoming, for instance, only requires a birth certificate, two pieces of mail with a current address, and proof of a Social Security number. Proof which can include a bank statement bearing the person's SSN," Vasilyev said with a grin.

Grishkov groaned. "A bank statement? A piece of paper that even a teenager with a computer could generate or alter, with no security features of any kind?"

Vasilyev simply nodded.

"Well, but hang on. Surely there is a requirement that the person requesting the birth certificate provide a valid ID that can be checked against a database," Grishkov said triumphantly.

"No," Vasilyev said simply. Then he held up his hand as Grishkov began to reply. "The requestor may provide a copy of such an ID. Or may, instead, choose to have their signature notarized."

Grishkov shook his head. "That means the only challenge is reproducing rubber seal images and a signature scrawl. Even I could manage that, and I'm no master forger."

"Yes, but once you have obtained it, you do have to ensure that the birth certificate has not already been used to obtain another government ID by the real person. There's only one way to be sure of that," Vasilyev said.

"Making sure the real person has already died. But the authorities must tie databases for birth and death together..." Grishkov's voice faltered as he saw Vasilyev's smile widen.

"In some states, yes, in others no. But there's a way around that. Find persons who died in states other than where they were born. Preferably as children, before they ever obtained a government ID," Vasilyev said.

"Ah, but our agent must still be running a risk with such purchases," Grishkov said. "Surely the Federal government ties all these local databases together somehow, particularly birth and death."

Vasilyev shook his head. "No. Only one agency, the State Department, does a significant number of searches against multiple state databases of birth and death. And that is only for cases of suspected passport fraud."

Grishkov sighed. "Over two decades have passed since the Americans suffered attacks in New York and their capital killing over three thousand citizens. You mean to tell me nothing has been done since then?"

"No, that's not right. There is now something called a 'Real ID' with more stringent requirements. But obtaining one is voluntary. Practically speaking, it's only essential to fly. Even then, many other IDs are still accepted to board a flight," Vasilyev said.

"Incredible. How do you explain this failure?" Grishkov asked.

Vasilyev shrugged. "Many Americans don't consider it a failure and would say privacy is more important than security."

Grishkov shook his head. "Who believes that their government doesn't already know anything they would provide for a national ID card application?"

Vasilyev shrugged again, but this time said nothing.

Grishkov shook his head. "Honestly, sometimes I wonder how we lost the Cold War to these people."

Vasilyev just cocked his head and smiled.

"Yes, yes, I know," Grishkov said with a sigh. "Our problems were even worse."

Five Kilometers Outside Columbus, Nevada

Anatoly Grishkov shook his head. "So many things surprise me here. I have seen many abandoned towns and bases in Russia but somehow never expected to see them in America."

Mikhail Vasilyev nodded. "The Western region has many, most from now terminated mining operations. Some towns supported mining precious metals such as gold and the one most commonly mined in Nevada, silver. Columbus, though, was a center for mining borax. It's been deserted for well over a century, making the area ideal for our purpose."

"Borax. Primarily a cleaning agent, yes?" Grishkov asked.

"Correct. Still used in America, Russia, and most other countries. Banned in the European Union, though. Some studies have shown it is dangerous for reproductive health," Vasilyev replied.

Grishkov grunted. "Well, I think it ranks low on the list of hazards we've faced. So, you don't think it will take long to zero your new rifle?"

Vasilyev shook his head. "No. Or anyway, less time than it took you to ensure our security. Are you sure the step was really necessary? From all appearances, there is no one anywhere near for many kilometers in every direction."

"Right now, I think that's true. But you plan to use the rifle without a suppressor to ensure maximum accuracy. That means its sound will carry a considerable distance," Grishkov replied.

"Well, that's true. I suppose it might draw the curious," Vasilyev said.

"I'm more concerned about attracting the greedy," Grishkov said. "We're completely exposed out here and could be quickly overwhelmed by a superior force."

Vasilyev cocked one eyebrow as he looked around the desolate landscape. Nothing moved.

"I see the habits you picked up in Chechnya have stayed with you," Vasilyev said, finally.

Grishkov shrugged. "Better safe than sorry. Let's get this over with, so you can spend our long drive back telling me I worry too much."

Then Grishkov gestured towards the McMillan TAC-50 rifle Vasilyev was readying to fire. "One question. I looked up this rifle online, and it looks a bit different than the picture I found. Has anything about it changed recently?"

Vasilyev nodded. "Observant as always. This is the updated 'C' model, which features a new folding chassis system. It has an adjustable cheek-piece with vertical adjustment and an adjustable buttstock. The stock includes a smaller pistol grip to fit a wider range of hand shapes, with and without gloves."

"Very nice," Grishkov said. "Now, let's see if you still remember how to shoot," he added, pointing at the distant target.

Vasilyev wasted no time answering, instead sending a round to the target. Grishkov looked through his locally purchased Japanese 20x50 binoculars and called out the result. He then heard the "clicks" that followed as Vasilyev made the necessary adjustments.

After multiple corrections led to repeated bullseyes, Vasilyev finally said, "I think that will do it," just as Grishkov shook his head.

"We have company," he said flatly.

"What do you mean..." Vasilyev said and then fell silent as he also heard the sound of the engines.

"That's the problem with an exercise like this," Grishkov said calmly. "We've been making so much noise that it's hard to detect an approaching enemy until it's too late."

Vasilyev sighed. "You mean too late for us to flee."

Grishkov nodded. "Yes. You might try getting in some real practice with that rifle, but they could be police. If they are and we eliminate them, it's unlikely we could avoid a subsequent search."

"Very well. So, we hope these men are simply curious, or if not that your preparations are effective," Vasilyev said.

Grishkov shrugged. "I see no better option."

Grishkov and Vasilyev both stood and watched as the sound's source turned out to be two pickup trucks, each carrying two armed men.

Grishkov noted with professional approval that both pickups stopped well out of comfortable pistol range. But within range of the rifles each man who first dismounted was carrying. At this distance, he couldn't be sure, but both men appeared to be holding AR-15s.

Another man left one of the pickups, but his AR-15 was slung over his shoulder. The last man remained in his vehicle.

The man with the AR-15 slung over his shoulder walked towards them but still out of easy pistol range.

Then he stopped and said in a loud voice, "Howdy folks! My name's Gary. We came to see what was making all the noise. I'm guessing it was that beauty there behind you?"

Vasilyev nodded and said, "Yes."

Gary smiled. "Mind if me and my friends take a closer look?"

"Yes, I do," Vasilyev said evenly. "We were just leaving."

Now both of the men behind Gary lifted their rifles and pointed them directly at Grishkov and Vasilyev.

"Sorry, but that doesn't work for me," Gary said. "I need you both to put your hands up and walk back ten paces and then stand very still while I go and pick up that rifle. Then stay right where you are while we leave. As long as you do exactly what I say, we'll leave you unharmed. Of course, if you try to follow us, all bets are off. Clear?"

"Clear," Vasilyev replied.

Then both Vasilyev and Grishkov walked slowly backward with hands up as instructed.

Grishkov knew the real reason they weren't both dead already was that "Gary" didn't want any chance of the rifle they were stealing being damaged by a stray round.

It made him feel better about what would happen next.

Once Gary had walked far enough forward, Grishkov said, "Drop."

Grishkov had calculated well.

The men with Gary didn't have time to react to Grishkov and Vasilyev's movement downwards.

Because the Claymore mine Grishkov had planted earlier and covered with just enough dirt to conceal it exploded as Gary's right foot made contact with its tripwire.

Neither Gary nor the two men standing behind him had a chance. All were well within the Claymore's effective kill radius of fifty meters.

The seven hundred steel balls ejected by the mine were each about three millimeters in diameter. Propelled by the explosion of seven hundred grams of C-4 explosive to twelve hundred meters per second, the steel balls were joined by hundreds of fragments from the mine itself.

Prospects were better for the lone man who had remained inside one of the pickups, since it was just over fifty meters away from the explosion.

However, he had made the mistake of parking his vehicle sideways with the window rolled down so that he could cover his three companions with his rifle from a distance. Two of the seven hundred steel balls struck him in the head, killing him instantly.

By contrast, Grishkov and Vasilyev were quite fortunate. Though the Claymore was designed to eject all of its steel balls forward, the laws of physics said that some of its case fragments would be propelled backward.

Towards them.

Thanks in part to the instruction to walk back ten paces, Grishkov and Vasilyev were well out of the greatest danger zone, the sixteen meters behind the mine.

Unfortunately, troops were cautioned to be under cover for a full one hundred meters behind the Claymore.

Mine fragments struck Grishkov and Vasilyev, but they were small, and their speed had dropped by the time both were hit. As a result, neither received more than cuts and lacerations.

Painful, but not disabling. And not enough to slow down their departure.

It took only a few minutes to change their clothes and bandage the most serious cuts. The dirty and damaged clothes went into the same hidden compartment in their SUV as the McMillan TAC-50 rifle.

They had already collected all the rifle's spent shells before the thieves arrived. The rounds that had passed through the targets might be found somewhere in the desert beyond by a truly determined search. But neither of them thought that likely.

There was no need to discuss the dead men, their weapons, and their vehicles. Nothing would be gained by examining any of them. They were clearly no more than common thieves who had believed Grishkov and Vasilyev would be easy prey.

And paid the price for their miscalculation.

Vasilyev tapped the GPS and said, "I have set it for Benton, a small town close to the other side of the California border. We should make it there in about an hour, hopefully before local authorities come on the scene we just left. From Benton, we should reach San Francisco in under seven hours. That will give us plenty of time for my questions."

Grishkov said nothing and nodded.

For the following hour, Vasilyev concentrated on driving, making sure he was going the same speed as the rest of the right-lane traffic. There were few other vehicles on US Highway 6, so they crossed the California border in well under an hour.

Grishkov had been tuning the radio to local stations, and they also had an app on their phones allowing them to monitor local police radio bands. There was no indication so far that anyone had come across the scene they had left behind in Nevada.

"OK, first, I recognized that as a Claymore mine from the shape and the 'front toward enemy' stamped on it. It's not a Russian Army device, so how did you even know about it?" Vasilyev asked.

"First, we do have a variant that's quite similar, the MON-50. There are a few minor differences, such as the type of explosive it contains, but the basic device is familiar to me from my time in the Army. As it happens, years ago, one of my men picked up a Claymore from a dead terrorist in Chechnya and used it to help defend my family from an attack led by a North Korean agent."

Vasilyev nodded thoughtfully. "My father told me about that attack, though not how your men and your family were able to survive it. He just said to remember that even inside Russia, an attack by foreign agents was always a real possibility."

"Yes. You may also be wondering what a Chechen was doing with an American mine. I certainly did, so I checked. It turns out Claymores were reported stolen from American military depots in Middle Eastern bases supporting their troops in the Gulf War. From there, I suppose they ended up in the hands of arms dealers ready to sell to anyone with the necessary cash," Grishkov said.

"And how did you obtain this particular Claymore?" Vasilyev asked.

"The Defense Attaché at our consulate in San Francisco is Colonel Geller. He happens to have been my commanding officer in Chechnya and credits me for saving his life there. I believe that is why he agreed to obtain the Claymore for my use. It had to be an American weapon to preserve mission security," Grishkov replied.

"A remarkable coincidence, wouldn't you say? That your old friend from Chechnya just happened to turn up here in California?" Vasilyev asked.

"I had the same thought," Grishkov replied. "I asked, and Geller told me he arrived for his new job just two weeks ago. Director Smyslov told us this mission was critically important to Russia. I think either he or someone working for him has done everything they could think of to help us, including Geller's assignment."

"So, when we report this incident, how will we square it with our instruction to ensure that no American other than the target is killed?" Vasilyev asked.

Grishkov shrugged. "I think an honest report of the circumstances will make it clear there was no alternative. Besides, these criminals are likely known as such to the authorities. If I'm right, suspicion will fall first on rival criminals. Even if the police eventually realize that's not true, I expect by then we will be back in Moscow. And we used no weapon that could be traced back to Russia. Plus, there were no surveillance cameras at our desert location."

"That's true," Vasilyev said with a nod. "Nearly every city in all but the poorest countries now has cameras everywhere. We are fortunate we were attacked in such an isolated area."

"Yes," Grishkov agreed with a sigh. "One more detail we will have to be sure to remember as we stage our attack. And as we make our escape."

Chapter Thirty-Nine

Jiuquan Satellite Launch Center
Gobi Desert, China

General Yang Mingren looked around the Mission Command and Control Center with satisfaction. It had taken a lot of planning to get ready for today's operation, but it had all come together. Barely in time, but in Yang's experience, it seemed as though it was either that or failure.

Then he scowled as he remembered the Americans had managed to destroy a satellite with a missile fired from a fighter in 1985.

Well, today's operation represented a far more significant challenge. The Americans' target had been a satellite in a long-established orbit, in effect a sitting duck.

By contrast, the satellite payload they would target today would be going at high speed along an unknown trajectory.

The most difficult technical challenge hadn't been adding a new engine to the Russian Kh-47M2 Kinzhal missile. Yang had thought swapping it for one that could operate both in atmosphere and in the vacuum of space would be quite tricky, particularly since the new engine had to fit precisely in the Kinzhal casing.

But no. That was the only part of the project to finish ahead of schedule.

Instead, the greatest and most expensive challenge had been developing the capability to track a small, rapidly moving object through space. The Americans had spent billions over decades to do so because of their anti-ballistic missile (ABM) program.

The Americans had their first successful ABM test in 1999, though there had been failures as well. Most galling, they had even managed to shoot down a ballistic missile from a ship in 2020.

China's most advanced interceptor missile, the just deployed HQ-19, was only effective against medium-range ballistic missiles. Practically speaking, that meant against rockets fired from India or eastern Russia.

The problem was that intercontinental ballistic missiles, or ICBMs, built up far greater speed over their higher and lengthier trajectory. Though an ICBM only reached its top speed of seven kilometers per second in the terminal phase of flight, even earlier, its speed made it difficult to track with precision.

Yang had received funding to build additional space tracking capabilities only with great difficulty. In particular, because he hadn't been willing to explain in detail why he wanted it. Security for the antisatellite weapon program was paramount since it was a top American espionage priority.

By contrast, ensuring security for the SU-34's launch with its new antisatellite missile had been relatively easy. Qingshui Air Base was only a few hundred kilometers away from Jiuquan Satellite Launch Center.

Even better, for years, Qingshui's only purpose had been training pilots to fly the Chengdu J-7, a fighter based on the ancient MiG-21. Despite numerous upgrades and enhancements since its introduction in 1965, production of J-7s had finally ceased in 2013. Though some later model J-7s were still flying, it had caused no comment even within the Air Force when Yang had declared Qingshui "surplus to requirements."

Only a small security detachment and the antisatellite missile's engineers were now based at Qingshui, living in rather spartan conditions. Yang would have never reached his present position as Air Force Commander if he hadn't recognized the danger those conditions posed to both morale and security.

Unhappy troops complained to anyone who would listen in any country's military.

Yang had promised everyone at the base an immediate promotion once he had successfully deployed the antisatellite missile. He had every intention of keeping that promise.

Besides, Yang knew if the attack on the American rocket's payload failed, he wouldn't be around to worry about it.

Yang smiled as he looked at the feed from the American news network shown on the massive display screen that dominated the Mission Command and Control Center's front. Kind of the Americans to give them real-time updates on the Spaceship's launch.

Just like the Chinese, the Americans announced some launches and provided full details and video images of the rocket as it climbed into space. For others, they didn't.

Yang had no idea how Lin had managed the destruction of the rocket in Florida. On the one hand, nothing had been said publicly by the Americans to suggest they thought China had been responsible. "Under investigation" had been the only public comment so far.

Well, however Lin had done it, it seemed the method couldn't be repeated.

Two SU-34s, each with the new antisatellite missile, were at Qingshui. One was scheduled for deployment and was now on the runway.

The other was a backup in case anything was reported wrong by the instruments onboard either the first plane or its missile.

So far, according to the monitor sitting in front of Yang relaying reports from those instruments, everything was green.

Yang was unhappy to have only a single backup. But though he had plenty of SU-34s, only three antisatellite missiles had been produced so far.

And Yang had reluctantly authorized one of them to be fired in a test that only evaluated the missile's in-atmosphere performance. He would have preferred a real test that sent the missile into space. But Yang had to agree with his engineers that the chances of detection outweighed the value of what they might learn.

Those engineers seemed very confident that their missile would work in space. Well, it was time to see whether the engineers' confidence was warranted.

Launch! Yang watched as the Americans' newest rocket made its second ascent. This time, nothing would interfere with its climb into space.

But with luck, its purpose would still fail.

Yang's eyes flicked to one of the half-dozen monitors in front of him showing data relevant to the mission. This one showed the countdown for the SU-34's launch.

It was a delicate calculation. On the one hand, the American rocket was fast indeed.

On the other, it first had to climb into space. Then, the rocket had to travel the distance between America and China before it could deploy its satellite payload.

His SU-34 had enough fuel to climb to the high altitude needed for missile launch and then return to base. It didn't have enough additional fuel to loiter indefinitely at high altitude.

More important, Yang wanted to minimize the time the SU-34 was aloft at precisely the same time as the American rocket. He doubted the Americans were able to track his fighters so far inside China.

But why take the chance?

And the Russians were always a concern. True, they might no longer have military bases in Mongolia, a mere one hundred fifty kilometers north.

Nevertheless, the Russian President's 2019 visit to Mongolia's capital and his signing of a "permanent treaty of friendship" showed that relations were still close. And why not, since Soviet troops had been responsible for Mongolia's independence from China in the first place?

And Russia still supplied over ninety percent of Mongolia's energy needs.

Was data from Mongolian radars relayed to Russia? Who knew?

But why take the chance?

So, for now, the SU-34 sat ready on the runway. But not for much longer.

There! With the rocket's launch, the intercept calculation was now complete and showed the time had arrived.

Yang transmitted the order for the SU-34 to set off on its mission.

Then he sat down, dreading to hear that there was some problem with one or, even worse, both SU-34s.

No. One of Yang's displays showed the flight telemetry being received from the mission SU-34. No need to deploy the backup fighter.

So far, so good.

Now it was time to see whether the engineers had overcome what they considered their greatest challenge. Continuous real-time communication allowing precise control of the missile once it was launched.

As a practical matter, this meant a data link from the engineers monitoring the rocket from the Mission Command and Control Center to the SU-34. And then another data link from the SU-34 to the missile while it was in flight.

The engineers had given Yang a long and complex explanation when he had asked the obvious question. Why not control the missile directly from the Mission Command and Control Center?

Yang believed the answer amounted to one fact he reluctantly had to accept. It would have taken too long to reproduce the Russian targeting system in the SU-34 and install it where Yang was sitting for this mission.

There were so many possible points of failure. The SU-34. Its pilot. The Kinzhal missile. The equipment tracking the American rocket. The communications system between that equipment and the SU-34. And between the SU-34 and the Kinzhal missile.

Yang grit his teeth and tried to will away those thoughts. None would help him now. He had worked for months to solve every problem he could foresee.

And so far, it looked like those efforts had paid off. The SU-34 had reached its launch altitude, and the American rocket appeared to be right on its expected course. All communication links were working just as they should.

Five minutes to go.

No matter how hard Yang tried, his mind persisted in showing him ways the mission could still go wrong.

Including the most frightening thought of all. That just as with the laser weapon, something would go wrong Yang had entirely failed to predict.

At last, the five minutes were up.

Yang ordered the firing of the modified Kinzhal missile.

Now the massive display screen in front of the Mission Command and Control Center split into two side by side images. On the right, the American news network's real-time coverage of the rocket's progress.

On the left, the computer's estimate of their missile's location relative to the American rocket.

Now came the final challenge. If the missile hit the rocket too early, his engineers had admitted the payload might still survive and deploy. Particularly if the missile struck a lower stage of the rocket.

Too late, and some of the satellites could deploy and escape destruction.

It was the first time this Spaceship model had survived to leave the atmosphere, so Yang had only his engineer's estimate of the right time to strike.

When the missile had been at the design phase, Yang and his engineers had debated whether or not the tungsten warhead should detach. Yang had pointed out the warhead would be much harder to detect from the ground than an entire powered missile.

Also, a missile making course corrections couldn't be mistaken for anything else. Like a piece of space debris or asteroid fragment.

The problem was that this decision had been made when the missile's task had been destruction of a satellite with a known and static orbit. Now it had to hit a target moving at high velocity.

Using what amounted to an educated guess. Yes, backed up by billions invested in ground tracking stations and computers.

But still a guess.

Yang was swept by a wave of anxiety. Had he been mad to risk his future on the accuracy of that guess?

Warhead separation from the missile was announced on the left side of the display. Moments later, the right side reported the imminent deployment of the rocket's satellite payload.

Yang sat ramrod straight in his chair and did his best to project the confidence he absolutely did not feel.

After all, if this worked, Yang would get the credit. Even more, if it appeared he'd never had any doubts about success.

And if the missile failed, nothing else would matter.

The tungsten warhead was on its way, and nothing anyone did could change its course. They had only been able to track the missile's progress because of its data link to the SU-34, which had been relayed to the Mission Command and Control Center. Now that the warhead had detached, there was no longer a link.

All everyone present had to do was watch the display.

And hold their breath.

The American news network announced that with the rocket's successful deployment of its payload, they were about to switch back to their regular programming. Yang knew they had only stayed with it this long because the rocket was a new model, and its first launch had ended in a spectacular and camera-friendly explosion.

Yang went numb. Had they failed?

"We're getting breaking news on the launch. SpaceLink's launch center lost contact with the rocket just as it was putting its satellite payload into orbit. Or with the payload itself. It's not clear right now. We'll take a break and have more for you shortly."

With that, the American news anchor's face was replaced by an ad for detergent.

Yes, Yang thought to himself. This is why we are destined to replace the Americans on the world stage. Even during their greatest moments of crisis, they still chase money.

The news anchor's face returned. "It's still not clear what happened. But something is definitely wrong with SpaceLink's satellite deployment."

"High-speed tungsten is what's wrong!"

One of the engineer's voices cut through the broadcast with a clarity that its owner appeared to immediately regret.

Every head turned to Yang for his reaction.

Yang wanted to curse the engineer for jinxing the operation. There were plenty of reasons the Americans could have lost contact with their rocket's payload that had nothing to do with the warhead carried by the modified Kinzhal missile.

But it was an impulse Yang immediately suppressed. Confidence and determination were what he wanted to project.

So he laughed.

And as his laughter grew louder, pointed at the engineer who had spoken and said, "Comrades, I think he's right!"

A wave of relieved laughter washed across the floor as everyone dared to believe the mission had been a success.

The next few minutes crawled by as the laughter died, and many words were spoken by the American news anchor that amounted to just one thing.

He knew nothing besides what he had already reported.

Then his expression suddenly became more serious as he evidently heard more over his earpiece.

"It looks like another disaster for SpaceLink. They've confirmed losing all contact with their rocket's satellite payload, and every attempt to deploy the satellites has failed. This will be the second misfire in a row for the troubled company..."

The rest of what he had to say was rendered inaudible by the cheering that started spontaneously and quickly included everyone across the floor.

Including, Yang was surprised to find, him as well.

And why not, Yang thought to himself.

Today was not just a victory for China's military and space program.

It was also a critical step towards placing China's future safely in the hands of the only people proved competent to lead this great nation.

Its Generals.

Chapter Forty

Zhongnanhai Compound
Beijing, China

President Lin Wang Yong looked up from the papers on his desk as General Yang Mingren was escorted into his office.

The expression on Lin's face could hardly have been more different than on Yang's last visit.

Wreathed in smiles. Not a thundercloud ready to erupt.

"General, welcome! Please, have a seat!" Lin said, beaming.

"Thank you, sir," Yang said. He did his best to keep any trace of resentment from his tone or posture.

But it wasn't easy.

"Congratulations on a great success! First off, let's take care of this matter," Lin said as he lifted one piece of paper from the many on his desk. Then, he showed it to Yang.

It was his resignation letter.

Lin slowly and ceremoniously ripped it first in half and then in quarters.

Next, he tossed the pieces over his shoulder to the floor behind him.

"China needs men like you to protect it from the threats that assail it from all sides. Sadly, though you have dealt one of those threats a crushing blow, it yet lives," Lin said.

"Sir?" was all Yang could think of to ask.

"You told me the last time we met there was a third Spaceship being readied to launch from Florida. Just before you walked in, it was announced that its scheduled launch had been pushed up. I fear you will have barely enough time to return to Jiuquan to oversee its destruction," Lin said.

As though he could do so as easily as ordering another bowl of rice with his dinner, Yang thought furiously.

A thought he was careful to keep off his face.

Aloud, Yang replied with a question.

"Sir, that rocket was due to conduct a test of delivering supplies to the American military who have just returned to Afghanistan. It isn't supposed to even carry real military items, just ballast, and monitoring instruments. Apparently, the American military didn't want to risk any real supplies on a test flight. After two failed launches, I'm sure they consider that a wise decision. Has that changed?"

Lin shook his head. "No. That's still what they're saying publicly. But I don't trust the American billionaire who owns the rocket. He could change what it carries. Maybe without telling his military."

Yang had trouble believing what he was hearing. He was no expert on the Americans. But even he was sure no person, not even a billionaire, could change a rocket cargo on his own that had been contracted to the American government.

"And I'm taking steps to make sure he won't be around to trouble us much longer," Lin said darkly, more to himself than to Yang.

Then Lin looked up as though realizing he'd said his thoughts aloud. And regretted doing so.

What madness was this? Had Lin sent assassins after Eli Wade?

Yang didn't know very many things with absolute certainty.

One of those few things was that China wasn't ready for war with the Americans.

Was Lin about to start one?

Lin hurried on as though hoping to erase Yang's memory of his last words. "The fact is, that rocket could still carry four hundred satellites to beam lies and sedition into our country. That is a risk we can't take."

Yang nodded as though agreeing, while he thought as quickly as he could. He had to convince Lin to change his mind.

Yang had only one missile left, and it would be at least two weeks before more were delivered.

And he knew how much luck had been required for the success of the last missile strike.

"Sir, I suggest we monitor the launch, with our attack at the ready. We will track the rocket's progress. If it is indeed delivering cargo in Afghanistan, this will be clear from its launch profile. If instead it matches the course of the last rocket and attempts to place satellites in orbit, we will destroy it then," Yang said.

Lin cocked his head suspiciously. "Wouldn't it be simpler to destroy the rocket either way?"

Yang shrugged. "We must consider the Americans' reaction to the explosion of three rockets in a row. It might lead to a much closer investigation of their cause. On the other hand, if the third rocket carries out its mission successfully, they may believe the first two disasters were simple accidents."

Lin looked at Yang with surprise. "You mean an American military reaction! Do you believe that's possible?"

Yes, I do, you jackass. Was the thought Yang absolutely had to keep off his face.

He managed it with some difficulty.

Aloud, Yang said, "Sir, the Americans have sometimes acted unpredictably. They certainly have the capability to damage our forces. It seems prudent to attack only if it is necessary."

Lin scowled but finally nodded. "Very well. But understand this, General. You are personally responsible for ensuring that no satellites are launched by that rocket. Based on your past success, I'm sure that you are up to the task."

Yang stood and saluted. "I appreciate your confidence, sir. You won't be disappointed."

A few minutes after Yang's departure, the door to Lin's office opened again.

Ministry of State Security Song carefully closed the door behind him.

Good, Lin thought. This is certainly a conversation I don't want overheard.

"Welcome, Minister," Lin said. "Congratulations on the success of the first action promised by the Russians. I have seen nothing that suggests the Americans believe we were responsible."

Song nodded, though Lin's words alarmed him. Did he think the Americans didn't suspect a connection between the satellites destroyed by the laser weapon and the destruction of the rocket in Florida carrying more satellites?

Since both the satellites they'd destroyed in space and the ones carried by the rocket that exploded beamed an Internet signal that could be received in China?

Song considered pointing this out to Lin but instantly discarded the idea. Lin didn't like being told bad news.

He liked being told he was wrong even less.

So, Song just said, "Thank you, sir."

"Now that the Russians have delivered on the first action they promised, it's time for them to carry out the second. I understand their team is in place, correct?" Lin asked.

"Yes, sir. But I understand the next American rocket launch won't carry satellites. Also, the American media reports SpaceLink hasn't yet been able to produce enough satellites to fill the Spaceship's capacity of at least four hundred. Since they lost a total of eight hundred satellites in the last two rocket explosions, that certainly seems credible," Song replied.

"So, you believe we should wait?" Lin asked.

"Yes, sir. Our reports say that even if rushed, the next Spaceship after this one won't be ready for at least another month. We have already found many of these so-called Gateways with our new detection drone and expect to find many more. Why take the risk of assassinating Eli Wade if we can avoid it?" Song replied.

If Lin hadn't just dealt with pushback from Yang, Song might have had a chance.

As it was, he had none.

"No, Minister, my mind is made up. Eli Wade is an enemy of the Chinese people and must die. Communicate with the Russians that the assassination should happen as soon as possible. And of course, to be certain nothing can be traced back to us," Lin said.

Song nodded and said, "I will do so immediately."

Then Song smiled. "Ordinarily, I would tell you I will report as soon as it is done, but I think we can count on the American media to do that more quickly than I possibly could."

Lin smiled back and said, "I look forward to it."

Once Song had left Lin's office, though, the smile quickly left his face.

When he had proposed the Russian's involvement, Song knew about the Air Force's antisatellite laser weapon.

But he had known nothing about the antisatellite missile until it had been used against the second Spaceship launch.

This meant three separate attacks against American satellites China objected to would be followed by assassination of the man behind their manufacture and launch.

Taken together, it was simply too much. The Americans would react. The only question was how.

Just as troubling as that prospect was the fact that Yang had somehow concealed his antisatellite missile project from State Security.

What else was Yang hiding?

CHAPTER FORTY-ONE

USS *Oregon*
Under the South China Sea

Captain Jim Cartwright frowned as he looked over all of the reports Lieutenant Commander Fischer had just given him. As Fischer had said, they all showed the USS *Oregon* was ready to launch the modified Tomahawk.

"Have we confirmed that the JSDF's AWACS is on station to monitor Chinese activities in the area and the success of our attack?" Cartwright asked.

"Yes, sir," Fischer replied. He knew as well as Cartwright did that the cooperation of the Japanese Self Defense Force (JSDF) would be critical for this operation. The JSDF had been keeping one of their Airborne Warning and Control Systems (AWACS) on station in the area for over a year, as China had kept pushing its military activities towards Japanese-claimed islands.

This meant the JSDF could be their eyes for the attack without raising Chinese alert levels. And since they would only observe and report, the JSDF had decided their AWACS could participate without violating the "self defense only" provisions of Article 9 of the Japanese Constitution.

This was fortunate since JSDF AWACS were the only ones in the world to use the newer Boeing 767 airframe. Japan had placed its AWACS order after the old Boeing 707 airframe used by AWACS in all other countries had ceased production. So, JDSF AWACS were capable of additional mission time aloft and included extra room for AWACS crew and equipment.

"Very well, Commander. Launch modified Tomahawk at the designated target."

"Yes, sir," Fischer replied as he relayed the order. There was a barely perceptible tremor as the Tomahawk left the *Oregon*.

After a few moments, Fischer said, "Launch successful, Captain. Missile is on course to target."

Cartwright nodded. "Now, I've read the reports on this weapon, but you've seen it tested. Is it really the game-changer for the Tomahawk that's being claimed?"

Fischer shrugged. "I saw it tested under nearly ideal conditions. The biggest drawback for the weapon is that its effectiveness drops if there's substantial wind over the target."

"Well, that makes sense. The missile is dispersing a cloud of highly volatile gas over the target and then igniting it with a laser. If wind blows some of the gas off the target, it would have to be less effective," Cartwright said.

"Yes, sir," Fischer said, nodding. "Especially since the Tomahawk has to fly far enough past the target to ignite the vapor cloud with its laser and still survive. The whole point of the weapon is deniability. With no weapon shrapnel on-site, there's no evidence to point to an attacker."

Cartwright frowned. "But what about the missile itself? If there's no deep water available within the Tomahawk's remaining range after it attacks, then it would be the proverbial 'smoking gun' wouldn't it?"

"That's right, sir. It's programmed to self-destruct once it travels as far as possible from the attack site. But deniability is based on the idea that those Tomahawk fragments will be scattered on a seabed and impossible to recover. That should work out fine for this attack on a tiny island, but wouldn't for many inland targets," Fischer said.

"But a Tomahawk's not that big. Can it carry enough 'volatile vapor' to do much damage, even if it's highly pressurized? In short, can it really knock out the airfield on that base?"

Fischer shrugged. "The missile did a lot more damage than I thought it would when I saw it tested. But I've seen the satellite pictures of the base just like you have, sir. Weather reports say winds will be calm, sure. But even under ideal conditions, the new weapon will just cause some damage to a base that size that will probably be repaired pretty quickly. I'd also be surprised if there were many casualties."

Cartwright nodded and then frowned even more deeply. "Well, launching that missile was like ringing a dinner bell to any subs the Chinese have out here. Any hint so far that we have company?"

Fischer shook his head. "No, sir. Sonar knows what to look for, including the new *Sui* class. They also know to inform me immediately if there's so much as a peep."

"Very well. Let me know as soon as we hear from that AWACS. In the meantime, set course back to base, best possible speed," Cartwright said.

"Yes, sir," Fischer replied.

Cartwright and Fischer had already discussed the course and speed the *Oregon* would use to exit the launch area based on one central guess. That any submarine the Chinese had in the area would be between them and the Chinese base they had just attacked.

They both thought it likely at least one Chinese submarine would have detected the Tomahawk launch. But Fischer figured it would wait for confirmation that the launch had been an attack rather than a test before engaging in pursuit.

Cartwright was sure they would pursue either way. He agreed, though, that any Chinese submarine captain would probably wait to fire on the *Oregon* until the attack had been confirmed.

Even then, if the attack caused few casualties, Cartwright thought the Chinese might hesitate to respond. After all, they had launched only a single missile.

And the *Oregon* wouldn't be so easy to find. The *Virginia* class was the first to incorporate an advanced electromagnetic signature reduction system. The latest sound-absorbing coating applied to the *Oregon* worked without peeling off, as it had on earlier *Virginia* class submarines.

Most important, its pump-jet propulsors created a high-pressure flow of water to move the *Oregon* forward. This method was far quieter than a traditional propeller.

As a propeller turns, it creates an area of low pressure at the trailing edge of each blade. And engineers had discovered decades ago that water could boil due to low pressure just as it could be boiled with high temperature and produce bubbles.

These bubbles are called cavitation, a deadly source of noise for most submarines.

The bubbles are cavities of vapor inside a liquid. Since propeller blades keep moving, they take the low pressure with them and leave the cavitation bubbles in the high pressure of the deep ocean. Where the bubbles pop and create noise.

Cartwright looked at a map of the area and frowned.

China had been pushing America and its Pacific allies in the South China Sea for years. Forcing down an American military aircraft flying in what everyone but China called international airspace. Building artificial islands in what everyone but China called international waters. Or waters that were claimed by American allies.

So far, there had been no response. From anyone.

Maybe it was only natural that China had kept right on pushing.

Cartwright wasn't surprised that America was finally responding.

He was amazed it had taken this long.

Chapter Forty-Two

Changzheng 20
Under the South China Sea

Captain Wen was annoyed every time he thought about the name of the submarine under his command. It was not that he objected to the name itself. Changzheng or "Long March" was a perfectly appropriate reference to a critically important event in Chinese Communist Party history.

If the Long March had not succeeded, China would not now be ruled by the Communist Party.

So maybe it was no surprise that the most remarkable feats of Chinese technology, both rockets and submarines, were named "Changzheng."

But every single operational Chinese nuclear submarine, regardless of class?

There were still three old Type 091s operating that the Americans called the *Han* class. Plus nine from the newer Type 093 class, called *Shang* by the Americans.

They were all named "Changzheng," followed by a number. Just like his submarine.

Giving his Type 095 command the same name as a Type 091 submarine commissioned in 1984, before most of his sailors had been born, was like giving the same name to both a Ferrari and a donkey cart.

Wen's musings were interrupted by his Executive Officer, Commander Duan.

Wen had a very high opinion of his abilities, which would have surprised nobody in China's Navy. Modest men did not reach the rank of Captain.

Wen respected few officers of lower rank. Duan was one of the rare exceptions. He was the only officer who Wen believed knew as much as he did about the real capabilities of the new Type 095. Both good and bad.

Maybe more than Wen did, though he had trouble admitting that even to himself.

Duan had just one failing. He sometimes questioned both orders and established regulations.

Wen tolerated this weakness for several reasons. First, Duan never pushed questions into outright disobedience.

Second, Duan's questions weren't born of stupidity or obstinance. His concerns were always reasonable, and sometimes Wen even shared them. On one occasion, Wen had drafted a new regulation based on one of Duan's objections and forwarded it through channels.

Wen was hardly surprised that he never heard back. The Chinese Navy's admirals were not known for their concern over input from lower ranks.

"Captain, sonar contact. Likely Tomahawk launch, sir," Duan said.

"Tomahawk launch! How many, Commander?" Wen asked.

"Just one so far, Captain. Sonar knows to report immediately if more launches are detected, sir," Duan replied.

"One," Wen repeated and sat thinking for a moment.

Duan stood by respectfully. Another thing Wen liked about him. Duan knew there were moments a leader needed to be free to think without interruption.

"One Tomahawk sounds like a test of some kind. I have seen Naval Intelligence reports suggesting the Americans are trying to add new capabilities to those old weapons. And a single Tomahawk could hardly do much damage, even to bases as small as the ones we have out here," Wen said.

Duan nodded. "I agree, Captain. There is another possibility, though. If the Tomahawk targeted our newest base, it might be meant to send a signal of American displeasure at the steps we have taken to assert our territorial rights."

Wen grunted and thought some more. Yes. Duan had also risen in rank despite asking questions because he always said the right thing politically.

"Assert our territorial rights?" Wen had wondered for years when the Americans would finally respond to being pushed around by China's Navy and Air Force.

Had the day finally come?

It wouldn't have surprised Wen even a little to learn that an American submarine captain not too far away was having similar thoughts.

"How good is our fix on the submarine that launched the Tomahawk?" Wen asked.

"Only a general bearing, Captain. Nothing solid enough to allow a torpedo launch," Duan replied.

Not a surprise, Wen thought. The Americans would have one of their most modern submarines carry out such a mission. Whether it was a test or an attack. Maybe a *Virginia* class?

If that guess were right, he would have to be careful not to turn from hunter to hunted.

"Rig us for ultra-quiet running until further notice, Commander.

Once that is done, set best silent speed towards the American submarine. Assume they are headed east back towards their base," Wen ordered.

"At once, Captain," Duan said and hurried off to carry out Wen's orders.

"Ultra-quiet running" meant taking every possible precaution to avoid making a noise that could be detected by the enemy submarine. All routine maintenance work was suspended. No cooking meals. No showers. In short, any activity not absolutely required to keep the submarine operational stopped.

"Best silent speed" meant that instead of relying on the submarine's nuclear reactor for propulsion, they would use power from lithium-ion batteries to approach the Americans. Those batteries were one of the new capabilities of the Type 095 that made it superior to its predecessors.

The batteries were also a real worry to Wen. They had already been used in China's much cheaper and more numerous diesel subs. But until now, they had been considered too risky to install in its nuclear submarines.

Lithium-ion batteries could leak hydrogen gas. Colorless and odorless, hydrogen gas could only be detected by special instruments. It could build up quickly and lead to an explosion powerful enough to rupture the hull.

Wen had been told that the batteries in his submarine would not leak hydrogen gas. And that even if they did, the instruments the Navy had installed would detect it. And that if hydrogen gas were detected, it could be safely vented out of his submarine before it caused an explosion.

Wen wanted to believe all three assurances.

But today would be the first time he put them to the test. Because Wen was sure of one thing.

Hydrogen gas might pose a real hazard to his submarine.

But a *Virginia* class opponent was an even greater danger.

Chapter Forty-Three

Ziyou Island
South China Sea

Colonel Xia smiled to himself as he walked down the makeshift runway. Though it was a dark and moonless night, lights blazed up and down both sides of the runway. This meant he could see the runway in detail, but nothing outside it.

It was the first time since he'd arrived at "Freedom Island" that anything close to a smile had touched Xia's lips.

But finally, things were starting to go right.

He'd overheard a joke this afternoon. Since it was at his expense, some might have wondered why he liked it so much.

It went, "Want to find out if there really is a God? Lift a match!"

Xia understood the key point immediately. Not "light a match," which would have meant the joke was about the consequences of lighting a match in the presence of temporary fuel lines.

No, the soldier had been joking about what would happen if you merely "lifted" a match.

Xia had every soldier and construction worker searched upon arrival.

So far, only one soldier had been found with a pack of matches that only had two remaining. The soldier had sworn he hadn't intended to bring them to this assignment, let alone use them.

Xia had the soldier held under armed guard until the next transport off the island for immediate court-martial.

But not before mustering every soldier and worker on the island for an assembly where he displayed the handcuffed soldier. And explained – again – what would happen to anyone caught with anything that might ignite the temporary fuel lines.

This morning the missiles and bombs needed to arm the fighter jets that would use the runway here had been offloaded and stored in one of the prefabricated buildings that had just been slapped together. In spite of Xia's repeated pleas that munitions storage wait for the construction of proper concrete weapons bunkers.

An Air Force officer had explained to Xia that it was safer to launch aircraft coming to the base without weapons. Unarmed planes also had a greater range, making it easier to reach this distant base.

But the clinching argument had been that without munitions on-site, this base could not be declared "operational."

Xia had placed the munitions as far from the fuel storage as he could. However, with much of the island already occupied by the runway and all the finished structures, that wasn't very far.

Tomorrow Xia would finally get the pumps, reinforced pipes, and qualified work crew necessary to replace the fire hazard that lay all around him. He understood why his superiors had done it this way. To report as quickly as possible that the base was "ready" to the politicians.

But Xia deeply resented the danger that everyone on this island had been exposed to as a result. It simply wasn't professional.

Along with the immediate prospect of ending the danger of fire engulfing the base, Xia was also enjoying his walk.

Xia smiled at the solid feel of the metal mats under his feet. Yes, it wasn't a paved runway. But he had walked the length of the runway twice already and seen no flaw or gaps.

On this third walk, Xia was still looking for problems. But by now, he was confident that if he found one this time, it would be minor and easily fixed.

What was that?

It sounded like something had flown overhead, but no nighttime helicopter flights had been authorized since the base had been built. And a helicopter would have made much more noise.

Xia frowned as a mist settled on his skin and all around him.

His first thought was that no precipitation of any kind had been forecast for the rest of the week, and if that was wrong, it might interfere with construction.

Almost immediately, though, Xia knew this wasn't water. It had a sharp smell that reminded him of...gasoline.

Xia had just completed the thought when the Tomahawk's laser ignited the vapor it had dispersed moments before.

Everything around Xia turned as bright as the sun. He felt as though he were flying.

And then he felt nothing at all.

Japanese Self Defense Force AWACS
South China Sea

Haruto Takahashi had pioneered the concept of integrating data from multiple sources on a single airborne platform. Ordinarily, an Airborne Warning and Control System (AWACS) would rely exclusively on its massive rotating radar to detect possible threats.

However, Haruto had been the first in the JSDF to spot the opportunity provided by their Boeing 767 airframe. It offered more room than the older Boeing 707 model used by the Americans and all of their other allies.

Haruto smiled to himself. Sometimes, it paid to be late to the party.

Additional computer and communications modules of Haruto's own design, as well as one extra crewman, made all the difference. In previous missions, he had been able to integrate data from other JSDF aircraft and drones into a single package.

Haruto had spent the past several years building on this accomplishment. In particular, he had managed to improve the stability of the interface linking the different platforms. This meant each data source, such as a drone's visual image or radio intercept picked up by a JSDF reconnaissance aircraft, would display along with their AWACS radar return.

Just as important, if a single data source was interrupted, it wouldn't affect the display of the others.

But Haruto was starting to think this latest project might be a bridge too far. No sooner had the thought crossed his mind than Kaito Watanabe appeared at his side. His supervisor since the start of the project, Kaito knew little about its technical details. But as the AWACS commander, he knew its original capabilities inside and out.

Kaito also had a disconcertingly deep understanding of his crewmen, which he now demonstrated.

"Have we bit off more than we can chew?" Kaito asked.

Like all AWACS commanders, Kaito's initial JSDF training on AWACS operation had been supplemented by additional courses in America. He had brought a slew of American idioms back with him. Just when Haruto thought Kaito's store must be exhausted, he came up with another.

At least this one was easy to understand. "More than one way to skin a cat" wasn't just a horrifying image. It was also difficult to fathom. Who besides a sociopath would want to devise a single way to do so, let alone many?

Haruto also had to admit reluctantly that this time, the idiom was apt. Japan had signed a defense pact with Australia in 2020, its first bilateral military agreement since its 1960 agreement with the Americans. The pact's initial focus had been on base visits, joint exercises, and disaster relief coordination. The agreement had since expanded to information sharing.

Like the data collected from the MQ-4C Triton drone operated in the South China Sea by the Royal Australian Air Force (RAAF), one of six it had purchased from the Americans.

The RAAF Triton had several declared purposes, none of which China could find objectionable. Protection of Australian commercial shipping. Detection of drug and people smuggling on its way to Australia. Early warning of threats to Royal Australian Navy ships.

This particular Triton had been launched from the RAAF base at Tindal in Australia's Northern Territory. Not far from the South China Sea.

The Chinese had complained bitterly about Triton overflights of their claimed airspace in the South China Sea. Australia had rejected these complaints. Given the importance of Australian-produced raw materials for China's economy, so far, its leaders had been unwilling to authorize its military to shoot down an RAAF Triton.

After first getting their Australian allies to agree, the Americans had asked the JSDF to relay data from the RAAF Triton to one of its submarines. The Americans had also provided the JSDF with full technical details on the Triton. Details they said would be sufficient to carry out their request.

Haruto looked up from his display at Kaito and nodded. "Yes, sir. It looks like the Australians have been tinkering with the Triton's systems since they purchased it from the Americans. I've had no trouble obtaining useful data from the drone. However, fully tapping into its data feed has been difficult so far. It's been very frustrating."

Kaito smiled. "Tinkering, you say. You mean, the way someone in the JSDF has been monkeying around with the original design of the American AWACS?"

Haruto sighed. "Monkeying around?" He could guess what this American idiom meant, and it didn't sound very complimentary.

But Kaito was right. He was in no position to complain about whatever the Australians had done to their Triton after buying it from the Americans.

"I'll put it this way, sir. The Americans want a damage assessment sent directly to their submarine as quickly as possible. I can get that to them. Fine detail, though, will have to come from the Australians," Haruto said.

Kaito nodded. "Understood. Not long now, right?"

"Yes, sir," Haruto replied, tapping a large monitor to his right. "This is the Triton's visual feed, currently trained on the Chinese island base targeted by the Americans. In a matter of minutes, their weapon should strike it."

Kaito frowned. "We have waited many years for the Americans to respond to Chinese provocations. So have the Australians. I wonder whether the Americans really needed our help on this operation or if they're doing things this way so we can see their attack for ourselves."

Haruto shrugged. "Maybe a little of both. You've spent a lot more time with them than I have. How often have you said their real intentions are not so easy to read, even though they pretend to be what you call an 'open book'?"

"Well, from what the Americans have told us, this won't be much more than a slap on the wrist. A single missile that will take out their runway for a day or so. Since the Chinese have still got a full construction crew there finishing up the base, maybe only a matter of hours. Honestly, I'm not sure why they're even bothering to launch such a limited strike," Kaito said.

"I suppose they have to start somewhere. At least the Americans will be sending a clear signal that more island-building will come at a price," Haruto replied.

"And there's the signal," Kaito said, as a pinpoint of light appeared on the center of Haruto's display.

The pinpoint almost instantly widened to a brilliant rectangle.

And then expanded far enough that the dazzling light shining from the display made them both look away.

But only for a few moments. Almost immediately, the bright light was replaced with a sullen red glow.

That appeared to encompass the entire island.

"What was that!" Kaito was the first to exclaim. "That was no lone missile!"

Haruto's fingers were flying over the keyboard, and at first, he was too busy to say anything.

Finally, Haruto looked up at Kaito. "I've cut the image brilliance so we can stand to look at it as the replay unfolds. I've also slowed down the attack's progression by a ten to one ratio. Maybe most important, I've zoomed in on areas with data, and I'm putting it up on the main display," gesturing towards the massive screen mounted on the wall behind them.

Haruto began the replay.

Almost immediately, Kaito gestured for Haruto to stop the playback.

"The Americans somehow managed to engulf the entire runway in fire with a single missile. But if we imagine the runway as a rectangle, look at how the rectangle widens almost instantly on both sides. What would explain that?" Kaito asked.

Haruto frowned. "What if the Chinese ran temporary fuel lines so they could gas up planes on the runway?"

Kaito shook his head. "No way. No fighter pilot I know would land his plane anywhere near a plastic hose full of aviation fuel. We'll have to think of some other explanation. Resume the playback."

Both sat silently as two thin lines of fire stretched from the runway towards...what?

The answer appeared almost immediately, as more light bloomed on the screen.

Kaito sighed and gestured for Haruto to pause. "My apologies. You were right. That must have been fuel lines leading back to the tanks that supplied them. Continue."

Now that they had slowed the playback, they could see multiple fires' progression rather than a single inferno.

Seconds later, there was another brilliant flare of light. This one, though, was...jumpy?

"Back up twenty seconds, and refocus on the source of that last light flare. Slow down playback again by half," Kaito ordered.

Haruto nodded, and a few moments later, the display resumed.

"Stop," Kaito said seconds later, shaking his head. "Those are munitions exploding. At first, a few, but then nearly all detonate at once."

Kaito paused. "What can we use besides these visual images to confirm what happened?"

Haruto frowned. "Ideally, I'd want an analysis of multiple light wavelengths, and all the other data picked up by the Triton's active electronically scanned array. But because of the Australian modifications, I don't have it here. The Australians will need to pass that data to the Americans for a detailed analysis. For what it's worth, though, I agree with your interpretation of the information we do have."

"One last point before you relay our assessment to the American submarine. What would you estimate the casualty rate to be, based on the extent of the fires and the power of the explosions we witnessed?" Kaito asked.

Haruto looked at him soberly. "I think the real question is, how many bodies will the Chinese be able to identify?"

Kaito shook his head. "I'd like to argue with you but can't. I think we're going to be flying more missions in these waters for a long time to come."

Chapter Forty-Four

Shanghai, China

Chen Li Na had read the news coverage of Forward's successful attack on the Shanghai Stock Exchange twice. First, the version in China's state censored media. There, the outage that followed was portrayed as a minor technical issue, quickly fixed the same day.

Chen's Gateway gave her access to coverage from the foreign press, where the story was very different. With only about three hundred billion US dollars invested, foreign investors accounted for less than ten percent of the Exchange's value.

But you wouldn't know that from how loudly they complained when they lost money.

Chinese investors were mostly in for the long term. Nobody wanted to attempt living on the meager retirement benefits provided by the government. With interest rates low, the Exchange was the only practical alternative, and daily fluctuations were seen as routine.

Not by foreigners. And once there was even a hint that the Exchange itself had been robbed, the unexplained "technical outage" had become a major news story outside China.

Gateway owners tried to upload the foreign press stories through social media, but nearly all were swiftly removed. Hacking "shame signs" at traffic intersections was one thing.

But now, this was about real money.

Chen smiled to herself as she walked to work, pushing herself without much thought through the usual morning crowds. It was a route she could take in her sleep.

Her subway trip took her past only a few stations before depositing her at one just two blocks from the office building where Chen worked.

Nobody with sense would walk the rest of the distance at street level, though. It was much safer to avoid the heavy traffic there and go through the underground walkways.

Some of the walkways downtown had been designed with small shops on either side from the start. Others had vendors occupying part of the walkway in little kiosks. Their products ranged from packaged foods suitable for a quick lunch at an office desk to scarves, ties, umbrellas- anything light enough to be easily carried by a busy person on their way to work.

Busy with her thoughts, Chen suddenly became aware men were walking on both sides of her. Though both were wearing suits and ties, their build and bearing said these were not office workers.

No. Her heart racing, Chen's first thought was – police?

The man to her right spoke in a calm, low voice. "Do not be alarmed. We have been asked to escort you to a meeting with Mr. Pan. His office is not far from here. Your employer has already been advised that you will be out sick today."

The man then spoke a phrase that sent a wave of relief washing over Chen. It was the phrase sent to Chen through her Gateway, changed weekly, that told her whoever spoke it was a member of Forward.

Chen nodded, and the man gestured to the next set of stairs to the right that led to street level. Where a large and expensive foreign-built sedan was idling against the curb. Despite the many prominent signs along the street forbidding any such action.

A glance revealed at least four policemen in plain view. Chen was more impressed by their studied failure to spot the illegally placed vehicle than the sedan itself.

Whoever owned it must be powerful indeed.

At least they were telling the truth about one thing. It was just a couple of minutes before the sedan left the street and descended into the garage level.

Chen took careful note of which building stretched above her head before they began their descent. It would be easy to remember because it was one of the tallest in Shanghai.

And then shook her head with chagrin as the sedan made multiple turns between several interconnected subterranean garages. Chen knew she was still in downtown Shanghai.

But that was all.

Their vehicle pulled up in front of an elevator with no button or any other visible device next to it.

Instead, a camera pointed down from the wall on top of the elevator door.

The man who had spoken to Chen earlier, but remained silent since looked up at the camera and remained perfectly still.

The elevator door slid open.

The man gestured for Chen to enter. Though she expected both men to enter the elevator with her, they remained outside as the door closed, and it began moving upwards.

There were no buttons inside the elevator either. Apparently, it was controlled by whoever or whatever was operating that camera, Chen thought.

As the elevator's speed increased and her ride continued, she realized the answer was probably more straightforward. This elevator only had one destination.

The top.

When the door opened, she immediately realized her guess had been correct. Directly in front of her was a panoramic stretch of glass revealing a view of Shanghai from a dizzying height. The vista was undoubtedly designed to impress anyone visiting the man who had his office here.

Chen smiled to herself wryly. Yes, she was smart enough to know when she was being manipulated.

She was also smart enough to know it was still working.

While she was standing momentarily transfixed by the view, a well-dressed man appeared at her side.

"Welcome, Ms. Chen. I am Mr. Pan's private secretary. Please allow me to escort you to his office," the man said with a slight bow.

Moments later, Chen was standing inside a vast office, blinking to adjust her eyes to its dimness after the brilliantly lit vista just outside. Pan sat behind a handsome dark wood desk at the opposite end, with several stacks of paper piled in front of him in three black metal trays.

Chen noticed immediately there were no electronic screens in view anywhere and nodded to herself.

Old-school security. Paper couldn't be hacked.

He looks younger than I expected, Chen thought. Maybe in part because his hair is cut a bit longer than the current business fashion. Quite handsome, too.

Pan took the piece of paper in front of him, moved his pen in a way that Chen guessed correctly meant he was signing it, and then placed it in the tray to his right.

Then he looked up and gave Chen a brilliant smile that made her think Pan was either genuinely pleased to see her or a world-class actor.

"Ms. Chen!" Pan exclaimed. "I'm so glad you could come!"

Then he bounded forward from his desk to her side so quickly that she was taken aback on several levels.

Chinese businessmen didn't "bound" anywhere. Because they would consider it undignified for a start. And because, like their Western counterparts, few were in the physical shape required for more than, at best, a brisk walk.

Chen could see at a glance that Pan's suit and shoes cost more than she made in a year. But they were cut to let him move like an athlete.

The next surprise was Pan's arm around her shoulders, propelling her side by side towards the sofa and chair set occupying the office's center.

Oddly, it didn't make her uncomfortable. Why not, Chen wondered?

Putting one hand on each of her shoulders, Pan guided Chen to a seat in the sofa's center.

The table in front of the sofa held what had to be the most beautiful tea set Chen had ever seen. Including the many she had seen in museums.

Pan sat next to her. Shortly, steam and a wonderful aroma rose as Pan went through the tea ceremony's familiar steps.

Minutes later, a fresh cup of tea was warming her hands, and its delicious taste had led her to one conclusion.

Nobody who made tea this good could be all bad.

Chen's involuntary sigh of pleasure brought an even broader smile to Pan's face.

"It's my favorite blend! I'm so glad you enjoy it! Now, first, I must thank both you and Ms. Tang for your contributions to Forward. I have decided that you, in particular, are ready to advance to our leadership ranks," Pan said.

So, that's why his touch didn't raise any alarm, Chen thought. I'd felt that it expressed comfort and affection, not anything sexual. Of course, he knows about Tang she thought, and briefly felt embarrassed.

Then that feeling disappeared as Chen remembered plenty of men who had made unwanted advances despite knowing about Tang. A few times, while Tang had been in the same room.

"There is a great deal I need to tell you in the short time we have. But don't hesitate to stop me if I say anything you don't understand. I'll start with a question. What is the greatest threat to the freedom of the Chinese people?" Pan asked.

Chen was startled by the question. Its answer was the only thing that united all the people she knew fighting against Party tyranny.

"The Communist Party," she said, making no effort to hide from her tone that she thought the question itself was puzzling.

Pan heard it and smiled. "Yes, what could be worse?" he asked softly.

Then Pan paused.

"What about military rule?" he asked quietly.

Chen frowned and shook her head. "Aren't the Party and the military one and the same? As Tiananmen showed, the military will stop at nothing to keep the Party in power."

"That was once true," Pan said with a nod. "But Tiananmen happened decades ago. The military is many times more powerful than it was then. In 1989 their annual budget was under twenty billion American dollars. It is now about three hundred billion."

Chen shrugged. "Guns and tanks are not enough to rule. Yes, tanks rolled over protesters at Tiananmen. But the real reason the Party remained in power was that most people believed they could deliver prosperity and feared democracy would unleash chaos. The military has no legitimacy, and without it cannot control a country with over a billion people."

Pan clapped his hands softly. "Excellent! You are right! But what if the Party appeared to remain in control, while the military was calling the shots behind the scenes?"

Chen cocked her head, trying to follow. "How would that work?" she asked. "And couldn't you stop it simply by alerting the Party to the danger?"

Pan sighed and said, "Both of your questions are good ones, and the answer to both is linked. We don't know enough to answer the first question fully. And until we do, any warning could do more harm than good. We might just alert the military plotters and make them postpone their plans, this time with improved preparations that may be impossible to stop."

"But you know at least some details about the military's plans. Isn't there anything we can do?" Chen said with obvious frustration.

Pan smiled. "We already have, with your help. The stock market investigation will reveal that some who made the greatest profits were certain Generals. They will protest their innocence, and in this case, they will be telling the truth. But once State Security begins a detailed investigation, they may uncover the plot's details independently. At a minimum, they will probably remove everyone suspected from command."

"And at maximum, execute them to be sure they don't pose a threat to Party rule," Chen said.

"Yes. But don't think this means the viper's nest will be fully cleansed. Adding funds to purchase suspect stocks on behalf of Generals with existing accounts on the Exchange was a simple matter. However, several of the Generals we believe are plot leaders don't have stock accounts. They will remain untouched," Pan said.

"So for now, we try to learn more about the military's plans while continuing to fight against Party control," Chen said flatly.

"Just so," Pan said with a smile. "Now, you spoke a moment ago about legitimacy. What has the Party done to earn it?"

Chen frowned. "Well, people like my parents give the Party credit for China's transformation from a poor country of farmers to a far richer country that manufactures more goods than any other."

"Well, don't you?" Pan asked, looking at Chen with a new intensity.

Chen could see her answer was important to Pan, but she had no idea why.

Chen didn't hesitate and said what she believed to be the truth. "China's economic miracle was produced despite the Party, not because of it. For thousands of years, the Chinese people have believed in the importance of family, education, and hard work. For most of human history, China's civilization outpaced progress anywhere else on the planet."

Pan interrupted Chen, who clearly had more to say, with a question.

"But your parents grew up in a China that was poor and agrarian. Why not give the Party credit for progress since then?"

Chen shook her head impatiently. "Some of China's problems were her own doing, especially civil wars and our failure to explore the world outside our borders. When first the British and then the Japanese attacked, we were weak and easy prey. The Japanese were only pushed out of China because the Americans defeated them. Another civil war between the Communists and the Nationalists cost us Taiwan, which is a separate country to this day. And what's more, a country that highlights the Party's failures."

Pan leaned forward. "How so?" he asked quietly.

"Taiwan had little in the way of natural resources or infrastructure when the Nationalists fled there in 1949. Yet today it ranks fifteenth richest in the world with a gross domestic product per capita of over twenty-five thousand American dollars, greater than Portugal's. China's GDP per capita is still under nine thousand dollars, less than Mexico's. I say that's because of the Party's repeated blunders," Chen said hotly.

Pan nodded. "Tell me what you consider the Party's greatest mistakes."

"The so-called 'Great Leap Forward' led to the deaths of as many as fifty-five million Chinese citizens by famine in the late 50s and early 60s, by far the greatest number to die of hunger in human history. Next, the Cultural Revolution killed as many as twenty million through a combination of massacres, individual executions, famine, and dam collapses. The Party's hands are coated with so much blood they can never be washed clean," Chen said, her eyes glittering with fury.

Pan held up both hands. "But wait. Even the Party has admitted responsibility for the failure of sixty-two dams due to Typhoon Nina in 1975, of which the largest was the Banqiao Dam. And that as many as a quarter-million Chinese citizens died due to the dam collapses, and about seven million homes were destroyed in history's greatest manmade disaster. But don't you give the Party any credit for all that has been built since?"

"Like the Three Gorges Dam? Which, when it collapses, will make the floods unleashed by the Banqiao Dam collapse look like a gentle shower?" Chen hissed.

Pan nodded. "So, you were not comforted by the arrest and swift trial of the Xiluodu Dam's manager? Or his subsequent execution? Even though by his actions, he certainly put the Three Gorges Dam at risk?"

Chen shook her head vigorously. "The Party executes people for reasons good and bad as easily as I blow my nose. That's the first thing we have to stop after the Second Revolution."

"The same fate appears to await the two managers arrested for shutting down the Qinshan nuclear power plant. That cut power for a while right here in Shanghai. Do you feel the same way about them?" Pan asked.

Chen looked at Pan incredulously. "You think I'd like to see those men executed just because I was inconvenienced? Anyway, there's another version of what happened at Qinshan circulating via Gateway. Plant workers at Qinshan are saying the men the Army arrested were heroes who prevented another Fukushima disaster."

Pan nodded. "Yes, I saw that too. But for now, at least, most people will believe the Army's claim that they are the ones to be thanked for avoiding catastrophe. Because first, the lights are back on. And second, people mostly believe what they see on their television screen. Where they saw two men the reporter said were guilty being arrested by the Army."

Pan paused. "Very well. You've convinced me the Party isn't fit to rule, and you certainly don't seem eager to be ruled at gunpoint by the military. So, what government would you see in its place?"

Chen looked genuinely startled by the question. "That will be up to the people, after free elections. Everything in our movement's manifesto, as well as Forward's charter, says so."

"Yes. The activists you led before joining Forward all believe in democracy. And so does everyone in Forward, including me. But I'm asking you a more complicated question. A constitution will be drafted. The people will vote. Then, who will be in charge?" Pan asked.

Chen frowned. "I'm not naïve. I know many revolutions that started with high ideals, like the French Revolution in 1789 and the Russian Revolution in 1917, ended in failure. I believe our own Chinese Revolution, which ended with Communist victory in 1949, was an even greater disaster. But the Second Chinese Revolution will be different."

"I'm sure you're right," Pan said, with a smile Chen found very irritating. "First, tell me why you call it the Second Chinese Revolution. After all, there have been many in our history."

"Of course, there have been many," Chen replied. "But if you talk about 'the Revolution' with anyone alive today, they will understand you to mean the Communist takeover in 1949. This will be the next revolution since then. So, I am not the only one to describe what we plan as 'the Second Chinese Revolution.' It's even called that in Forward's charter."

Pan nodded and slowly clapped his hands. "Good. You have not only read our charter but understood one of its most important points. Now, tell me how the Second Revolution will be different than the first."

"Leaders like you and me won't get power just because we helped cause the Second Revolution. People will have to vote to put us in office, and anyone who has different views than ours will be free to stand for election," Chen said.

Pan nodded. "Well, that will make a change. Does 'different views' include Communists?"

"Yes," Chen said immediately. "East Germany's Communists ran for office in free elections after Germany was reunified. They did very poorly. I don't think ours will do any better."

"Let's say you're right. We've talked about the Party and the military. Who else holds power in China today?" Pan asked.

Chen looked slowly and deliberately around Pan's immense, well-furnished office. She let her gaze linger on its museum-quality art and statuary, placed at tasteful intervals within its expanse.

Then Chen looked at Pan and silently raised her right eyebrow.

Pan laughed. "Yes, the rich. The ones who are still here, anyway."

Chen nodded. "I've heard that many have gone to countries like America and Canada. But surely the numbers aren't high enough to matter."

Pan shrugged. "I'm not surprised you think so since the Party works hard to deliver that message. But in reality, over ten thousand American dollar millionaires flee China every year."

Chen stared at Pan in disbelief. "But doesn't the government try to stop them? Or at least, stop them from leaving with all their money?"

"Yes to both," Chen replied calmly. "But being part of the capitalist world means that people like me must have some freedom to travel and the ability to move at least some of their money out of China. And if you give a rich man an inch..."

"Soon, he'll have crossed the Pacific and be laughing at you from Vancouver," Chen finished with a scowl.

"I would have said San Francisco, personally, but yes," Pan agreed with a nod. "So, what place do you see for people like me after the Revolution?"

Chen looked at Pan thoughtfully. "I'll be honest. There was a time when I thought the rich were just as much oppressors as the Party. Then someone subsidized my purchase of a Gateway. You, I'm guessing? And probably the others who got Gateways in our movement?"

Pan nodded silently.

"So, as I said before, I'm no innocent. I know the rich have many reasons to want to be free of Party rule. Maybe even take power themselves, the way they have in most Western countries. But that's for the people to decide for themselves in free elections. I trust them to make the right choice," Chen said confidently.

"So, let the best person win?" Pan asked with a smile.

"Exactly. And until the day comes when we can finally have free elections in China, all of us who hate the Party will work together to bring it down," Chen said.

And thrust her right hand towards Pan, who immediately recognized it as that most American of gestures.

Pan shook Chen's hand gravely and said, "With the help of patriots like you, I am sure that day will come soon."

Once Chen had left, Wang Yan entered through a side door.

Pan smiled. "You heard all that, yes?"

Wang smiled and nodded. "I did. A real idealist. Are you sure we'll be able to get her to do everything you want?"

Pan laughed. "That's what I have you for. You did say you believe you can seduce her?"

Wang shrugged. "I've met no one yet, man or woman, who can refuse me. But there is always a first time. She is in a relationship, after all."

"Yes. But that will just make Chen a more interesting challenge for you. And once you succeed, help to increase our hold over her. After all, Chen wouldn't want this other woman to find out about you, would she?" Pan asked.

Wang shook her head. "Remind me again how we're supposed to be better than the Party."

"Oh, you know better than that. Once we're in charge, we won't be locking people up just for speaking against us. No more forced labor camps. People will be liberated from the thousands of controls on what they can do and say," Pan said.

Wang nodded thoughtfully. "And so will you and your companies. As well as those of your friends."

"Of course. I never pretended otherwise. You shouldn't pretend either. I can tell from how you talk about her that you actually like this woman," Pan said.

"It's true," Wang acknowledged. "But don't worry. I never forget the difference between an assignment and reality."

Pan nodded approvingly. "And that's why you're so valuable to me. I'm willing to share you for a while."

Then he paused and looked at Wang intently.

"But never forget, I do want you back."

Chapter Forty-Five

Near the Chinese-Indian Border

Sergeant Xu had taken familiarization with the Barrett sniper rifle one step at a time. It helped a lot that he'd already read quite a bit about the rifle, as well as watched hours of online video of Americans using it.

Xu thought to himself wryly that he'd have to do something to thank his cousin Deshi the next time he saw him. Yes, he'd been right to be angry that Deshi had risked their whole family by using a Gateway to obtain the information.

But it was indeed coming in handy now.

Step one had been disassembling, cleaning, and then reassembling the rifle. The Barrett had a solid, reassuring feel to it. Everything about it said quality.

Well, it made sense. For a long time, Americans had said that General Motors was inferior in quality to its competitors such as Ford. But GM sold more cars in China than in America.

Why? Because Chinese customers correctly considered its cars superior to those produced by its many Chinese-owned and run competitors.

Even though all GM's factories producing cars sold in China were in country, and all their workers were Chinese.

Xu carefully checked the armory's inventory of Barrett ammunition and then relaxed a fraction. There was enough here for a multi-year deployment.

No sooner had the thought crossed his mind than he did his best to stamp it out. Xu had been told their unit would be at the border for no more than a few months, and as far as he was concerned, that was plenty.

Zeroing the rifle was easy. Its previous owner had all the settings almost exactly right, as far as Xu could tell.

Then he remembered this rifle had been used to kill a Night Tiger commando and shook his head.

Yes. Its accuracy had been proven.

Xu spent the rest of the day firing at targets, with Corporal Guan calling out his results. They improved steadily as Xu became more familiar with the rifle.

Normally Xu would have spent several more days practicing with the Barrett before taking it into combat. But nothing about this situation was normal.

Xu and Guan once again avoided the trail that led to their previous sniper perch. As well as the perch itself. Xu had picked out a different spot, certain their previous one had already been plotted by the Indians.

They also set out even earlier than usual. By the time Xu and Guan arrived at their new perch, the sky was just beginning to lighten. It would be a while before there was enough light to attempt a shot.

Trying to hit an enemy sniper at this range with night optics was out of the question.

And this was exactly how Xu framed the challenge in his mind. His target was enemy snipers, not their spotters.

Xu's training had emphasized that spotters were just as much legitimate targets as the snipers they assisted. Any time the topic came up, he'd pretended to agree.

On one level, Xu understood the point. A sniper with a spotter to help him identify both targets and threats was far more effective.

But even if the spotter was armed, in practice, he was no threat. His job was to look, not fire. As far as Xu was concerned, that meant he wasn't a legitimate target.

Xu had made sure Guan understood that from everything he had seen and heard, their Indian opponents had no such scruples.

Before picking this spot for today's patrol, Xu had given plenty of thought to its location. If he were replacing a sniper team that had been ambushed and wiped out by commandos, how would he react?

Would he seek a safer but probably less effective location? Or would he move forward, eager for revenge?

Xu went back and forth until he finally realized he had no way to know. So, he used two factors to guide his choice. First, topography and the Barrett's range limited available spots to just a handful.

Second, Xu thought that only a fool would try to reuse the sniper base that the Night Tigers had wiped out. The Indians were many things, but they weren't idiots.

Soon, Xu thought, we'll see whether my guess pays off. The sky was getting lighter by the minute.

Guan had become much quieter after his hospital stay, Xu thought. Well, nothing like a brush with death to make you realize just how serious their situation was here at the border.

Almost as though the thought had provoked him to speak, Xu heard Guan's low voice.

"Movement, twenty degrees right," Guan said.

Xu shifted his scope and, at first, saw nothing. But Xu didn't doubt Guan's abilities. If he said he'd seen movement, it was there.

Xu just had to be patient.

The minutes crawled by. But Xu still had faith in Guan. Wait, wait...

There!

A rifle barrel. At this range, Xu couldn't be sure, but he thought it was another Barrett.

Xu quickly calculated where the enemy sniper had to be and fired. He didn't have to tell Guan anything.

Time to go.

Xu had too much respect for the Barrett's capabilities to try to see whether his round had found its mark. But there was no answering round.

When they were both sure they were out of view of the Indian side of the border, Guan startled Xu by patting him on the shoulder.

"You got him!" Guan said with a grin.

Xu nodded back and smiled but said nothing. Partly because he was out of breath from their crouched run to safety.

Partly because he knew the sniper he'd just shot had been a person, too. The first one he'd ever killed.

And Xu knew better than to kid himself that maybe he'd just wounded his Indian opponent. The Barrett's .50 caliber round was large enough and traveling at such a high speed that it could punch through light armor. Anywhere it hit a person would be nearly sure to cause enough shock and blood loss to kill him.

Winded as they both were, it took them a while to make it back to base. Still, it was quite a shock that there had apparently been enough time to organize a reception when Xu and Guan arrived.

Captain Yin greeted them as they walked in and escorted them to the mess tent. As soon as Xu saw him, he remembered hearing that Colonel

Chang had been ordered to Beijing for consultations and was expected back tomorrow.

Xu hadn't thought about it before, but now he realized that had left Yin in command. What was he up to?

Xu hadn't had much to do with Yin, but what little he knew he didn't like. He came across as a Party lackey with little interest in the men he commanded, who cared only about his career.

Fortunately, Yin could do little damage as long as Chang was around. Was that about to change?

A white cloth had been rigged up against one interior side of the mess tent, and now a digital projector whirred to life. It looked like almost everyone in the camp had been packed into the tent for the show.

What were they going to see? Besides calling for silence and attention, Yin hadn't said anything.

It took a moment for Xu to recognize the scene that appeared. He had just seen a much smaller view of it through his scope.

A drone! Yin must have ordered one to observe the area.

That would have been nice to know, Xu thought acidly. Even nicer to have had whatever the drone operator saw relayed to them.

Now the view zoomed in to the figures of an Indian sniper and his nearby spotter. They were both cautiously moving.

Yeah. It would have been really nice, Xu thought.

He'd barely completed the thought when Xu saw the sniper thrown backward into the tall grass behind him. The spotter crawled towards him.

And then crawled away without doing anything. As Xu had guessed, a hit from a Barrett round was very unlikely to be survivable.

Up to now, everyone in the tent had been silently staring at the screen with rapt attention.

Now, though, Yin began to clap loudly. Then he stood between Xu and Guan and shouted, "Congratulations to our newest heroes!"

Everyone in the tent stood and joined in the clapping, along with yelled congratulations.

Xu's feelings were mixed. On the one hand, many of the men crowding around him were friends who knew the Indians had put Xu and Guan in the hospital and come close to killing them both. Xu had no problem accepting their praise as sincere.

Yin was another matter. What he was doing couldn't have been more obvious. He was trying to make their success his own.

For a moment, Xu wondered if he was being too hard on Yin. After all, maybe he was just trying to raise camp morale the way Chang had by giving them the Barretts.

Xu immediately saw the difference. There had been a military purpose to giving them the captured rifles. And Chang hadn't staged a spectacle to do it.

No, this felt uncomfortably close to dancing on the enemy's grave while his body was still warm. The thought sent a wave of nausea washing over Xu.

After all, probably no more than a second or so of reaction time had prevented that still figure in the grass from being him or Guan.

Xu had to get out of here.

"Sir, I need to secure my weapon," Xu told Yin. Yin had dragged them into the tent before either he or Guan had been able to put anything away.

Yin nodded absently, busy with accepting congratulations from soldiers looking to curry favor with the base's second in command. Xu was relieved to see none were friends of his.

Guan was surrounded by his friends and didn't seem in any hurry to leave. Xu didn't blame him.

After all, he hadn't killed anyone today.

Xu shook his head as he hurried to the armory. He had to snap out of it. Killing that Indian sniper was his job.

And if he hadn't, Xu had no doubt the Indian sniper would have taken the first available shot. Particularly after the Night Tiger attack.

"Hey, Sergeant! Great shot! Way to go, sir!"

The words from the armory guard brought Xu out of his thoughts. "Thank you, Private. I need to secure my weapon."

"Of course, sir," the guard said, hastily unlocking and opening the door to the bunker. The only solid concrete structure in the entire forward base, it always made Xu feel claustrophobic. Even more than other bunkers Xu had entered, it was precisely as large as it needed to be. And not one square meter more.

Xu knew the guard hadn't been able to leave his post for the show and almost asked him how he could have possibly learned about what had happened.

Then he smiled to himself. As well, ask how the sun could shine. Soldiers always heard the news that mattered, one way or another.

Xu had just finished cleaning the Barrett and putting it back in its case when the floor suddenly rocked.

An earthquake?

The guard always left the armory door opened a crack when someone was inside. Partly because Xu wasn't the only one who had complained about feeling claustrophobic. But more because the door automatically locked when it was closed, and that meant the guard would have to go to the trouble of unlocking it again to let him out.

Now though the door slammed shut with a loud bang, as if it had been closed by a giant hand.

Next, the floor didn't just rock. It seemed to rush up to meet his face.

And then Xu saw nothing more.

301 Military Hospital
Beijing, China

Sergeant Xu blinked and tried to focus. Where was he?

What had happened?

Xu heard a voice to one side say, "Colonel, I've administered this stimulant against my better judgment. Keep this brief."

Colonel. Which Colonel, Xu wondered.

Colonel Chang! As his face came into view, Xu felt a wave of relief. Chang, at least, knew what he was doing.

But this wasn't the camp medical unit. What was going on here?

Before he had a chance to frame the question, Chang answered it for him.

"Sergeant, you're at the 301 Military Hospital in Beijing. You've already undergone surgery. The doctors tell me you're expected to make a complete recovery, but will be here at least another week, probably longer. At least, you can be sure you're getting the very best care available," Chang said.

Xu knew Chang wasn't exaggerating about the quality of care. 301 Hospital was famous as one of China's best hospitals, where both soldiers and many in the Party elite received care. A massive four thousand-bed facility, it was also a teaching hospital that turned out many of China's best doctors.

"Sir, what happened? Was anyone else hurt?" Xu asked.

Xu wasn't sure how to interpret the expression that passed quickly over Chang's face. Anger? Sadness? Shame?

Some combination of the three?

"The Indians attacked our base with drones firing from their side of the border. The drones had been patrolling there for weeks and done nothing but watch. There was no warning," Chang said and then took a deep breath.

"You and I are the only survivors from the men assigned to the base. You, because you were inside the armory. Me, because I was absent, having been ordered to report to headquarters here in Beijing," Chang said.

"That means Guan is dead," Xu said, almost to himself.

"Yes, I'm afraid so, Sergeant," Chang replied quietly.

"It's because I killed their sniper, sir," Xu said. This was all my fault, he thought.

Chang shook his head at once. "No. The drone attack came too soon after that. It must have been approved at the highest level of the Indian government, probably by their President. No, I'm afraid this was the Indian response to the Night Tiger assault. This is my responsibility, not yours."

Before Xu could respond, Chang said briskly, "And speaking of Presidents, there's one who wants to speak with you. I think I've kept him waiting long enough."

Then Chang surprised him by smiling. "Get some rest, Sergeant. You'll need it. There will be plenty of work for us to do, and soon."

Chang walked away, and Xu could see him nodding to someone in the hallway out of his view.

Xu hadn't even had time to wonder what Chang had meant by his "Presidents" comment when President Lin Wang Yong walked in.

Xu's first shocked thought was that Lin looked smaller than he seemed on TV.

His next, instinctive, response was to try to stand.

Lin appeared to have been expecting that because he smiled and grabbed Xu by his shoulders, pressing him gently back into bed.

"Take it easy, Sergeant. That's an order from your commander in chief, so I expect you to obey it," Lin said with an easy humor that made Xu think, yes.

Here is a politician.

Aloud, Xu said, "Thank you, Mr. President. I very much appreciate your taking the time to see me."

Lin shook his head. "The honor is mine, Sergeant. I am about to recognize your courage in facing Indian mines and snipers and your skill in using an Indian weapon against its former owners. Before I call in the cameras, is there anything you would like to ask me?"

Here was an opportunity Xu had never dreamed could be possible. Dozens of questions immediately crowded his head, especially the most obvious. Was there any real point to pressing the Indians at an arid, rocky, frigid, and high-altitude border?

Xu's survival instincts prevented any of those questions from passing his lips.

Instead, he quietly said, "Sir, I know the Army will take care of the families of the men who died at my base. But I would rest easier if I knew you were personally involved in that effort."

Lin looked at Xu as though he were seeing him for the first time. Xu could see the quick calculations being made and the result he expected.

The cost of generosity to the families of the men killed at the Indian border would be trivial, particularly since nearly all were unmarried, with at most one or two parents to support.

But a promise to see to the families' welfare would be very popular. And help rally the country for a conflict with India.

Lin smiled. "What you are asking couldn't be easier, Sergeant, because I had already planned to see to those families. But thank you for mentioning it because I will now take this opportunity to guarantee their welfare to the nation."

Xu had to admit he was impressed. No wonder Lin had made it to the Presidency.

But what was Lin going to do with that power? Did war with India make any sense at all?

Before Xu had a chance to think any further, his room was suddenly flooded with men holding lights and cameras of all shapes and sizes. He blinked in the sudden glare.

A sharp voice from a man Xu couldn't see said something, and some of the lights cut off, so at least he could see.

Now Lin was standing right next to him, holding a medal, and saying words Xu didn't follow about his bravery and heroism.

Xu was thinking, don't forget dumb luck. If I hadn't been inside that bunker at precisely the right moment, there'd be nobody in this bed to receive a medal.

Suddenly Lin had stopped talking, and everyone was looking at him. Xu said what he knew everyone was expecting.

"Thank you, Mr. President."

Lin patted Xu's shoulder and then said more words about how he would personally see to the families of the men killed at the base on the Indian border.

Then the lights all went out, and everyone disappeared as quickly as they had arrived.

Xu turned his head and saw the two medals in their cases on the small table next to his bed.

The first was the one he'd expected. The Medal of Loyalty and Integrity was for soldiers wounded in combat. Now that he was on his second hospital stay, Xu thought he'd earned that one.

The second one was a surprise, though. The Medal of Army Brilliance was for victory in combat. Did a single kill really qualify?

After a moment's thought, Xu realized that the medal wasn't actually for him. It was for a leadership looking for any victory to celebrate after his base's destruction.

As Xu drifted off to sleep, one thought kept circling around and around in his head.

Didn't the Indians have nuclear weapons?

Chapter Forty-Six

Shanghai, China

Chen Li Na had, against her better judgment, agreed to meet Wang Yan again at her apartment. Again, the reason given was to deliver a USB drive containing the information she would need to craft entry to a new target.

Chen had no idea what that target would be, nor did she care. Her main worry was how to get Wang out of her apartment as quickly as possible. Especially since her girlfriend Tan happened to be out of town at a business conference.

I love Tan, Chen told herself fiercely. I'm going to take the USB drive from Wang and then show her the door.

A soft knock announced that Wang was right on time. Swallowing hard, Chen walked to the door and opened it.

Wang looked just as she had last time. If anything, her clothes might have been a little plainer.

It didn't matter. Chen briefly froze as she fought to keep her reaction to Wang off her face.

Wang said nothing. But her smile told Chen that Wang knew exactly what was passing through her mind.

With an effort of will, Chen gestured brusquely for Wang to enter.

And flushed with embarrassment. Wang had done nothing to merit such rudeness.

Chen turned away and rushed to her tiny kitchen, saying, "Please have a seat. I will make us tea."

Make us tea? What happened to taking the USB drive and shoving her out the door, Chen asked herself.

Well, I had to make up for my earlier rudeness, Chen told her interior voice.

Sure you did, came the mocking answer.

Trying to silence her inner turmoil, Chen busied herself with the familiar routine of making tea. Far too soon, it was ready, and Chen walked the few steps towards her sofa and small table.

Wang was lounging comfortably on the sofa as though she was perfectly at home there. She smiled and said, "I appreciate your going to so much trouble. It's very kind of you."

Words from a guest that were nearly as much a part of the tea ceremony as the tea itself. From anyone else, Chen would have barely heard them.

So why did these routine pleasantries make Chen's smile so wide?

Chen nodded quickly and said, "You're welcome. Please, drink your tea while it's still hot."

And so I can get you out the door, which I should have done already.

And where is that USB drive, anyway?

Wang answered that question before Chen had the chance to ask it.

"I especially appreciate the break because you and I are going to be working together for hours. I'm the only one Director Pan trusts to do so. We must complete our work today because the access codes are changed daily," Wang said.

Then, she took a delicate sip of tea and sighed with pleasure. "It is good to know that in this way, too, your skills are admirable," Wang said with a smile.

The tea was nothing special, and Chen's mother had berated her many times for rushing its preparation. And one voice in Chen's head told her so.

That didn't stop a warm feeling of gratitude from sweeping over Chen.

Stop it, she scolded herself. Think about all the questions Wang has just raised.

Chen asked one first because it was the most important.

"Very few access codes are changed daily, so this must be a high priority target. What is it?"

Wang nodded gravely. "You're right. It's one that we know will get the attention of the Party. We're going to cut power to the entire Beijing district that includes the Zhongnanhai Compound."

Chen spluttered and nearly dropped her teacup. "Where the President and many other top officials live and work? Nothing could shock and embarrass the Party more!"

Wang smiled gently. "Yes, of course. You know that such a bold step will help us move closer to our goal. Did you think we would take longer to achieve it?"

So many questions crowded Chen's head, she hardly knew which to ask first.

To her horror, the one she heard herself asking next was, "You said Director Pan trusts only you to work with me. Is that because you're his lover?"

Wang's musical laughter was magic to listen to, and oddly Chen was sure it was genuine.

Then Wang shook her head and leaned towards Chen as she whispered, "No. I only like women."

Chen trembled, and only one thing kept her steady.

Wang had said the work had to be done today.

"You have the USB drive with the information?" Chen asked.

Wang nodded, and now her accompanying smile was different.

Chen didn't know why, but she felt as though she'd just passed some kind of test.

"Let me clean these things away, and we'll get to work," Chen said as she busied herself moving the remains of the tea service to the kitchen.

By the time Chen returned with her laptop, Wang had her own laptop set up. Wang then handed Chen the USB drive with the access codes.

"Entry to the system with the access codes will be fairly straightforward. I will take care of that part. The real challenge will be to keep them from restarting power, and you will need these codes again for that part. Just as important will be to ensure no attempt to trace the origin of the attack is successful. Of course, we expect you to launch this attack via a SpaceLink satellite, as we did for our last two. If possible, though, we would like to conceal that fact this time," Wang said.

"Why?" Chen asked, frankly puzzled. "I thought we wanted the Party to know that it was Forward attacking them. Don't we plan to claim credit if we're successful?"

Wang shrugged. "Director Pan didn't tell me the reasons for this instruction or whether Forward will claim this attack. Maybe he thinks it's good to keep the Party guessing? I didn't think about it much because no matter how hard you try, if we succeed, I'm sure the Party will know it was Forward."

Well, Chen thought, she was probably right about that.

"Very well," Chen replied. "We'd better get started."

Wang finished first. Chen was so deeply engrossed in her work that she hardly noticed.

At the same moment Chen finished, she smelled something oddly familiar but couldn't place it.

Wang put the teacup she had just filled in front of Chen with a smile and said, "It won't be as good as yours, but at least it's hot."

Chen's eyebrows rose as she drank thirstily. She wasn't sure how long she'd been working but knew it must have been hours.

"Did you add osmanthus?" Chen asked.

Wang nodded. "Yes, I found some in your cupboard. I hope that's all right. I haven't had it myself since I was a child, so I couldn't resist."

Chen smiled. "I keep it on hand for whenever my mother comes to visit. It's her favorite. It's funny. I hadn't made it for myself since I was a child, either. Maybe the peach-like flavor was too strong a reminder of a happier time."

Then Chen shook herself and said, "Speaking of time, we're running out of it. To get the maximum effect, we need to cut power while everyone is still at work. You look over my code while I check yours."

Wang simply nodded and passed her laptop to Chen and then slid Chen's to her side of the table.

It didn't take long before Wang was shaking her head with frank admiration. "So clean and simple! I'm just barely good enough to appreciate how much better you are. They'll be chasing their tails for quite a while trying to figure out what you've done."

Chen had been praised for her work many times before. Including, she realized with a guilty start, by her girlfriend Tang Yanfei. Tang also coded software but had nothing like Chen's skills.

So why did Wang's praise make Chen feel so much better?

"I like the work you've done, too," Chen said, meaning every word. Tapping the screen of Wang's laptop, she said, "I don't need to fix anything. What you've written should get us into one of China's best-guarded networks. I work with some of the country's best programmers, and I don't think I've ever seen completely error-free code before. And that's from software engineers who had days, not hours, to do their work."

Wang's answering smile was warm and genuine. "Coming from someone with your skills, that's high praise indeed. Now, your phone is connected to your old government monitored Wi-Fi network, right?"

Chen nodded, puzzled. Why would they need it?

Wang saw her confusion and laughed. "No, of course, we're not using that to launch the attack. I want you to access the President's public website. That's something, at least, that nobody watching online will find suspicious."

Chen shrugged, still confused. She almost asked Wang why but then realized she'd probably find out soon enough.

"I would have told you to turn on your TV, but I already saw you don't have one," Wang said.

Chen shrugged. It was true. Nothing shown on China's heavily censored broadcast TV had ever held any interest for her. That was doubly true now that she had access to the entire Internet through her Gateway, not just the fraction that made it through the Great Firewall.

Moments later, Chen's phone was displaying the Presidential website. She set the phone on the table sideways between the two laptops. Her case's built-in kickstand held up the screen, but so far, Chen saw nothing of interest.

"I don't understand. Why are we waiting? Shouldn't we execute the attack now?" Chen asked.

Wang shook her head. "Not yet," she said, holding up her phone. "Director Pan will let us know soon."

It didn't take long. A few minutes later, the screen on Chen's phone was refreshed, and the National Emblem appeared. It contained in a red circle an image of Tiananmen Gate, the entrance to the Forbidden City. Above the gate were the five stars found on the national flag.

Tinny patriotic music began to play from the phone's small speaker.

"The President will soon speak about the situation on our border with India," Wang said.

Chen frowned. "Really? I've heard nothing about it."

Wang just smiled.

"Of course," Chen sighed. "I'm sure Forward's leaders know about many things the rest of us don't. But..."

Before Chen could say more, the emblem disappeared and was replaced by President Lin's stern expression.

"Get ready," Wang said quietly.

Chen nodded and moved her hand over her laptop's keyboard.

Ready? All she had to do was hit one key.

President Lin began to speak.

"My fellow countrymen, I come to you tonight with grave news," Lin said.

Wang's phone vibrated to announce the arrival of a text.

"Now," Wang said.

Chen hit the key to execute the hack.

Seconds later, the phone's screen went dark.

It only took a few more seconds but seemed much longer before the National Emblem reappeared on the screen.

A voice said that there were technical problems that would soon be fixed.

Wang and Chen sat silently, staring at the National Emblem on the screen, as one minute became two.

And then three.

Finally, Chen heard Wang say in a soft, wondering voice, "You actually did it."

Chen turned to Wang and was surprised to see tears spilling from Wang's eyes.

"Why are you crying?" Chen asked as she gently brushed the tears away from Wang's face.

"I'm so happy," Wang said. "A part of me never really thought we could win. But that was before I met you."

Chen had left her hand on Wang's face while she spoke. Now Wang's lips moved to that hand, and she kissed it softly.

Chen felt as though an electric shock had just passed through not just the hand but her entire body.

"Thank you," Wang whispered.

Chen's other hand seemed to move by itself to the other side of Wang's face and pulled it towards hers.

Hours later, Chen woke up and saw Wang's sleeping form beside her.

What happened?

You know very well what happened, a fierce voice inside her said.

The sofa they had been sitting on had been pulled out into a bed. The table that had been in front of it had been shoved to the side. Laptops and phones were stacked on it haphazardly.

What time is it?

Chen's blood froze as she realized she had no idea whether the government had made any progress in finding out who had attacked it.

Well, nobody was pounding on the door.

The same fierce voice said that doesn't mean they won't be here in the next few minutes.

Chen's laptop was still powered and connected to the Gateway router. She shook her head.

I didn't even take the time to turn it off.

Now, though, that was a good thing. It took her only a few minutes to confirm that there had been no successful backtrace.

And five hours had passed since Chen had launched their attack. If the authorities hadn't succeeded in finding her by now, they never would.

Chen shut off the laptop.

Then she noticed Wang's phone was still on, too.

The text on the screen said, "Well done. Stand by for further instructions."

The time stamped on the text was over an hour after the attack had started.

Had it taken them that long to regain control of power at the Zhongnanhai Compound?

Did the President ever complete his address?

Why weren't there more texts after Wang failed to acknowledge this one?

Chen jumped as the string of questions flowing through her head was interrupted by Wang's arms encircling her from behind.

"Good morning," Wang said quietly.

Chen's blinds were closed, and it was too early for any light to penetrate them.

Still, Wang was right. Technically, it was morning.

Wang's arms were warm and comfortable. Why not just sit like this for a while?

Chen sighed and started to lean back.

Then she shook herself. No. What was she doing?

Chen turned and started to speak.

Wang's hair was tousled, and her makeup was smeared. Chen could still see traces of the tears Wang had cried hours ago.

None of it mattered. Wang was still beautiful.

Oh, no.

Not this fast.

Wang smiled and put one finger on Chen's lips.

"Breakfast first, talk later," Wang said.

Then Wang rose, dressed, and began cooking breakfast as though she had been living with Chen for years.

Chen shrugged, and began to tidy her living area. Sheets removed, sofa folded, table in front. Laptops and phones neatly side by side.

Then Chen went to her single bathroom. After a quick shower and change, she felt as though she were emerging from a fog.

Does Wang actually have any feelings for me, anyway? Maybe this was just how she reacts to a big success, Chen thought.

Wang was waiting as Chen emerged from the bathroom.

"My turn," Wang said and slipped inside.

Chen had barely had time to admire Wang's performance in the kitchen when she was back. The food she'd cooked smelled amazing. And she'd just used what Chen happened to have on hand.

Wang's appearance when she stepped to Chen's side was now perfect. But her makeup was just slightly different.

Because Wang hadn't taken her purse into the bathroom. She used my makeup.

Not even Tang did that, Chen thought.

And then immediately felt guilty.

Yet at the same time, pleased. Was this Wang's way of saying there should be no boundaries between them?

Stop grasping at straws, the fierce voice in her head said. You'll find out what she wants soon enough.

"Let's eat," Wang said.

Chen nodded and sat at her tiny kitchen table. Wang had filled it with so much food Chen had to be careful as she lifted her teacup.

Again, made with osmanthus. Just as before, it made Chen think of her mother.

And what would her mother think of all this?

Chen resolutely pushed that thought out of her mind and began eating.

Wang's food tasted even better than it looked and smelled. Very quickly, it was gone.

Chen flushed as she looked up at Wang. She had been eating like a villager just returned hungry from the fields. Without a word of thanks to the cook.

Wang smiled and put her right hand on Chen's. "I'm glad you liked it," she said.

Chen trembled at Wang's touch and then heard herself saying, "We need to talk," and gestured towards the sofa.

Wang nodded, and shortly they were back where they had been the previous evening.

Which felt like about a decade ago, Chen thought.

Wang spoke first. "Look, I know you have a girlfriend. If you don't want to see me again, I understand. But I know myself. I'm not going to spend time with someone unless I have real feelings for them. And I don't have a girlfriend and haven't for more than two years. I'd stopped looking and have spent all my time and energy on Forward. If you don't want me, I'll go back to that and ask Director Pan to have someone else work with you. I'm nothing special as a coder and can be easily replaced."

"No, you can't," Chen heard herself saying.

Then her arms were around Wang again.

I guess I've made my decision, Chen thought.

And then Chen stopped thinking about anything but Wang, and how she was happier than she'd ever been.

Chapter Forty-Seven

South Sea Fleet Headquarters
Zhanjiang, China

Admiral Bai was already in a foul mood when his staff car pulled up at his headquarters' entrance. His favorite perk of being an Admiral was that he kept regular hours. That meant for the first time in decades of Navy service, he was home for dinner and got a full night's sleep.

Bai had started to get used to it.

But now Bai was here while the sun was still struggling to get over the horizon. And if the news was as bad as initial reports made it sound, it was going to be a long time before things went back to normal.

Bai's executive officer, Senior Captain Ding, was at the headquarters door waiting for him.

Ding's wooden expression said no good news was waiting inside.

Ding was Bai's third XO after officers at both lower and higher ranks had proved unsatisfactory. So far, Bai thought he'd finally found an officer who knew what he was doing.

Ding had served his last tour as a submarine captain. He was waiting to assume command of a new Type 095 submarine, but unluckily for him, its completion had been delayed.

"Do we have a damage report from Ziyou Island yet?" Bai growled.

Ding nearly had to run to keep up with Bai's urgent stride towards his office.

"Yes, sir. Two helicopters from a Type 075 carrier we have on station in the area were sent as soon as radio communication with the base was cut off," Ding replied, at the same time as he opened the door to the Admiral's office suite and stood aside for Bai's entry.

Bai glanced at his desk as he walked towards it and saw the expected folder.

"Their report?" Bai asked.

"Yes, sir," Ding replied and then stood quietly as Bai read the report.

It didn't take long.

"No survivors?" Bai said, shaking his head. "What sort of attack could do that?"

"Sir, as you'd ordered, a Xi'an KJ-600 was on station in the area. It reports that no flights by aircraft capable of launching an attack passed anywhere near Ziyou Island last night," Ding replied.

Bai grunted. The Xi'an KJ-600's resemblance to the American Hawkeye early warning aircraft was no coincidence. Obtaining classified details on the Grumman E-2 Hawkeye to allow production of a Chinese version was one of the most critical successes to date for Chinese Naval Intelligence.

But the KJ-600 was a brand new aircraft. Had its crew missed something?

"No aircraft capable of launching an attack, you say. So, what was detected?" Bai asked.

"An Australian MQ-4C Triton naval surveillance drone was reported passing within fifty kilometers at seventeen thousand meters altitude on what appeared to be a routine patrol. A Japanese AWACS was reported at the edge of airspace claimed by Japan closest to our waters. Again, on what looked like a routine patrol."

Bai frowned. It was true that neither the Triton nor the AWACS had an offensive capability.

"Let's say there was no attack from the air. We'd have spotted a surface ship. That leaves an attack from a submarine. Only the Americans have both the ability and the will to launch such an attack." Bai said.

Ding nodded but said nothing. Bai was right. An attack from an American submarine was the only explanation that made sense.

"I also ordered a submarine to patrol near that base. Do we have any report from them?" Bai asked.

Ding shook his head. "No, sir. The *Changzheng 20* was assigned to the patrol you ordered, but we've heard nothing from them yet."

"A Type 095 submarine, like the one you're going to command, right? And the best we've got. Well, that's good news anyway. Let's get some use out of that new communications facility we built at such expense. Order that submarine to search for a potential attacker, and report its findings."

Ding said, "Yes, sir," and was careful to keep his expression neutral.

But not quite careful enough.

"OK, Ding, out with it. Why don't you think we should do what I just ordered?" Bai asked.

"First, sir, I recognize we will be asked why we did not use the Project WEM facility if we don't contact the *Changzheng 20*. But I know her captain. If the base were struck by a submarine, Captain Wen would have detected the attack and already be in pursuit. If I'm right about that, then contacting the *Changzheng 20* will interrupt its pursuit and likely alert the enemy," Ding replied.

"None of that sounds good. But you're going to have to explain further, Captain. Are you telling me that all the money we spent on Project WEM was wasted?" Bai asked.

The Wireless Electromagnetic Method (WEM) Project had taken over a decade to build before completion in 2018. Its Extremely Low Frequency (ELF) antenna array covered an area of central China greater than New York City. Officially its purpose was to map underground mineral resources and provide early warning of earthquakes. Which were both scientifically valid explanations.

And had nothing to do with the money spent on it. Its real purpose was communicating with submarines since ELF radio waves could penetrate seawater.

The Russians and Americans had both built ELF facilities during the Cold War, and India had built one in 2014. The Americans, though, had abandoned ELF technology in favor of Very Low Frequency (VLF) in 2004.

China had considered copying the American approach but decided on ELF because it preferred a single central facility. To make VLF communication with submarines practical, the Americans had to build a network of ground transmission facilities and deploy a fleet of sixteen E-6B Mercury strategic communications aircraft.

Ding's entire career had been in submarines, and he knew all this. He also knew Admiral Bai, who had spent his career commanding surface vessels, did not.

This would not be the best time to tell him so.

"Sir, Project WEM gives us the ability to notify a submarine anywhere in the world that headquarters has new orders for it to execute. That is a precious capability. However, its ELF technology only allows limited communication. In practice, we can only use it to order them to approach the surface to receive new orders through its regular communications antenna," Ding said.

Bai nodded slowly. "So, if they are already pursuing an enemy submarine, that would make them vulnerable."

Ding relaxed a fraction. Bai might not be a submariner, but he wasn't stupid.

His hopes were dashed almost immediately.

"But you're assuming this Captain Wen heard the attack. We don't know what new technology an American submarine might be using. Maybe he didn't hear anything," Bai said.

As he could see Ding getting ready to object, Bai held up his hand.

"And let's suppose he did. How would Captain Wen know about the results of the American attack? And if he didn't know, what would his orders say he should do? Would they allow him to attack the American submarine?" Bai asked.

That made Ding stop and think. Finally, he nodded reluctantly.

"You are right, sir. Captain Wen will have no way to know our base was destroyed unless we tell him. Unless the Americans fire on him, his orders will not allow him to do more than pursue them until they have left our waters."

Bai smiled. "Good, then we agree. And don't think I'm ignoring the risk to our first deployed Type 095 submarine. Find out which attack submarines we have closest to the *Changzheng 20* and send them an ELF message as well. Order them to assist in finding and destroying the American submarine that carried out the attack."

Ding saluted and hurried off to carry out his orders.

Then he was struck by a new thought. The damage assessment report had said there was no evidence of what had caused the base's destruction.

How was that possible?

Ding mentally added one more order to the list. Having whoever had been in charge of the damage assessment team report to him in person as quickly as possible.

If they were going to war with the Americans, Ding wanted to know everything he could about how it had started.

Chapter Forty-Eight

USS *Oregon*
Under the South China Sea

Captain Jim Cartwright had sailed on many missions with Lieutenant Commander Fischer and thought he'd seen every expression that could be on his face.

But not this one. Fischer's face showed nothing at all.

In fact, Cartwright thought with a frown, Fischer looked close to shock.

"What's wrong, Fischer?" Cartwright asked in a voice he hoped was too quiet for anyone else on the bridge to hear.

"Captain, we have the report on our attack from that JSDF AWACS," Fischer replied and handed a printout to Cartwright.

Cartwright didn't need long to read it. He understood immediately why Fischer looked so upset.

Cartwright had the same reaction but firmly pushed the feeling away. Time for regrets later.

First, he needed to understand what had happened.

"There's not much solid detail in this report. To get it, the JSDF says we're going to need to request follow up from the Australians. Do you have that request drafted via PACOM?" Cartwright asked.

"Yes, sir. I have it right here," Fischer replied.

The unified combatant command for all US forces in the Indo-Pacific region was officially renamed USINDOPACOM in 2018 to recognize South Asia's growing importance. That included annual naval exercises with India and Japan that were sometimes expanded to include Australia and other countries, to China's vocal annoyance.

But in the privacy of a submarine deployed thousands of miles from USINDOPACOM headquarters in Hawaii, "PACOM" was still good enough.

"Good," Cartwright said, barely glancing at the message before scrawling his approval. Fischer knew his business, and this needed to go out fast.

"The JSDF thinks just about all the damage done outside the runway was caused by secondary explosions. In short, that the Chinese left enough fuel and explosives improperly stored to let our weapon detonate the lot. Does that make sense to you?" Cartwright asked.

To Cartwright's relief, Fischer's shocked expression slowly became more thoughtful.

"That's a good question, sir. The Chinese military has become more competent and professional over the last decade or so, not less. There has to be a reason..." Fischer's voice trailed off, and his eyes lost focus for a moment as he thought.

Then Fischer's head snapped back up, and he said disbelievingly, "Sir, could they have been ordered to get the base ready for operations by a fixed date, no matter what? I can't imagine what else could account for what the JSDF is saying happened."

Cartwright nodded slowly. "I think that's a good guess. Include it in our request for further analysis of the Australian data."

"Yes, sir. One other matter. We still don't have a confirmed sonar return on any other submarines out here. But sonar does report intermittent noise that doesn't fit any known acoustic profile. Sonar also doesn't consider the noise significant enough to indicate a submarine and says it's not consistent enough to generate a bearing," Fischer said.

Cartwright nodded. "But you still think it's worth telling me about it."

"Yes, sir. Whatever the noise is, it's moving closer," Fischer said.

"Battle stations," Cartwright said immediately and smiled at Fischer's startled reaction.

"I know other things could account for the noise, and the sound's movement towards us could be a coincidence. But if I were a Chinese submarine captain, I know what I'd do when I heard us fire a Tomahawk. Move towards us on battery, and wait for our reaction. Designate the noise as *Sierra One*," Cartwright said.

"Yes, sir," Fischer replied and pulled the yellow oval handle that set off the general alarm, a series of fourteen gongs. At the same time, he said into his microphone, "Man battle stations torpedo."

Cartwright nodded to himself. If his guess was right and a Chinese submarine was approaching, they should know now that the *Oregon* had noticed.

That left two questions.

Did the Chinese submarine captain know that the island base they had been protecting was now a smoking ruin?

And if so, did his orders allow an immediate attack on the *Oregon*?

Changzheng 20
Under the South China Sea

Captain Wen looked up at Commander Duan's approach. Duan didn't look happy.

"Sir, we have received an ELF message from headquarters to establish contact to receive new orders," Duan said.

Wen knew better than to ask if the ELF message contained any further details. Due to the limitations of the technology, he knew an ELF message would never say more than "establish contact to receive new orders."

But he could see Duan had something else to say.

"Something else, Commander?" Wen asked gently.

"Yes, sir," Duan said glumly. "Sonar reports an increase in noise from within the target submarine consistent with their assuming battle stations. But our fix on the American's position is not yet close enough to fire on them with confidence of a hit."

Wen nodded thoughtfully. Well, he could see why Duan was unhappy. If they obeyed orders and headed towards the surface, they would lose what little tactical advantage they possessed.

"So, Duan, do you think the Americans know for sure we are here?" Wen asked.

Duan immediately shook his head. "No, sir. We have been quiet enough on battery that I see no way they could have a torpedo lock or anything close to it. No, I think their sonar has heard something, and their Captain is making an educated guess."

"Yes," Wen said. "He knew firing that Tomahawk would draw the attention of any submarine nearby and that our new base would have a submarine nearby on patrol."

"So, Captain, do we obey orders and turn the American's guess into certainty?" Duan asked.

Wen frowned. "Commander, I have already made my decision. But tell me, if you were in my chair, what would you do?"

Duan was silent for a moment. Good, Wen thought approvingly. The decision merited some thought.

Finally, Duan made a face that reminded Wen of the last time he'd tasted spoiled fish.

"Sir, we have no choice. Not only must we obey this ELF notice from headquarters, but they might also be sending us orders to attack the Americans. If we don't receive such orders, we can only pursue the enemy submarine until it leaves our waters. Unless it decides to fire first."

"Excellent, Duan. I knew I'd picked the right man to be my XO. I'm glad to have that confirmed once again. Order us to rise slowly to the depth needed to extend our communications antenna. Maintain all precautions against noise generation," Wen said.

"Yes, sir," Duan said gamely.

Of course, Duan knew as well as Wen did that their precautions would do little good. In rising, the *Changzheng 20* would pass through multiple thermal layers and changes in water pressure. Doing so would cause noise. The only question was how much.

No effort had been spared to make the lifting of their antenna as silent as possible. But, it was still a mechanism moving through seawater. It could never do so in total silence.

So, until now, the Americans might have been guessing that the *Changzheng 20* was keeping it company.

Very soon, they would know for sure.

In minutes, Wen had received his new orders.

Duan had, of course, read them before passing the orders to his Captain. So, at first, he was surprised by Wen's next directive.

"Resume pursuit on battery. Maintain all noise precautions. Keep me advised of any change in the target's course and speed," Wen said.

Duan slowly nodded. "Yes, Captain," he said automatically.

Then he smiled.

"You want to keep their Captain guessing about the orders we've received," Duan said.

Wen nodded. "Correct, Duan. I think sonar is right, and the Americans are at battle stations. Let them stay that way for a while, with their nerves stretched to the breaking point. As we resume battery operation at a constant depth, their fix on our location will again become less and less precise."

"And when the moment is right, we will launch our attack," Duan said softly.

"Yes," Wen said just as quietly. "And avenge the deaths of all those killed at our base by the Americans."

CHAPTER FORTY-NINE

USS *Oregon*
Under the South China Sea

Captain Jim Cartwright could guess what news Lieutenant Commander Fischer was bringing from his excited expression.

"Sonar has a fix on the enemy submarine," Cartwright said flatly.

The fact that it had taken this long suggested the new *Sui* class's ability to avoid detection had significantly improved over the previous *Shang* class of nuclear attack submarines.

The *Oregon* carried the best tools available to find enemy submarines. The horseshoe-shaped Large Aperture Bow (LAB) replaced the previous sonar sphere. It was surrounded by water instead of air and made of advanced composite materials. These three changes dramatically improved performance.

The new Light Weight Wide Aperture Array (LWWAA) used fiber-optic arrays instead of ceramic hydrophone sensors for another significant increase in performance.

Multiple upgrades to the AN/WLY-1 acoustic intercept and counter-measures system helped sonar technicians examine and interpret the data collected by these sensors more quickly. Just as important, in case of attack, the *Oregon*'s ability to emit signals designed to confuse and degrade an enemy torpedo's tracking ability had improved as well.

"Yes, sir," Fischer replied. "They tried to be quiet about it, but sonar got a good return as the target approached the surface to raise their communications antenna. They've definitely received new orders."

Cartwright nodded. "And based on their conduct since, any indication what those orders might have been?"

"Sir, they've once again tried to look like a hole in the ocean. Sonar thinks they must be running on batteries. Also, we don't yet know much about the new *Sui* class. But during the target's ascent towards the surface, they got enough data to make that the most likely identification," Fischer said.

"Well, that's what I'd expected. It makes sense to have your best submarine guard your most advanced base. Anything suggesting they're planning to attack?" Cartwright asked.

"No, sir. Sonar reports our fix is getting softer by the minute. They're keeping pace, but on battery, there's no way they'll overtake us. At our current course and speed, in a few hours, we'll be outside China's most expansive territorial claims," Fischer replied.

"So, then, cancel battle stations? Head to the mess for a cup of coffee?" Cartwright asked with a smile.

Fischer shook his head with an answering smile. "No, sir. I doubt the Chinese know we didn't intend to destroy their base. Even if they figure that out, they probably won't care. Frankly, I doubt we would either. I'm certain they've been ordered to attack."

"Agreed," Cartwright said. "But our orders still stand. Our guesses don't count. We don't fire on the Chinese submarine unless they fire first."

"Yes, sir," Fischer replied.

Cartwright could see Fischer was just as unhappy as he was to be playing defense. Submarine combat was like any other in one respect.

Firing first was a significant advantage. However, many computer combat simulations suggested it was a disadvantage that could be overcome.

Cartwright was not looking forward to becoming the first American submarine commander since World War II to find out whether those simulations were right.

Changzheng 20
Under the South China Sea

Captain Wen gestured towards Commander Duan, who was then immediately at his side.

"Commander, I know we're still out of torpedo firing range. How long will it take us to correct that if we move towards the target at maximum speed?" Wen asked.

"Sir, I've constantly been updating the answer to that question. About five and a half minutes," Duan replied.

Wen nodded. "And if we assume the Americans fire as soon as they can once they detect us moving towards them at high speed, how long would it take their torpedoes to reach us?"

"Sir, that is much more of a guess. Sonar believes we are facing a *Virginia* class submarine. Naval Intelligence has estimates of that submarine's capabilities, but we can't be sure of their accuracy. They carry the Mark 48 torpedo, but there are many variants. It is likely one able to reach about one hundred kilometers per hour, with a range of at least eight kilometers, probably more," Duan replied.

"Yes. About the same range but roughly fifteen kilometers per hour faster than our Yu-11 torpedoes. And we can only guess at their orders.

Moving towards them at high speed could be seen as evidence of intent to attack," Wen said.

Seeing Duan's raised right eyebrow, Wen had to stop and smile.

"Yes, should be seen as evidence of intent. But, do the American captain's orders say 'fire only if fired upon,' or do they say 'fire only if under attack.' And, will he obey them when faced with our advance?" Wen asked.

"Yes, sir. Those are all key questions. I can only say for sure that our chances of launching a successful attack increase substantially the longer the Americans wait to fire," Duan said.

Wen nodded. "Of course, there is the other difference between the Mark 48 and the Yu-11 to consider. Their torpedo carries a warhead with about eight times more explosive than ours. How many Yu-11s do you recommend we fire?"

"I think four is the best number. We can put that many in the water very quickly and then focus all our efforts on defeating the American torpedoes," Duan replied.

"Agreed. I have been impressed by the crew's performance in exercises with both electronic jamming and acoustic decoys. I think the enemy will find we are not so easy to kill," Wen said.

Duan smiled. "I think you're right, sir."

Wen nodded. "Very well. Full speed towards the target, and fire four torpedoes as soon as we are within range. If the enemy launches torpedoes before we reach firing range, maintain course until, in your judgment, we have a reasonable chance of scoring a hit. We must launch our attack before beginning evasive maneuvers. Once our torpedoes are away, we will change to an evasive course and deploy all countermeasures."

"Understood, Captain," Duan said as he hurried to carry out Wen's orders.

It helped that Duan agreed with them completely. Their priority had to be destroying the American submarine that had launched an attack killing everyone on China's newest base.

If to achieve that goal, it became necessary to sacrifice the *Changzheng 20*, so be it.

CHAPTER FIFTY

USS *Oregon*

Under the South China Sea

Captain Jim Cartwright had started to think that maybe their guess of the enemy submarine's intentions had been wrong.

Lieutenant Commander Fischer dashed that hope nearly the instant it was born.

"Captain, sonar reports *Sierra One*'s speed has more than doubled, and it is now on a direct intercept course."

In theory, the enemy submarine's actions could be a bluff designed to hurry their departure from claimed Chinese waters.

And his orders were precise. Fire only if fired upon.

Cartwright had no problem with dying to achieve his mission. That commitment came with the uniform. But he wasn't going to sacrifice his crew when he knew that the officer who had drafted his orders couldn't have imagined these circumstances.

"Latest report, *Sierra One*," Cartwright replied.

The sonar supervisor called out *Sierra One*'s bearing, estimated course, and range.

Cartwright then said, "Firing point procedures *Sierra One*, tubes one and two."

The weapons officer then designated *Sierra One* as the system contact and entered a target solution into his console. The target solution was then sent to the torpedoes in tubes one and two.

Both torpedoes were powered on, and their gyros rapidly spun up. Then an internal system check was run, and the fire control solution data set in memory. The fire control officer next confirmed, "Solution set!"

The flooded torpedo tubes were equalized to the current depth pressure, and the outer doors opened. Next, "Weapons ready!" was announced by the weapons officer. The diving officer declared, "Ship ready!"

Cartwright authorized launch by saying, "Shoot tubes one and two."

At nearly the same moment, the typical torpedo firing sequence was interrupted by the sonar supervisor calling out, "Torpedo launches by *Sierra One* confirmed! Likely Yu-11 model."

"Deploy countermeasures and continue with firing point procedures," Cartwright replied.

The first countermeasure to be activated was the torpedo jamming component of the AN/WLY-1 system. It had signals preprogrammed to attempt to throw off any enemy torpedo's tracking ability. It also had refinements specifically targeting the performance of torpedo models that US Navy technicians had analyzed.

There were many ways to obtain foreign torpedo models. The easiest was to purchase them. The Yu-7, the Yu-11's predecessor, had been based mainly on two sources. The first was the Italian A244/S torpedo, which China purchased from Italy in 1987.

Italy, a NATO ally, had no objection to America's purchase of several A244/S torpedoes for evaluation.

Another was fishing nets. Chinese fishermen retrieved an American Mark 46 Mod 2 torpedo in 1978. Some of its technology had also been incorporated in the Yu-7. Vietnamese fishermen had found a Chinese Yu-6 torpedo in 2018.

Other foreign torpedoes had been found over the years, including many never reported by the press. Unfortunately, these did not include the Yu-11.

The unmistakable rumble of thousands of kilos of air forcing hundreds of liters of seawater into and through two torpedo tubes confirmed launch of two Mark 48 torpedoes from the *Oregon*.

"Weapons startup" was confirmed by the sonar supervisor when two new traces appeared at the top of the sonar display.

The Mark 48 is a wire-guided torpedo designed to allow guidance from operators in the *Oregon* to take advantage of its vastly more powerful sonar. Even the upgraded Mark 48 carried by the *Oregon* with its Common Broadband Advanced Sonar System (CBASS) had its limits. The CBASS's instruments had to fit inside a torpedo.

So "wire-guided" meant that once the Mark 48s had been fired, it was necessary to confirm the submarine was clear of their command wires. But it only took a moment for the sonar supervisor to announce, "Wire clearance maneuver complete, weapons running normally."

The warning that *Sierra One* had fired meant the command wires had to be cut immediately. Updating the initial information on the enemy submarine's location would have to be left to CBASS.

The torpedo firing procedure was one of the most frequently drilled in not only the *Oregon*, but every American attack submarine.

That helped explain how the entire process took only about forty-five seconds.

Next to be launched were weapons designed to destroy the attacking torpedoes. Officially called the Anti-Torpedo Torpedo Compact Rapid Attack Weapon (ATT CRAW), they were usually called simply "mini-torpedoes" by the crews who used them.

Weighing only about one hundred kilograms, the mini-torpedo was about sixteen times lighter than the Mark 48s the *Oregon* had just fired. At just over two meters long and with a diameter of a bit more than seventeen centimeters, each mini-torpedo was also far smaller than the Mark 48.

Yet, each mini-torpedo was able to accelerate to half the speed of the Mark 48 in under twelve seconds and nearly match it in under a minute. This speed was produced by its Stored Chemical Energy Power System (SCEPS). SCEPS worked by bathing a solid lithium block in sulfur hexafluoride gas, creating a chemical reaction that produced steam to drive the mini-torpedo's turbine engine.

The *Oregon*'s crew was able to fire six mini-torpedoes in time to attempt an intercept of the four Yu-11s launched by the *Changzheng 20*.

One of the four Yu-11s had already been led astray by an acoustic device countermeasure (ADC) called the ADC MK5. A mere eight centimeters in diameter, it was the first time this model of ADC had been deployed in combat. Though it had cost over forty million dollars to develop the ADC MK5, today the *Oregon*'s sailors would call the expense well worth it.

Two of the mini-torpedoes failed to lock on to the three remaining Yu-11s in time.

The remaining four mini-torpedoes did successfully acquire Yu-11s as their target.

Unfortunately, two Yu-11s were each targeted by two mini-torpedoes. This happened because the mini-torpedoes were not wire-guided and had no way to communicate with each other.

This was not all bad. One of the targeted Yu-11s was hit by only one of the two mini-torpedoes, while the other passed it by harmlessly. The hit broke the Yu-11 in half, and it was no longer a threat.

The other targeted Yu-11 was hit by two mini-torpedoes, and reduced to fragments drifting onto the seabed.

But that still left one undamaged, on-target Yu-11.

That remaining Yu-11 was briefly sent off course by an ADC MK5. But the Yu-11 had a proximity sensor that told the torpedo the target it had been seeking was nearby.

The Yu-11's designers knew that targeted ships and submarines would try to confuse its guidance systems. So whenever it faced conflicting information, it was programmed with a simple solution.

It exploded.

On the one hand, the Yu-11's designers had definitely made the right decision. The Yu-11 was about to be led off course and cause no damage to the *Oregon*.

But as it was, the Yu-11 exploded too far away to inflict a mortal blow.

Not by much, though.

The *Oregon* rocked as the pressure wave from the Yu-11's explosion hit.

"Damage control crews, report," Cartwright said.

"Sir, a hit on *Sierra One* from one of the Mark 48s," the sonar supervisor reported.

"Damage estimate to *Sierra One*?" Cartwright asked.

The sonar supervisor listened to his headset intently for over a minute, while Cartwright received reports on the damage caused by the Yu-11 explosion from throughout the *Oregon*.

Then he looked up at Cartwright, who was now standing next to him.

"Sir, I can hear compartments collapsing. *Sierra One* has been destroyed."

There was no cheering from any of the sailors within earshot. They all knew it could just as easily have been them.

"Any indication of additional enemy torpedoes?" Cartwright asked.

The sonar supervisor would have told Cartwright immediately if any had been detected. But the question didn't bother him since he knew it was procedure, drilled countless times.

In the stress of combat, details were easy to miss. Even the most important ones.

"No, sir. No indication of either torpedoes or other vessels in the area," the sonar supervisor replied.

Cartwright turned to Fischer.

"Commander, continue on course to base at our best safe speed. Coordinate with damage control parties, and get me a report as soon as possible. In particular, I want to know if any damage could affect hull integrity, our top speed, or our acoustic signature," Cartwright said.

"Yes, sir," Fischer replied.

Well, it looks like we survived that battle, Cartwright thought. And, we should soon reach Japanese-patrolled waters.

But would his superiors consider this a victory?

CHAPTER FIFTY-ONE

South Sea Fleet Headquarters
Zhanjiang, China

Senior Captain Ding hadn't been happy with any aspect of the damage report prepared on the base at Ziyou Island. Most obviously, it failed to explain what had killed everyone on the island.

But after multiple exchanges, it had finally become clear that Captain Qin, the officer who had signed off on the report, had not even set foot on the island. A Chief Sergeant Class 2, who the Americans would call a Sergeant Major, had done the actual assessment.

In one sense, Ding had no problem with that. He had pulled Chief Sergeant Cao's file and saw that he was indeed the man for the job. Cao had investigated everything from accidental explosions caused by poor munitions storage to arson. Thankfully, nobody since China's brief war with Vietnam in 1979 could claim directly relevant experience. If anyone was still serving who had seen combat in that war, Ding hadn't met them.

No, what was bothering Ding was that Captain Qin had tried to refuse his request to have Cao report to him directly. Instead, Qin had said he would answer any questions about his report.

Ding knew that some officers would have agreed with Qin's request simply because it came from a fellow officer.

Not Ding. One of the reasons Admiral Bai had picked him as his deputy was he knew Ding was not impressed by rank. And gave zero priority to doing things "as they had always been done."

No. Qin was hiding something. And Ding was going to find out what that was.

The intercom on Ding's desk crackled to life. His assistant, a lieutenant, said hesitantly, "Sir, Chief Sergeant Cao is reporting as you ordered."

Ding mashed the reply button and said irritably, "Escort him in, Lieutenant."

"Sir, a Captain Qin is insisting that he come in as well," the Lieutenant said.

"Tell Captain Qin I will talk to him after I speak with his Sergeant. And if he has a problem with that, tell him I will have him wait in less comfortable surroundings," Ding snarled.

There was a pause, and then a relieved voice said, "He heard you, sir. On my way."

Moments later, the door to Ding's office opened. Cao entered, and Ding's assistant closed the door behind him.

Cao marched up to Ding's desk, saluted, and said in a confident voice, "Chief Sergeant Cao reporting as ordered, sir."

Ding looked Cao up and down while Cao stood at attention. Uniform in perfect order and groomed to correct military standards. In excellent physical shape, which was not a given. As a senior noncommissioned officer, Cao would spend a lot of time behind a desk. That meant on top of demanding responsibilities, Cao had the good sense to go to a gym.

Satisfied, Ding nodded towards the chair in front of his desk. "Have a seat, Chief Sergeant. You know you're here to answer questions about your report on Ziyou Island."

"Yes, sir," Cao said as he sat.

"Good. Now, your report says you could find no evidence of an attack. What did you look for?" Ding asked.

"Fragments that didn't belong there, sir," Cao replied immediately. "When I've investigated accidental ordnance explosions, for example, the scene was always littered with metal fragments from the weapon casings. They're easy to distinguish from other metal debris, like pieces of metal support beams."

Ding frowned. "Isn't it possible that the fragments were too small to spot? Or were blown off the island and into the sea?"

Cao nodded. "I had both thoughts, sir. That might account for some pieces of an enemy weapon. But to do the kind of damage I saw, no ordinary ordnance could have done it without leaving some evidence behind."

"And that's where the report leaves it. So, Chief Sergeant, what do you think happened?" Ding asked.

Cao hesitated and then said, "Permission to speak freely, sir?"

"Granted," Ding replied at once. Finally, he might get to the bottom of this.

"I did find plastic debris on both sides of the runway I wasn't expecting. When I looked through the construction records I discovered it was left by the destruction of fuel lines," Cao said.

"Plastic fuel lines?" Ding repeated, shaking his head. "That can't be right. We use those for temporary airstrips, like when we're airlifting supplies after floods have taken out regular airports. We wouldn't use them for a military base."

Now Cao looked uncomfortable. "Sir, I talked to an officer on one of the ships waiting to offload supplies to Ziyou Island. He told me that the day after the attack they were due to deliver metal fuel lines, pumps and other equipment to a Colonel Xia. Said Colonel Xia had been very anxious about getting the shipment. They also asked me how long they'd have to wait before they could deliver it."

Into the sudden silence, Cao nearly whispered, "I told him I didn't know."

Ding nodded thoughtfully. "So, if the fuel lines ignited, could the rest of the damage you saw be explained by secondary explosions?"

"Yes, sir," Cao replied. "The fuel tanks would have gone up first. Once those exploded, nearly every structure on that side of the island would have ignited. The fire would have spread quickly to the temporary structure they were using to store ordnance."

"Bombs and missiles, yes. I read the inventory. And once those exploded, any remaining survivors would have had no chance," Ding said, shaking his head.

"That's right, sir," Cao said soberly.

"Very well, Chief Sergeant. Any other detail you can think of that wasn't in the report?" Ding asked.

Cao hesitated again and finally said, "Well, sir, I can't be sure of this. But when I first came to the island, there was a smell that just wasn't right. At first, I thought it was burned aviation fuel, but it was different somehow. Like nothing I've ever smelled before. As the day went on, the smell faded, and by the time I left, it was hardly there anymore. So, there's no proof I could grab onto."

Ding nodded and sat still for a moment. Then he looked at Cao.

"What if a missile sprayed a volatile chemical over the airstrip and kept flying past the island. And then ignited it somehow from a distance, say with a laser? Would that fit what you saw and smelled?" Ding asked.

Cao's eyes widened with astonishment. Probably, Ding thought, at the fact an officer had managed an intelligent thought. He knew what senior NCOs like Cao thought of officers.

And given the many officers like Captain Qin, maybe that was no surprise.

"Yes, sir," Cao replied. "It would explain why there were no weapon fragments. And the odd smell. But there's still one thing I don't understand."

"Yes, Chief Sergeant?" Ding prompted.

"Well, sir, how could the attackers have known we were using temporary fuel lines? The attack you're describing would have only knocked out the airstrip for a few hours if the fuel lines had been properly buried metal pipe," Cao said.

Ding nodded, but at first, said nothing. Then he pressed the intercom button.

"Lieutenant, call Admiral Bai's office. Tell them I need to speak to the Admiral as soon as possible," Ding said.

"Yes, sir," the Lieutenant replied.

A few minutes later, his voice came again over the intercom.

"The Admiral will see you now, sir," the Lieutenant said.

Ding nodded towards Cao, who had been sitting silently and obviously expected to be dismissed.

"You're coming with me," Ding said evenly.

"Sir?" was all Cao could manage through his astonishment.

Ding smiled. "The Admiral may have questions for you. You were on Ziyou Island. I wasn't."

Moments later, Ding and Cao were both standing in front of Admiral Bai.

Ding said, "Sir, this is Chief Sergeant Cao. He wrote the damage report on Ziyou Island. He has also provided me with additional details that were not included in that report. I know you have already read the report. I thought you would like to hear the extra details directly from the Chief Sergeant."

"Indeed I would. Have a seat, both of you. Chief Sergeant, please proceed," Bai said.

Once Cao was finished, Bai nodded and said, "Very helpful, Chief Sergeant. I have only one question. Why did you omit those details from your written report?"

As he saw Cao hesitate, Bai added, "Chief Sergeant, I am giving you a direct order to answer my question completely and truthfully."

Cao swallowed and nodded quickly. "Yes, Admiral. All of that information was included in my original written report. I was ordered to omit details that I was told would reflect poorly on officers who had served at the Ziyou Island base. Because they were no longer alive to defend themselves. And the details being omitted were either irrelevant or based on guesses."

Bai nodded. "And who gave you that order, Chief Sergeant?"

Cao's face was expressionless as he replied, "Captain Qin, sir."

Bai pressed the intercom button on his desk.

"Lieutenant, get Chief Sergeant Cao a decent cup of tea and a comfortable place to sit nearby. Also, arrange for his quarters here at headquarters for the next few days," Bai said.

"Yes, sir," the Lieutenant replied.

Bai turned back to Cao and said, "Chief Sergeant, we may have more questions for you."

"Understood, sir," Cao said as he stood and saluted.

A few moments later, Bai and Ding were alone.

Bai lifted his phone and, at the same time, asked, "Captain Qin is still in your outer office?"

Ding nodded silently.

Bai said into his phone, "Security? Yes, this is Admiral Bai. A Captain Qin is in Senior Captain Ding's office. Arrest him and have him held for court-martial. I will forward charges later today."

Bai put down his phone and looked at Ding curiously. "Now, let's talk about the real reason you had me hear all this directly from the Chief Sergeant. Not to get this Captain Qin charged. You could have done that yourself, and you know I'd have supported you."

Ding nodded. "Yes, sir. I wanted it to be clear in your mind that the Americans did not intend to destroy our base."

Bai cocked his head. "Is it so clear? The Americans have satellites and drones. Perhaps they saw the airstrip fuel lines could be easily ignited."

Ding shook his head. "Sir, I think that's very unlikely. The temporary fuel lines were buried. Not deeply, it's true. But well enough that they wouldn't have been visible. And I don't think either of us would have imagined the Army men building the base could have been so careless. I doubt the Americans would have thought so."

Bai nodded. "Let's say you're right. Now, let's also say a man goes into a shop with a knife and demands money. Then the elderly shopkeeper has a heart attack and dies. Do we call that murder?"

Ding frowned. "I see your point, sir. I'm not saying the Americans aren't responsible for every single death on Ziyou Island. They are. But I believe their intent is crucial to how we should respond."

"Very well. What do you suggest?" Bai asked.

"Sir, we've already sent our best submarine to hunt down the Americans we believe launched this attack. Others are on the way to help in that search. I think we should propose to headquarters in Beijing that should be the extent of our response," Ding said.

"Because you believe the Americans didn't intend to destroy the base, just damage it in a way that would cause few casualties. But have you considered how this disaster could have been possible?" Bai asked.

"I don't understand, sir," Ding replied immediately.

Bai nodded. "The right question is this. Why were temporary fuel lines used at all?"

Ding sat quietly for a moment. Then he said, "You're saying that wasn't done by the Army construction crew commander on his initiative. But then by who, and why?"

Bai tapped on a folder on his desk. "Nothing happens in my command without my knowledge, no matter how much other officers may wish to hide it. Air Force Commander Yang and Army Commander Shi recently visited Ziyou Island and gave everyone involved strict orders not to report on their trip."

Ding slowly nodded. "They would only have come if high-ranking politicians were pressing them to have the base ready as quickly as possible. And it was declared operational two days before the Americans attacked."

"Correct. And to get both Yang and Shi to come to Ziyou Island, the pressure probably came from the President himself. Now, how do you think the politicians would react to our saying the American attack only killed everyone on our base because of their insistence it be ready as soon as possible?" Bai asked.

Ding sat quietly and then shook his head. "I see the problem."

"Good," Bai said. "As soon as I saw you had ordered the Chief Sergeant to report to you, I had the three other enlisted men who assisted him brought here to headquarters as well. They are in temporary quarters under guard, where the Chief Sergeant will soon be joining them."

Ding frowned. "Sir, how would you like me to proceed?"

"For now, do nothing. We need to see first whether we succeed in destroying the American attackers. Once we know that, we can decide what to do next," Bai said.

"Yes, sir," Ding replied. "Are there any options you would like me to prepare?"

Bai shrugged. "Anything beyond the submarine that attacked our base would amount to the same thing. A declaration of war against the Americans. Any such conflict would quickly escalate to a nuclear exchange, and this headquarters would be one of the first targets. For us, the war would be over quickly."

Ding was taken aback by the Admiral's casual fatalism. "Sir, there must be something we can do!" he exclaimed.

Bai shook his head. "No, Ding. We have already sent all the assets we have in the area in pursuit of the American submarine. But I doubt that any but the *Changzheng 20* will be able to reach the enemy before they leave our waters. So, everything now depends on a single submarine. You say you know its captain?"

Ding nodded. "Captain Wen, sir. He's one of our best."

"I've met him, of course, but can't say I know much about Captain Wen beyond his file. If he fails, we'll have to hope that the politicians in Beijing can keep this incident from getting out of hand. And there's nothing the military can do about that," Bai said.

Chapter Fifty-Two

USS *Oregon*
Japanese Patrolled Waters

Captain Jim Cartwright looked up from his bunk as he heard a soft tap at his door. He'd spent most of the past six hours trying to sleep, with little success.

"Enter," Cartwright said.

Lieutenant Commander Fischer poked his head in. "Sir, this is when you asked us to wake you. But nothing is happening at the moment if you'd like to get a little more sleep."

Considerate, as always, Cartwright thought. Especially since he knew that Fischer had spent no more time in his bunk than his captain since their arrival in Chinese waters.

Well, waters claimed by China. A claim that no other country recognized.

Cartwright shook his head. Pointing to the chair next to his small desk, Cartwright said, "Have a seat."

Privacy was a rare commodity on any submarine. But it was necessary for this conversation.

Still, first things first.

"Any luck tracking down what's amplifying our acoustic signature?" Cartwright asked.

"Well, we knew from the outset that battle damage probably included loss of SHT," Fischer said.

Cartwright did his best to suppress a smile. Special Hull Treatment (SHT) was the official term for the rubber tile anechoic coating that reduced the sound the *Oregon* produced as it traveled through the ocean.

However, from the outset keeping the tiles attached to *Virginia* class submarines had become a known problem. There were even publicly available photos of *Virginia* class submarines with missing tiles that had nothing to do with the nearby explosion of an enemy torpedo.

Inevitably, this had led to jokes about submarines "losing their SHT." Evidently, never within the hearing of one Lieutenant Commander Fischer.

This, though, wasn't the right time to go off on that particular tangent.

"Hull damage?" Cartwright asked quietly.

"The engineers think it's likely, sir," Fischer said, nodding.

"I suppose it will take an external examination to determine how bad the damage is," Cartwright said.

"That's what they say, sir. But, as long as we don't go down too far we should be able to stay submerged. And that's a good thing, sir," Fischer said.

Well, the whole point of a submarine's underwater existence was to avoid detection while it carried out its mission. Fischer knew this wasn't news to Cartwright. So...

"New orders?" Cartwright asked.

"Yes, sir. Just received. The only change is that we're to remain submerged, as long as our battle damage allows us to do so safely until we return to base," Fischer said.

Cartwright grunted thoughtfully. "Headquarters doesn't want the Chinese to be sure we've survived that encounter with one of their submarines. At least, not right away."

"Actually, sir, we've been directed to dock at a covered berth. I think they want the Chinese to keep guessing for quite a while," Fischer said.

Cartwright nodded. Interesting. Covered submarine berths weren't cheap to build and maintain. The fact there were publicly available photos of *Virginia* class submarines testified to that reality.

But over the past several years, the Navy had built at least one covered berth at every major submarine base. Someone at the Pentagon had realized that other countries besides Russia had satellites monitoring the world's oceans and naval bases.

Like China.

"Any questions about our battle report?" Cartwright asked.

Fischer shook his head. "No, sir. But I want you to know I'm going to back your decision to fire on that Chinese submarine all the way. It's the same one I would have made."

Cartwright frowned. "That's the last thing I want you to say. You're about to get your own command. Declaring you're ready to disobey orders from headquarters is certain to change their mind."

A stubborn look settled on Fischer's face that Cartwright had seen only a few times before. Great, he thought.

I'm not going to be able to budge him on this.

Still, he had to try.

"Look, I'm asking you this as a personal favor. I have no regrets about my decision. If I'd waited to start firing procedures until we'd confirmed the Chinese submarine's torpedo launch, I don't think we'd be having this conversation. But the Navy needs good captains in charge of its submarines. I'd hate to see it lose one because you insist on backing a lost cause," Cartwright said.

"That's another thing I wanted to talk to you about, sir. You are in no way a 'lost cause.' I've gone over the records with the sonar supervisor. The Chinese submarine did fire first, sir. Not by much, but they did," Fischer said triumphantly.

Cartwright shook his head. "But at the time I ordered us to fire, I didn't know that. That's all the admirals at headquarters will care about."

Fischer scowled. "Sir, this doesn't make any sense. These submarines cost over three billion dollars to build. We have a crew on board of one hundred thirty-five sailors. When it's obvious to you, me, and anyone else with a bit of sense that the enemy is attacking, how could you be expected to sit on your hands?"

"Simple. China has nuclear weapons. They could decide our sinking their submarine was an act of war and use those weapons against us. Don't forget that the battleship *Maine* sinking in Havana Harbor was one of the reasons the Spanish-American War started, even though it turned out Spain didn't do it. To avoid nuclear war, the Navy would be ready to sacrifice any one ship or submarine," Cartwright said.

"Shouldn't that work both ways, sir? Our nuclear forces are still superior to China's. They have to know that they'd lose such a conflict," Fischer said.

Cartwright shrugged. "I think you know as well as I do that in a nuclear war between China and America, there'd be no winners. Except maybe Russia. And don't forget, we did destroy one of their bases."

"I still don't understand how that happened, sir. A strike by one Tomahawk, even with its unique design, shouldn't have led to such massive damage," Fischer said.

"Maybe, but whatever the explanation, the results are undeniable. The Chinese are going to want payback. Court-martialing me would be one way to provide it," Cartwright said.

Fischer looked stunned. "Do you really think that's what will happen, sir?"

Cartwright shook his head. "I have no idea. But I do know that as captain, the decision to fire was mine alone. That's final."

There's that obstinate look again, Cartwright thought with a sigh.

"With respect, sir, it's not. If I'm called upon to testify, and we both know I will, I'll be under oath to tell the truth. That's exactly what I intend to do," Fischer said.

"Very well. I guess I can't argue with that," Cartwright said, shaking his head.

And it would take days for the *Oregon* to reach its base, Cartwright thought.

Who knows what might happen by then?

Chapter Fifty-Three

SpaceLink Pacific Mission Command Center
Vandenberg Air Force Base, California

Eli Wade waved towards the glass wall of the conference room, beyond which was the floor containing the dozens of SpaceLink employees trying to understand what had gone wrong with the latest launch.

"So, has anyone managed to find out more than we knew yesterday?" Wade asked.

SpaceLink project manager Mark Rooter tapped the thick folder sitting in front of him on the conference room table. "The main thing we've been able to confirm is that this isn't a repeat of the attack in Florida. With all the extra security measures we put in place, I was sure no one could compromise our network. All our checks show that didn't happen."

"OK, so what did?" Wade growled.

"We're also sure something struck the payload module just after it separated from the rocket and moments before satellites were going to start deployment. What we don't know is exactly what hit the module or where it came from," Rooter replied.

"I can answer both questions right now. Who cares, and China," Wade said with a scowl.

Rooter shook his head. "I have to disagree with you there, boss. We need to figure out what hit the module, or we can't prove China did it. Everybody knows there's plenty of junk in orbit, and this could have been an accident."

Seeing Wade's gathering fury, Rooter held up both hands, "You and I don't believe that. We both think China did it. But if we're going to get government help to do anything about China, we need proof. I've asked my Space Command contacts to look over their tracking records for evidence to help us do that."

Rooter saw with relief that Wade's anger ebbed as quickly as it had grown.

"OK, that makes sense. What else are we doing?" Wade asked.

"Bob Hansen and the rest of his FBI team are on their way and should get here later today. Maybe they'll find something we missed. He'll also bring us up to date on what they've learned about the Florida attack," Rooter replied.

"Good. They're not going to interfere with the charity event I'm hosting, are they?" Wade asked with a frown.

"No, sir. Just as you directed, the contractor I hired will be the only supplement to your regular security detail. He's promised to be discreet, and I trust him to do that," Rooter replied.

"Fine. Now, you've got one of our old workhorse rockets, the Eagle, ready to launch satellites tomorrow from here at Vandenberg. Right?" Wade asked.

"Yes, sir, targeted to replace the ones China destroyed plus adding many more. As you know, it will be a much lighter load than the one on the rockets China just destroyed, but we haven't announced this launch. It should come as a complete surprise," Rooter replied.

"And what about our cover story on the NOTAM? Is that ready?" Wade asked.

A NOTAM was a "Notice to Airmen" sent by the Federal Aviation Administration to all pilots about any event that might interfere with a flight. Like a rocket launch.

"Yes, sir. We'll have proof we sent the draft NOTAM to the FAA through our email system but that there was a technical problem preventing its receipt. I don't think they'll be able to prove we caused the problem. Airspace over Vandenberg is always restricted anyway, so failure to issue a NOTAM shouldn't pose any real danger to flight safety," Rooter replied.

"Excellent. Now, did we swap out the payload module on the Spaceship launch due to take off from Florida tomorrow? And will it take off at the same time as the Eagle launch?" Wade asked.

"Yes to both, boss. And as we arranged, it should all happen the same day you're in San Francisco hosting that charity event," Rooter replied and then hesitated.

Wade saw it immediately and quietly said, "Out with it, Mark."

Rooter shrugged. "Look, boss, these are your rockets. What you want in them and where you want them to go is your call. But is anyone in the government going to back us up when what we're doing comes out?"

"Well, you're right to be worried. Especially since the government isn't going to have to prove what we did in court. Once both launches have been completed, I'm flying to DC to tell Hernandez exactly what I did and why. After that, the government may decide to seize all our assets, give the launch business to NASA, and sell the rest. Honestly, I'm not sure I'd blame Hernandez if he did," Wade said.

"And you're not asking first because you don't think the President would agree with what we're doing," Rooter said with a nod.

"Let's be very clear about this, Mark," Wade said. "There is no we. You're doing what I ordered you to do. You had no idea the government hadn't approved. The military could sue me for breach of contract. I'm probably also violating a dozen or so Federal criminal statutes, not to mention conducting my own foreign policy."

Rooter grinned. "You mean because we're going to ring China with satellites giving everyone in it access to uncensored high-speed Internet and thousands of Gateways to access it for free?"

Wade shook his head. "There's that 'we' again. Get this through your head. You just followed my orders, like any good company employee. I'm not taking you down with me, and that's final."

Rooter's smile disappeared, and he said, "That's not your call, boss. I don't like what China is doing to our life's work any better than you do. Maybe it makes me even madder."

Indeed, Rooter had to stop for a moment while he got his anger under enough control to keep speaking.

"You've got other businesses to take care of like electric cars and solar roofs. SpaceLink is my only child. If jail is the price to do something about the people attacking it, then I'll go to prison. I'm with you all the way, boss, and I don't care who knows it."

Wade drew a deep breath and was about to argue with Rooter but then looked at his expression and thought better of it.

"Well, then all I can do is thank you for your support. I had this image of myself as the captain going down alone with his ship. I see now that was pretty selfish."

"No, you were looking out for me, and I appreciate it. But I'm going into this with my eyes wide open, just like you. And besides, you never know. I doubt the President likes what China's doing any better than you do. Maybe this will work out after all," Rooter said confidently.

"Maybe so," Wade said automatically in response.

While thinking that if he knew Hernandez at all, the real question was whether the President would even finish hearing him out before having him arrested.

Wade didn't care. China wasn't going to get away with destroying five of his satellites and his two newest rockets.

Not if Eli Wade had anything to say about it.

Chapter Fifty-Four

Downtown Office Building
San Francisco

Mikhail Vasilyev and Anatoly Grishkov looked around the office space, and both nodded with satisfaction, though for different reasons.

Vasilyev was pleased that his primary requirement had been met. There had been no shortage of tall office buildings close enough to Eli Wade's downtown charity event to let him make the shot.

Particularly with the McMillan TAC-50, it should be no challenge at all, Vasilyev thought.

But only one building met another critical requirement. That the windows be as close to jet black as possible.

The human eye was excellent at noticing objects that didn't belong, even from a great distance. Like, say, a black rifle barrel poking out from a clear glass windowpane.

Against a dark background, however, spotting that barrel became a much greater challenge. The windows weren't totally black, but Vasilyev had known that would be unlikely.

But they were dark enough. His rifle would never be found by chance. Vasilyev thought it unlikely even someone searching for it with a scope would find it in time.

He wasn't going to leave the barrel sticking out of the window for long.

Grishkov's concerns were completely different. First, that their vantage point be easy to secure.

There was a single door leading into the office suite. Grishkov had replaced the door lock's cylinder with a German one from the consulate's stock, which had several advantages.

First, it worked. Designed for precise interaction between the cylinder body, pins, balls, and springs, it would open to Grishkov's key. A stuck or jammed door wasn't something they could afford.

Any American criminal seeking entry would find his usual tools wouldn't do the job. Top-ranked even among German cylinders, these locks were as close to tamper-proof as possible.

Since he had only replaced the door lock's cylinder, Grishkov doubted any investigation once they had gone would discover the alteration. And even if it did, the German product would do nothing to implicate Russia.

Even more important, Grishkov had discovered an excellent escape route out of the building. He scowled briefly as he thought about the capsules Alina had given him, as well as Vasilyev. Along with their orders, just before they had boarded their flight to San Francisco.

Grishkov was going to do everything possible to avoid taking them. He was returning to Arisha and his sons, and that was his top priority.

Keeping his partner alive would be nice too.

Grishkov's gaze swept around the office space. Also high on his security list had been a clear and unobstructed view of the door from all vantage points. No matter how good the lock, any door could be forced.

The office was completely unfurnished. The sharp chemical smell that had pervaded the space on their first visit from the carpet's cleaning had thankfully dissipated. There was nothing but lighting overhead and carpet underfoot.

Ideally, Grishkov had wanted to rent an entire floor but knew that was unlikely. Not for financial reasons, since Smyslov had told them their budget was virtually unlimited for this mission. But because downtown office space was in high demand in this city.

But the agent in charge of obtaining this space for them had done as well as he could. Only two other offices on this floor were occupied. Neither dealt directly with the public and so could be expected to have few visitors.

So far, that expectation had proved accurate. On the short walk from the elevator to their office door, Grishkov and Vasilyev had never encountered anyone. Even better, when Grishkov had been forced to stand in the doorway for several minutes to change the lock's cylinder, he had seen no one.

The building's lobby, though, always had plenty of people. And cameras.

The low-tech solution Grishkov used for both of them was windbreakers with attached hoods. In rainy, foggy San Francisco, they certainly weren't the only ones wearing them.

Grishkov knew using a hood had a significant advantage over the classic "cap and sunglasses" approach from his time in law enforcement. One of the key reference points used in facial recognition was the ear, fully concealed by a hood but not a cap.

They both wore thin leather gloves to avoid leaving fingerprints. Since they had worked with the Americans before in Afghanistan, Grishkov and Vasilyev assumed their facial images and prints had been collected by an American intelligence service, either CIA or DIA.

It's what they would have done.

"I think it's time," Grishkov said.

Vasilyev glanced up from his position next to the TAC-50 and nodded.

Grishkov had only one regret starting out on this mission. He knew he would have to leave behind one of his favorite tools from his days as a detective.

It was a German glass circle cutter he had bought with his own funds. He had used it many times to cut out a hole in a windowpane for two different purposes. The most common was to insert a monitoring device, either video or audio, to collect evidence in criminal cases.

Grishkov has also used it to enter homes after unlatching a window without breaking the glass and alerting those inside. Twice he believed coming upon heavily armed criminals from behind thanks to this technique had saved his life.

Grishkov counted the money he'd spent on this German tool as very well spent. Especially when, thanks in part to its help, he became the youngest ever Chief Homicide Detective for the entire Vladivostok region.

He sighed as he attached the suction cup to the glass pane in front of Vasilyev's rifle and began turning its six-wheel turret. Given the scene they'd be leaving behind, Grishkov knew he couldn't leave with the tool.

If police stopped them, it would be difficult to explain.

It didn't make him any happier about parting with his old friend.

There, Grishkov said to himself with satisfaction as he could feel the glass give way but remain firmly within the suction cup's grip. Carefully, he pulled the newly created glass disc inside the office suite.

One of the first times he'd used the tool, Grishkov had failed to pull straight back and dropped the cut glass on the wrong side of the window. That time he'd been lucky. The room inside had been carpeted and unoccupied, and the glass hadn't shattered.

If a glass disk dropped dozens of floors onto a San Francisco street, though, Grishkov expected people to notice.

Wind rushed through the hole, as both Grishkov and Vasilyev had expected at this altitude. This time, it had been up to Vasilyev to select the solution to the problem.

The Swiss-made wind meter Vasilyev had used before was no longer in production, but an American equivalent was readily available. For security purposes, it was probably better to use a meter any American could purchase anyway, Vasilyev thought.

The consulate had ordered Vasilyev's selection, a highly accurate meter including a barometer for the most precise wind measurements. It measured current wind speed, average wind speed, maximum gust, temperature, local barometric pressure, and altitude. All this information was shown on a digital display. Obtaining a reading only required pressing a single button.

As far as Grishkov was concerned, the meter's most important feature was its attached lanyard. Before going anywhere near the hole in the window, he had it securely knotted around his wrist.

Vasilyev had read the device's promotional materials. They said its 90-degree rotating anemometer head would let him measure how much crosswind would be applied on the side of his bullet without having to move the wind meter or do angle calculations.

Vasilyev had Grishkov move the meter several times. Then he did his own angle calculations.

And came up with the same result as the meter.

Both Vasilyev and Grishkov still considered it time well spent.

Grishkov trained his Japanese 20x50 binoculars on the building entrance across the street where Wade was expected to make his appearance. Reporters and their equipment were there, which was a relief.

It had been clear from the outset that Wade could avoid the assassination attempt they were planning. All Wade had to do was enter the building where his charity event would be held through its underground garage.

Grishkov and Vasilyev, though, agreed that everything in Wade's file suggested such a decision was doubtful. Wade's egotism and stubbornness may well have been critical to his success in business.

But they were about to prove less than helpful when it came to security planning.

The Internet had once again demonstrated its value as a research tool. They had set up for their attack well in advance of Wade's expected arrival. But Grishkov knew from reviewing video footage of Wade's appearance at the same charity event in earlier years that Wade would be late.

So, when first ten and then twenty minutes after Wade's announced arrival time passed, Grishkov wasn't concerned. Instead, he made productive use of the time by carefully examining the surrounding buildings.

If a counter-sniper team was operating anywhere nearby, Grishkov could see no sign of it.

As thirty minutes stretched to forty, though, Grishkov began to worry. Had they miscalculated?

Though Grishkov had said nothing, his concern was still obvious to Vasilyev. He glanced up at Grishkov and smiled.

"If Wade decides not to come or goes in through another entrance, there's nothing we can do. So, why worry about it?" Vasilyev asked.

Grishkov shrugged and nodded. Why indeed?

Vasilyev's father could well have made the same observation, Grishkov thought. Instead of saddening him, the thought was oddly reassuring. Despite the limited time that Alexei had been able to spend with his son, he had still managed to pass on the most important lessons.

Grishkov could at least see that the reporters were still there. If Wade had appeared inside after arriving through some other entrance, they would undoubtedly have learned about it and departed.

At last! A long black vehicle slowed and finally stopped in front of the building. Reporters quickly converged around it and just as rapidly were pushed back by the men who emerged from the vehicle.

And who were joined by more men exiting a smaller vehicle that had pulled up directly behind the larger one.

The professional in Grishkov approved. One team charged with keeping the reporters at a distance where they could take good quality photo and video and call out questions. But not threaten Wade's security.

Another team serving as a moving physical barrier to attack.

"Two guards on sides, two more front, and back. Target in center," Grishkov called out.

"Target acquired," Vasilyev replied.

Grishkov knew that meant Vasilyev would fire as soon as he had a clear shot.

Charity Event Building
San Francisco

Retired Commander Dave Martins had used the Knights Armaments SR-25 rifle over nearly his entire Navy career. Called the Mk 11 Mod 0 by the Navy and the M110 by the Army, it had been used by Seal Team snipers to carry out many challenging missions. Martins thought its use to kill the terrorists holding Captain Phillips hostage on a pitching lifeboat in 2009 was probably the most impressive example of the rifle's capabilities.

Not to mention the skill of the Seals firing the rifle, Martins thought with a grin.

The Mk 11 wasn't the longest-range sniper rifle available. But the distance to the three buildings with a line of sight to the building he was in wasn't that great and certainly within the MK 11's range.

Rooter had come through on every count. It turned out there were about a dozen vacant or recently rented offices in each of the three target buildings. Martins and his two other men, both retired Seals, had maps of each building showing their locations.

None of them needed the maps now. Each of them had committed the office locations to memory. It was the sort of capability each of them had demonstrated countless times throughout their careers.

Rooter had also obtained access to the offices Martins had requested as the ideal spots for him and his men to surveil each target building. Each of them covered one building. Martins had naturally taken the building that he would have selected if he had been planning to assassinate Wade.

Bob Hansen had turned out to be surprisingly helpful. Martins had expected him to insist on taking over the counter-sniper operation, but instead, he had promised full cooperation. That had included giving him a radio to connect directly with an SFPD captain if Wade was attacked.

Only an amateur would reveal his position by extending his rifle barrel outside an office window before Wade's arrival. And Martins doubted very much that people who had managed to blow up a rocket in Florida would hire any but the most qualified professional.

But never take anything for granted. So, Martins and his men had been systematically sweeping the possible target offices in their assigned building for over an hour when the word finally came over their radio earpieces.

Wade was arriving.

There had been no hint so far that any attack was imminent. Was this going to turn out to be a big waste of time?

No sooner had the thought crossed Martins' mind than he saw movement at an office window just as he moved his scope on to look at another location. He immediately moved back to where he had seen something move and...yes!

It was a rifle barrel, pointing down to where Wade had just exited his vehicle.

Martins quickly calculated where he thought the sniper would be relative to the rifle barrel and fired.

He heard a clamor of voices over his earpiece. Martins had been too late.

Whoever it was had already fired on Wade.

The rifle barrel was no longer visible.

Cursing, Martins reached for the radio to call the police.

Was Wade dead?

Chapter Fifty-Five

Downtown Office Building
San Francisco

His training told Grishkov to stay focused on the target area since Vasilyev would fire any second.

But some instinct told Grishkov to do another counter-sniper sweep, though the many he had done over nearly an hour had turned up nothing.

And this time, all he saw was a distant glint of light that vanished almost as rapidly as it had appeared.

Grishkov launched himself at Vasilyev and landed on him an instant before a shower of glass was accompanied by a rush of wind and a distinct "*thwock*" some distance behind them. The momentum of Grishkov's leap carried them both about a meter from Vasilyev's former position.

Grishkov was spared having to ask whether Vasilyev had been hit when he heard his wry voice say, "Time to go!"

Hunched low, both of them rushed towards the exit door, half expecting more rounds to follow.

None did.

Grishkov wondered whether it was because the shooter could no longer see them or was merely content with stopping their attack.

As Grishkov closed the office door behind them, he shrugged. It didn't matter. At least, they had survived.

Now to see if they could escape. Whoever had fired at them had certainly contacted the authorities, who would be here in minutes.

Or seconds.

At least there were no curious neighbors in sight. As they walked the short distance to the elevator, the other doors in the hallway remained firmly closed.

Testimony to excellent soundproofing? Or to American caution at exploring whether an unexplained sound meant a gunshot?

Grishkov's money was on a call from his neighbors that would help pinpoint where the police should go.

The elevator opened promptly and didn't stop until depositing them at the building's basement level, below even the parking garage. The locked door directly in front of the elevator quickly yielded to Grishkov's tools and experience.

In fact, Grishkov had picked this door's lock several days before and thoroughly explored the level. Filled with pipes and equipment, it had no offices, and Grishkov was sure nobody ventured into the level unless it was necessary to conduct repairs.

As they walked quickly to their next destination, Grishkov asked in a low voice, "Did you have time to take the shot?"

Vasilyev nodded and replied in an even lower voice. "Yes, just as you slammed into me. But I have no idea whether I hit the target."

Then he quickly added, "Not that I have any complaints. In fact, thanks."

Grishkov nodded absently. "A simple act of self-preservation. Between them, Neda and Arisha would have left nothing but bones if I'd failed to bring you back intact."

Vasilyev grinned. "Yes, we're both fortunate to have found such formidable women."

His smile disappeared as they arrived in front of a bare metal door set into the basement's far wall.

"I have to tell you, I'm still not too fond of your escape plan," Vasilyev said.

Grishkov nodded. "I'm not either. But I think it's our best chance."

With that, he used his tools on the lock, which was even easier to pick.

Well, Grishkov thought, what was it really protecting?

A short distance past the door was a metal grate, which once removed revealed a set of metal handholds leading down into darkness.

Grishkov had been inspired to look into this means of escape by his father, who had fought in the Second World War as a very young man. He had told Grishkov several stories about one of his friends who had survived months of guerilla fighting against occupying German and Romanian forces in Odessa.

In large part, because of Odessa's two thousand five hundred kilometers of underground tunnels. With about a thousand known entrances. Though some were natural, most of the tunnels had been created as a byproduct of limestone mining.

Remembering those stories, Grishkov had checked on whether San Francisco had a substantial network of tunnels. He had been delighted to find that its one hundred twenty-seven square kilometers were home to about one thousand six hundred kilometers of walkable tunnels. Tunnels that were to be found underneath every city block.

Grishkov had been less excited to find that they were sewer mains, some dating back to the 1840s. Fortunately, the city's sewer mains also happened to be the only ones in California combining waste and stormwater transport. This dilution didn't quite make their upcoming walk a pleasant prospect.

But according to the accounts of many unauthorized explorers, it did make it survivable.

Fortunately, they didn't have too far to go. San Francisco's subway system had fifty stations, and they were headed towards one about two kilometers away. Not the closest station available, but instead one Grishkov had picked because he expected it to be outside the initial police search perimeter.

Grishkov had spent hours committing the route to memory, and his recollection proved accurate. Within minutes, they stood in front of another set of metal rungs and began to climb.

Grishkov breathed a sigh of relief as the metal grate at the top lifted away both smoothly and quietly. He had the tools to defeat a lock, but time was critical.

They had no way to know how quickly the police would react to their attack or how widely their net would be spread. But seconds were likely to count.

Grishkov and Vasilyev found themselves in a small room occupied by pipes and what looked like a meter. And no hint that anyone was likely to come here soon.

That was good because they needed privacy.

Grishkov zipped open his tool bag and removed its other contents.

Clothes and shoes for both of them. After their stroll in the sewers it was a critical step in the escape plan.

Once they had changed, Grishkov nodded to Vasilyev, who nodded back and closed his eyes. He also knew to hold his breath.

Grishkov did the same and emptied the contents of an aerosol can over both of them. The KGB's 14th Department had been tasked decades before with developing a method to conceal even the most pungent odors, including decomposing bodies. The agent at the consulate who had given Grishkov the can had assured him it worked.

He'd been grinning as he said it, though.

"I think that's enough," Vasilyev said quietly.

Grishkov set the can down gently on the cement floor. No need to risk drawing attention.

He carefully opened his eyes, which stung sharply enough that he closed them again immediately. Grishkov next risked a quick breath.

And suppressed an urge to cough and perhaps reveal their presence. Who knew who might be just outside their small room?

Grishkov waited a few moments. Then he wiped his eyes with his sleeve and risked opening them again. Better.

Then he drew another breath and was relieved the urge to cough was gone. Now, though, he could distinguish at least one of the active agents used by KGB scientists.

Lemon oil.

Well, it could be worse. Wrinkling his nose, Grishkov amended that. Moments ago, it had been worse.

Grishkov looked across at Vasilyev, who he saw was still rubbing his eyes. Shortly, though, he nodded.

Ready to go.

Grishkov carefully opened the door and peeked outside.

Nobody in sight.

A few minutes later, they were standing in front of an elevator with only one button. Grishkov assumed correctly that was because "Up" was the only direction available.

The elevator doors opened, and they entered just as a voice behind them said, "Hey, who are you guys? You're not supposed to be down here!"

Grishkov's finger stabbed the "Door Close" button as he turned to see the source of the voice running towards them.

The man had close-cut graying hair and was wearing a leather tool belt. As the elevator doors closed, Grishkov could see him pull a walkie-talkie from it.

On the bright side, they didn't have to deal with the man.

On the other, Grishkov was certain building security had just been alerted.

Had they already been notified that the police were searching for assassins in the area?

Grishkov had pressed the button for the next level, hoping it would lead to a ground-level exit. This time, though, as the doors opened, he could see he had miscalculated.

The lack of windows said they were still underground. The large white machines, rising steam, and cloth baskets full of sheets made it immediately clear this was a laundry. Probably for the hotel that was supposed to occupy this building.

They stepped back into the elevator and pressed the button for the next level.

Nothing happened.

Apparently, security had already locked down the elevator.

Not good.

Grishkov spotted a door some distance away with the word "Exit" over it, and ran towards it, Vasilyev close behind.

Just as Grishkov's hand closed on the door's handle, they could both hear shouting behind them.

The door wasn't locked. It opened on a stairwell, with steps leading both up and down.

Well, they weren't going back into the sewers. Up it was two steps at a time.

The next door had a narrow glass pane set into its top half. Grishkov looked through it and immediately saw the level lacked what he needed.

Windows.

Grishkov continued bounding up the stairs, with Vasilyev right behind. Now they could both hear someone on the stairs below them.

Grishkov didn't bother looking before opening the next door. Still no windows, but quite a few people walking around. On his right, Grishkov saw a glass-sided room filled with exercise equipment. A strong chlorine smell announced the presence of an indoor swimming pool on his left before he even saw it.

Grishkov and Vasilyev walked as quickly as they thought they could without attracting attention. So far, it seemed to be working.

But how were they going to get out of here?

Grishkov's heart leaped as he saw a sign even better than the "Exit" sign he'd been hoping to spot. It had an arrow pointing straight ahead and the word, "BART."

Bay Area Rapid Transit. The subway. As he had thought, there was an underground walkway leading from this hotel directly to a station. Until now, though, he hadn't been sure he could find it.

Grishkov had to suppress the urge to look behind him. He knew if they were still being pursued, it would merely help remove any doubt that they were the trespassers being sought.

A sign directly over a heavy metal door on their left once again said "BART," and Grishkov opened it to find an empty corridor, with another door at its end.

As soon as the door closed behind them, Grishkov nodded at Vasilyev, and they both began to run. Just as they reached the next door, they could hear the one behind them swing open.

"Hey, you there!" was all Grishkov heard before the second door closed behind them.

And revealed a swirling mass of people in front of the subway station. Grishkov and Vasilyev quickly merged with them and arrived at the entrance. Both had smartcards provided by the consulate, allowing entry with just a tap on a reader.

Grishkov had seen that all four subway lines available here at "Embarcadero" led to their destination station called "Civic Center/UN Plaza" as long as they picked one going in the right direction. Moments later, a train had arrived, and they were on their way.

There was no indication building security had pursued them to the station. Probably their authority ended at the last door they had opened, Grishkov thought.

He was sure, though, that they had called the police. Grishkov doubted the police would attach a high priority to trespassers who had stolen nothing and caused no damage.

With luck, the police wouldn't connect that trespassing report to their attack on Wade. At least, not in time.

Annoyed looks from some of the other passengers encouraged them to maintain their distance to the extent possible. It seemed the smell of lemons still lingered.

Grishkov sighed and said, "I don't know if I'll ever be able to look at a bottle of cognac again."

Vasilyev looked at him curiously and then smiled. "I get it. I remember my father drinking a glass of cognac once with a side of sliced lemons. I thought he was crazy. I'll never forget how surprised he was at my reaction."

Grishkov snorted and shook his head. In a low voice, he said, "I'll add that to the long list of things I liked about Alexei. You youngsters have a lot to learn about real Russian culture."

Vasilyev smiled again, but Grishkov could see the worry in his eyes. "Think there'll be a reception party once we get there?"

Grishkov shrugged. "I doubt it. They have no way to know which station we'd use to leave the subway system, so would have to put men at every exit. And with what description? I picked these clothes to be as anonymous as possible."

Vasilyev nodded. It was true. They had on solid-colored khakis and polo shirts that matched those worn by several other men in this very subway car.

Though not everyone was wearing caps and sunglasses. Since it was one of San Francisco's rare clear sunny days, Grishkov had been forced to abandon their usual hooded windbreakers.

It took less than ten minutes for the subway train to reach their destination. As they exited the station, Grishkov and Vasilyev looked around as unobtrusively as possible for any police who might be searching for them.

Neither saw anyone suspicious.

Instead, they saw exactly what they needed.

A taxi.

Both of them piled into the cab, and Grishkov said to the driver, "Pier 39, please."

The driver nodded and put the car in gear. After a few minutes, he glanced in the rearview mirror and asked, "You guys been polishing furniture?"

Grishkov didn't understand the question but decided it was safest to nod.

"Yeah, that's what I thought. My wife loves the stuff. I'm not a big fan of the smell, but I know better than to complain. I mean, it could be worse, right?" the driver asked.

Vasilyev and Grishkov both smiled and nodded. Grishkov added, "My father always said keeping complaints to yourself is the secret to a long marriage. I never heard him say it while my mother was around, though."

The driver laughed. "Sounds like your dad was a smart guy. I've been following his advice for almost thirty years. Well, mostly. Whenever I forgot and opened my big mouth, I always regretted it."

Grishkov nodded. "It helps that my wife is nearly always right, anyway, so I'm not often tempted to argue."

The driver smiled. "Sounds like the son is just as smart as his father. How many years do you have in?"

Grishkov correctly guessed he meant years of marriage. "Eighteen, so I'm not quite up to your record."

"That's OK," the driver said. "I'm sure you'll get there. Now, what are you guys planning to do at Pier 39?"

Grishkov shrugged. "A friend told us it was a good place to walk around. Said we'd see some sea lions. Lots of restaurants to choose from when we get hungry."

The driver nodded. "Your friend was right. And you're in luck. Traffic has been a breeze today for a change, and we're just about there."

Indeed, less than a minute later, the taxi slid to a stop in front of the pier.

"The fare's twenty-five bucks," the driver said.

Grishkov nodded and handed the driver two twenty-dollar bills, saying, "Keep the change."

"Nice!" the driver exclaimed. Then he handed Grishkov a card with a name and a phone number.

"If you guys need any other rides, call me anytime! Have a great day!" the driver said and pulled back into traffic.

Grishkov pocketed the card and walked with Vasilyev towards the nearby boats. Both of them looked from side to side but saw no one noteworthy among the throng of visitors.

"Well, I must admit I thought it odd to travel away from our ultimate destination at first. But I can't argue with the results," Vasilyev said.

Grishkov shrugged. "What mattered was putting distance between ourselves and the event. If anyone is thinking about someone leaving San Francisco in a hurry, I hope they'll think first about airports and trains."

Vasilyev frowned. "Airports, plural?"

"Yes. The subway system we just left could have taken us to two different international airports. The first, designated for San Francisco, is one of America's largest. The other across the bay in Oakland is much smaller but still has multiple flights to both Mexico and Europe," Grishkov said.

"But not good options for us," Vasilyev said quietly, glancing at the crowds of nearby tourists.

"No. Now, we just have to find the right slip. They're supposed to be grouped by size. The boat we're looking for is about fifteen meters long. I have the boat's name and slip number, so it shouldn't be too hard to find," Grishkov said.

"Perhaps I can help," a familiar voice said behind them.

Grishkov and Vasilyev both wheeled around to find a grinning Alina, resplendent in a smart white outfit with a matching white hat.

"Let's go fishing," she said.

Chapter Fifty-Six

Jiuquan Satellite Launch Center
Gobi Desert, China

General Yang Mingren had mixed feelings as he watched the hum of activity all around him at the Mission Command and Control Center. The last time, he had been eager to score a victory over the American billionaire Wade that would save his career.

And it had come, a success that had cost him years of effort to achieve.

But now, it left him with a single missile and no backup. Worse, Yang feared he had used up his store of luck on the last mission.

So now Yang was hoping he had been right to tell President Lin the Spaceship that Wade was launching today from Florida would contain a test cargo of ballast and monitoring instruments, not satellites.

Wade had been saying for months that his new rocket could deliver cargo anywhere on Earth on a same day basis. The American military was one of the few organizations, though, requiring such a capability that could afford to pay the price Wade needed to make delivery profitable.

The American billionaire would never risk the money to be made from this new business.

Or would he?

Yang shook his head with irritation. Pointless to speculate when in a few minutes, he would know.

As before, the massive display screen in front of the Mission Command and Control Center split into two side-by-side images. On the right, the American news network's real-time image of Wade's Spaceship sitting on its Florida launch pad.

On the left, the display that would track the rocket's progress towards its landing point in Afghanistan.

Assuming it went where it was supposed to go.

Mercifully, there were no last-minute delays to the countdown. And it took only moments for the track on the display showing the rocket's progress to illuminate, indicating that China's newly enhanced capability to detect and track foreign missile launches was working correctly.

A few minutes later, a beaming man reported to Yang.

"General, I am Lead Technician Jiandan. Our analysis of the rocket's trajectory shows it is on a flight path to land cargo in Afghanistan, exactly as the Americans had announced," he said.

At nearly the same moment, a harsh klaxon sounded. Jiandan paled and ran to his terminal.

Rapid typing followed.

Now the display screen dominating the front of the Mission Command and Control Center split into three side-by-side images.

The third showed a second rocket's ascent being tracked from California.

"General, the Americans have launched another rocket from Vandenberg Air Base in California. We're analyzing its trajectory now," Jiandan said, as the activity around him increased to nearly frantic.

Yang sat rooted in his chair. What was happening?

"Is it another Starship?" Yang asked.

"No, General. It is one of their old Eagle rockets, with a much smaller payload. The American media reports that no one, including their government, anticipated this launch," Jiandan replied.

The image on the screen that had been occupied by the American news network's coverage of the Florida launch had now switched to California.

A twisting trail of smoke and vapor was on the screen that looked as though it had been captured from a distance.

The news anchor's voice said, "We've still been unable to get any comment from either NASA or the FAA about today's rocket launch from Vandenberg Air Base. The Pentagon has confirmed that it's not a launch conducted by the US military. We'll bring you more details as soon as they become available..."

Yang turned away from the display and asked Jiandan, "Do we know where this second rocket is headed?"

Jiandan nodded nervously and said, "Yes, sir. It's on track to the same satellite deployment point as the last rocket we destroyed. However, its possible payload is much less, sixty or so instead of four hundred satellites."

Yang wasted no time replying. Instead, he typed the command in his keyboard for the SU-34 to launch from Qingshui Air Base with their last modified Kinzhal missile.

When he looked up, Jiandan was still standing there, shifting nervously from one foot to the other.

"Something else?" Yang growled.

Jiandan nodded miserably. "The first rocket, the Spaceship, has changed course. We're not sure yet, but it looks like it might land within China."

Yang stared speechlessly at Jiandan for a moment. Then he asked, "How long before you know for sure?"

"Assuming it doesn't change course again, just a few minutes," Jiandan replied and hurried off to his console.

Within China? Not even Wade would dare. And what could he hope to accomplish?

The answer came to him immediately.

The Spaceship was a distraction, meant to draw him away from the Eagle rocket that would deploy more satellites.

Well, it wasn't going to work.

No sooner had Yang made his decision than Jiandan announced, "The Spaceship's course has been fully plotted. If it makes no additional change in direction, it will land in northern Myanmar, not repeat, not China."

Of course, Yang said to himself with a nod. Myanmar, which many in the West still called Burma, was a poor country with no ability to impose any real penalty for Wade's "accidental landing" on their territory.

Bordering China.

But by making it look like the Spaceship might land in China, Wade had hoped to draw attention away from whatever had destroyed his last rocket.

Yang quickly typed in the orders directing the SU-34 to fire its modified Kinzhal missile at the Eagle rocket's payload as soon as a lock had been achieved.

Nice try, Mr. Wade, Yang thought with a sardonic smile.

Against a more gullible opponent, it might have worked.

Yang sat back to wait for the announcement that a lock against the Eagle rocket's satellite payload had been achieved.

And waited.

Yang frowned and looked up at the main display, where the Eagle rocket's progress was being tracked.

The satellite payload had separated from the rocket.

"Why has no lock been transmitted to the SU-34?" Yang asked with a cold fury that made everyone near him duck.

Except, to his credit, Jiandan.

Jiandan kept his eyes focused on his monitor and maintained his rapid typing as he replied.

"The Eagle's payload is much smaller than the Spaceship's. So it is harder to track. But our ground stations are doing all they can. I am almost ready to transmit our best guess as a lock to the attack plane unless you object," Jiandan said evenly.

"Has the payload begun deployment?" Yang asked.

"As far as we can tell so far, no. But if we wait, yes," Jiandan replied.

"Transmit the lock as soon as you are ready," Yang ordered.

Jiandan didn't bother acknowledging the order and kept typing.

Moments later, Jiandan sat back and nodded, rubbing his hands together as though his fingers were sore.

Well, Yang thought, maybe they were.

At almost the same instant, the message came to Yang's terminal that the SU-34 had fired.

Yang leaned forward and fixed his gaze on the small dot on the main display representing the satellite payload. With an intensity that looked to everyone nearby capable of destroying the payload on its own.

Seemingly endless moments passed as Yang felt a sickness in the pit of his stomach. A missile launched on Jiandan's "best guess" against a target in the vastness of space? What had he been thinking?

The voice in his head answered promptly. If he'd waited for a better lock, satellites might have started deploying. And then he'd be fired at best.

Prison was only the beginning of a long list headed "at worst."

The small dot on the display wavered and then disappeared.

Jiandan shouted, "Target destroyed!"

Everyone present cheered and clapped. Just like the last time, Yang was one of them.

This time, though, there was one difference.

Still smiling and cheering, Yang walked up to Jiandan and put his arm around his shoulders.

"Congratulations to you and your team!" Yang said in a loud voice as he led Jiandan away from the happy, cheering crowd.

Once he thought they were safe from being overheard, Yang asked in a low, intense voice, "Did any of the satellites deploy?"

Jiandan immediately shook his head. "I don't think so, General."

Yang's smile disappeared, and he asked even more quietly, "When will you know for sure?"

"Let's go to my office, General. I have a monitor there that will let us see if any deployments have been detected," Jiandan said.

Yang nodded, and moments later, they were in an office that reminded him of one he had been assigned as a Lieutenant. Enough room for Jiandan, a desk, and a monitor.

And, barely, one very impatient General.

Yang hadn't imagined it possible to type more rapidly than Jiandan had before. Well, Yang mused, I suppose having someone standing behind you with the power to have you arrested on the spot is a superior motivator.

A black screen with numbers marching across the bottom appeared on the monitor.

Jiandan tapped the numbers at the bottom of the monitor's screen. Yang realized with a start that they were all the same number.

Zero.

"This display shows tracking station data from the area of space where the payload was destroyed. I directed them to look for any signals being broadcast in the area. As you can see from the zeros on the screen, none have been found so far," Jiandan said.

Yang looked at the screen intently. "Couldn't surviving satellites be waiting unpowered, in case we launch another attack? And can't we see them whether they're powered or not?"

Jiandan shook his head. "SpaceLink has had many complaints from astronomers about their satellites interfering with astronomical observations. So, they have done everything possible to reduce their brightness. To the point where seeing them from the ground is now impossible. But I doubt very much that any surviving satellites are deliberately waiting unpowered."

"Why?" Yang snapped, his temper starting to fray.

"Because of how satellites work," Jiandan replied. "They need to remain in contact with a ground station to function properly, especially just after deployment. In short, if you lose contact with a satellite, there's no guarantee you'll ever get it back."

Yang felt the sick feeling in his stomach that had never really gone away, starting to ease.

"How long before we know for sure?" Yang asked.

Jiandan shrugged. "Unless some number other than zero shows up on my monitor while we're sitting here, I'm ready to call it now. Remember, General, our primary job at this launch center is satellite deployment. If this long had passed since deployment with no signal transmission sent by a satellite launched from here, we'd consider it lost. I'm going to draft a report to my headquarters in Beijing for your approval right now. Unless we intercept a satellite transmission before I'm done, it's going to declare the Eagle's satellite payload confirmed destroyed."

The icy hand that had been massaging Yang's stomach now released its grip almost entirely.

Yang nodded brusquely and hurried back to his terminal, ignoring the curious looks from the staff who had been cheering with him moments before.

As promised, it only took a few minutes before a soft chime announced the arrival of Jiandan's report.

Which said the satellites carried by the Eagle rocket had been completely destroyed.

A wave of relief passed through Yang as he added his authentication code to the report and pressed the button that would send it on to several destinations in Beijing.

Including the Office of the President.

Now Yang focused on those faces all around him, clearly wondering what was happening. And for once, satisfying the curiosity of people he didn't know was no trouble.

"We have just informed the President of our success!" Yang called out in a voice loud enough for all to hear.

Yang had thought the massed technicians were loud before. Now they threatened to damage his hearing.

Yang smiled, relaxed, and let their cheers and raucous laughter wash over him.

He didn't mind the din. Not at all.

Chapter Fifty-Seven

Myanmar-China Border
Near Ruili, China

The Forward agent driving the semitrailer had picked the pseudonym "Lishi" when he joined. Both because the name was uncommon and since he liked its meaning. After all, anyone taking the risks involved with Forward membership had to be hoping to make "history."

So far, everything had gone as well as he could have hoped. The Spaceship's cargo module had floated to a nearly perfect landing in a clearing just out of sight of the nearby road. A road just twenty kilometers away from this border crossing point.

Smuggling had been the lifeblood of this region for centuries. Hiring a team of men to move the cargo using small four-wheel-drive vehicles to the semitrailers had been both easy and cheap. Particularly after Lishi had repeated several times that, no, he wasn't smuggling drugs.

Apparently, anything to do with drugs was much riskier. And so more expensive.

In the dead of night, Lishi hadn't been expecting much traffic on the road. And indeed, only a few cars had passed by as his team loaded the cargo module's boxes from their 4x4 vehicles into the two standard forty-foot containers he was hauling.

Lishi had driven a "B-double" before, but this time was happy he wouldn't have to do so for long. The B-double combined the prime mover where he was sitting attached to two semitrailers, linked together by an additional wheel. The additional wheel provided a level of extra stability, though that was a relative term.

Fortunately, none of the passing vehicles had contained police. But Lishi had wondered whether any drivers from the passing cars would call the police. After all, the scene they were passing could fairly be described as suspicious.

Apparently, nobody cared. Or wanted to risk becoming involved. After all, cell phone numbers might be traced back to their owner.

Because Lishi had driven without incident right across the Ruili Jiegao bridge, marking the border between Myanmar and China. A new border crossing point had been built specifically for the transport route Lishi planned to use.

Lishi eased his semitrailer into the designated lane, leading to the right as soon as he crossed the bridge into the Chinese city of Ruili.

Lishi could also see the flashing lights of a checkpoint directly ahead for any vehicle not making the turn.

At this hour, there were only a few vehicles ahead of Lishi, all semi-trailers, but none B-doubles. It didn't take long for his turn to arrive.

"Papers," the armed border guard said impatiently as soon as Lishi brought his semitrailer next to the inspection station.

Lishi mutely handed a thick sheaf of documents through the vehicle's window to the scowling guard.

The guard's scowl deepened as he flipped through the documents.

"These documents don't make any sense! They say no customs duty is due because everything you're shipping was made in China! So, then, why are you bringing them from Myanmar into China?" the guard asked.

Lishi shrugged. "If you look through all the documents, you'll see these are wireless routers that were made in China and then shipped to Europe for sale there. The European wholesaler who bought the routers stopped distributing them after the first ones sent to retailers were rejected by consumers, who said they didn't work. The wholesaler has paid to return them to the manufacturer in Dali and is demanding a refund."

Then Lishi grinned. "My boss told me they plan to sue the manufacturer in our courts."

The guard's expression cleared as he took in Lishi's explanation. Finally, he laughed.

"They must be idiots," the guard said. "Still, I need you to open up for inspection."

"Of course, officer," Lishi said politely and hurried to open the doors to both containers. As they swung wide, he added, "If you wish to confiscate the shipment, you are more than welcome. I get paid either way."

The guard said nothing in response, and for a moment, Lishi thought he might have overplayed his hand.

With an agility that surprised Lishi, the guard clambered into the back of each container. Ignoring the cargo stacked in the front, he methodically moved boxes around until he had nearly reached the far end of the first container.

Then, he reached out and picked up a box. It took him only moments to repeat the procedure with the second container.

Moments later, the guard was back at Lishi's side. Then, he snapped a command in a loud voice.

Out of the darkness, two uniformed soldiers were suddenly on both sides of Lishi, guns drawn.

"This is your last chance to admit you have been attempting to smuggle prohibited items and perhaps obtain a reduced sentence. Do you wish to confess?" the border guard asked, fixing Lishi with a piercing stare.

Lishi shrugged. "No. The boxes contain exactly what I said."

The guard grunted and took a knife from his belt, and with a single deft stroke, opened first one box and then the other.

Then, he lifted out one of the Gateways and looked at it curiously.

"I have a wireless router at home. This one looks different. It's a little smaller. And the antenna is odd," the guard said.

Lishi shrugged again. "I asked the friend who got me this job whether he'd taken any for himself, knowing the answer. He told me the Europeans weren't lying. They don't work. The antenna is supposed to distribute the wireless signal around the home more efficiently, but it doesn't. You and your men are welcome to take as many as you like to try them for yourself. Maybe you'll have more luck."

"What's this?" the guard said with a frown as he looked intently at the Gateway's underside.

Then he scraped at it with a fingernail.

Lishi felt as though his heart had stopped.

A tiny rectangular piece of paper fluttered to the ground.

The guard cursed and pulled a small flashlight from his belt. Then he trained it on the ground.

Lishi tried to look unconcerned. He doubted very much that he was succeeding.

Fortunately, the guard's attention was entirely focused on his search for the small slip of paper.

Which after a few seconds, he held up triumphantly and laughed.

"It's a 'Made in China' sticker! I can't remember the last time I saw one of these. The factory was too cheap to print it directly on their product! No wonder their junk doesn't work," the guard said, shaking his head.

Then the guard contemptuously tossed the Gateway into the nearest forty-foot container.

"So, now I'll answer your questions. No, we don't want any of this technotrash. And we won't confiscate and hold these containers. Let the stupid Europeans pay to ship them to Dali. It's a brand new line, and I'm sure they could use the money."

The new rail line from the Myanmar border to Dali had just opened after seemingly endless years under construction. Stretching over more than three hundred kilometers, three-quarters of its length was composed of bridges and tunnels. One tunnel under the Gaoligong Mountains was over thirty-four kilometers long.

Lishi nodded and said, "Yes, sir." In fact, he had no doubt that the Railway Authority would welcome Euros.

Lishi's documents only listed the two containers' travel as far as Dali. But payment had already been wired to the Railway Authority to send them on from there to Guangzhou, on China's heavily populated southern coast. From there, the Gateways would be easy to distribute for maximum effect.

Fortunately, the Chinese government made no effort to monitor ordinary commercial shipments' movements within its borders.

The guard snapped, "Close it up," and Lishi rushed to obey. By the time he hurried back to the semitrailer's cab, the documents Lishi had given the guard earlier were in his hand.

Now Lishi could see a large stamp had been affixed to the documents, with an attached metal grommet transfixing the entire sheaf of paper.

"Move along," the guard growled.

Lishi didn't have to be told twice.

As he drove the short distance to the train station, the same thought kept rolling around his head. Lishi's boss had said the Gateways he was carrying would help bring revolution to China.

How? He said free access to uncensored information through satellite Internet would let the people know how badly China was being ruled. Satellite Internet would also let them organize an effective movement to overthrow their oppressors, out of sight of government spies.

A China where you didn't deal with men like that border guard every day? People who were able to wield power without accountability of any kind, who considered it their right to command?

Lishi would believe it when he saw it.

CHAPTER FIFTY-EIGHT

The White House
Washington DC

President Hernandez's expression could hardly have been more different than the last time Eli Wade and General Robinson had been shown into the Oval Office. Then he had been all smiles at seeing his most prominent campaign contributor and his favorite advisor.

Now Hernandez's glare as he looked up from the papers on his desk could have stripped paint.

Because now Hernandez saw Wade as the man who might force America into war with China.

And Robinson as the man who had failed to stop Wade, or even warn Hernandez that Wade posed such a danger to American national security.

Hernandez coldly gestured for both men to sit on the sofa while he took the large chair opposite them.

Then he took in Wade's bandaged face. Yes, Hernandez had been told that Wade's injuries weren't that serious, just bruises and stitches. Stitches from flying glass and bruises from being pushed to the ground by his security detail.

Still, he had to say something.

"How are you feeling?" Hernandez asked and immediately kicked himself at the note of genuine concern he heard in his voice.

Well, Wade didn't look good and had looked even worse when cameras had zoomed in on his bloody face right after the attempted assassination.

That was one reason why rather than having Wade arrested after his unauthorized rocket launch yesterday, Hernandez had decided on this meeting.

Plus, Hernandez thought he had a better chance of getting the truth than FBI interrogators could from a billionaire like Wade flanked by the best lawyers money could hire.

"I'm fine, Mr. President," Wade answered. "I may have a scar or two, but I can live with that."

Hernandez had to work hard to keep what he was thinking off his face. That Wade could afford the world's best plastic surgeons, and the only reason he would have any scar on his face is that he wanted it there. To remind everyone of the assassination attempt.

Hernandez instead nodded and said, "I'm glad to hear that."

Then he turned to Robinson and asked, "General, since this attack may be linked to recent rocket launches by Mr. Wade's company from Air Force facilities, I asked you to coordinate with the FBI on the investigation. Any news to report?"

Robinson nodded. "The FBI briefed me on an important discovery they made just before I came here, sir. They matched the round they recovered from the attack on Mr. Wade to another one in their ballistic database. That round was found near the recent incident in Nevada."

Hernandez frowned. "The one with the Claymore mine and the four dead bodies?"

Robinson nodded. "Yes, sir."

Hernandez shook his head. "That was days ago. So you're telling me this was no spur-of-the-moment attack."

"That's right, sir. It now looks like the assassins were test-firing their rifle out in the desert, and the dead men tried to steal it from them," Robinson said.

Hernandez nodded absently. "Yes. I remember that all the dead men had criminal records, so that fits."

Robinson continued, "The FBI has had no luck tracing whoever rented the office space used to stage the attack. The funds were wired to the rental agent, and he never met whoever paid in person. Everything was in the name of a bogus company, and payments were routed through a string of shell companies and offshore banks. The money was real enough, and that's all that mattered to the people renting the space."

Hernandez grunted. "We've had Presidential candidates with offshore accounts. Nothing financial surprises me anymore."

Then he paused. "You said 'assassins' plural. Do we know that for sure?"

"Yes, sir," Robinson said. "We suspected it from the start because snipers often operate with a spotter. Video footage from the office building they used is still being analyzed, but we think we've got images of the two men who carried out the attack."

Hernandez nodded. "Good. Any hope of identifying them through facial recognition?"

Robinson shook his head. "The FBI has already tried. The men were wearing windbreakers with hoods anytime they were on camera, plus sunglasses. With their eyes and ears covered, there's no hope of getting a match, even if we already have their images on file. All we can say for sure is that they were white and middle-aged."

"And not Chinese," Hernandez said flatly.

"Of course, that doesn't mean the Chinese couldn't have hired them, sir," Wade said.

Hernandez turned to Wade and started to say something but then visibly reconsidered.

"We'll get back to the Chinese in a moment," Hernandez said.

Turning back to Robinson, Hernandez asked, "Any trace of the assassins so far?"

Robinson shook his head. "Local police searched for blocks in every direction, but it looks like they escaped through San Francisco's sewer system. There was a report of trespassers in a hotel basement blocks away that may or may not be related. Since that hotel was next to a subway station, if it was them, it's safe to say they're now far from the scene. The FBI has passed on what little we know to all other law enforcement and border security agencies."

"But you think it's unlikely we'll find them," Hernandez said flatly.

Robinson nodded. "Yes, sir."

Hernandez turned back to Wade. "OK, Eli, you told the press that your Eagle missile launch was a test flight carrying nothing but instruments. That a communications snafu accounted for your failure to request authorization for the launch. And that you got the readings you were looking for during this so-called test, and everything went well. We both know none of that was true. What were you really up to, and what really happened?"

Hernandez could hear his voice rising towards the end and had made an effort to control his growing anger.

An effort that, he knew, had not been entirely successful.

"Mr. President, I'm going to tell you exactly what I did and why I did it. First, the Eagle rocket was carrying a payload of sixty SpaceLink satellites to provide Internet service to the countries around China," Wade said.

"And within it," Hernandez added quietly.

Wade nodded. "Yes. Believe me, when this all started, that wasn't my intention. But after the Chinese used a laser attack to destroy my satellites in orbit and then blew up two of my rockets, I'll admit my intentions changed. Every satellite I've launched or attempted to launch before this was headed for an orbit designed to provide Internet service to countries bordering China. But yes, I know now that there were and are Chinese citizens using those satellites to access the Internet free of their government's censorship."

"And what happened to the Eagle rocket's satellite payload?" Hernandez asked.

"It was struck by an object just like my last Spaceship's payload and was also destroyed. Mostly," Wade said with a smile.

"So, you're saying some satellites survived?" Hernandez asked.

Wade nodded. "Yes. Thirteen had time to deploy before the Chinese weapon struck the rest of the payload."

Hernandez sighed. "I'm going to pass over the fact you have no proof China was behind the strike on your satellites because I think it's likely they were. Do you think the Chinese government knows thirteen satellites survived?"

"No, sir, I don't. Because of astronomers' complaints, every generation of SpaceLink satellites has been less visible from the ground than the last. And no satellite has emitted a radio signal since deployment," Wade said.

Robinson frowned. "Mr. Wade, we both know that satellites must remain in contact with a ground station to remain viable. How can you be sure you'll be able to reestablish contact?"

Wade smiled. "Because we're still in contact with those satellites. I said they're not emitting any radio signals. But all of them have a tight-beam laser onboard. Too low power to communicate with a ground station, but able to reach other powered SpaceLink satellites I already had in orbit."

"Ingenious," Robinson said, nodding. "Not enough bandwidth for operation, but fine to maintain constant steerage contact."

"So, what do you plan to do with these thirteen satellites, assuming they still work?" Hernandez asked.

Wade shook his head. "I'm not planning to do anything. I've had time to think during the flight here. Risking my companies is one thing. But other people besides me could have been hurt or killed yesterday. From what I heard you say about Nevada, I guess they already have. If the Chinese are setting off mines, blowing up rockets, and sending assassins to stop my satellites now, who knows how much further they're willing to go? It's time for me to step back and let you handle this."

"I'm glad to hear you say that," Hernandez said.

Seeing Wade's expression in response, he added quietly, "Do you have something else to tell us, Eli?"

Wade nodded. "Yes, sir. It's about the Spaceship launch yesterday."

Hernandez frowned. "The one that went off course and landed in Myanmar near the Chinese border. We assumed you did that deliberately to distract the Chinese from the Eagle launch."

"That's right, sir. That was one of its purposes. But the other was to deliver a cargo of Gateways to Forward," Wade said.

Hernandez stared at Wade. "Forward. The Chinese organization that's been calling for the overthrow of the Communist Party. That's claimed responsibility for the cyberattack on the Shanghai Stock Exchange. That Forward."

"Yes, sir," Wade said stoically.

"How many Gateways did you send? And anyway, I thought you said Gateways were being made by people you didn't authorize inside China. Was that a lie?" Hernandez asked.

"No, sir. I've never lied to you and never would. All the Gateways except the ones I sent yesterday were made in China without my knowledge or permission. I had these made and sent because I couldn't stand by while the Chinese government blew up my rockets without paying a price of any kind," Wade said quietly.

Wade paused and then added, "I think it's worth remembering the Chinese had already decided to kill me before I sent the Gateways. To answer your first question, enough Gateways to fill two forty-foot shipping containers. I don't know the exact number offhand, but thousands. We've managed to make them pretty small."

Hernandez shook his head. "Are they in China now?"

Wade nodded. "Yes, sir. Just before I boarded the flight here, I was notified that the Gateway shipment cleared Chinese customs at Ruili and is on a train bound for Guangzhou. From there, Forward will distribute them all over China."

"And even with the satellites that were destroyed, can people within China still use the ones that remain to access the Internet using these Gateways without government censorship or monitoring?" Hernandez asked.

"Not in a few areas within China's interior. But we estimate that over ninety percent of Chinese residents can still access a usable SpaceLink signal. That will improve a little once our Gateways are distributed. They're a higher quality product than what the Chinese produced," Wade replied.

"Of course they are," Hernandez said acidly, shaking his head. "Do you have any idea what you've done?"

"If you mean taking action to support Forward's call for free and fair elections in China, yes, I do. I don't support government censorship, and I don't think you do either. If my Gateways make it harder for the Communist Party to impose it, isn't that a good thing?" Wade said defiantly.

"But that's not all they're doing, is it? What about the Shanghai Stock Exchange cyberattack? Americans lost money in that too. And who knows what else Forward is planning? Isn't one of the points of these Gateways that Forward can plan and execute more attacks without any chance the Chinese government will find out?" Hernandez asked.

Wade shrugged. "Sure, they could be used that way. But I'll tell you something I didn't on my last visit. I talked with my SpaceLink chief about finding a way to cut off Chinese users without a paid account when their government attacked my satellites with a laser weapon. And then destroyed two of my rockets, plus most of the cargo on a third. If they hadn't, we wouldn't be where we are now."

Hernandez sat back, suddenly thoughtful. "Of course. You've always been able to cut off users inside China if you decided to do it."

Wade held up his hands and shook his head. "I said we were talking about how to do it. It's not like flipping a switch. We also have to be sure we're not shutting off any legitimate users in the countries bordering China by mistake."

"Frankly, your customer service reputation isn't my priority here. We're talking about a country with thermonuclear weapons and the means to deliver them to where we sit. Governed by a Communist Party that made it clear how far they'll go to stay in power by running over Chinese citizens with tanks at Tiananmen. The safety of American citizens is what I care about most, first, last, and always," Hernandez said.

Wade nodded. "I can't argue with that. Especially after finding myself in China's crosshairs. So, do you want me to shut off satellite Internet service to the Gateways in China?"

Hernandez shook his head. "For now, no. What you will do is coordinate with General Robinson and whoever he designates to accomplish two things. First, to ensure that if I decide to shut off the Gateways, it will happen as soon as I give the order. Second, to be sure I am the only one who can decide to turn on the last thirteen satellites you deployed."

Wade looked puzzled. "Yes, sir. I have to admit, though, I'm confused. You mean there's a chance you'll want to improve Gateway access in China?"

Hernandez nodded. "One of the first things I've learned in this job is not to foreclose options. Today I don't think I'll want to turn on your satellites. But who knows what will happen tomorrow?"

Wade stood, correctly guessing that their meeting was over. "Understood, sir. I'll get right on it."

"Thanks, Eli. General, please come back after you see Mr. Wade out. There's a lot we need to discuss," Hernandez said.

"Yes, sir," Robinson replied.

Once they were gone, Hernandez almost called for another cup of coffee but stopped himself. It would be his fourth today, and it wasn't yet noon.

The Chinese government wouldn't be able to prove America was behind its lost base and submarine. Or the satellite Internet devices letting thousands of its citizens avoid Chinese censorship and tracking.

Any more than Hernandez could prove China was behind destroying American satellites and rockets. And trying to assassinate one of its leading citizens.

Yes. Probably best to keep his nerves steady while discussing options with General Robinson.

CHAPTER FIFTY-NINE

Zhongnanhai Compound
Beijing, China

President Lin looked at General Yang, the Air Force commander, and shook his head.

"You told me that a review of radar tracks after the attack on our base at the Indian border established that the drones were launched from Jorhat Air Force Station, correct?"

Yang nodded. "That's right, sir. In India's Assam province, close to our border. Jorhat AFS has been active for decades as a transport base and currently has two squadrons of An-32 aircraft on station. It's only recently that drones were added."

"So, tell me why you think attacking it in retaliation for the Indian attack on our base would be a mistake," Lin said.

Yang could see from Lin's scowl that he would need to tread carefully.

"Sir, we have the ability to strike Jorhat or any other base in India. However, you asked us to avoid civilian casualties. Our analysis shows that may not be possible. Jorhat's rural area is heavily populated, with a total of about a million residents. Farming is carried out nearly to the air force station's fence line. But that is not the only issue," Yang said.

Lin sighed. "What else?"

"Well, sir, those transport aircraft I mentioned are there primarily to carry out airdrops of food and medicine to people living in remote villages. Our strike will certainly destroy many, if not most, of those An-32s. The Indian government is likely to focus attention on that aspect of our strike, rather than the drones," Yang said.

"You let me worry about that," Lin said. "The Indians can spin this any way they want. They started this, but I'm going to finish it. After Forward interrupted my broadcast announcing we will take action against India, we looked weak. That cannot stand. Notify me as soon as planning for the strike is complete and you're ready to launch. Make sure you tell no one besides the men in your command who will be involved in the actual mission."

Yang wanted to point out that the Night Tiger's commando strike on the Indian sniper outpost had started this. And that it was nearly certain the Indians would respond to an attack on Jorhat AFS with one of their own against a Chinese airbase.

But he could see that Lin was in no mood to listen to any of that.

Instead, Yang said, "Yes, sir," saluted, and left.

Once Yang was in the President's reception area, he saw Admiral Bai was waiting to see Lin.

Why does the commander of South Sea Fleet Headquarters need to see the President, Yang wondered.

Too bad he couldn't ask.

Instead, they just nodded at each other politely and exchanged wry smiles.

As Yang realized, Bai was probably wondering why Lin had wanted to see him.

One of Lin's assistants called Bai to come forward. At least, Yang thought, now Bai would have the answer to one question.

Admiral Bai saluted as he entered Lin's office. Lin acknowledged the salute with an irritated wave and gestured for Bai to sit.

"Admiral, I understand you believe the American submarine that attacked our base has escaped after sinking one of our newest submarines," Lin said.

Bai nodded. "Yes, sir. At least, we have confirmed that our submarine was sunk from debris retrieved at sea. No such debris has been found from an American submarine. Though the possibility exists that it was sunk without trace, I think that unlikely."

Bai wanted to add that there was no real proof that the Americans had destroyed the base at Ziyou Island. Or that they had meant to do so. Or that they had sunk the *Changzheng 20*.

First, because he didn't think Lin would listen. Also, because Bai thought the Americans had some responsibility for their actions, no matter what.

Bai assumed he was here to make an appropriate response. Say, sink an American submarine, or perhaps even two.

He quickly discovered his assumption was wrong.

"I want you to prepare a target list for my approval. We are going to destroy an American naval base. I don't care which one. I suggest a method that will keep our sailors safe, like cruise missiles fired from a distance, but that's your call. I'm not the expert," Lin said.

Bai was stunned. There were no American bases within China's range as small as the one at Ziyou Island.

And what about retaliation?

And escalation?

Bai rapidly thought about the many American military bases in the Pacific. All with thousands of personnel. Okinawa. Yokohama. Guam.

Hawaii.

Bai's thoughts raced forward. The Japanese had paid a terrible price for attacking the Americans, and American troops were still on Japanese soil all these decades later.

What could he say that might change Lin's mind?

Bai knew the answer to that question as soon as it came to him.

Nothing.

But Bai did have another question to ask.

"Sir, I understand that this attack will take place using the forces under my command. Should I expect to coordinate with higher headquarters here in Beijing?" Bai asked.

Lin immediately shook his head. "No. When I called you for this meeting, I told you to tell no one, and I have a reason for that order. Operational security must be paramount if our attack is to be successful. The Americans have spies everywhere and are always watching and listening to all we do. Our only hope of victory is to keep this mission secret. You must inform no one of this order except the sailors in whatever ships or submarines you select to carry it out."

Outwardly Bai nodded his understanding and said, "Yes, sir."

It wasn't easy, though. An icy realization had just struck Bai.

Lin was keeping this order secret from the Politburo. The only ones in China with authority to remove Lin.

Which they might do if they realized Lin was about to start a war with the Americans.

But if the war were already underway, they would have no choice but to rally behind him.

And Bai had no way to legally refuse Lin's orders since he was Commander in Chief.

Bai hoped he had been successful at keeping this realization off his face.

Apparently so, because Lin smiled and said, "Excellent, Admiral. I look forward to seeing your target list soon. Let's say by this time two days from now."

"Yes, sir," Bai said as he stood, saluted, and left Lin's office.

Bai was still deep in thought as he reached the building's entrance and reached in his pocket for his phone. A Navy driver was on call for him while he was in Beijing but was not allowed to idle in front of the President's office.

"May I offer you a ride, Admiral?" Yang asked.

Bai was startled, having been so occupied with his dilemma that he hadn't even seen Yang was there.

He must have been waiting for me, Bai realized.

On the one hand, Yang was outside Bai's chain of command.

On the other, Yang certainly outranked him as Air Force Commander, while Bai only commanded a single naval force.

There was only one possible reply.

"Thank you, General. I'd be honored," Bai said.

Besides, Bai was curious. Why did Yang want to speak to him?

Once Yang's car was underway, he leaned over and said to his driver, "Xijiao Airport. Take your time getting there."

Bai nodded. Of course. Yang hadn't had any trouble guessing that Bai would be using Beijing's military airport to return to his headquarters after seeing the President.

Then Yang turned to Bai and smiled. "You may speak freely. My driver is one of the few men with my absolute trust, and this car is swept for listening devices daily."

Bai nodded his understanding but said nothing.

Yang's smile widened. "Good. If I were you, I'd be cautious too. So I'll go first. The President wanted to see me to order an attack on an Indian air station. One that sits in a heavily populated area, where civilian casualties will be impossible to avoid. Casualties that will make an Indian response inevitable and may quickly escalate to a wider war with a nuclear-armed opponent. He's ordered me to tell nobody but the men in my command involved in the mission."

Bai nodded. "So, why then are you telling me?"

"Because I'm guessing the President just gave you a similar order. And that he gave the order to you rather than your superior officer here in Beijing because he wants to keep the order secret from the Politburo," Yang replied.

"Let's say that's true," Bai said. "What prevents you from going to the Politburo? Wouldn't they listen to the Air Force Commander?"

Yang shook his head. "Under my leadership, the Air Force has had some recent successes. It has also had one failure. Though still secret from the public, that failure is known to the Politburo. Whatever I say could be taken by some there as an attempt to salvage my position. The President knows all this."

Bai frowned. "Then what's to be gained from telling you what the President has ordered me to do?"

Yang smiled. "That depends on the orders, doesn't it? We're both military men. We know that no problem can be solved without all the information available. And that we're stronger together."

Bai sat silently for a moment.

He didn't trust Yang. At all.

But Bai didn't trust his superiors in Beijing either.

At least he knew Yang thought attacking the Indians was a mistake.

Bai made up his mind. Yang was undoubtedly a far more influential figure in Beijing than he was. Maybe he could do something to stop this before a wider war began against two countries with nuclear weapons.

"The President wants me to destroy an American naval base. One of our bases was attacked a few days ago, killing a few dozen men, and one of our submarines was sunk. We think the Americans did both but have no proof. Since they don't have any bases as small as ours we can reach, I'll be forced to attack a larger American target," Bai said.

Yang looked at Bai speechlessly for a moment.

"Lin has to be stopped," Yang said finally. "The Americans will retaliate at once. And their conventional and nuclear forces are still far superior to ours."

Then Yang paused. "How long before this attack is supposed to happen?"

"I was given two days to provide the President with target options," Bai replied.

Yang nodded. "My deadline was less specific, but I know he'll expect a response by then from me too. Very well. Stall if you can. I'll try to get you word on what I and anyone I can convince are doing to stop this."

"Understood," Bai said.

Though he couldn't imagine how anyone could stop war now.

Chapter Sixty

August 1st Building
Beijing, China

The Central Military Commission (CMC) was housed in the Ministry of National Defense compound, which everyone called the August 1st building. The date was a reference to the People's Liberation Army's founding during the 1927 Nanchang Uprising.

The August 1st building was the closest Chinese equivalent to the American Pentagon. It was most similar in one way. Civilian leadership was paramount. Though the Central Military Commission included generals like Yang and Shi, it was chaired by the Commander in Chief, President Lin. And its most important positions were held by top Communist Party officials.

The building was also full of listening devices installed by Song's Ministry of State Security.

Air Force Commander Yang and Army Commander Shi were taking a chance today that all the listening devices in the building's sauna had been successfully discovered and temporarily disabled by one of Yang's technicians. Both of them had made a habit of using the sauna to relax after a long day, so no one would be surprised to learn they had been there.

They had both been mindful of the ever-present bugs on previous encounters and kept their conversations innocuous. The sauna's use was restricted to generals and admirals, and any that ranked lower than Yang or Shi who happened to be there when either came quickly found a reason to be elsewhere. So, they could be sure of privacy for today's conversation.

A bonus to this meeting's sauna setting was that Yang and Shi both knew neither of them could be hiding a recording device on their person.

Yang began by explaining what he had learned from Admiral Bai about President Lin's plan to attack the Americans. Plus, Lin's orders to have Yang strike an Indian air station in a heavily populated area.

Shi was still for nearly a minute, and Yang could see he was close to shock.

Well, who could blame him?

Then Shi slowly shook his head. "You were right all along. I see that now. Lin must be stopped. But don't you think the CMC might be willing to overrule his plans? Recent events at the Indian border have raised serious questions about his leadership. As well as Forward's successful attacks."

Yang frowned. "But Lin remains CMC chairman unless and until the Politburo strips him of that title. And that won't happen before Lin launches his attacks. If we go to the CMC and try to make our case while Lin is still chairman, he'll remove and replace us before we're even able to speak. And you know what will happen to us then."

Shi was still again, but he didn't need long this time to decide. "You're right. We will need to use the more direct method we previously discussed. The device, as well as the technician, will be ready tomorrow morning. I will make sure the bomb threat call cannot be traced."

Yang looked at Shi intently. "And the technician will not be the same man who built the device."

Shi smiled. "Please. Give me that much credit, at least."

Yang nodded. "Sorry, but you know how many things could go wrong with this plan. And your supposed medic will be ready as well?"

Shi shrugged. "Yes. But you know as well as I do that it could all fall apart there. All Lin has to do is insist on seeing his regular doctor."

"That's true. If you have a better plan to suggest, I'm ready to hear it," Yang replied.

And Yang meant it. The assassination plan as it stood was too complicated. But the plan had to do more than just kill Lin. It had to do so in a way that couldn't be traced back to Yang and Shi. And Lin couldn't die before he gave one crucial order.

Shi immediately shook his head. "No. I have given the problem as much thought as I know you have. I see no better alternative."

"Very well," Yang said. "And your troops in Beijing are ready for the next phase once Lin is dead?"

"Yes," Shi said shortly. Then he cocked his head and looked at Yang. "Do you think Song will order his men to resist no matter what? They're nearly as well-armed as my troops, and here in Beijing almost as numerous."

"Impossible to know," Yang replied with a shrug. "We'll find out tomorrow."

Zhongnanhai Compound
Beijing, China

President Lin stood impatiently next to his desk as General Yang was shown in by his assistant.

"General, I hope you're here to tell me that your forces are ready to strike that Indian base as we discussed," Lin said.

"Yes, sir," Yang replied. "We will be striking tomorrow as you ordered."

"Excellent," Lin said. "I presume you're now on your way to the weekly CMC meeting?"

"That's right, sir. I'm sure I will see you there. As you ordered, I will say nothing to the Commission."

"Good. Since I have you here, why don't you come with me?" Lin said.

Said, not asked. Though it would have looked like a question on paper, Lin's tone made it clear it was an order.

"Of course, sir," Yang replied automatically. While his mind was racing furiously.

This shouldn't derail the plan. Should it?

As they walked together out of the building, Yang's cell phone rang.

"I'm sorry, sir, but my office knows to call me here only in case of a true emergency. I must answer," Yang said.

Lin stopped and turned, one eyebrow arched with surprise. "I believe you. I've never heard your phone ring before. Answer, and then tell me about this emergency."

Yang tapped his phone and then put it to his head.

"Yang here. What? Is the threat credible? An Army bomb technician is already here? Very well. Tell me as soon as you know more."

Yang tapped his phone again and said, "Sir, we must reenter the building."

Then he pointed to the President's limousine, where a man could be seen underneath it doing something with a piece of equipment.

"Sir, there is a credible bomb threat from Forward. The Army has a technician examining your car because they fear your regular security detail has been compromised. But it's not safe here. We must..."

Yang wasn't able to finish his sentence.

The explosion's shock wave pushed both Yang and Lin to the ground.

After a brief moment of blackness, Yang opened his eyes.

The President's limousine was in too many pieces to count. Presumably, so was the man who had been under it.

As soon as he could move, Yang went towards Lin, cursing. The bomb wasn't supposed to have been that powerful.

Though otherwise, its detonation had been carefully planned. The man who had just planted it had been told he was to go through the motions of disarming a fake device.

Obviously, not one that would be detonated by remote control as soon as Lin had exited the building.

Yang hadn't expected to be standing with Lin when the bomb went off. But now that he'd survived the explosion, Yang thought that fact should help deflect suspicion.

But Yang's curses were still genuine. Because Lin had to be alive. There was one order Lin had to give, or all this had been for nothing.

Lin groaned, and his eyes fluttered open. Yes!

"Sir, there's been an explosion. Are you injured?" Yang asked.

Lin sat up, dazed. Then he looked at the smoking wreckage that was all that was left of his limousine.

Yang looked at Lin carefully. No shrapnel damage he could see, but who knew what internal injuries he might have suffered.

Finally, Lin shook his head.

"Let me help you into the building where you'll be safe," Yang said.

Right on cue, Shi's troops were everywhere, pushing back the men from Lin's regular MSS security detail who had tried to come to his aid.

"Why are these soldiers here?" Lin asked in a weary voice as Yang helped him up.

"Sir, the Army has information that Forward may have infiltrated MSS. General Shi has sent troops to protect you until an investigation can determine what happened and who was responsible," Yang replied.

Lin swayed a little as he thought over what Yang had just said and finally nodded.

"I want to go to my office," Lin said.

Perfect, Yang thought.

Aloud he just said, "Yes, sir."

Moments later, they were back in Lin's office. Lin sank into the sofa closest to the door.

Yang snapped at the nearest soldiers, "Guard the President's office. We need a military doctor in here!"

Lin looked up tiredly. "Can't you find my regular doctor?" he asked.

"Sir, I don't think we have time to waste," Yang replied.

Lin didn't answer but nodded in agreement.

Yang's heart jumped. One hurdle passed. Now for the next.

Yang waved to Lin's chief of staff, Meng, who had been hovering anxiously near his office door.

"Meng, come in, please," Yang said.

Then Yang said, "Mr. President, I believe immediate action is needed to safeguard you after this attack. I recommend that responsibility for your security and the other members of the Central Military Commission be placed in the hands of military police reporting to General Shi. Reports General Shi has received that Forward has infiltrated the Ministry of State Security must be investigated. If you agree, I recommend that Meng issue the necessary orders in your name, putting General Shi in charge of CMC security and beginning a military investigation of the MSS. Today's attack may not be over. We must act."

Lin looked uncertain, and for a moment, Yang feared he would refuse.

Then Lin sat back tiredly and nodded. "Meng, do as he recommends," he said.

"Yes, Mr. President," Meng said and hurried off to give the necessary orders.

An Army doctor appeared at the office door holding a black case. Yang waved him forward.

"Doctor, please examine the President immediately. He has been close enough to a bomb explosion to be forced to the ground by the blast. I am concerned that there may be internal injuries," Yang said in a voice he was sure was loud enough to be heard by everyone in the outer office.

The doctor nodded and said, "An ambulance is on its way with a military escort and should be here any minute. I will examine the President in the meantime."

Yang raised his voice even higher. "Meng, close the door and no interruptions while the President is being examined. Tell us as soon as the ambulance is here."

Meng had a phone pressed to his head but waved his understanding and closed the door.

The doctor said, "Mr. President, first I am going to take your blood pressure."

Lin nodded and sat still as the doctor placed the cuff on his arm and took the reading.

A look of concern appeared on the doctor's face, and he said. "Sir, your blood pressure is far too high. In your state, I don't want to risk an injection."

Then he reached in his black bag and pulled out a clear ampoule, a hermetically sealed small bulbous glass vessel. Next, he snapped off the top.

"This medication will reduce your blood pressure almost immediately. Please drink it, sir," the doctor said calmly.

Yang did his best to keep his composure. It probably helped, he thought, that worry about his plan's chances for success could be mistaken for concern about Lin's health.

Lin looked at the ampoule dubiously, and Yang held his breath. Would he refuse?

Then Lin said, "Well, I suppose it's better than a shot. I've always hated needles."

Lin reached for the ampoule and swallowed its contents.

The result was indeed almost immediate.

Lin's right hand reached for his throat while his left waved frantically.

Then Lin collapsed onto the floor, where he lay twitching on his side while Yang and the doctor watched.

In seconds, Lin was still.

The doctor rolled Lin onto his back and shined a small light into his eyes.

"Fixed and dilated," he said.

Then the doctor took Lin's pulse and quickly said, "No pulse."

Yang tapped his phone and said, "Have the ambulance arrive."

Then Yang walked to the office door and flung it open. The doctor behind him had begun to go through the motions of administering CPR, though he knew the untraceable poison he had handed Lin would make it futile.

"The President has had a heart attack!" Yang shouted. "Where is that ambulance?"

No sooner had he said the words than an ambulance pulled up to the building's entrance, followed by three military vehicles bristling with guns and soldiers.

Two men in medical uniforms ran from the ambulance carrying a stretcher. In just a few minutes, Lin was in the ambulance and on his way to 301 Military Hospital.

Or rather, his body was. Accompanied by two men who would make sure that in the unlikely event Lin revived, his recovery would be short-lived.

One hour later, Presidential chief of staff Meng was notified by a doctor at 301 Military Hospital that Lin had died of complications from internal injuries suffered in the bomb blast, which had provoked a heart attack.

Meng then notified Vice President Gu that he was to assume the duties of the Presidency. He also told Gu of Lin's last order placing responsibility for his security and the other members of the Central Military Commission in the hands of military police reporting to General Shi and opening a military investigation into the Ministry of State Security.

Gu told Meng he would proceed to the Presidential office immediately and confirmed Lin's last order.

Yang's plan had worked.

Gu held the title of President, and the Communist Party would still control China's economy and society.

But from now on, General Yang and General Shi would decide how China's military power should best be used.

Chapter Sixty-One

SS Sunny Day
En Route to Ensenada, Mexico

Anatoly Grishkov gripped the boat's railing tightly as it bobbed up and down on the Pacific Ocean. He thought his stomach was now completely empty but would stay here for a while, to be sure.

Grishkov had thought his seasickness was over earlier, only to be proved wrong.

Mikhail Vasilyev passed Grishkov a damp washcloth, which he accepted with a grateful grunt. After using it to clean his face, he felt better.

Then Grishkov looked at Vasilyev and shook his head. It wasn't fair. Neither he nor Alina appeared bothered in the least by the boat's endless rolling motion as it made its way south.

Craning his head, Grishkov could just see Alina at the back end of the boat. What was she doing back there?

"So, are you ready to undertake the next stage of our mission here on the *Sunny Day*?" Vasilyev asked gravely.

Keeping his right hand on the railing, Grishkov turned to see whether he could guess what Vasilyev meant.

The *Sunny Day* was a Navigator 400 boat built in 2008. About sixteen meters long, Alina had said the *Sunny Day* had a top speed of forty-five kilometers per hour, though she planned a more sedate cruising speed of thirty KPH.

Grishkov finally decided he could risk stepping away from the railing and took a few steps towards Alina. Now he could see what was in her hands.

A fishing pole.

No, there were actually three poles, side by side. Grishkov could see the rods were mounted on brackets of some sort from his new vantage point.

"Feeling better?" Alina asked with a wave.

Grishkov made his way unsteadily towards Alina, followed by Vasilyev. Once Grishkov was within a couple of meters, he answered.

"Now you see why I joined the Army rather than the Navy. This is only my second time on a boat, and I sincerely hope it will be the last."

Alina smiled and shook her head. "And yet you have parachuted from great heights and been on many helicopter rides, including one where the pilot was doing his best to outrun a nuclear blast."

Grishkov smiled back, though Alina noticed the smile was a bit shaky. "Yes, but none of those experiences included water. Now, are these poles just for show, or do you really expect me to try my hand at fishing?"

Alina shrugged. "Up to you. Normally I'd say if you don't fish, you don't eat, but I suspect that won't be much of an incentive for you at this point."

Grishkov shook his head. "Certainly not. After all the effort I've made to empty my stomach, I have no interest in repeating the exercise."

Then Grishkov noticed several red plastic tanks nearby and pointed at the closest one.

"Extra fuel?" he asked.

Alina nodded. "And by now, we've burned enough that we can empty these small tanks into the boat's main fuel reservoir. These should give us more than enough range to make it to Ensenada."

"Good," Grishkov said. "That's a task I can handle. Just point me towards the main fuel tank, and I'll take care of it."

Vasilyev cocked his head curiously. "Ordinarily, I would offer to help my ailing friend, but I'm guessing there is some purpose to fishing beyond recreation and our next meal."

"Correct," Alina replied. "These waters are regularly patrolled by the US Coast Guard. There is a good chance we will be boarded at some point, and if we are, I would like us to look as innocent as possible."

"Very well. As it happens, I've gone fishing several times, including once on the Caspian Sea with my father. So, I at least know the basics," Vasilyev said.

"Good. I've leave you to it, then, while I show Anatoly the way to the main fuel tank," Alina said as she turned towards Grishkov.

Then Alina added over her shoulder, "If you get a strike before I return, remember that there are sharks in these waters. Try not to pull up anything on deck capable of fighting back."

Vasilyev laughed and said, "Thanks for the reminder. Though the people who live on its shores insist otherwise, scientists say there are no sharks in the Caspian Sea. Certainly, I never caught one. I'll try to keep that record intact today."

There were high, cushioned stools bolted to the deck behind each pole. Vasilyev soon had a baited line in the water and a comfortable perch to see whether anything was interested.

A few minutes later, Alina returned alone. "We're refueled. I sent Grishkov below to get some sleep."

Then she nodded with approval at Vasilyev and said, "I can see you have indeed done this before."

Vasilyev shrugged. "This pole is a little bigger than what I'm used to, but I suppose the fish out here are a bit larger as well. The only really large fish in the Caspian Sea were sturgeons, but it was illegal to catch them."

Alina smiled. "I've heard that doesn't stop many people on both the Russian and Iranian sides from doing just that."

Vasilyev frowned. "Yes. As well as fishermen from Azerbaijan, Turkmenistan, and Kazakhstan. My father Alexei was with me in a restaurant in Derbent when we overheard one of the customers ordering sturgeon made into sushi. An "off-menu" item, of course. Alexei was good friends with the police chief there, and so a quick text later, the customer and the owner were both in custody."

Alina laughed. "I hope you went elsewhere for your meal!"

Vasilyev grinned back. "Yes. I wouldn't have risked anything that came out of that kitchen."

Then Alina looked thoughtful. "Derbent. Why does that name sound familiar?"

Vasilyev nodded. "It should. Derbent claims with some justification to be the oldest city in what is today Russia, with documentation dating back eight centuries before Christ. It's also the most southern city in Russia."

Alina nodded. "Makes sense. Right on the coast, next to what used to be some of the best fishing in the world. And certainly warmer than Moscow!"

Then she pointed at his line. "I think you've got something!"

Moments later, a wriggling fish that Vasilyev guessed weighed about three kilos was in his net.

"What sort of fish is this?" Vasilyev asked. "Is it good to eat?"

"See these stripes? That's how you know you've caught a striped bass. And yes, they are very tasty. An excellent start!" Alina said.

Vasilyev smiled. "I think this fish will be enough dinner for both of us. I very much doubt Grishkov will be joining us at table."

"I'm sure you're right," Alina said with a laugh. "But keeping us fed isn't the main point, remember."

Vasilyev nodded. "Of course. The more fish we catch, the less suspicious we will seem."

Alina shrugged. "You may think my caution excessive. But I've always believed in taking every step possible. It's not as though we have anything else to do."

Vasilyev couldn't help then but think about his failure to assassinate Wade. The truth was, though, he had mixed feelings about the outcome.

Wade was no enemy of Russia. He understood the logic that had put Wade in his crosshairs. But that didn't mean he agreed with it.

Vasilyev had never failed to achieve a mission objective before. What did that mean for his future career in the FSB?

And would Neda's success with her mission be enough to shield her from the failure of her spouse?

Alina's voice cut through his dark thoughts. "I think you've got another customer," she said.

Vasilyev looked up, startled, to see that the pole next to him was bent forward. Then he realized that Alina had baited and cast the line while he was thinking about Wade and Neda.

Vasilyev could see from Alina's understanding smile that she had guessed his thoughts or at least some of them. He approved of her method of dealing with them.

Show sympathy, and keep the agent busy.

This time the fish put up more of a fight, and Vasilyev was surprised at its size. He guessed its weight at about fifteen kilos.

"Your father taught you well," Alina said. "You have caught a California halibut. In my opinion, it's even tastier than the bass, and that's saying something."

"California halibut," Vasilyev repeated. "That implies there are other types?"

"Correct," Alina said. "The female Pacific halibut can reach well over two hundred kilos."

Vasilyev's eyes widened. "Are these poles up to such a creature?"

Alina laughed. "Well, there's nothing to do but keep fishing and see!"

Then she frowned and looked to her right. "I think we're about to have company."

Vasilyev followed her gaze and nodded. "Yes, I see it too. A fairly large ship. Perhaps a hundred meters long?"

Alina looked through her binoculars and then said, "Yes," with a sigh. "With a crew of over a hundred. It is one of the first of the Coast Guard's new *Heritage* class. Only a few have been built. It has a cannon, machine guns, and a helicopter."

Vasilyev shrugged. "So, it appears we will not be able to outfight or outrun them."

Alina looked at him sharply but then saw from the twinkle in Vasilyev's eye that he was joking.

"Well, I was careful not to include weapons of any kind onboard. And I don't think we can beat its helicopter's top speed of over two hundred KPH. So yes, I think we should get ready to welcome our visitors. I will cut the engine. You can wake up Anatoly," Alina said.

A few minutes later, Vasilyev, Grishkov, and Alina were all on deck looking at the cutter as it came alongside.

"Let me do the talking," Alina said.

Vasilyev and Grishkov both nodded silently.

An officer holding a loudspeaker said, "Permission to come aboard" in a way that, while polite, made it clear it was not a request.

Alina waved her arm in a welcoming gesture and then stepped back from the boat's side facing the cutter. Vasilyev and Grishkov followed her lead.

In a low voice, Alina said, "Make sure your hands are visible at all times."

Moments later, four Coast Guard sailors were standing in front of them.

"Good afternoon, ma'am. My name is Lieutenant Foster, and we're here to conduct a safety inspection of your boat. Do you have any weapons on board?"

"No, Lieutenant, we don't. Please feel free to check anything on board. It's not a very big boat, so I hope it won't take long," Alina said.

Foster nodded to the three other sailors, who moved on to begin their inspection.

"It should be pretty quick. I don't see any violations yet, and overall your boat looks to be in excellent shape. Have you had her long?" Foster asked.

"Not long," Alina said. "In fact, we're headed down to Ensenada, where we plan to sell her on behalf of the Russian Consulate."

Foster nodded. "That's the one in San Francisco?"

"That's right," Alina replied.

Foster nodded again. "Do you all have any identification?"

"Of course," Alina said with a smile and pulled three Russian passports from a plain brown envelope.

Foster held up each one in turn, matching the photos to the three people in front of him. Then he took pictures of each data page and returned the passports to Alina.

"So, Mr. Vasilyev and Mr. Grishkov. Sorry, but I'm not sure how to pronounce your last name," Foster said to Alina.

"Please, just call me Alina," she said with a smile.

"Do your friends speak English?" Foster asked.

"They do, but not as well as I can. We agreed that it's best I alone speak to avoid any possible misunderstanding," Alina said.

Foster nodded. "Interesting that you're planning to sell this boat in Ensenada, by the way. It should get a good price there. But have you thought about how much you'll lose converting pesos to dollars?"

Alina smiled. "We have an Embassy in Mexico City with many expenses payable in pesos. There will be no need to convert currency."

Foster smiled back. "Well, that makes sense."

Then he gestured to the open cooler where Alina had put the two fish Vasilyev had caught.

"I see you've been fishing. You've got some real beauties there. Do you happen to have California fishing licenses?" Foster asked.

Vasilyev and Grishkov both struggled to keep their expressions impassive. What nonsense was this? They were well outside the territorial waters claimed by the Americans.

"Certainly," Alina said, reaching inside the same brown envelope and handing three documents to Foster.

After glancing at them, Foster nodded and handed the fishing licenses back. "Well done. You'd be surprised how many Americans don't know that anyone on a boat leaving from a California port is required to have a California fishing license to put a line in the water. Now I'll be able to tell any American who complains about being reminded that if Russians know, they should too!"

The three other sailors now returned. Foster asked, "Any issues?"

One sailor handed Foster a flare gun and said, "Just this, sir."

Foster looked the flare gun over and nodded. Then he handed it to Alina.

"The cartridge in this flare gun expires next month. You may want to replace it before you make your sale. Have a good trip to Mexico, ma'am," Foster said.

"Thank you, officer," Alina said.

A few minutes later, Vasilyev, Grishkov, and Alina were alone again, watching the cutter as it rapidly resumed its patrol.

"So, was that true? Are you really selling this boat in Ensenada?" Vasilyev asked.

Alina nodded. "Yes. Well, not me personally. I'll be flying with you to Mexico City and from there back to Moscow. But we have an agent who will meet us in Ensenada and take charge of the sale."

Grishkov shook his head. "Seems like there should have been a simpler way to get us out of America. That didn't involve emptying my stomach into the Pacific."

"That's because you don't have the whole picture. Our operational funds in Mexico were recently depleted by the need to extract one of our agents. Think of this boat as a quick emergency replenishment. And as you heard me discuss with that Coast Guard officer, we should both make a profit on the sale and avoid paying a hefty currency conversion fee," Alina said.

Vasilyev grunted. "You told me you saw Neda safely off in Mexico City. So the money was spent on getting Kharlov back to Moscow?"

Alina nodded. "Yes. But I'll let him tell you the details himself. I think we'll all have quite a bit of catching up to do once we're back."

Vasilyev nodded silently.

Yes. But once they were finished talking, would Vasilyev still have a job?

Chapter Sixty-Two

FSB Headquarters
Moscow, Russia

Boris Kharlov smiled as Mikhail Vasilyev and Neda Rhahbar walked into the secure basement conference room.

"Good to see you both!" he said.

Vasilyev smiled back. "And you as well! I understand getting back was something of an adventure."

Kharlov sighed. "Yes. But I've been told to keep my mouth shut about the details. I think it's about time I started following orders."

Neda frowned and shook her head. "I'm not sure that's the right lesson here. If you hadn't taken some initiative, we would have failed in our mission."

The conference room door opened, and in walked Anatoly Grishkov. As he closed the door behind him, Grishkov said, "I see we've already started arguing. What is today's topic?"

Before anyone could respond, the door opened again to admit an unsmiling FSB Director Smyslov.

They all murmured greetings, which Smyslov dismissed with a wave.

"I will get right to business. I have just met with the President, and most of what I am going to tell you comes straight from him."

Smyslov paused and pointed at Neda.

"You alone in this group both followed orders and succeeded in your mission. The President, and I, both congratulate you on your success. He will award you the customary one million American dollars from his personal funds."

"Director, I am grateful. If I may, I would like to ask just one question. What became of the mission we prepared to carry out in Kazakhstan? Will we go there next?" Neda asked.

Smyslov started to speak and then frowned and said nothing for a moment.

"I was about to say that you have no need to know, and the fact that you and Kharlov spent more than a year preparing for that mission entitles you to nothing. Which would have been true," Smyslov said.

Smyslov paused for a moment to let that sink in.

"But I am going to tell you nevertheless. Because some here need to learn that there is often more than one way to reach an objective. Sometimes, without making the objective explode," Smyslov said.

Neda nodded and remained quiet.

"You and Kharlov were both ready to carry out a complex mission that would have destroyed several nuclear missiles held back by the Kazakh government from the Soviet period. We were confident we could gain you entry to the missile complex and that you would succeed in your mission. The mission planner, however, rated your chances of escape afterward as low," Smyslov said.

"Alina," Vasilyev said shortly.

Smyslov nodded. "Yes. Based on her recommendation, we looked for another way to achieve the objective. After some research, we found one.

The opportunity arose during the Kazakh Vice-President's recent unofficial trip to Thailand."

Vasilyev nodded. "Kompromat."

"Just so," Smyslov said. "I will not go into the details of the blackmail material, which were quite sordid. But they were more than enough to ensure his execution if they had become known to the Kazakh President, Sadykov. Confronted with the video, he agreed to provide us with the access we needed to Sadykov's kitchen to carry out our alternate plan."

"Poison," Vasilyev said softly.

"Yes. Mind you, even with access, it was not simple. We suspended one of Sadykov's favorite vegetables in a solution containing the poison for several days until it was infused without visible trace. Of course, colorless and odorless," Smyslov said.

Vasilyev frowned. "Doesn't Sadykov have a taster?"

"Indeed he does," Smyslov said with an approving nod. "I hope the rest of you are paying attention to this lesson because the method may come up again. We administered the antidote to this poison to the taster without his knowledge before he ate the test portion of Sadykov's meal."

Neda asked hesitantly, "But Director, can we be sure the Vice-President will hand over the warheads after he becomes President?"

Smyslov nodded. "As I said, the kompromat was quite sordid. We could place it on Kazakh websites, and since his country borders Russia, he knows we could have it broadcast on Kazakh TV sets. But none of that will be necessary. The warheads were flown to Russia a few hours ago. You will hear about Sadykov's death from a heart attack and his replacement by the Vice-President from regular media channels later today."

"And if the new Kazakh President ever gets out of line, we still have the kompromat," Vasilyev said.

"Just so," Smyslov said with a smile.

Then he made a wave that included both Vasilyev and Grishkov. "You failed in your mission but followed your orders. As far as we can tell, the Americans have no idea we were behind the assassination attempt on Eli Wade. And, the new Chinese President has told our President that he is satisfied with your efforts. More, that he is happy you failed, and he would have never authorized your mission. Most important of all, he will honor his predecessor's deal to import our oil and gas. So, the President has awarded you each half a million American dollars."

Vasilyev and Grishkov both looked at each other with relief. Neither of them had been expecting any bonus. Vasilyev, in particular, had been worried about whether he would even be able to continue his career with the FSB.

Finally, Smyslov turned to Kharlov.

"Your performance is mixed. On the one hand, you accomplished your mission. On the other, not only did you fail to follow orders. By bringing unauthorized explosives, you were very nearly captured by the Americans. If Alina had not intervened, you and your comrades might have been identified and linked back to us. The consequences could have been catastrophic."

Kharlov nodded. "Alina has explained this to me. I have no excuse. I can only say that if I am given the opportunity, I will not repeat my mistake."

Smyslov grunted. "It was only with great difficulty that I persuaded the President to give you that chance. Only my proposal to have Alina take charge of your retraining convinced him."

Then Smyslov paused and shook his head.

"Alina was one of the last agents the President personally recruited when he was FSB Director. He has great respect for her capabilities. Remember that if you fail again, it will reflect directly on her."

"I will not fail either you or her, Director. I swear it," Kharlov said, looking Smyslov in the eye.

Finally, Smyslov shrugged. "We shall see. In the meantime, you must reimburse the State for the money expended on your rescue. I convinced the President to allow this to be done by forfeiting your salary for the next several years. In the meantime, I believe you have enough saved to get by."

Kharlov was sure Smyslov knew how much he had in his Moscow accounts down to the last kopeck and simply nodded.

"Now, I know you have all seen the classified reports about the increased influence of China's military after recent events," Smyslov said.

They all nodded.

"However, what you don't know is that the military's influence is even greater than we had first believed. The Communist Party still runs China's economy and sets domestic policy with little military interference. But military and foreign policy are firmly in the hands of China's two leading generals," Smyslov said.

Then Smyslov paused and waved his hand around the room. "You will be wondering, what does this have to do with us? Well, this. China plans to invade Taiwan, and soon."

There was a moment of silence, and then Vasilyev asked hesitantly, "But why does that matter to us? And hadn't we seen that as inevitable at some point?"

"Inevitable, no. There was always the possibility that as China became increasingly prosperous, Taiwan might agree to reunification voluntarily. Taiwan has, after all, invested billions in manufacturing goods in mainland China. Not so long ago, such investments would have been unthinkable," Smyslov said.

Then he took a deep breath and shook his head. "But we have unmistakable evidence of China's intentions. In particular, a large Chinese order of our planes, helicopters, and other military equipment that can have only one use. Now, you are right that a Chinese takeover of Taiwan doesn't appear to affect us directly. But if you think a little harder, maybe you will see why the President is so concerned."

Grishkov said, "Won't adding Taiwan's economy and military resources to their own make China a more formidable adversary?"

Smyslov nodded. "The short answer is yes. Taiwan's lead in several areas of computer technology may be even more important. However, China's sheer size reduces Taiwan's relative importance. So, while we would never have welcomed a Chinese takeover of Taiwan, that's not why the President believes we must act."

Kharlov said, "Once China is no longer focused on Taiwan, where will its gaze turn next?"

Smyslov nodded vigorously. "I'm glad to see my instincts were right, and it was worth the trouble to give you another chance. Yes, indeed. The President's predecessor made numerous deals with the Chinese dating back to 2018, giving them a foothold in the Russian Far East. Nearly all focused on resource extraction, and staffed by Chinese citizens."

Neda said, "I've read about those deals. Weren't the Chinese supposed to be in Russia just temporarily? None of them were made Russian citizens, were they?"

"They were not," Smyslov replied. "Neither did they return to China. As a result, the Chinese population within Russia, which started at about a million, has roughly tripled."

Now Vasilyev shook his head. "But Russia is a nation of one hundred fifty million. Surely the President's worries are exaggerated about only a few million Chinese."

Smyslov shrugged. "Perhaps. But let's start with the figure you just quoted. Russia's population has now dropped to one hundred forty million."

Vasilyev stared at Smyslov. "How is that possible?"

"Our population has been dropping for many years. Societal changes, like those in most industrial countries, have resulted in a declining birth rate. Unlike America, true immigration, including citizenship, has not made up the difference. Abuse of drugs and, particularly, alcohol has led to a decline in Russian life expectancy. Finally, the death toll from the pandemic several years ago was more severe than was ever officially acknowledged," Smyslov replied.

"So, shouldn't we try to address those factors?" Vasilyev asked.

"Of course," Smyslov said. "But even with our best efforts, with available resources, the current projection is for Russia's population to drop to one hundred twenty-five million by 2050."

Kharlov nodded. "And with their focus no longer on Taiwan, China will step into that vacuum."

"Fine," Vasilyev said with a frown. "Let's say the President has some reason to be concerned about the Chinese. Will we then intervene to support Taiwan?"

"Certainly not," Smyslov replied. "Remember, China is now by far our most important customer for oil and gas. In fact, another reason we are so sure action against Taiwan will come soon is an increase of Chinese orders for fuel types used by military ships and aircraft. Plus, we are making good money selling military equipment to the Chinese. No, we will do nothing overtly."

"That's where we come in," Grishkov said, shaking his head.

Smyslov laughed. "Yes, indeed. The President, once again, wishes your assistance. But the burden will not fall on you alone. We are still working on the details. But here is what I know so far..."

Chapter Sixty-Three

Apartment Building
Moscow, Russia

Boris Kharlov looked up at Alina's apartment building and had to admit he was impressed. All glass and steel, he thought it would have been more at home in a city like London or New York.

Kharlov might have been amused if he'd known that this was the same building housing a man who had provided critical information for his first FSB mission in Ukraine.

And that Vasilyev and Grishkov's reaction to the building had been much the same as his.

It would not have surprised him, though, if he'd known that several other top FSB agents resided in the building. Not once he saw its security.

The building's lobby was dominated by a chrome and glass reception desk. A fit man with dark, close-cropped hair sitting there was, to Kharlov's practiced eye, obviously ex-military. As was a man in a suit sitting on a nearby leather sofa reading a newspaper. And the more casually dressed man looking over a digital display mounted to the wall on the far left corner of the lobby.

None had the tell-tale bulges in their clothing that would announce concealed weapons.

Nevertheless, Kharlov was certain all three men were armed and knew how to use their weapons.

Kharlov paused in front of the desk and took one more look around. Impressive. He wasn't armed. But even if he had been, the three men's tactical positions wouldn't have given him any chance.

The man at the desk smiled and said, "Mr. Kharlov! You're expected. Please go right on up."

Then he gestured towards the bank of elevators nearby.

Moments later, Kharlov was standing at Alina's door. As he lifted his hand to knock, Alina's voice over the intercom next to the door said, "Come in," and a "snick" announced it had been unlocked.

Kharlov walked through the door and closed it behind him. The bright lights in the hallway left him unprepared for the dimness of the apartment's interior, and he stood still for a moment to give his eyes time to adjust.

Then Kharlov grinned. Very good. Use every tactical advantage.

Alina's voice came from a room off the main living area where he was standing.

"I will be with you in a moment. Feel free to look around."

Kharlov did just that, being careful to touch nothing or go anywhere but the living room.

He guessed, correctly, that cameras were letting Alina see his every move.

Kharlov had spent nearly all of the million American dollars he had earned from his last mission on buying and furnishing what he had thought was a very nice Moscow apartment.

This one made his look like a dump.

Kharlov couldn't put his finger on the reason. He had hired a professional decorator, and until this moment, thought she had done an excellent job. There was nothing obvious about the furnishings, flooring, or decorations that could account for it either.

Kharlov shook his head. Maybe Alina's taste was simply superior.

Evgeny's comments about Alina's interest in him had stirred conflicting feelings in Kharlov. On the one hand, Alina was undoubtedly attractive.

On the other, if their relationship became anything but professional, what would happen to Kharlov's career in the FSB if their liaison went sideways?

Kharlov knew the answer to that.

Nothing good.

Maybe Evgeny's guess had been wrong. After all, how well did he really know Alina?

On the other hand, Kharlov had been told to report to Alina's apartment. Not an office at FSB headquarters.

Despite his best efforts, Kharlov had been unable to find out anything about Alina besides what he already knew from their missions together. Agents that Kharlov had approached outside the team shut him down as soon as he spoke Alina's name. The last one had warned Kharlov that if he persisted, the agent would be forced to report him.

All of them showed genuine fear. Of punishment from the FSB?

Or from Alina?

Kharlov didn't know. It would plainly have been a mistake to ask.

A lecture from a Spetsnaz trainer kept running through Kharlov's thoughts. It had been on the psychological aspects of killing. He had emphasized that few women were capable of dealing with the stress of killing people, especially more than once. As evidence, he noted that there had been very few female serial killers.

Yet, Kharlov knew Alina had killed at least once on their last mission. Rumors said she had killed many more.

The trainer had also underlined the difference in stress produced by killing someone in combat and doing so when the victim was unarmed and the killing premeditated. As was sometimes necessary during Spetsnaz covert missions.

One point worried Kharlov above all others. The trainer had said that a woman could only engage in premeditated, repeated killing outside of combat with armed opponents if they had been subjected to trauma. Severe enough to detach them from normal psychological restraints.

Kharlov wasn't sure he believed that. Was this part of the lecture only there to justify why women were so rare in Spetsnaz?

Besides, the FSB entrusted Alina with some of its most critical missions. Surely they would not do so if she were unstable.

What if she were able to conceal that condition? Wouldn't the FSB overlook anything as long as Alina produced results?

Sudden movement at one of the interior doors interrupted his thoughts. It was Alina.

But what she was wearing, her makeup...she was almost unrecognizable.

In particular, her dark eyeshadow and carmine lipstick triggered two conflicting feelings in Kharlov.

On the one hand, desire. On the other, a deep, primitive part of Kharlov's brain was warning him of mortal danger.

That part quickly proved correct. Faster than Kharlov would have believed possible, he was pressed against the nearest wall with Alina's right hand on his throat.

Alina's face was inches from his as she hissed, "Do you have any idea how much I risked to save you? The damage to my reputation? The danger I put my best friend in to rescue you?"

So, Evgeny was Alina's best friend. It made sense. How many others in the FSB could she really respect?

Kharlov was able to breathe, but just barely. So instead of saying anything, he did his best to nod without making it seem he was trying to break Alina's grip.

Though Kharlov wasn't sure how easy that would be, even if he tried. He was certainly bigger and stronger. But he had seen those qualities fail against those better trained before.

And he remembered what Smyslov had said about obeying Alina if he wished to remain in the FSB. Which he wanted very much indeed.

Alina's eyes glittered as she said, "You will make it up to me."

Kharlov did his best to nod. Dots were beginning to dance at the edge of his vision.

Dispassionately, he thought to himself that before long, his reduced oxygen intake would end up with him unconscious on the floor.

Before that happened, though, Alina's face moved even closer until it seemed all he could see was her eyes.

They were blue, cold, and devoid of sympathy or feeling.

"Your training will begin now," Alina said, her breath hot on Kharlov's face.

Kharlov once again did his best to nod but wasn't sure he'd been successful.

Yes, apparently so, because Alina's face moved back a fraction, and now he could see her crimson smile.

A smile with no trace of humor.

"There is one thing you must learn above all others. It is where your training will begin. Do you know what it is?" Alina asked.

Her grip tightened, and the dots in his vision multiplied and danced harder.

It took everything Kharlov had to shake his head. No, he didn't know.

Now Alina's eyes were back against his as his vision began to blur and consciousness fade.

Her grip relaxed a fraction, and his eyes came back into focus.

Alina's eyes were still as blue and cold as before. He felt as though he were falling into them as she said a single word.

"Discipline."

Chapter Sixty-Four

Zhongnanhai Compound
Beijing, China

General Yang closed the door behind him as he walked into President Gu's office. "Good morning, Mr. President," he said as he took a seat in front of Gu's desk.

No salute. No pause for Gu to invite him to sit.

Both of them knew the point Yang was making. Gu might be President. But he wasn't going to be giving Yang orders.

On paper, Gu still had that authority. But Yang had evidence Gu knew about the plot that had led to President Lin's death.

Could Yang leak that evidence without implicating himself as well? Maybe not.

But both of them knew it was a risk Gu would never take.

"Good morning to you, General. I understand you wish to brief me on an operation against Forward?" Gu said.

Yang nodded. "Yes, sir. It is now underway. We judged that the threat posed by Forward was too great to delay action. Several non-nuclear weapons have been detonated close enough to disable satellites they have been using for communication and propaganda distribution through Gateway devices."

Gu frowned. "Non-nuclear, you say. I'm not an expert, but it sounds like you're talking about weapons using an electromagnetic pulse. I thought an EMP had to be generated with a nuclear weapon."

Yang did his best to hide his surprise. As well as his flash of anger against, well, himself.

A fool would have never reached Gu's position. If Yang failed to remember that, he and his allies in the military could quickly lose the power they had so recently gained.

"You are correct, sir, that a nuclear weapon is by far the most efficient and powerful way to generate an EMP. However, we needed to ensure the pulses from our missiles did not affect our own satellites. The weapons we fired used an explosively pumped flux compression generator to create an EMP. No nuclear warheads were involved," Yang replied.

Gu shook his head. "These were American satellites. Don't you think you should have consulted with me in advance so that I could plan for the Americans' reaction?"

Yang nodded. Well, that was a critical point, wasn't it? Was the military free to do as it liked, or not?

"Sir, given Forward's role in the assassination of President Lin, we thought no delay could be tolerated," Yang replied.

Gu looked at Yang silently for a moment. They both knew Forward had nothing to do with Lin's death.

But Gu could hardly say so aloud.

Finally, Gu said, "That may be, but we can still expect an American protest. And what about the countries neighboring us that relied on those satellites?"

Yang shrugged. "I suggest you remind the American President that they destroyed one of our bases and sank one of our submarines. They should be grateful that we have done no more than retaliate against a few satellites. Ones owned by a private American company, not even the American government."

Gu frowned. He knew Hernandez and doubted that Yang's last point on SpaceLink's private status would impress him.

But Hernandez would understand that the destruction of the base at Ziyou Island and the sinking of a Chinese submarine required a response. Yes, this could be considered a proper settling of accounts.

Yang continued, "President Lin offered the Americans a deal where we would launch satellites to replace the ones our citizens found so easy to hack. Ones that we control to provide Internet access to our neighbors. We could repeat that offer to our neighbors, and since SpaceLink's satellites are no longer available, perhaps this time it will be accepted."

Gu nodded. Yes, maybe it would, he thought.

"Please pass on my congratulations to General Shi for the role his men played in avoiding disaster at the Three Gorges Dam and the Qinshan nuclear power plant. Without his foresight, we might still be recovering from disasters greater than any others in our history. You may tell him that the entire Politburo has taken notice. And, of course, they also appreciate your role in dealing with the threat posed by the American satellites. I'm sure, even more after today," Gu said smoothly.

"Thank you, Mr. President," Yang said stiffly. Message received, he thought. Shi's accomplishments were considered greater than his.

Never mind that all Shi's men had done at Qinshan was arrest the two managers who had actually prevented the nuclear power plant from killing thousands in Shanghai's southern suburbs. And maybe even some in Shanghai itself.

Yang suddenly realized why Shi had sent video crews as well as troops to the Xiluodu Dam, the Three Gorges Dam and the Qinshan nuclear power plant. Like people everywhere, Chinese citizens believed what they saw.

And what they had seen in all those places, according to the Army reporters speaking over the video footage, was Army troops rescuing them from disaster.

On the one hand, the Xiluodu Dam's manager had certainly deserved execution for risking the collapse of the Three Gorges Dam.

On the other, the execution of both Qinshan managers appeared to be a poor reward for preventing a disaster that could have killed more people than Fukushima.

Well, it did stop them from protesting their innocence, Yang thought. And so far, it looked like Shi and the Party had managed between them to keep the truth from getting out.

But I wonder how many brave and competent men we can afford to sacrifice before we end up regretting it.

"On a personal note, I join the Politburo in congratulating you on spotting the danger of striking an Indian air station. The risk of escalation to a nuclear conflict was, as you thought, indeed too great," Gu said.

Well, Yang thought, maybe his standing was better than he'd thought.

Yang had thrown the dice and sent a classified report detailing his objections to attacking an Indian air station to the Politburo just before Lin's car was due to explode.

Admiral Bai had sent his classified report to the Politburo on Lin's order to attack an American base as soon as Lin's death had been confirmed. It included the fact that Bai had done nothing to carry out Lin's order. Because, Bai had claimed, he was waiting for confirmation of those orders from Navy HQ in Beijing.

Yang wondered what the Navy brass in Beijing had thought of the revelation that Lin had asked Admiral Bai to launch an attack on an American naval base. Without their knowledge or approval.

Well, in a way, it didn't matter. The Politburo had found a way to thank Bai for dragging his feet on carrying out Lin's orders without Politburo or Navy HQ approval.

Admiral Bai was now in command of the entire Navy.

Too bad Yang couldn't claim some of the credit for stopping Lin's attack on the Americans. Since killing Lin had been the only way to do it.

The Politburo's appreciation for what they did know, though, helped explain their relatively easy acceptance of the military's new independence. For now, at least.

Gu interrupted Yang's thoughts by saying, "Good work, General. You are dismissed."

Yang took his time standing and even more walking out of Gu's office.

Yes. They both knew that for now, Gu wouldn't be giving any orders to the military. At least, any the military didn't like.

Chapter Sixty-Five

FBI Headquarters
Washington DC

Bob Hansen looked up from the report just filed by the Mexico City's legal attaché, as the FBI field office there was called, and shook his head.

It simply didn't fit.

He'd been excited to see a Coast Guard report that said three Russians with diplomatic passports had been intercepted off the coast of California.

Two men, and one woman.

Maybe the sniper, his spotter, and their handler?

Too bad Coast Guard procedure for a routine inspection was just to take pictures of identifying documents, not the boat's passengers. The general description of the two men in the report could have fit the security camera images from the sniper's building in San Francisco. What could be seen through hoods and sunglasses, anyway.

So could the photos in the passports.

But there were agents in Hansen's office who could have matched the security camera images too.

Hansen had been less happy to see that all three Russians had California fishing licenses. And had actually caught fish.

OK, fine. Their backstory was better than average. That didn't make them innocent.

But now the rest of their story had checked out. They really had gone to Ensenada. Their boat really had been sold in the name of the Russian Embassy in Mexico City.

Just as they had told the Coast Guard they would.

How likely was it that the Russians had all that lined up to support agents leaving the country after one assassination? Sure, their intelligence people were supposed to be good.

Were they really that good?

The biggest problem, though, was motive. Why would the Russians work for the Chinese?

Hansen sighed and shook his head. There was nothing here to take to his boss.

But Hansen still didn't like it.

On both the rocket explosion in Florida and the assassination attempt in California, all they had was a big fat zero.

Hansen made a note of the three Russians' names to enter into a special Homeland Security database.

The next time these Russians came to America, Hansen was going to check up on them personally.

Chapter Sixty-Six

Downtown Office Building
Shanghai, China

Director Pan beamed as Wang Yan walked into his office. "So good to see you! Please, come and sit with me."

Moments later, they were both sitting on Pan's sofa, with a tea set before them.

I wonder why Pan's office always smells of sandalwood, Wang thought. She saw a few carved wooden decorative pieces that could be made of sandalwood.

No, she thought, too small.

Wang had read that American casinos pumped tailored fragrances through their ventilation systems to make their customers stay longer. Would Pan spend his money on something so foolish?

Or was it just Pan's cologne?

Wang shook herself. Why was her mind spinning on such a useless tangent? She had to focus.

"So, tell me everything. Have we secured Chen as an asset?" Pan asked as he poured Wang's tea.

Wang warmed her hands on the cup and inhaled the tea's delicate bouquet.

Yes. Money had its advantages. Wang knew Pan's personal blend cost as much per pot as she spent on monthly rent.

But, when you were a billionaire, who cared?

Wang nodded. "We have. And her coding skills are improving even more rapidly than you predicted. Her work for us started at world-class. Now Chen is moving into a league of her own. It's as though each challenge we set her spurs her on to greater heights."

Wang paused and shook her head.

"You hired me years ago as Forward's first hacker before you learned I have other skills. I am barely good enough to understand just how much better she is, and she's still improving. We must keep her at all costs."

Pan nodded. "I am already paying one far heavier than I expected. Was it really necessary to move in with her? How can you breathe in that tiny apartment?"

Wang smiled. "We should have both predicted that outcome. Chen couldn't sneak around behind her old girlfriend's back. That's not who she is. I'm glad that you took my advice and sent another Forward agent to comfort Tang after their breakup."

"It wasn't difficult, according to the report I got back. A rebound relationship that may not last too long, but it should keep the way clear for you. I don't want you to have to deal with any reconciliation attempts," Pan said.

Wang smiled. "I don't think you have to worry. Chen seems happy enough."

Pan looked at Wang intently. "And what about you? Are you happy?"

"Are you asking if I've forgotten this is all about making sure Chen keeps working for us? No, I haven't," Wang said, looking pointedly around Pan's opulent office.

"You mentioned Chen's studio apartment. It's not 'Another Heaven.' At all," Wang said, shaking her head.

Pan immediately recognized the reference to the famous Chinese love song, a staple at wedding celebrations, and laughed.

"I'm sorry to make you suffer in such a small cage, but it won't be forever. Now, do you think there's any chance Chen suspects I arranged for her girlfriend Tang to be away at a conference while you seduced her?" Pan asked.

The question, put so bluntly, almost took Wang off guard.

It doesn't sound too pretty when it's put that way, does it? But it's exactly what happened.

Yes, Pan had his own set of skills. Wang would forget that at her peril.

Those thoughts flashed through Wang's mind in less than a second.

While Wang's head was already shaking.

"No," she said calmly. "If Chen had any such suspicions, she'd have already confronted me, and she hasn't. She's very direct. It takes some getting used to, in fact."

Pan grinned. "Compared to me, you mean. Do you think she has any suspicions about our real goal?"

Wang didn't have to think before again shaking her head. "No. You were wise to tell her most of the truth at your last meeting with her. She is far from stupid."

"I've found the most effective lie includes as much truth as possible. I meant every word I said to Chen. I did use the Shanghai Stock Exchange attack to implicate certain generals in corruption. There too, the truth was an important element. Nearly every general has broken the law in various ways while supplementing their official salary. I just threw the spotlight on some of them and let government investigators do the rest," Pan said.

"But all that did was clear the way for Yang and Shi. Those generals will be able to consolidate their power and free the military from Party oversight..."

Wang's voice trailed off as Pan's smile widened.

"That's what you wanted," Wang said wonderingly. "But why?"

"First, until now, the Party held all the levers of power. By taking away its absolute control of the military, we made the task of overthrowing the Party that much simpler," Pan said.

Wang nodded slowly but then frowned.

"But what's to stop the outcome you told Chen you feared? That the military will replace the Party, and institute a rule that's even more oppressive? Surely that is not the Second Chinese Revolution we planned, is it?" Wang asked.

"There too, I told the truth. That is indeed a risk we must avoid. But the military's reputation will never survive a crushing defeat. And that is what it will suffer when they attempt to invade Taiwan," Pan said.

"How can you be so sure? I remember what you told Chen about how the military has grown. What if the invasion of Taiwan succeeds?" Wang asked.

Pan smiled. "Some secrets I cannot yet share. But believe me when I say, they will fail."

Wang shrugged. "Fine. Say the invasion of Taiwan fails. And that the people blame both the Party and the military for that failure. Who then will replace them?"

"Again, I told Chen the truth. We will hold elections. I just left out the part about money and gerrymandering," Pan said.

"Money is clear enough, and you've talked about it before. I get how money can buy campaign ads. And pay for projects to curry favor with voters in a particular district. But what is gerrymandering?" Wang asked.

Pan laughed. "A new term I've just learned from the Americans. Well, it's actually just new to me. Do you know when they invented it?"

Wang shook her head.

"In 1813! A cartoonist drew a map of a voting district a party had created to ensure their candidate would be elected, which was shaped like a salamander. The party's leader was a Governor Gerry. And so, the 'gerrymander.' Truly, as so often, Americans lead the way," Pan said with frank admiration in his voice.

"Is this technique really so valuable? Won't our opponents object?" Wang asked.

Pan nodded approvingly. "Yes, they will. But even though Americans have been objecting for over two centuries, gerrymandering still happens. Thanks to computer-drawn districts, it has become even more effective. One American state had over half of its voters select one party, but the other party sent over three-quarters of its candidates to Congress. All because of how the successful party had drawn the electoral map."

"But what about the courts? Surely they will stop such a travesty!" Wang said.

Pan grinned. "You would think so. But no. Even the American Supreme Court has refused to intervene. Because the party that uses gerrymandering most has succeeded in naming the majority of the Supreme Court's members. We will follow this example. Our people must believe that after the Second Revolution, China has achieved true democracy. But it will be an illusion."

"You and the other billionaires will be in charge. Just as in America," Wang said softly.

"Well, it's not that simple. Even in America, sometimes things happen that the billionaires don't like. Their control is not absolute. For example, some of the billionaires who've run for President have lost. Here in China, though, we can do better," Pan said confidently.

"How?" Wang asked.

"You still insist I reveal my most precious secrets?" Pan asked with an easy smile and paused.

"Why not? You need to understand how deeply you have my trust. Here's how it will work. After the Second Revolution, we will be the ones who draw the first electoral map. And make whatever subsequent 'adjustments' we decide are necessary. We will also have the world's best coder to help ensure the outcome we want," Pan said.

Wang looked up with alarm. "So you don't just want Chen to help make the Second Revolution a success. You also need her for its aftermath. But Chen will never agree to what you plan."

"Yes, she will. Because you will persuade her," Pan said with a smile.

"You overestimate my powers. No matter how much Chen believes she loves me, she will never betray her ideals," Wang said decisively.

"Of course not," Pan replied. "You will have to convince her that the alternative is even worse. A return to Communist rule, for example."

Then Pan paused. "Except for the attack on the Shanghai Stock Exchange, what we have done so far with Chen's help has only embarrassed the Party. Or so it seems. In fact, by hacking the shaming signs and interrupting the President's address, we raised Forward's visibility throughout China. Many others with the access codes and other information we need to attack much more important targets have contacted us. But Chen's talents are still critical to making the best possible use of what we have been given by the many who desire a free China."

Wang frowned. "Do you really think getting Chen to help will be so easy?"

Pan shook his head. "Not at all. Remember, the best lie always has an element of truth. The Communist Party will remain a threat, even after we drive it from power. After nearly a century in charge, how could it not be?"

Then Pan paused and smiled. "And we both know how persuasive you can be."

Wang smiled back. "Let me remind you."

As she knew Pan expected.

But as she removed her clothes, Wang asked herself where her loyalties truly stood.

And how long it would be before she had to choose.

Chapter Sixty-Seven

Beijing, China

Mark Bishop smiled to himself as he walked to his car, parked just outside his daughter Katy's high school. Beijing was one of the rare posts offering a student a choice of several English-speaking high schools issuing a diploma that any American university would accept.

Though when he sought his assignment at the Embassy in Beijing, where he was now the highest-ranking CIA representative in country, Bishop already knew which high school Katy would choose.

The one with the best girls' basketball team.

Bishop had just spent the early evening cheering himself hoarse for Katy and her team, which had won again. Katy had been the team's lead scorer. She was good enough that Bishop thought she had a real shot at a university basketball scholarship.

Too bad Katy was only a junior. Bishop had been able to get the extra months added to his assignment to let her finish the school year, but Katy would have to do her final year of high school in Virginia. Bishop's home, currently occupied by renters, was in Fairfax County not far from CIA headquarters at Langley.

Katy had insisted on having a friend on the team take her home after the game. Since her friend lived in the same apartment building as Bishop and her father would be driving, he had no good reason to say no.

It was just one of many signs that Katy wasn't his little girl anymore.

As he walked down the sidewalk towards his car, Bishop's thoughts were so preoccupied with Katy that he almost missed seeing him.

But not quite. Bishop had been well trained and had years of field experience before his Beijing assignment. Yes, as first deputy station chief and then as chief, the Chinese had known exactly who he was. With few exceptions, that meant an end to field work.

Still, a part of him was always alert to his surroundings.

Even with all his experience, Bishop almost missed seeing Minister Song, head of the Ministry of State Security (MSS). It was dark, and Song had a hat pulled down low that obscured his face.

Bishop did spot him, though. Mostly because Song was walking right towards him.

Bishop automatically looked for Song's security detail. He thought to himself it might help that he'd seen at least some of those guards before, at the meal they had shared not so long ago.

He couldn't see anyone else on the street other than a parent headed, just like Bishop, for his car.

Bishop knew that didn't mean anything. This was the MSS' home turf. Not just China, but the Chinese capital. Song could have two dozen security agents within easy reach, and if he wanted to hide them, Bishop wouldn't see a thing.

But Bishop didn't think so. Song was now close enough that Bishop could see his expression.

Not that Bishop was sure what Song's expression meant. Or that he could be certain Song wasn't putting on an act.

Song looked like a man being hunted. Who knew he didn't have much time left.

Bishop had nearly reached his car and slowed. Song was close enough now for him to speak if that's what he wanted.

Was he going to ask Bishop to go with him somewhere?

Did Song want to defect?

No. Song walked right past him and didn't say a word.

Bishop opened the door to his car and started the engine.

Then Bishop looked in the sedan's rearview window. Song was still walking in the same direction and wasn't looking back.

Bishop drove his car away from the curb at a normal, slow speed. This was a residential area, and Chinese police were diligent at enforcing speed limits.

Never mind that no foreign diplomat posted to America ever paid a traffic ticket. The State Department insisted that any American official abroad pay for every infraction.

That's not why Bishop was such a careful driver, though. It was basic tradecraft. Do nothing that might attract attention.

The car approaching Bishop from the front was a Wuling Hong-guang. Produced by a joint venture between General Motors and a local company, it had one primary virtue for State Security.

It was the most popular car in China, with over a half-million annual registrations. Nobody would give one a second look.

Except that this one was going nearly double the speed limit, with no lights or siren.

So probably not police.

MSS.

Bishop made a point of looking straight ahead as the car sped past him.

It didn't matter. From the corner of his eye, he could see that the driver had been staring straight at him.

Bishop looked in his rearview mirror and cursed as he saw the speeding car had braked and wheeled around in a maneuver too smooth to have been executed by an untrained civilian.

Had they recognized Bishop? Or were they after Song and had been ordered to pull over anyone in the vicinity?

It didn't matter. Bishop was going to the Embassy and wasn't stopping for anyone.

He had just figured out why Song had walked past him without speaking.

Keeping his right hand on the steering wheel, Bishop had checked his left jacket pocket, the one that had been closest to Song.

It now contained a USB drive.

A brush pass.

Bishop had to give Song credit. He hadn't seen or felt a thing.

Ordinarily, Bishop's diplomatic status would have kept him safe. The Chinese knew that targeting an American diplomat would have serious repercussions.

But whatever China's top security official had passed him on the USB drive would be worth any price to recover.

And I'm in a car, Bishop thought.

Over a quarter-million people died in traffic accidents annually in China.

An American diplomat happened to be included in that statistic? Regrettable.

Very regrettable.

Bishop had only one advantage. Not by coincidence, Katy's school was close to the Embassy. He didn't have far to go.

Then Bishop realized he might have one other advantage and punched the button on the dashboard that connected his phone to the Embassy. Next, he said, "Post One."

This connected Bishop to the Marine staffing the security booth in the Embassy closest to the main entrance, called "Post One."

"This is Bishop. Do you know who I am?" Bishop asked.

Beijing was one of the largest Foreign Service posts, and Marines cycled through frequently. If Bishop's luck was bad, he could have drawn a newly posted Marine who had not yet been read in on key Embassy personnel.

But his luck tonight was good. "Yes, sir," came the immediate response.

The Marine then added, "Sir, I have the Gunny here with me. Would you like to speak to him?"

Jackpot, Bishop thought. The Marine commanding an Embassy's Marine Security Detachment (MSD) was often, but not always, a Gunnery Sergeant. A very old tradition had that MSD commander informally called "Gunny" by everyone at post regardless of his actual rank.

"Yes, please," Bishop said as he looked in his rearview mirror.

Bishop was driving as fast as he safely could on the narrow residential street. But the car behind him was gaining.

"Gunnery Sergeant Watkins here," came the familiar gravelly voice over the car's speakers.

Familiar not just because it was always a good idea to get to know the men who protected you. Bishop regarded staying in shape as vital for any agent posted overseas. The Marines always had the best workout equipment and were happy to share.

"Gunny, it's Bishop. I'm being pursued by Chinese security. I'll be arriving in a few minutes at the cargo entrance with them right behind me. I'm in my own vehicle with dip plates. I need the gate open with security in place."

"Got it," Watkins replied. "We'll be ready."

"Dip plates" had been key to Watkins' willingness to agree to Bishop's request. Watkins' console at Post One told him that the phone being used to call was Bishop's. He knew Bishop's voice. On top of that, diplomatic license plates on the car speeding towards the cargo gate would tell Watkins it was Bishop's vehicle.

First, though, Bishop had to get to the Embassy.

A vehicle emerged from each side of the intersection two blocks ahead and swung towards him.

Then stopped with headlights blazing on high, each one angled toward the middle of the street.

An improvised roadblock.

They had made just one mistake. By being a few seconds too early.

Bishop reacted instantly, turning left on the only intersection that lay between him and the new roadblock.

On this street, though, he was no longer headed towards the Embassy.

Instinct, though, told him to wait. Bishop had to stay focused on the road ahead. But quick glances confirmed his guess that a right turn at the next two intersections would have run him into vehicles obstructing his way to the Embassy.

At the third intersection, though, Bishop decided to take a chance and turned right.

Clear.

They hadn't yet had time to block every intersection between Bishop and the Embassy.

With luck, they'd think he was headed to the main entrance, not the cargo gate. Especially since at night, the cargo gate would usually be locked tight and unmanned.

Bishop grimaced. He wasn't giving Watkins much time to change that. Even at a dead run from the other side of the massive Embassy,

Bishop wasn't sure Watkins and his men could get to the cargo gate before he did.

Well, he was about to find out.

Bishop made one more sharp right turn. If his memory served, the cargo gate should be right ahead.

Yes! Even better, it was starting to swing open, and security lights snapped on at both sides of the gate.

Bishop could see Watkins and two other Marines at the gate and accelerated towards them.

No! A sedan lurched into the intersection ahead and slammed on its brakes.

There was no room to avoid it.

In America, everyone had heard about defensive driving. For agents like Bishop, another course was part of initial field training, with mandatory refreshers over the rest of a career.

Its unofficial name was Offensive Driving.

Bishop had only a couple of seconds to calculate trajectories and weights. And, crucially important, to remember to press the button on his dashboard that turned off the airbags.

Because without that custom switch, those airbags would have been sure to deploy.

Bishop hit the blocking car near the facing rear wheel. He knew the Chinese car's model and that it was front-wheel drive. Slamming into the car near its trunk gave him the best chance to swing it out of his way.

It worked! The way to the cargo gate was clear!

Suddenly, Bishop's rear windshield shattered, and he ducked.

He hadn't heard any shots. They'd been fired from silenced weapons. MSS, Bishop thought again, not ordinary police.

Glass fragments and cold night air washed over Bishop as his car passed through the cargo gate and approached the loading dock.

Bishop could hear the gate humming closed behind him as he brought the car to a stop and opened the door at his side.

Bishop cautiously raised his head to check what was happening before he exited, just as he heard a familiar voice.

Watkins.

"You OK, sir?" Watkins asked.

A reasonable question, Bishop thought, as he looked himself over. He knew from experience that sometimes gunshot victims weren't immediately aware they'd been hit due to shock.

But not this time.

"I'm fine. Are they still out there?" Bishop asked.

Watkins shook his head. "No, sir. As soon as your car made it through the gate, that vehicle you hit took off. Gate's closed, and we shut off the lights. No point giving a sniper an easy shot."

Bishop nodded. "Thanks, Gunny. You and your men really saved me tonight."

Watkins shrugged. "What we're here for, sir."

As Bishop exited the car, Watkins gestured towards the smashed front end and shot-out rear windshield and shook his head. "Hope it was worth the risk, sir."

Bishop fingered the USB drive in his left jacket pocket.

Yes. Still there.

"Me too," Bishop said.

Chapter Sixty-Eight

The White House
Washington DC

President Hernandez scowled as General Robinson walked into the Oval Office.

"General, I've just finished a telephone call with President Gu. He invited me to climb a tree when I complained about their destruction of SpaceLink's satellites near China. Says they were a threat to Chinese national security. When I demanded compensation, he asked about compensation for their base at Ziyou Island and their missing submarine," Hernandez said.

"And how did you reply, sir?" Robinson asked with a worried frown.

Hernandez shrugged. "How do you think? What island? What submarine? But even if China has no proof to take to a world audience, they know it was us. I think Eli Wade is going to have to eat the cost of those satellites."

Robinson nodded. "And what about China's neighbors? They can't be happy about losing their satellite Internet service."

"Gu said that they're willing to launch replacement satellites to provide free Internet service and that several countries have already accepted the offer," Hernandez said.

Robinson grunted. "Satellites that will be controlled by the Chinese, of course."

"I don't think most of those countries will care whether anything critical of the Chinese is censored. Not if they can get satellite Internet access for free," Hernandez said.

"You're probably right, sir. Did you see my report on the thirteen SpaceLink satellites that survived the previous Chinese attack?" Robinson asked.

"I did," Hernandez replied. "So, because of the contract the Air Force just signed with Wade to have SpaceLink satellites serve as backup military communications, those thirteen satellites were hardened against an electromagnetic pulse. And SpaceLink has confirmed that those satellites are still functioning, though they still haven't been turned on for users."

"Yes, sir. I propose that we let Forward know about those satellites. At a minimum, so they won't throw away their Gateways quite yet," Robinson said.

Hernandez grunted. "And at maximum, to coordinate their activities with us? That could be a dangerous road."

"Agreed. But we could keep cooperation limited. For example, by turning on just one SpaceLink satellite for the short time needed for a specific Forward attack," Robinson said.

"Or turn them all on if, say, China invaded Taiwan," Hernandez said, and frowned.

"It would give us the ability to distract the Chinese government at what could be a critical time, sir," Robinson said.

Hernandez paused, and for a moment looked uncertain. Finally, he shrugged.

“Fine. Coordinate with the CIA to pass the word to Forward that SpaceLink satellites capable of communicating with Gateways have survived. But their use will be on our schedule, not theirs. And if they want those satellites to continue to be available, they had better ensure word of their survival doesn’t reach the Chinese government,” Hernandez said.

“Yes, sir,” Robinson said, as he wrote notes on his pad. “What did you think of the intelligence report on China's intentions towards Taiwan?" Robinson asked.

"I think intentions are one thing, and capabilities another. I want an updated report on whether China can invade Taiwan successfully and what the Air Force could do to stop them. Coordinate with the State Department to find out which other countries would be willing and able to act against a Chinese invasion of Taiwan. We'll lead, but I'm not going to try to stop China alone," Hernandez said.

"Understood, sir. Shall I send in Admiral Bartlett?" Robinson asked.

"Yes, please, General. For us, any conflict over Taiwan will be an Air Force and Navy joint operation. I'm not putting any soldiers on the ground in either Taiwan or mainland China, so the Army will sit this one out."

"I completely agree with you, sir. I'll have some answers for you by tomorrow," Robinson said.

A few moments later, Robinson had left, and Admiral Bartlett, the Chief of Naval Operations (CNO), took his place.

Bartlett's job title made it sound as though he had operational command authority over ships and submarines. He didn't, any more than Robinson did over aircraft. That authority was exercised by the combatant commanders, who were organized by region. For the coming conflict over Taiwan, that would be the Admiral commanding USINDOPACOM, which covered the Pacific and South Asia.

However, as the Navy's professional head and its highest-ranking officer, CNO Bartlett was the one Hernandez turned to for advice when he had questions about the Navy and its assets.

There were previous CNOs who had careers in submarines, including two who'd served in the same one, the *Los Angeles*-class attack submarine USS *Honolulu*. Bartlett, though, like most CNOs, had spent his career either on or commanding surface ships.

"Admiral, I'd like to start with some old business and then move on to our next challenges. I've read through your report on the *Oregon*'s last deployment, and it looks like we're lucky the crew is still with us," Hernandez said, tapping on the thick folder in front of him.

"Yes, sir," Bartlett said. "Once it reached port and we were able to do a complete examination, we determined that the hull damage caused by the Chinese torpedo's explosion was even more severe than the crew thought. It looks like the decision to use a tougher, though thinner, structural steel in its construction was a good one. I doubt a *Los Angeles*-class submarine would have survived."

Hernandez grunted. "But the report says that it might not be possible to repair the hull, at least at a reasonable cost. Explain that to me."

Bartlett frowned. "I'm not surprised that puzzled you. That section of the report was preliminary and is missing a detailed analysis because there hasn't been time for it. The *Virginia*-class submarines were the first built using modular construction techniques. That would make salvaging everything inside the *Oregon*'s hull far easier than with an older submarine."

"So, it's like an insurance company deciding whether to total a car," Hernandez said. "If the value of what you can salvage plus the cost of building a new hull is a lower figure than the cost of repairing the existing hull..."

"Exactly, sir. Another consideration is whether, given the serious damage to the hull, we could ever have sufficient confidence in the repairs' quality. Honestly, sir, I don't think it's worth the risk," Bartlett said.

"I'm glad to hear you say that, Admiral," Hernandez said.

Bartlett looked startled, and Hernandez smiled.

"You were expecting me to push back on that, right? I know I've acquired a reputation as a President who's not a fan of defense spending," Hernandez said.

Bartlett shrugged. "Sir, I understand choices have to be made. But I'm guessing this time there's another factor I don't know about."

Hernandez nodded approvingly. "That's right, Admiral. You've kept the *Oregon* in a covered berth, right? And her personnel under wraps?"

"Yes, sir," Bartlett replied. We've restricted all *Oregon* personnel to base and ordered them not to communicate with anyone off base. They were due to be on deployment for at least another two months. So, nobody's expecting to hear from any of them. I have to be honest, though, and say that with well over a hundred men, the chances are good that word of their presence will leak to someone off base."

Hernandez waved his hands dismissively. "I expected that. All I want is for the Chinese to keep guessing. They've already asked unofficially about that submarine we sank. At some point, they're going to ask officially. I want to be able to answer that I don't know."

Bartlett nodded slowly. "And that's why you wouldn't mind our salvaging the modules inside the *Oregon*, and scrapping her hull. Rather than taking the *Oregon* to a repair yard, which would be impossible to conceal."

"That's right," Hernandez said. "And that brings us to the prospect of an inquest into the damage done to the *Oregon*."

"You mean, whether her captain fired first in violation of orders," Bartlett said flatly.

"Part of this report seems to contradict that directly. I see the *Oregon*'s sonar supervisor says that given the time it took him to detect and identify the Chinese sub's firing, he's sure they fired first," Hernandez said.

"Even if that's true, sir, the issue is what Captain Cartwright knew at the time he fired. And it's clear Cartwright hadn't been notified that torpedoes had been fired at the *Oregon* when he fired on the Chinese submarine," Bartlett said.

"And if he'd waited?" Hernandez asked.

Bartlett hesitated and looked uncomfortable. Finally, he said quietly, "The *Oregon* would have been destroyed."

Hernandez nodded. "So, why doesn't that settle the matter?"

"Sir, it's not that simple. Those orders were given for a reason. Firing before being fired upon risked starting a war with a nuclear-armed adversary. Did waiting increase the risk to the *Oregon*? Yes, it did. But that risk had a purpose," Bartlett said.

Hernandez, though, noticed Bartlett hadn't put much conviction into the words he'd just said.

"Very well, Admiral. Now, what would defense counsel say on Captain Cartwright's behalf?" Hernandez asked.

Now came a much longer hesitation.

"Sir, the Chinese submarine had come close enough to the surface to receive new orders after Captain Cartwright fired the Tomahawk missile that destroyed a Chinese base. Its later behavior, particularly its high-speed pursuit of the *Oregon*, would lead any submarine commander to believe the Chinese submarine had been ordered to destroy the *Oregon*," Bartlett said.

"We both know the Tomahawk the *Oregon* fired wasn't intended to destroy that Chinese base. If it had been, isn't it fair to say the *Oregon*'s orders would have been different?" Hernandez asked.

Bartlett reluctantly nodded. "Yes, sir. A lethal Chinese response would have been anticipated, and the *Oregon*'s captain would have been given greater latitude to defend against it."

"You mentioned a minute ago the risk of nuclear war with China. I want to avoid that. But I'm not ready to see the Pacific turned into a Chinese lake to do it. So, do you understand why for now I want to keep the Chinese guessing about the *Oregon*'s status?" Hernandez asked.

Bartlett nodded. "And why you don't want an inquest into how the *Oregon* came to be damaged."

"That's right," Hernandez said. "If the fact that the *Oregon* sank a Chinese submarine becomes part of a military trial record, I'll no longer be able to deny it to the Chinese government."

Hernandez paused. "Even though I'm the commander in chief, ordinarily, I wouldn't interfere in matters of military justice. This time, though, I think we have to conclude national security takes precedence. I know I can make this an order, but I want your honest opinion. Do you agree?"

Bartlett sat quietly for about a minute, though it seemed much longer.

"I do, sir. There are plenty of arguments to make either way. But in the end, national security has to come first. It's the whole reason we have a military, after all," Bartlett said.

"Good. Now, let's talk about what this intelligence report out of our Embassy in Beijing means. This Chinese minister may have disappeared, but the information he put on that USB drive certainly gave us a lot to think about. 'Second Chinese Revolution' sounds like an exaggeration. But if the Chinese military's power and influence have increased as much as he claims, I think the Navy is going to be asked to help defend Taiwan sooner rather than later," Hernandez said.

Bartlett nodded. "It's a challenge we've been preparing for since before I joined the Navy. I'll start by saying we're not going to put any surface ships between Taiwan and the Chinese mainland. China has spent quite a bit on developing air and land-based missile capabilities that would make such a deployment suicide."

Hernandez nodded. "Understood. But you do have other ways to make a Chinese invasion of Taiwan more difficult."

"Oh yes, Mr. President. We certainly do," Bartlett said, with a wide smile.

Chapter Sixty-Nine

August 1st Building
Beijing, China

General Yang, the Air Force Commander, looked across the conference room table at General Shi, the Army Commander. For the moment, Shi seemed content to let Yang take the lead in crafting the military's new role in China's government.

But they both knew where the real power was to be found. With over two million active-duty soldiers, as well as more than another half-million in reserve, China's army was the world's largest by any measure.

Yes, China's air force was potent as well. But when it came to real power, Shi's troops and tanks were what counted.

If Shi moved against him, the best use of Yang's air assets would be to fly the fastest plane he could find out of China.

When the bomb that blew up the President's limo had turned out to be powerful enough to flatten him as well as the President, for a moment, Yang had thought that Shi might have been trying to eliminate both of them.

But no. Shi knew as well as Yang did that Song's security forces had to be told to stand down by the only man whose orders they would obey.

President Lin himself.

Shi had even apologized to Yang, and told him he was pleased Yang had escaped serious injury. Yang couldn't be sure, but Shi had seemed sincere.

Well, maybe Shi was happy to let Yang be the bigger target for the many in the Communist Party who resented the military's new leading role.

Yang did his best to push these thoughts firmly away, at least while Shi was sitting in front of him.

Plenty of time to brood later.

At least now they could talk freely. Yang had used Forward's supposed infiltration of the Ministry of State Security to justify removing all MSS listening devices from the August 1st Building.

"I have read your report on the Army's preparations for the invasion of Taiwan. Are you confident the timeline is realistic?" Yang asked.

Shi nodded. "Yes. Of course, much will depend on the success of the initial landings conducted by the Marines. If they can secure the ports we need to land troops, tanks, and heavy equipment in quantity, the Army will meet every target."

"Understood," Yang said. "Let's assume for the moment that they fail. What do you think of the contingency plan to seize airfields using paratroopers and then bring in the occupation force by air?"

"Not much," Shi said immediately. "You've received nothing in writing from me on that proposal and won't because I'm not going to have my staff plan for disaster."

Yang frowned. "Are you so sure that method has no chance of success?"

"Yes," Shi said. "Even if we assume your planes have swept all opposition from the skies. Taiwan's military has had decades to plan against a paratrooper assault targeting its airfields. As long as the enemy has the will to fight, any air-only assault is doomed to failure."

"Very well," Yang said. "Admiral Bai agrees with you. The Navy is busy building more Type 071 landing platform docks, Type 075 amphibious assault ships, medium landing ships, and tank landing ships. I appreciate your agreeing to assign a dozen of your attack helicopters to the Marines to help with training and doctrine development for amphibious operations."

Shi nodded. "Happy to do it. Marines are soldiers too. Just a little wetter."

Yang looked up from his reports, startled. Had Shi just made a joke?

Yang couldn't help himself and started laughing. Shi joined in, surprising Yang even more.

Finally, they both stopped. Then Shi, wiping his eyes, said, "Don't hesitate to ask me for anything else needed to make this operation a success. Our new role in China's future depends on it."

Yang nodded. "Not to mention our lives."

Shi smiled. "Yes. That too."

Yang pointed at the large map of the world that dominated one wall of the conference room.

"I will tell you, though, that once we have achieved reunification with Taiwan we have much more work to do. There may be little our enemies can do to stop us. But they will not quietly accept our success. I do not propose to sit back and wait for their blows."

Shi cocked his head quizzically. "What do you intend?"

Yang shrugged. "First things first. I hope to get Taiwan to surrender without destroying all their military assets, or losing many of ours. If we can do that, incorporating the best of Taiwan's equipment and troops in our armed forces will see us emerge even stronger."

Yang paused, and gestured again towards the world map on the wall.

"It's a big world. It's long past time the Americans and the Russians were reminded they're not the only ones living in it."

First, thanks very much for reading my book! I sincerely hope you enjoyed it. If you did, I'd really appreciate it if you could leave a review - even a short one - on Amazon.

If you found a typo or some other error despite my best efforts, please let me know with details. I will fix it!

If you have questions, please send those to me too. You can reach me at my blog, https://thesecondkoreanwar.wordpress.com or on Twitter at https://Twitter.com/TedHalstead18

Or if all else fails, you can e-mail me directly at thalstead2018@gmail.com

I'll answer a few questions now that I received after my first four books and one for a reader of an advance review copy of this book. I'll start with the newest questions and then repeat answers to a few old ones, in case this is the only one of my books you've read.

Your books have always portrayed Russian agents as protagonists. Why did they turn into villains in this book?

In my first four books, the Russian characters always act in Russia's interests. But, in many cases, those interests either coincided with America's, or at least didn't contradict them.

Not this time.

Why the change? Well, I've enjoyed imagining that Russia and America could work together on some level and set these books in the near future in part to make such cooperation a bit more credible. Judging from the reaction of most readers, they enjoyed the idea of cooperation too.

However, even the most optimistic among us have to acknowledge it's inevitable that at some point, the interests of two great powers will conflict.

Will Russian and American interests ever realign? You'll have to read my next book to find out!

Is any of the information in your books classified?

For the benefit of anyone in the national security apparatus of which I used to be a part, the short answer is an emphatic NO.

Now, the longer and more detailed answer.

I was aware when I started writing these books of the danger that I might inadvertently include classified information. Of course, that danger has receded as time has marched on since my retirement. But it's still there.

The way I dealt with it was simple. I made sure that absolutely every detail that could possibly have been classified when I learned of it has since made it into public knowledge. In short, if I could find out about it through Google, I could put it in the book.

For instance, I first read about the idea of arming US subs with anti-aircraft missiles long ago. But before I included it as a near-future capability in my first book *The Second Korean War*, I did a Google search. Here's what I found in an article from an editor at Time's "The War Zone":

"During the late 2000s, the US Navy, Raytheon and Northrop Grumman worked to migrate the highly flexible AIM-9X short-range air-to-air missile to the undersea world under the Littoral Warfare Weapon program. The AIM-9X would be vertically launched in a canister from a submarine, then the missile would climb into the sky when the canister broke the surface, locking onto its target after launch.

Tests during the mid 2000s had the AIM-9X fired from a vertical launcher as a proof of concept demonstration. A few years later, an

AIM-9X was launched from an actual submarine as part of a series of integration tests. Since then the program seems to have disappeared from public view, but it's likely development has continued on in the classified world—especially considering that submarine-launched unmanned aircraft have been an operational reality within America's nuclear submarine fleet for some time."

In one of the book's first reviews, I was called out by a reviewer who said:

"The author could have done a little research using Google. A *Virginia* class submarine with stern tubes that carry fire AIM-9 air to air missiles? Puhleaze...."

After I responded by posting the quote from the article I used as the basis for including a sub-launched AIM-9 in the book, later the same day, another reader had this comment:

"Re: the author's reply: very nicely done. You just sold another copy of your book."

Satisfying? Well, yes! Sadly, Amazon no longer allows authors to respond to reviews or readers to react to those author comments.

Information about the Soviet SS-24 test involving anti-tank mines described in *The End of Russia's War in Ukraine* was indeed classified when it happened almost thirty years ago. Reports of the trial made quite an impression on me at the time, and I always thought the SS-24 would make a great element to include in a novel.

And of course, now all the details about that incident are available to anyone with Internet access.

What inspires you to write these books?

Sometimes it's 100% personal experience. I worked in Seoul for four years, and almost every day at the Embassy we had reason to think about what would happen if the North Koreans attacked.

Also, every day at work, I talked to South Koreans applying to immigrate to America, in numbers that made Korea one of the top ten source countries at the time. Why were they leaving when Korea was already an economic powerhouse, and prospects seemed to be bright?

Applicants were blunt when we asked them. They were worried about the prospect of a North Korean attack for themselves. They were even more concerned for their children.

So, I had the ideas that eventually became *The Second Korean War* in my head for a long time.

Are any of the stories in the books from my own experience, and if so, which ones?

You can usually apply common sense to answer that one.

In my first book, *The Second Korean War*:

Characters set mines, throw grenades, and attempt to defuse nuclear weapons.

None of that was me.

Characters describe kicking up tear "gas" powder on a Seoul subway platform and not enjoying the results, and dealing with poorly aimed golf balls hit by American military officers landing in their yard at Yongsan Army Base in Seoul.

Yes, that was me.

In my second book, *The Saudi-Iranian War*:

Characters fire rockets, and drive a truck off a pier.

Not me.

Characters in Saudi Arabia go through traffic experiences themselves and recount others. They describe the treatment of women in Saudi Arabia. Hulk Hogan makes an unexpected appearance in the narrative.

All from my experience, all true.

Sometimes, though, it's a bit trickier. In my third book, *The End of America's War in Afghanistan*, one character describes a person nearly being bisected by the wing of a Harrier jump jet. Looking back, it's hard to believe it, but that person really was me!

Again, as noted on the book listing page, all of my books are set in the near future, not the present. Please keep that in mind when deciding whether the technology described in this book is plausible. If you still think not, remember that not so long ago, widespread GPS capability in cars and phones wouldn't have been just science fiction. It would have been not very credible science fiction.

Thanks again for reading my book, and I hope you will enjoy my next one in 2022!

Cast of Characters
Alphabetical Order by Nationality
Most Important Characters in Bold

Chinese Citizens

Admiral Bai, Commander, South Sea Fleet Headquarters

Chief Sergeant Cao, soldier who prepared report on destruction of Ziyou Island base

Colonel Chang, commanding temporary base at Indian border

Chen Li Na, hacker and pro-democracy leader

Deshi, cousin of **Sergeant Xu**

Senior Captain Ding, South Sea Fleet Headquarters

Commander Duan, executive officer of submarine *Changzheng 20*

Vice President Gu

Corporal Guan, spotter at Indian border

Lead Technician Jiandan, Jiuquan Satellite Launch Center

Dam Manager Jiang, Xiluodu Dam

President Lin Wang Yong

Lishi, Forward agent transporting Gateways into China

Director Ma, Ministry of State Security (MSS) Science and Technology Investigative Division

Director Pan, billionaire secret leader of Forward

Hydropower Director Peng, in charge of all Yangtze River dams including Three Gorges Dam

Captain Qin, officer signing report on destruction of Ziyou Island base

Dam Manager Shen, Three Gorges Dam

General Shi, the Army Commander

Minister Song, Ministry of State Security (MSS)

Senior Manager Tan, Qinshan Nuclear Power Plant

Wang Yan, Forward Agent

Captain Wen, commanding submarine *Changzheng 20*

Plant Complex Director Wu, Qinshan Nuclear Power Plant Complex

General Yang Mingren, the Air Force Commander

Captain Yin, deputy commander of temporary base at Indian border

Minister Yu, Ministry of Public Security (MPS)

Colonel Xia, commanding construction of base on Ziyou Island

Sergeant Xu, sniper stationed at Indian border

Captain Zhong, helicopter pilot for **Hydropower Director Peng**

Russian Citizens

Alina, FSB Senior Field Agent

Evgeny, FSB Field Director

Anatoly Grishkov, FSB agent, former Vladivostok homicide detective

Boris Kharlov, FSB agent, ex-separatist Ukrainian warlord

Neda Rhahbar, FSB agent, former Iranian citizen

FSB Director **Smyslov**

Mikhail Vasilyev, FSB agent

Japanese Citizens

Haruto Takahashi, JSDF Crewman

Kaito Watanabe, JSDF AWACS Commander

American Citizens

Captain Jim Cartwright, commanding submarine USS *Oregon*

Lieutenant Commander Fischer, executive officer of submarine USS *Oregon*

U.S. President Hernandez

Retired Seal Team Six Commander Dave Martins, now security contractor

General Robinson, the Air Force Chief of Staff

Mark Rooter, SpaceLink project manager

Eli Wade, President and CEO of SpaceLaunch and SpaceLink

Made in the USA
Middletown, DE
18 June 2021